Under the Orange Tree

Three Stories of Misfortune
and the Triumph of the Human Spirit

New Hanover County Public Library
201 Chestnut St.
Wilmington, NC 28401

Nimfa Hakani

outskirtspress
DENVER, COLORADO

This is a work of fiction. The events and characters described herein are imaginary and are not intended to refer to specific places or living persons. The opinions expressed in this manuscript are solely the opinions of the author and do not represent the opinions or thoughts of the publisher. The author has represented and warranted full ownership and/or legal right to publish all the materials in this book.

Under the Orange Tree
Three Stories of Misfortune and the Triumph of the Human Spirit
All Rights Reserved.
Copyright © 2016 Nimfa Hakani
v3.0

Cover Image by Zamir Mati

This book may not be reproduced, transmitted, or stored in whole or in part by any means, including graphic, electronic, or mechanical without the express written consent of the publisher except in the case of brief quotations embodied in critical articles and reviews.

Outskirts Press, Inc.
http://www.outskirtspress.com

ISBN: 978-1-4787-5053-6

Outskirts Press and the "OP" logo are trademarks belonging to Outskirts Press, Inc.

PRINTED IN THE UNITED STATES OF AMERICA

Contents

Introduction i

Under the Orange Tree 1

Rina 217

The Awakening 281

Biography 352

Introduction

The three narratives of this collection have a special place in my heart and a strong sentimental value. They are related in some ways with a distant family acquaintance. She was a very old woman, older than my grandmother at the time I first made her acquaintance. She was born at the dusk of the 19th century and lived a long life.

She was an icon among the young female generation of my family. She represented the times we did not have a chance to live through, the times we looked back at in awe, admiration, and wonder.

And to think of it, we look at the times that preceded us as the ideal times when history was made, bravery was displayed; values of the human society were at their highest. Moreover, not experiencing in person the events of those times, a certain harmonious mystery surrounds that past, and that illusionary harmony entices us, draws us toward the mystery of the unknown, and we worship the past in veneration in the same way we sometimes strongly despise, resent, and have a sharp, critic eye for the present. The difference is, our sentiments are directly connected with the times in which we live, while, we often, save our passions, our adoration, our compassion for the past. By experiencing the reality firsthand, we lose sight of its present greatness, and the ability to see the past with practical sense as we developing a strange blindness to see its flaws.

We are blindfolded by the hardship of the reality of our times and cannot be unbiased when we judge it. It takes the future generations to evaluate the traces, the history of our times leaves behind, when we reach the dusk of our age or we simply have become dust. Only then we are seen as perfect, without any flaws, and our stories make the young wonder about the distant past where we were a protagonist of some sort. It seems as the veneration for the past helps humanity to balance the hardship of the reality perceived in the presence.

That's how we listened to her stories, with amazement for the unknown past. She used to enjoy the storytelling very much. She had a gift for it. Every time we would visit her, she would tell a new story. It was her thing and her great enjoyment. We stood around her in silence listening to her voice that carried us back to times unknown to us. Her stories were mostly narratives about the country life she had witnessed firsthand, or she had heard from others. I often thought that some of her stories were entirely of her own making.

We listened with a deep curiosity for the distant past without passing any judgment; on the contrary, we used to absorb each word that came out of her mouth with unquenched eagerness. Her style gave each of her narratives an aura of perfection, and as youngsters we saw only the mystery and a flawless past in each one.

As I think of it today, she could have been a great writer if she had lived in a different era.

Among the stories I heard from her, and in my family gatherings, the fascinating life-story of three women and one man who lived in countryside of South Albania between the first and second world war, stood out, stirred my curiosity and remained with me for almost four decades. I always thought to write about the women and the man who were the epicenter of each story, and I did not find the right moment until...

In the month of October of 2006, I sat down and began writing the first one without having a particular plot in mind, just the main facts of the story itself. *Under the Orange Tree* was born.

A unique woman is the focus of *Under the Orange Tree*, a woman whose life story was told and retold until it reached my ears during the seventies of the last century. If alive, she would have been beyond my grandmother's age when I heard about her grand gesture. However, I wrote this story to honor not only this particular woman's exceptional life but also to honor all Albanian women who lived through times of hardship, accordingly, honoring women everywhere, women who never had or have a chance to have a normal life but stoically accepted and accept their fate. Women who raise their children by themselves, surviving day in and day out, facing drawbacks and carrying out extraordinary tasks in a very simple, silent way for anyone to notice, till their last breath.

One year later, in 2007, I wrote the second story, *Rina*, the perplexed story of a young widow.

In 2008, I wrote *The Awakening*, the story of a simple man and an unfortunate woman, for whom life goes through some quite intriguing challenges.

The three short stories describe, with a good brush of imagination, the dynamism of the existence of four vulnerable, but at the same time very strong women, and one exceptional young man. A labyrinth of occurrences, thrown at their feet, twists the thread of life of each protagonist, determining the direction their life-path, and ultimately leads them to their destiny. The vehemence, the vivacity, the anguish, the anger, the cruelness, the odds, and survival they have to face, are astounding.

Dear readers,

I hope you will enjoy the ride you will take wandering through the pages of *Under the Orange Tree*.

Sincerely,

Nimfa Hakani

Under the Orange Tree

The story of a mother and a daughter in law!
December 2006 - March 2008

Part One

The news spread all over the village: "A newborn was abandoned inside the church!" The word spread from mouth to mouth, from house to house in whispering tones at first. Then loud, intense discussions, "Who could have done it?", "Who's baby is it?" followed the news. The hunches were of all kinds. Every household was analyzed. Every single young lady was considered a suspect. Distrust became an ordinary thought among the villagers. The suspicion fell especially on families who had young daughters. People looked at one another through their eyelashes. The dirt had fallen upon the village. Dishonor was the word to describe the elusive sense of indignation that had lurked in every household.

"How could someone do such a thing?" people would ask. The Elders would shake their heads and keep silent. When it came to matters of this extent, they were very careful on what they had to say. They knew these kinds of things had happened in other villages from time to time, but it never befell in their village. "There is a first time for everything", they would say, shaking their heads in wonder. After a thorough examination of the situation, the convocation of the Elders unanimously decided that it had to be someone out of the village. "People who have done this," they concluded, "to cover their tracks, came and brought the child into our church so no one would know who was who."

After reaching that conclusion, some felt as if someone had thrown mud at their faces. But, most of the people felt the burden lifted off their shoulders. Relief was the word. Villagers stopped looking at one another suspiciously. The young ladies felt more relieved than anyone else. Although they knew they were not at fault, the fact that people looked at their private lives through the eye of a needle, made every one of them feel uneasy; as if they were at fault somehow for the abandonment of that poor child. The mothers, relaxed, took the opportunity to have the "chit chat" with their daughters. They found the courage to tell their daughters how important it was to save themselves for marriage.

But, the discussion continued. No one could figure out how the person got inside the church. Everyone knew the deacon closed the door every evening at dusk. He found the child as he was making his early, morning rounds, and he swore the door was closed. But a certain rumor was spread around the village about him lately. He was discreetly seeing a woman. No one knew who she was, but they knew he would sneak out of the church at night to go somewhere. Probably he left the door open on purpose to sneak back inside.

The newborn was crying hard when the deacon found him. He boiled water, added a little sugar, and gave it to the infant after it cooled off to calm the child down. Right away, the priest made a social call on all women who were lactating to make their rounds and come in to feed the baby. He even set a schedule for four women, while his maid took charge of grooming the little one.

The parish was living at a high intensity that was very rare for a hamlet. The abandoned infant had changed the small village's ordinary, daily routine. Electrifying sparks were flying all over. The child had stirred up live discussions and had awakened the consciousness of people about life in general. No matter what the conversation would on, it would end up about that poor, deserted, tiny boy. Some even talked about what turn the life of the abandoned newborn, which fell out of the blue on their doorstep, would take.

After the first round of shock, people began to wonder who was going to raise the baby. In a meeting with the elders, the priest had said, if no one wanted to make a Christian gesture of compassion, his maid would take care of the child, and he was going to look after the child. That statement stimulated more passionate discussions. Someone said that the only way to hide a pregnancy was having a large body.

The fact that the priest's maid was a big, round woman, made people go on and on in another round of inquiring and seeking the truth, as they put it. Somehow, in the middle of all that talk, a suspicion came up in conversation that everyone had for a while but kept quiet: the priest was having an affair with his maid. The size of her body made it very credible for the maid to cover up her pregnancy. "Maybe the infant is the priest's child after all?!" someone expressed a suspicion out loud under that assumption. That stirred another round of strong gossips, mostly involving the maid.

This turnover of new speculations unsettled the village again. The Elders would shake their heads and say, "No, it is not possible!" But others would say, "Who else could have access to the church without breaking the door?"

The presumption of someone from another village dropping the child at their church held no more credibility.

The Elders resumed their inquiry. They were seeking for evidence. One of them came up with the fact that the maid was not lactating. Another pointed out the fact that the priest had asked other women to come and feed the baby, and none of the women feeding the child saw anything doubtful about the maid. But they knew, people wanted proof to take the suspicion off the priest. After a heated debate, the Elders decided to ask the priest to allow the midwife to examine the maid. They needed substantial proof on whether she had given birth recently to prove her purity. That would once and for all stop the rumors about him having an affair with her, or, just the fact that she was the mother of the child.

Two years earlier

Mariána was on her way to church. She had never put her foot outside the borders of Kalasa. All her life revolved around this village, its roads, and its orchards. That's where she grew up. She fell in love, got married, and had her first and only child in Kalasa. Women very rarely had a chance to travel out of the villages they lived in. They would only go as far as to their relatives while men took trips around the neighboring villages for trade purposes. The roads of this area allowed only the use of a single animal or a caravan of animals, mules and donkeys, as the most suitable animals to ride through the villages of the township of Himara. A woman would endure a traveling of sorts only if she had no choice. There was no way carriages could travel on the bumpy mountain roads of Kalasa. Mariána loved her village. Coming down from her orange orchard, she always enjoyed the view that unfolded ahead of her. Kalasa was built on the side of a mountain. It was located on the other far side of a cliff from where one could see the Ionian Sea. The only things that could be viewed from the vertical height of the cliff was the vast area of blue sea; the gulls flying in and out the dark caves underneath the cliff that couldn't be seen covered by wild bushes—their deafening cries disrupting the tranquility of the air and reaching the ears of those who were on the top of the cliff; and at the bottom of it, a shiny, white foamy strap created by the waves crashing on the steep, rocky cliff. The villagers could sometimes feel the breeze of the sea reaching their hamlet when high winds whirled over the water. But it was impossible to walk on foot down to the seashore, as the mountain went on in length along the sea.

She had never seen the Riviera, but the way people who had seen it from the sea and described it to others, the glimpse she, herself, got from the cliff, made her wonder. She often thought, one day, she would be able to visit the villages next to the seashore. She heard that many people went bathing in the sea in those villages to get absolution from their sins. But some bathed in the sea just for the fun of it. People told stories about the water being so crystal clear; they could see the white stones and the fish at the bottom even when they swam far from the shore. She felt mesmerized every time listening to the tales of the sea. Time and again, she dreamed of entering the water on a sunny summer day—a long white linen covering her body—dipping slowly until her head was under water. In her dream, she could feel the water dripping off her body when she would come out. Water droplets would fall all around her when she threw her wet, long hair over her head, and she would feel the magic of the moment. It was just her, the sea, and the sun. After she would wake up, the mesmerizing feeling would stay with her throughout the day.

There were stories about a village, Dhermi, built not far from the water. Its villagers would go down to the shore to watch the magic nights when the moonlight created a bright, glittery, broad path over the sea, that looked so real, they would feel like walking on it. There were stories of a pod of dolphins, huge sea animals, gray and white. There were three or four of them, showing once in a while at the shore.

Villagers would rush at the shoreline, to see the creatures when the news spread around the villages. The dolphins' appearance was the most extraordinary story she had ever heard.

The dolphins would stay around for a few days, at most a week, and then they would disappear for a couple of years, sometimes for more than a decade.

It was considered good luck to see the dolphins. People described them as beautiful creatures and very amicable who released some sweet, odd sounds and who swam as if they were giving a show to the people on the shore. They would jump out of the water high in the air and release friendly noises. There were stories about a man, Kozmái, who was crazy enough to swim far in the waters to reach the pod of dolphins. Strangely, he befriended them, and he started to swim with the pack and even play with them. Kozmái was fierce enough to climb on the top of the largest dolphin and swim around on its back. The people at the shore were terrified the first time Kozmái approached the dolphins. They screamed for him to turn around. But Kozmái, as wild as he was, always took chances no other would.

There were many stories told about him. He would take risks, from climbing the most dangerous sides of the mountains, to jumping into the sea from the highest, steepest cliff in the area; or doing things no one dared to do around the region of Himara. He would go out of his way to find danger, wherever it was. The boldest thing Kozmái ever did, as the Elders would comment, was going into the sea with just his short underwear on, showing his bare upper body and his legs. Other men could not even dream of doing it. They wore a long-sleeve shirt and long underpants, all covered up when getting into the water. It was considered promiscuous to show the body in the way Kozmái showed his.

Kozmái had earned the status of doing things differently from everyone else since he was very young. His ways were received little by little by most, no matter how crazy the things he did—sounded to others. If another man acted the same way Kozmái did, as in appearing in front of others just in short underwear, he would be regarded unfit by the commune's kinship. But no one was surprised anymore by what he did and what he would do next. People would just tell the exciting story about whatever new, crazy thing Kozmái did. Some called him foolish or insane. Some others said he was too wild for their taste, and the rest said he was just bold. And the Elders would say, "Kozmái is a brave, wild man who dares to do things out of the ordinary, things others don't have the slightest courage or even dream of doing in their lifetime."

Kozmái and the dolphins made big news in the daily, ordinary life around Himara. His friendship with the dolphins and his interaction with them were told over and over as a nighttime tale to children. She heard he was one of the most handsome men in the whole area. He was described as having sharp, strong features, dirty blond, long hair, blue piercing eyes, and a tall, toned, and tanned body. It was told, he even used to get into the water and take a good swim in the middle of the winter when it was freezing cold. Doing that, he reached his highest madness, people would remark. The word around was, he was strong as a bull, and he looked much younger than men his age.

Dolphins showed up three times during Mariána's lifetime. If the dolphins ended up by accident the first time in their coastline, people were convinced they came back so often in the last decades not by chance, but because of their camaraderie with Kozmái. People would swear that they were the same dolphins that came back for the three past showings.

There was a strange friendship established between the man and the astonishing animals, they would say. Kozmái knew how to approach and deal with them creatures. He was seen petting them and talking to them. The first time the dolphins showed up, no one knew what kind of sea animals they were and what to call them. Some were afraid and even saw their appearance as a bad sign. No one had seen such large sea animals in the area before. The biggest they had seen were sea turtles.

But the fear disappeared after a man who returned from America told everyone that they were harmless, very human-friendly creatures, and they were called dolphins. He had seen them in a place called aquarium in America. People, unable to pronounce the name correctly, transformed the name into "*delfins.*"

Mariána, like everybody else, was fascinated by Kozmái's stories. She had sometimes a strong desire one day to go and see the sea and the dolphins, and maybe see even the crazy Kozmái in person. For no reason, she often thought of him, the sea, and the bizarre animals.

Mariána had heard from others that Kozmái had dared to come once to Kalasa to see her just before the Sunday Mass. Not many had seen him though. Only a few people had noticed him while he was leaving. One of the Elders swore he had an interaction with the man that day. The rumor has spread fast in the village.

The Elders enjoyed telling about that exchange between Kozmái and one of their own over and over again. They had spiced it up and exaggerated a little bit as they usually did with all the narratives they told.

The villagers liked that particular story. Every time they heard it, they identified themselves with the Elder, who spoke to Kozmái, and it made them feel for some reason superior to the popular man. A grin would show on their faces at the end of it. Sometimes they'd ask to hear it from the beginning (over). Right away, one of the Elders would start:

That day, Kozmái was standing at the corner of the church leaning on the wall, watching the villagers coming to Sunday's mass. A few of them, curious, looked at the tall man with long, dirty blond hair, whispering to each other, wondering who that stranger was.

After a while, Kozmái noticed from afar a woman in her mid-thirties coming by herself down the north road. At one point, she stopped and greeted a couple, and then, chatting with them, walked in their company toward the church.

When they got closer, he saw how beautiful the woman was. Her dark brown, silky, long and wavy hair amazed him. It was unusual for a woman to keep lengthy hair below her shoulders. Most of the women in the countryside combed their hair in braids and fixed them in circles around the back of their heads, except the youngest ones who let their braids to fall over their chest. Only in the city the poor Kozmái had seen women with their hair down, but never as long and as beautiful as their Mariána's. *Never in his dream Kozmái had thought he would find such a rare beauty in a far village, hidden in the mountains.* He was stunned.

One of the Elders, heading to the Mass, was walking toward the corner where Kozmái was standing. He greeted him raising his hand at the side of his hat and bending his head slightly.

"Zoti[1] Kozmai! Mr. Kozmái!

Startled, Kozmái, instead of greeting back, asked:

"How do you know my name, old man?

"We don't often have strangers visiting our village young man. And, my boy, it is not so difficult to recognize crazy Kozmái! Your fame precedes you," the elder had the answer on the tip of his tongue.

Looking toward Mariána, Kozmái had responded without paying much attention to the old-timer.

"Hum! Thanks, old man!"

As the elder had walked by him, almost whispering, he asked a rhetorical question:

"Our Mariána is beautiful, isn't she?"

Kozmái, startled again by the straightforwardness of the old man, released a sigh. Smitten by her beauty he responded back:

"Oh yes! Yes, she is! She is as fine-looking as they have described her."

"That's our Mariána all right!" the elder had replied.

Then, the old man had given him a jest-like look.

"You had come all this way from Vunoi just to see her, didn't you?!"

Kozmái didn't respond; he just sneered.

---

1 Zoti- Mister

Passing past him, the elder saluted: "So long Zoti Kozmái!"

And, going away slowly, leaning on his cane, he couldn't help himself but throwing in the air his last words with a smirk on his face.

"She is way out of your reach young man!"

Kozmái had shaken his head and moved his right eyebrow up. A sly smile had appeared on his face. Then thoughtful he answered:

"Hum! Maybe you are right old-timer! But who knows for certain what the future might bring!"

"Oooh yes, my boy! Oh, yes! I know!" the elder, unable to keep his mouth shut answered back as he walked away from him. "You will ever, ever get her, even if you pull out of your sleeves the Othello trick; telling her your mighty stories about the dolphins, and the cliffs you jumped, and all the other stuff you've done!"

Kozmai had waved his hand in disregard.

He watched Mariána until she entered the church, and then, left slowly with his head down as if a burden had fallen on the unlucky fellow.

In a triumph tone, with that sentence, the elders would finish the story.

At the words, "even if you pull out of your sleeves the Othello trick", everyone would burst into laughter. They had heard the Othello story from a man who had worked in Italy for a few years. He had seen the play in a theater there and had liked so much; he told it over and over again at the evening gathering under the oldest olive tree in the center of the village. The first time the story was told, at the part of Othello's marriage to Desdemona, one of the Elders, the

Under the Orange Tree

oldest of the lot, and the jokester of the village, shaking his head, had blurted out, "What a cunning fox that Othello guy! What a cunning fox! Some tricks he had up his sleeves!" laughing heartily. At that moment, his usual jovial face had become funnier with his open, toothless mouth, and a strong hilarity had broken among those present. And, the expression, the Othello trick, had become famous since then.

The Elders' interpretation afterward about the exchange, was, "Even the boldest man's courage will vanish when it comes to confronting a beautiful, exceptional, pretty woman like our Mariana!" They enforced that by saying, when Kozmái had seen their Mariána, he was left speechless and intimidated to the point that he did not have the guts to approach her. And everyone knew Kozmái was no loser when it came to women.

Kozmái lived four villages away, and coming to Kalasa from his far village was a very daring thing to do, Mariána thought at the time. It took twelve hours by mule and more than a day on foot from his village to Kalasa. The saying was, Kozmai traveled only on foot. No one had seen him on a carriage or a mule.

A warm smile appeared on her face as her thoughts wandered about Kozmái. His image was surrounded with an aura that made him desirable to women and sort of a symbol for men. Some women would whisper in each other's ear; they would have Kozmái's image in their mind while making love to their husbands. Mariána heard he had never been married. The word around was as he, himself, had put it; he never met the woman of his dreams. On the other hand, many fathers would not consider Kozmái suitable for their daughters. "He," they would comment, "wouldn't make a good father or a decent husband. He is too distracted and busy doing crazy, strange things to focus on family matters." But no one ever heard a word on his behalf asking for anyone's daughter's hand though. There were rumors of him having affairs with widows, and sometimes with women whose husbands were away in America. But, no one ever heard of him getting involved with unmarried young maidens.

Nevertheless, when Kozmái's name would come up once in a while in the midst of the Elders' evening-gatherings at the big bench, under the olive tree, a slight envious squirm would show almost undetected in their wrinkled faces. "Kozmái was strange indeed for a man in his mid-forties", they would say, and add. "A man marries for consolation and not for love!" But secretly, they deemed him in high regard.

Mariána's looked down at the view unfolded in front of her. It looked especially marvelous if you were over at the church, or from her house on the north side of the village. Most of the houses were two stories and at a fair distance from one another. The white walls and the red roofs created an absorbing sight to look at. The narrow cobblestone roads meandered nicely through the village. But, what made the view of her village more exceptional, were the citrus plantations around it, numerous orchard oranges, several lemons, grapefruits, and a few tangerines groves. There were some groups of olive trees here and there, but the orange orchards dominated the area. The blend of the green leaves and the orange color of the fruits gave the surrounding a striking effect during the season. It all displayed in front of her eyes see it all every time she had to go down in the village.

The church itself was the most fascinating and grotesque building in the entire area. The shape of the church always made her wonder who were the masters that built it and why the church stood out above everything. It was opposite of her house on the other part of the village on the south side of it. It stood taller, bigger, and more imposing than anything else around, and one could see everything from standing in front of the church. The view of the massive white structure of the church with the cross rising high toward the sky drew her as a lodestone as she headed to the church.

It was the same thing everywhere with the churches, she had heard. She wondered how the master builders managed to do it. "How did they find a spot in every village to build a church so one could see it from everywhere, and everything else to be below it?" she wondered.

Mariána loved the sound of the church's bells. The echo of their chiming sound would diffuse all over the village three times a day. People could hear the echo of them bells even if they were in the furthest orchard. Their sound made them feel the existence of their village even if they were alone working in their orange groves or on a remote location in the mountains. It made the villagers feel connected with the rest of the villages around as well. It reminded them the time of the day while they were lost working in their orchards. It made them stop, take a break from whatever they were doing, and have their meals. It kept them on alert what to do next. And once in a while it reminded them that life was indeed precious.

As for the inside of the church, the colorful paintings of the saints around the walls, the hemisphere-high ceiling covered with frescos, the mesmerizing scattering of the sun's rays into the church, and the translucent light through the colorful small pieces of the stained-glass windows made it very pleasant to be there during the Sunday Mass.

The rays of the sun would enter the church at a particular angle through the windows dispersed around the church's space, creating a heavenly sensation. The stained windows would bring the light on the face of each saint. An hour or two before midday, while Mass took place, passing just above the head of people, the sunlight would become stronger. The sun rays would come alongside together at one point, the altar. A cluster of rays would illuminate the priest's figure, and an aura would appear around the priest's head. At that point, the music played by the deacon on the small organ would reach a higher pitch. The priest's strong, masculine voice reading the prayers would rise, and the Mass would reach its climax. And the spirits of the villagers would be captivated almost to ecstasy. It was like their souls were almost rising up and reaching the heavens. In those occasions, Mariána felt as if she was lifted up in paradise.

Once in the middle of the Mass, on a rainy gray day, as the priest was addressing his sermon with nothing interesting to say, feeling a little bored, she remembered watching around. As she sat her eyes on the frescos, the saints' pictures, the shape of the dome, she realized the sunlight was not entering the church that day to enlighten the saints or the altar. Only the candle-lights were illuminating the church creating a shadow-light proviso.

The church did not seem the same on rainy days she became aware. The magic was not there. On rainy or cloudy days, it looked like mysterious, transient forces were going about the aisles. The high winds outside found their way in once in a while, making a muffled, whistling sound. The slightest motion of an air current inside the church made the flames of candle-lights move from side to side as if to show the existence of the wicked souls through the game of light and shadow they created. In those instances, it seemed as if the mystic spirits were hissing in people's ears, almost putting people in a hypnotic state.

She didn't like the trail of her last thought and tried to think of something else. Her mind drifted again, and she began thinking about the people who built the church, mostly about how the light created the magic on sunny days. She had noticed that sunbeams dispersed from the sun shone over all objects on earth, while in the church it was different. Did the stained-glass windows originate that trick? Maybe it was a make-believe stipulation, she considered.

In the meantime she made it to the church and went in. She looked up at the high ceiling and wondered how the painters got up there to paint the frescos. She would have liked being part of the crafting crew who built this church and see with her own eyes how they did it all.

She had heard that their church was small compared to other churches, like the one in the township of Himara, but she couldn't imagine how another church could be bigger than this one. She greeted her neighbors and took a seat waiting for the Mass to start. Her thoughts shifted, and she looked around at her fellow villagers. Their outfits caught her attention. She noticed they all wore plain black, gray, or blue colors, men and women alike. Most of the outfits were discolored by extended use. *Why spend all this money to build this beauty in a village as poor as Kalasa, where people dress as colorlessly as a gray day?* The question popped in her mind, and she looked down at her old blue dress, with not-so-white-anymore dots, and tucked up her lips in dislike.

As usual she wondered about the things that surrounded her. Her contemplation, always brought her thinking to curiosity of discovery; but, as it often happened, she had no direct answers of her rational thinking. *Would I wander off like this if I had Socrates beside me?* She thought, but the church absorbed her attention once again and her eyes became aware of the surrounding. She noticed Andrea entering the church with George, and after waving at her, sitting on the last bench on the other side. She smiled at the sight of her handsome son. He and George were always the last to come and the first one to leave. She turned around and faced the altar.

Despite her spontaneous, rebellious quests, she enjoyed the Sunday Mass. She took pleasure in the interior decorated walls and the beauty of the altar; and if not for the priest, she would have attended Mass every Sunday.

After Mass, the ritual was to go around and kiss the portraits of the saints. She did not do it often. But that day, she considered staying a little longer and making her rounds with the saints. She stood in front of *Shën Thomai*, Saint Thomas' portrait. She clasped her hands in front of her chest and prayed silently. As she was praying, she felt the warmth of a bunch of sun rays coming from of the windows and landing right on her cheek. She experienced an instant retreat from reality mixed with a slight form of dizziness. She was almost reaching to kiss the saint's face when she suddenly felt the presence of the priest, who had emerged next to her from nowhere and startled her.

His eyes were fixed right on her lips. They were bright and piercing. It felt as he silently was saying, "Am I not good enough for you to be kissed? I am alive, right here in front of you; the saint is not!"

Staring at her, Father Niko suddenly raised his hand to give her his blessing.

Mariána blushed under his intense gaze. She clasped her palms in front of her chest, bent her knees slightly, lowered her head in sheer respect, and left quickly, not looking back.

He had ruined the sanctity of the magic moment of her feeling immortal, feeling light with no weight, feeling as a sole existence in the universe. Just she and the saints for an instant back there, and it were all gone. He had taken away that moment, and had brought her back to the mere reality of daily routine; men looking at her with the wish she would give them a sign of hope somehow after all these years. She was so tired of all their nonsense.

Kissing the Saints was a blissful ritual. She felt the strength passing through her body every time she did. And it was not an earthly kiss, it was a divine one. It was the kiss of saints. It was the kiss of purification. The painters made the Saints look human, but at the same time, even if you could touch their faces, they seemed so unreachable. Their eyes, with the small little sacks around them, their head bent slightly to the side, made them look supernatural and mystical. It seemed to her sometimes they were making judgments upon her every time she looked in their eyes. She felt their gaze entering her soul to examine intimately the struggle and suffering she had to go through every day but safeguarded her at the same time. After the divine kiss, she always felt as if the look in *Shën Thomaï*'s eyes softened, and he would bestow absolution on her soul.

She had always blamed her lips for the priest's reaction. Her pink curvy lips were famous in the village. Other women envied Mariána since she did not need to do anything to have rosy red lips. They had to torture themselves to give them, the lips, some color every time they had to participate in an important event such as the Sunday Mass.

The Elders would chuckle in that regard, "Mariána's lips would revive even them, the dead, and who could blame them, the saints, if they are resuscitated and act like real men when she approached to kiss them?" Despite the Elders' humor, Mariána was determined to keep her pinkish lips untainted, saving them only for the man in her life and the saints.

She walked away from the church and headed to her house. The trail of her thoughts brought her back to the church.

The church was the center of her village's life. The priest, a middle-aged, tall man with a gray aura around his handsome face, was the only one in the whole village who knew what was happening around the area. He was the only man

Under the Orange Tree

who received news about and around the villages in the area, in the township of Himara, in the city of Vlora and Saranda, or even in Greece. If the villagers were in need of anything, they went to him. No one else knew how to write and read. There was no school in the village.

Not only was the priest a spiritual leader who brought the word of God to them, but he was also the man who took care of their earthly needs and affairs. If they needed to read or write a letter, from or to overseas, he was the one reading the incoming message and writing the outgoing one. He also took care of their deeds or filled out other legal documents for them. They were appreciative to his endeavors. They recompensed him for his unholy services with payment in nature—a dozen eggs, a hen, cheese, honey, smoked lamb meat, or other items the priest considered acceptable.

The letters weren't that long, sometimes just a few sentences. Most people didn't have much to say while "writing" to the loved ones overseas. In that case, the priest was pleased with a few eggs or a small chicken or a reasonable portion of feta cheese. Milk and butter were also accepted. The priest had a slender body, and the villagers wondered how he digested all that food he received from them on the top of the goods he produced himself on his small farm behind the church. His wife had died a few years back, and he never remarried. He did not have any children. And all the cracks fell on his poor maid, who had become the target of the elder's mockery. They would joke about her body size. "She is as big as a two-hundred-year-old walnut tree, and she eats all the food she can take in," the old-timers would joke. Looking around, with a sly smile on their wrinkly faces, they would add in a low voice, "She also makes the priest very joyful in a way she should make only her future husband." The eldest of the group would add with a grin, "She has a bulky appetite about everything." The poor girl was a celibate woman of forty-five who had been big since everybody remembered her and for some reason never got married. She earned her living as the priest's housemaid, but after the priest's wife passed away, the rumors about her status in the priest's house were very imaginative.

Mariána did not take into account the gossips, but she avoided meeting the priest outside the church. After the Mass, as it was the routine, the priest went outside and stood by the main door to greet his parishioners, as a shepherd counting his sheep, and giving them his blessing. The way he looked at her had made her feel uncomfortable. She attended Mass every other Sunday, finding a pretense of having too much work to do around the house with the sheep and hens, her small orange orchard and all. Thus, she always sat in the last row of the aisle next to the door so she could be the first one out. She did not want the touch of his hand on her shoulder or head. She did not want to see his face close next to hers. She did not want to hear his voice up close. It was enough she had to hear it during the Mass. He had a very deep, masculine voice that confused her profoundly sometimes, and she felt something that if she were to explain it, it would have been too close to the word "sin." She did not want to feel that way about her priest, and she did not want his piercing eyes on her. She did not like the flare in those eyes every time she couldn't avoid an encounter with him.

Part Two

Mariána was happy and sad at the same time that day. Her only son, Andrea, was getting married. Finally, her house would be filled with children voices. She was going to be a grandmother soon. A sparkle appeared in her beautiful hazel eyes. Mariána was a charming, beautiful woman, but age and hard life had left marks on her face. Visible lines like a bunch of rays appeared on the sides of her mouth and eyes that reflected the hard years of loneliness. She was no older than thirty-nine, but she looked like her mid-forties, yet her beauty reflected a roughness that made her a very attractive woman.

When she was younger, many men asked for her hand in marriage, but she refused every single man who showed up at her doorstep. Her beauty, even now, drew the attention of both men and women. Hearing about her legendary beauty, widowers or unmarried men from far villages would take the risk to travel and see in person if the myth about her beauty was true. And they would, without a blink, ask for her hand. But she never accepted any of the offers.

It had been years and years, and she had not heard from her Socrates. He had left a month after their wedding night to take a long journey to America. It had become common the last decades for young men in the area to make the journey to America after getting married. The line of single mothers celebrating their only child's wedding on their own was becoming a little too long lately. In almost two decades the young bride would become the mother-in-law of another promising, lonely new spouse. The ships took a lot of young men abroad, but very few of them would be on board on the way back home fifteen or twenty years later. The vital force of the villages in the region was succumbing more and more to the ocean. The chance of a man returning from overseas was very slim. And yet the number of people migrating, instead of decreasing, had increased as far as she remembered. Only a few had sent for their wives, to join them in the New World—as everybody called America. *But why get married if they planned to go?* The question had tormented her often throughout the years.

Some of the wives never heard back from their husbands. Somewhere in the long journey to that wonderland they found something better or maybe some bad luck. Some of them would send money every other month to support their wives and a child usually born six to eight months after their departure, but they chose for whatever reason not to return. At times, along with the money there would be short letters that did not tell much about their lives, just a simple greeting to the wife, parents, and other people in the village. The letters were kept as the precious, valuable possession somewhere in a chest along with the woman's dowry and other personal possessions dear to her. There were new tear marks on those letters every time they were handled. Nevertheless, the women remembered every word written in each letter after hearing the priest reading it out loud to them. Sometimes they asked him to read it twice. Afterward, they would recite it by memory a thousand times when no one was around.

What baffled Mariána most about all of this, was the young bride; from the moment she got married, she would be called in an informal way by her husband's first name. Usually, the young woman's first name would be forgotten with time. Only her family members would call the married young ladies by their first name. For the rest of the villagers, they were *Moj e Thanasit*, O Thanasis', Moj *e Nikiforit*, O Nikifori's, or *Moj e Sokratit*, O Socrates'.

She wondered how it all began. Why should a woman be called by her husband's first name after marriage, especially if the husband was not even around? Was it because men liked to proclaim their owner rights over their women even if they were far away, in a land beyond the big ocean? The ironic part was, a lot of women around spent the rest of their life alone, without the ones whose name they were given upon the marriage.

In Mariána's case, the villagers, for some reason, did not follow suit. She was called by her first name even after getting married. Only the priest followed the code and was more formal calling her "*Zonja*[2] *Socrates,* Mrs. Socrates." As for the villagers, it seemed as if they were in the denial of the fact she got married.

She was considered the precious gem of the village. They were proud of her. But it was not only her beauty that made them break the rule of calling her by her first name. It was also the way Mariána had carried herself since she was in her early youth.

Men, old enough to get married, envied Socrates after their engagement. For that matter all men, married or not, envied him. Mariána was held in high regard as the prettiest and the smartest young lady of all the villages around Himara's township. "The soul of a person depicts the beauty of their face," the Elders would say about her. After Socrates stopped writing, some widowed and unmarried men's hope rose fast, but it died quicker than it took place.

Many women, after their husbands took off to the far land, were left with no choice but to do hard labor in their orange or olive orchards, taking care of the harvest of the honeybee hives, taking care of vineyards and wineries. There was a satiric poem going around addressing the fact that women were working more than men throughout the countryside of the homeland. It was written by a scholar, Mariána had heard. The part she loved most from the poem was the verse:

---

2   Zonja- Mrs, missis

Burrat ndënë hije,
    Lozin, kuvendojnë,
pika që su bie,
    se nga gratë rrojnë![3]

Men, under shades,
playing cards,
chatting all day long,
shameless living
on their women's
laboring incomes!

The families who had money, mostly sent from the men abroad, were fortunate to hire seasonal workers. The rest of the women had to work hard to keep their family property intact. Generation after generation, their possessions, the fruit, the olive orchards, the vineyards, or the wineries, were lost one by one to the prominent family of Komnenis. The Komnenis were the richest family in the region. As the vigorous young men migrated more and more overseas, the Komnenis got richer and richer. The best vineyards, honey hives, wineries, citrus and olive orchards became their possessions. Most of the people were working the same land that they once owned, but now they were getting paid a very low daily wage that most of the time ended up as a payment in natural products. A woman would be lucky to find a job as a maid inside the Komnenis' mansion. No matter how hard

---

3 Verses in Albanian of a poem by the Albanian poet, satirist, writer, essayist, play writer, lawyer, renaissance man, and activist Andon Zako Çajupi (1866 - 1930)

the cleaning and cooking or other chores in that big house, it was much better than working outside in vineyards or orchards. Mariána lost her husband's olive grove to Komnenis years ago when her son was an infant, and she couldn't afford working so hard on both the orange and olive orchards.

Socrates had been gone for more than twenty years, and she had no one to give her a hand in her daily struggle until Andrea grew up. She knew she could have exploited the help many men had offered her during the years after Socrates left. But she had refused the idea of a man other than her husband, with obvious ill intention as she called it, to give her "a hand" in order to make her life easier.

Mariána shook her head, as she wanted to depart from the sad thoughts. Today was the happiest day of her life. She was going to celebrate the wedding of her son. A smile appeared on her face.

Andrea looked exactly like his father. His handsome face held Mariána high-spirited throughout the years of loneliness. It made her strong-willed enough to reject all the men who showed up at her door to ask her hand in marriage. His little face gave her hope; his father would show up one day, tall, muscular, and handsome. She remembered as if it was yesterday Socrates making love to her for a long August month, night after night, several times each night. She had a vivid remembrance of his robust body, his feverish eyes on her, his hands all over her, his sweaty skin rubbing hers, as his strength flowed into the innermost part of her being.

The presence of her son, the love and care for him, had helped her to repress the pain inside her chest, and in the deeper parts of her young body. If not for him, she could not imagine how she would have kept herself composed from one day to the other throughout the first years of her loneliness.

It was that little boy, his face, his deep brown eyes, just like his father's, who helped her to contain the strong desire of having her husband at night in the bed; his body next to hers. But as the time passed by, with her son growing up and her in-laws and her parents passing away, the hard work on the orchards, and the miniscule daily worries had drained her strength. Her desires faded away, and her memories of being with him became blurry as if they belonged to someone else.

She wanted a better life for Andrea. She wanted a better life especially for her daughter-in-law. She made her son promise he would not migrate. She made him promise he would stay and have a life with his sweetheart here in the village.

Everyone had helped with the wedding. Her son was excited and nervous at the same time. It was his first time with Ana. He looked just like his father. Tall, dark features, lean body, with well-formed muscles from the hard work. She was lucky to have a son. Some women, who had girls after their husbands' departures, had a hard time making ends meet. Her life had become easier these past few years since Andrea became capable of doing most of the work around.

The music had filled the village with joy. Weddings were the days when people would forget about their daily problems and enjoy themselves to the point of drunkenness. The community would come as one to make that day the best entertainment they ever had.

People had enjoyed themselves at her son's wedding. They had left more than two hours ago, but not before pushing her son and his young bride into their bedroom and banging the door to cheer his manhood and her womanhood finally taking place. Afterward, no one wanted to leave without the proof that the bride was a decent girl who did not give up her virginity before the wedding day. They danced their way until a white linen cloth, stained with the young bride's fresh blood, was hung out of the window in her son's hand.

Then, satisfied with the proof of her innocence and purity, pleased that she was untouched to the day she had to give herself to the man she would marry and to whom she pledged forever love—they cheered and screamed, wishing the couple, "May you have happiness and many children in your life! May the firstborn be a boy!"—Then, with very loud, merry conversations, that a good wedding and alcohol would furnish to people, they left, and disappeared through the narrow cobblestone roads to go their own beds, and start their usual, ordinary lives all over the next morning.

Everyone in the village was asleep but Mariána. The wedding had brought back very vivid flashbacks of her own wedding. Her son's young bride was as beautiful as she was on her wedding day. Looking at the bride and her handsome son beside her, she felt like someone else was looking at herself and Socrates a lifetime ago.

Today she sang and danced and showed great happiness

at her son's wedding. She was the best hostess this village had ever seen. Resonating mature beauty, joy, and grace, she pleased everyone. Many people were glad to see her so happy after such a long time. Some men, including the priest, tried to get her attention, but she did not pay regard to any of them. The priest brushed against her once when the crowd became dense on the dancing floor, but she carefully arched her body and moved away and enjoyed the night the best she could.

For the first time in some twenty years, she was going to sleep in the fire-room downstairs. She gave up her bedroom, on the second floor, to the newly married couple. The only thing she had brought downstairs from the bedroom was her chest, which she had put it in the corner of the fire-room. She opened it, picked up her nightdress and put it on. She did not want to hear the noises coming from the young couple's room. She cut two small pieces of gauze and put them in her ears. She rolled her son's old mattress next to the fireplace. After, she took out the chest a clean pair of white bedding, a cushion, and arranged them over the mattress, and lay down. It was a warm summer night. It was awhile past midnight, and the village was awfully quiet after the noisy, cheerful wedding day.

Alone with her memories, suddenly, hot, burning tears came down on her cheeks, and she wept quietly for a while alone in the darkness of the room. She remembered when the white linen with the bloody stain on her young, untouched body had left on it came out of the same window twenty years ago.

After a while, her eyes ran out of tears, and short sobs

followed. She stood in the darkness, unable to sleep at her thirty-nine years of age, feeling ancient and very young at the same time. Her body, as always, spoke a language she did not like, but her spirit felt like a hundred-year-old woman at the moment. She got out of the covers, lit a candle, and opened her chest. The flavor of the apples reached her nostrils and filled the room. For the apples not to spoil and to preserve their aroma, she always put unripe persimmons next to them. She didn't know how that helped. She was told to do so by her mother, and her mother was told by her own mother, and generation after generation, the unripe persimmon had to go along with it. Both apples and persimmons were replaced from time to time, to keep the fruits fresh, and have apple fragrance infiltrate the fine linen clothes. She picked up the only shirt she had left from Socrates. The shirt was the only item she kept from the man she slept with only a single month. While Socrates was packing, she hid the shirt in her chest to keep something that belonged to him when he was away.

She buried her face in the shirt and inhaled intensely whatever smell was left in its fabric. His body odor was no longer there. The apple flavor had replaced his masculine smell a long time ago. A very sharp and painful sensation inside her brought tears to her eyes again. There had been occasions when she would be aware of his scent as if he were standing right there, next to her. The smell of his body would reach into her nostrils in those moments as if it was real. *How could it be stored in the memory of her senses in such a powerful way, so the occurrence of it would make her experience his presence?* she wondered. *How could it arise time and again into her perceptions after so many years as if it had entered her system yesterday?* She had no explanation. She dropped the shirt back in the chest, closed the lid, and walked outside.

The dark sky was bright around the full moon, and she could see clearly everything about the house. It appeared as if the moon were joyfully celebrating her son's wedding night. It seemed as if it was observing from above, with great curiosity, the instant act of creation inside her modest home, and, its discretion, was witnessing the beginning of the new life of another being among humans.

Wrapped up in her own thoughts; Mariána did not pay much attention to the moon's delight as she usually normally would. She was lost in the memories of her twenty something years. She spotted the Great Bear. Socrates used to bring her out of the house and show her the sky. They would look at the stars, and he would teach her how to spot the Great Bear and the North Star in the zenith. Then, they would go running into the citrus orchards, playing around and teasing each other. The aroma of the citrus buds and flowers that were blooming would fill their lungs and tease their nostrils, and their sensuality would reach a climax. He would make love to her, over and over again, right there under their favorite orange tree, just a layer of green grass underneath. After their passionate lovemaking, he would promise her that he would come back once he had made enough money to afford a decent life. Then other times, he would promise her he would take her back to the faraway land and they would build a life together there, or, he would say, he would come back and build a house in the middle of the orchard, right there, next to their favorite tree. Thus, their new home would have the citrus smell all over it, and their children would grow breathing the fresh scent of it. He would tell her, they would have four healthy sons who would not need to migrate to America. He would tell her right there and then; they would have a girl among boys. That way, she could pass her beauty into her and cherish her, and he would watch a small Mariána growing up into a beautiful woman like her own mother.

As the memories were pouring in her mind, a deep sadness overcame her. This strange, faraway country, America that had swallowed her husband from the surface of the earth was back in her life again. America, the unfamiliar country that meant loneliness for her and many other women, would not go away. America, that remote soil with no news of her Socrates, was soon to swallow her son too, taking another dear one from her life, leaving her emotionally handicapped again.

Her son, the little boy who had grown up, was following his father's footsteps. And all this because his father did not keep the promises he had made to come back and build a life with her.

For the first time after all these years, she felt irritated, angry, and bitter. She could not bear the fact that her son was going away too. And he told her today, the same as his father did. She could not deal with the fact that she couldn't prevent it from happening again. The most important man in her life was going to be taken away from her by the same place who swallowed his father; by the dreamy place on the other side of the world, where everyone wanted to go, a place so far, she had no way of knowing what actually could happen to her loved ones.

Suddenly, she realized, *Socrates is never coming back!* For the first time, she understood that her life was wasted on false pretenses. She had waited for something that never would happen. Despite the promises, the man she trusted with all her heart made so solemnly to her, he was never coming back. For twenty years, she did not receive even an official statement or a death certificate. Not even an announcement of abandonment. For the first time, it crossed her mind that probably he had built another life there, another family, and did not want to be found. Dumbstruck, she realized that he didn't even care about the existence of his son.

"*He had found another wife,*" an inner voice whispered to her the ruthless truth. She felt a sharp pain just thinking it might be true.

Finally, the clarity of her reality, which others for years tried to make her understand, struck her hard. Even her mother tried many times to open her eyes to the fact that Socrates was not coming back. But she would reply, "He promised me! He promised he would come back! And he is going to keep his promise!" When her friends would indirectly imply that he would not return, to block their voice from entering her senses, she would think about the way he was with her. She knew. The way he used to make love to her was very special. Women would talk among themselves about their husbands' lovemaking habits. And it wasn't even close to the way Socrates had made love to her.

The way he spoke to her, the way he worshiped her and her body, made her believe in him for twenty years. It made her trust his words. It made her go on, be in denial, and not see the reality for what it was. *No man who makes love to his young bride that way abandons her*, she thought all these years. He loved her in a way she did not have words to describe. He wrote her three letters within the first year. In the letters, he made the same promises. She could smell his scent through those letters. She would relive their special moments while citing his letters by memory every time she opened her chest. After, she waited for more letters. And she waited! And waited! But there was none! Not a single one after the third! Nothing whatsoever!

Not even a word with people who came back and forth from the promised new land. Not one single person had seen or met him. No one had heard of him. The letters she sent to the address shown on his three first letters were returned with no forwarding address, noting, "No such person lives at the above address." Despite it, for twenty years, she believed he would come back one day. She waited day after day, for so long, she couldn't even count. She waited and waited for him to show up at last on the doorstep. She would sometimes see his image in broad daylight coming down the main road, tall, big, and handsome.

In the endless nights, she anticipated the knock on the door. But it never happened. Then she hoped he would make it to his son's wedding. She was so convinced he would. *Hopeless wishful thinking!* She scoffed inwardly.

Strangely, she felt something she never did before. Suddenly an alien feeling overcame her. A feeling she never thought she would experience about her Socrates. She heard many women expressing hatred now and then for their husbands. Their faces showed even more than the words coming from their mouths. She never understood how would they talk ill about the men they shared their life and bed with. But at that very instant, for the first time, she was experiencing an unfamiliar sentiment. She was having a hard time accepting that she could feel that way about him; the man who had nourished her spirit year after year, day in and day out, without even being around her for twenty years.

She realized she had turned the only month with Socrates into a lifetime with his image; his depiction living vividly in her mind and her senses for years and years. Ironically, she converted one month with the man into twenty long years of hopeless daydreaming and disheartening expectations.

She did not understand herself much at the moment, but the words "You bastard!" came out of her mouth, and angry, bitter tears filled her eyes this time. The wild reflection in them, made them look like the eyes of a provoked, fearless female wolf. She went inside, lifted the lid of her chest, and moved a box from the bottom. She opened it, took out the only three letters she had received from him, then the dry rose that came with the first letter, and threw the empty box back inside. She picked up his shirt, a pair of scissors and went around the back of the house to the stream. Everything was bright outside. The water was reflecting the moon's shining light. The loud moans coming from the open window of the bedroom on the second floor spoiled the serenity of the night. She turned her head toward the window. Her eyes had a strange look, a look that never had been there before. She took her eyes off the window and began cutting the letters and the shirt in pieces with an unstoppable fury. Tiny pieces of white paper and white clothing fell in the stream and floated slowly away.

With nothing left in her hands, she watched how the last pieces of his letters and shirt disappeared in the darkness, and she walked back to the front of the house. She started to fix the mess from the wedding by putting things in order with a feverish intensity. After she finished, she stood in the middle of the yard in confusion. The sleep had left her body for the night. She succumbed to deep pain again. Suddenly she started running away from the house.

She found herself under the orange tree in the middle of their orchard, where Socrates used to bring her often at night. She had visited this spot a thousand times throughout the years. She couldn't even count how many times she had come up here and sat under the tree. The orange scent would fill her nostrils, making his presence so real; she would feel he was right there beside her. The flashes of them being together physically would be so powerful she would almost lose her mind. This tree had helped to keep her love for him alive and lasting. She remembered some strange sighs would come out of her every time she came here. They were like feeble, whimpering sounds an animal would release when wounded and unable to escape its predator's claws, sensing death was sinking in.

Suddenly, the cruelty of the reality she just came upon to finally understand, hit her hard somewhere deep inside as a thunderbolt. She felt extreme pain, and an intense scream came out of her mouth. She screamed and screamed and screamed like a person who had lost their mind, releasing the pain and the profound suffering she had accumulated within her all these long, lasting years.

Some people in the village heard a bizarre cry that night. They wondered where the unusual yell came from. The wolves were not around during the summer nights, and it wasn't even their mating season. But, whoever heard that outcry and wondered for a short while about the hollow she-wolf, too exhausted from the busy, merry wedding day's affairs, rolled on the other side and went back to sleep.

Part Three

It had been seven months since her son had left, six months after his wedding. Mariána loathed herself for allowing her son to get married before leaving and for allowing the same thing to happen to Ana. She did not understand why the men were going so far away from their loved ones. Were they taking a long journey because of necessity, or perhaps going to America became a habit, or maybe because whatever stories were told about that place strangely attracted them to take the long journey to the mysterious land?

How did she allow this to happen with Andrea too? She had promised herself she would never let him go away. And she did! Had the whirlwind madness of going away from this beautiful land possessed her too in some ways she was not aware off?

Ana was having such a hard time dealing with her husband's departure. She seemed lost. She would do the chores around the house and obediently carry out whatever Mariána asked her to do. She helped her at the orange orchard, but it seemed to Mariána that her spirit was not in the present. The cheerful, vivacious young lady she used to be before the wedding was gone. Ana became quiet, almost silent. Mariána felt as if she was experiencing her own pain all over again. Watching her son's bride, Mariána could not help but see her own reflection embodied in Ana in a time gap of twenty years.

Mariána kept an eye on the young woman, constantly looking for signs of missing menstrual cloths, or the familiar sounds of vomiting in the morning. In a few months after Andrea's departure, Mariána gave up. Ana was not pregnant.

A sense of great concern swept her upon the harsh, unpleasant realization. She began to worry about the young bride. A child would have occupied her time and, most of all, her young spirit. A child in her arms, a small mouth on her breast, a tiny face with two miraculous little eyes looking into her mama's eyes, the tiny pinky fingers wrapped around her thumb would have changed her life into a sensational miracle. Mariána had Andrea to balance the pain she had experienced for more than two decades.

Usually, most women got pregnant the first day or at least during the first month. Very rarely would it happen the second month. Her Ana wasn't lucky in that regard for whatever reason. It was going to be just Mariána and Ana for twenty-four hours every day, every week, every month, and every year. Two women alone in the house! No child to cherish, no melodious sound, for the mother's ears, of cooing or babbling or giggling of an infant in the house. No baby's crying during the day or in the middle of the night. No baby bathing and or washing baby pads. No breastfeeding for Ana! The sound "Ba-ba" obviously was out of the question, but even the sounds of "Ma-Ma" or "Na-Na" were not going to be heard either. The house seemed cursed! Mariána wanted a child more than anything else. Poor Ana! She did not know what she was missing. An infant would have eased her suffering.

The child, the desire for a future grandchild, she came to realize, was maybe the real reason she allowed her son to marry. She didn't realize how strongly she, herself, wanted to hold an infant in her arms again. With Andrea's marriage, deep down she had hoped for exactly that, a grandchild. She had experienced motherhood only once. Other women usually bore three to four children and more in their lifetime. She genuinely missed the feeling of motherhood. A woman is supposed to experience motherhood more than once. It was the best sensation she ever experienced in life. Even what she experienced with Socrates during the month of their honeymoon, or, for that matter, the only month they spent together, she thought sarcastically, could not be compared with the beautiful, powerful feeling of bearing and raising a child.

Andrea and Ana had been inseparable since they were little kids. Everyone in the village enjoyed seeing the two of them together. Andrea had made it clear since he was very young; Ana was his girl. No other young man dared to approach her. She, on the other hand, enjoyed his protectiveness and being called Andrea's girl. They were young, beautiful, full of energy, and full of love for each other, and they wanted to get married. But she should have known better. Yes, it was purely selfish. She did not want to be alone with Andrea gone. She wanted to have a child of her son's flesh and blood in case he did not come back as his father did not.

Feeling slight remorse for not stopping their marriage, she made Andrea afterward promise he would come back for Ana and her and his future children. She made him promise right there in front of Saint Thomas. She also made him promise in front of their house, the home he grew up in, the home where he gave his mother some sweet, beautiful years. But now she was not sure if Andrea would keep his promise. Many men had made that promise, but many of them did not hold on to it. Whatever it was in that land of the New World, it kept most of the men from coming back. Whatever they found there, it had to be better than what they left behind, she thought for the first time.

Tears came down on her cheeks. How could they forget their beautiful village? How could they get out of their minds the orange orchard, the smell of the lemons, the tangerines, and citrus flowers? How could they not miss the fresh air, the taste of the olive oil in the food, the traditional cooking that couldn't be compared with anything else?

From what men wrote in their letters, she learned they lived in small apartments, six or more men sometimes in the same small one-bedroom place; they worked all day from early morning till late at night, and they even worked on holy days, like Saturdays and Sundays. What did they find there that made them stay? *Other women!* she chuckled nervously.

From what she had heard, there was nothing in that

land that could be compared to the beauty of their mountains, to the crystal water fountains, to the blended orange and green colors in the their orchards, to their juicy oranges, the honey and the wine they produced. They wrote about dusty streets, all day hard work in the back of a place where people went to eat during the day or in the evening called a restaurant. They wrote about hard work in mines, a place under the ground with no proper air to breathe, digging out coal. They talked about hard work in constructing homes with many, many stores called buildings, where many families that were not even blood related lived; or working hard under the sun or rain on building the railroads, with some strange metallic beasts moving on it, transporting people to far places; or working twelve to fourteen hours in a place they called a factory. In those huge buildings, they would manufacture cars—strange, metallic moving things that had replaced the wooden carts pulled by animals in transporting people around.

So, what was it then that kept them there? What was there that made her Socrates not come back? *Women?!* she wondered again. *If women over there do not cook but go to that place called a restaurant and have their men pay for a cooked meal, what kind of women are they?*

Again, Mariána knew she never would be able to find the answer to her questions about things that she could not know or explain, things that were out of her reach, no matter how hard she tried to figure it out.

Mariána and Ana grew more silent and worn out by the day. The communication between them was mostly about simple things. With no other person in the house, the place sounded empty, huge, and depressing.

One night Mariána woke up and heard Ana crying in her room. She went upstairs and put her ear behind the door for a while, then reluctantly entered the room. Ana was shaking in her bed and sobbing hard. Mariána sat on the side of the bed. She took Ana in her arms and started to rock her gently and stroked her hair tenderly as if she was a small child who just had a bad dream and needed her mother's affection. Ana put her head on her mother-in-law's shoulder and did not reject her gentle hand petting her hair, and voiced her pain more with loud weeping.

The shed, hot tears of the two women mixed, and a strong connection was established between them at that moment, a bond that would survive years of hardship to come. After that night, the two women felt closer and began to communicate more about their strange fate and their feelings. Mariána shared her experience of loneliness with Ana. The loneliness of being married, with no husband to fulfill their dreams and needs, made their friendship stronger.

They received Andrea's first letter in three months' time. After that, his letters came every two months. Their arrival had become the peak of their lives, and both women waited anxiously for every single one. All the letters were addressed to the church. They had to go to the priest, Father Niko, to get the letter and had him read it for them. Andrea wrote long letters, and Ana would blush when the priest read the parts that were mostly about her. It was rare that a man would write to his bride in such an intimate way. Mariána would slightly smile and appreciate her son giving Ana so much attention in his letters. Andrea wrote in his recent letters, he had learned to write and read in English and Albanian. He sent the last letter written in Albanian using the Latin alphabet. He wrote he was taking lessons from an Albanian priest, Bishop Noli.

But Father Niko, was not familiar with the Latin alphabet. He knew only the Greek alphabet as he studied in an Orthodox Greek school in Athens. In the letter he wrote back in the name of the two women, he complained to Andrea about him using the Latin alphabet. He urged Andrea to go to the same person who wrote his previous letters in Greek if he wanted his new wife and his mother to know what he was writing about. But Andrea insisted on writing in Albanian, and the priest had no choice. He was forced to learn the Latin alphabet, to be able to read Andrea's letters. The letters became the new amusement for the Elders in the village. "Our Andrea is becoming so bright that even the priest needs to become smarter to read his letters," one would say smirking. Another would add to that with a sly smile, "Andrea doesn't want Father Niko to know what he is writing to his missus, but our priest is eager to learn what is going on, and that's why he is learning the Albanian alphabet" and a loud, warm-hearted laugh would burst among the Elders.

Andrea's letters made the life of the two women easier and pleasant. They would talk about what Andrea wrote in his letters, his job, Boston, the city where he was settled, the ocean, the big electrical wagons moving around the streets, the small private cars that would release white smoke, the money he was saving and putting it in a bank so one day he could get on a ship and come back. Recently he started to send even some money. When Andrea explained what a bank was, the Elders, after a rational debate, came to a bitter conclusion: in their village their bank was the Komnenis. Whatever they made, whatever earnings they managed to make, for some reason it ended up in Komneni's hands. The only difference was, they couldn't get their money back, like in the banks Andrea talked about.

Mariána and Ana memorized the letters and read them to each other if one would see the other was a little on the downside. Andrea's letters gave them a sense of hope for the future. The letters even became famous in the community. No one wrote letters the way Andrea wrote. Mariana was very proud of her son. Lately, she began to walk again with her head high, a thing she had not done in years.

Everyone in the village followed the old routine. Everyone was working hard, either on their property or over at Komneni's mansion, or at their citrus orchards, winery, or bee hives. No dolphins had showed up recently, and there was no mention of crazy Kozmái doing something odd to give their ordinary life some excitement. Andrea's letters, having a cheerful tone, lifted the people's spirit once in two months, and became the only thing everyone looked forward to.

Life for Mariána and Ana was no different. It had been more than a year since Andrea had left. The winter passed by, the summer too, and the autumn was fully in. Assembling the oranges required more workforces, and seasonal workers became regulars around the village. The villagers took pride in their oranges. They claimed their oranges were the best ones around the region, and even sweeter and bigger than the fruits produced in Greece, although they knew the Greek oranges were most famous. The usual way to grow juicy, delicious oranges was to follow some basic steps, the Elders would advise.

The orchard oranges were located in the warmest part of the mountainside, a sunny side where the soil was rich, and the wind was not too strong. Also, they would say there was much more than that into farming delicious, big, juicy oranges. They would emphasize; it was the essence of the soil in their village that gave the oranges the proper nutrition ingredient for the right sweetness. It was the sun that was warmer in this part of the country. It was the love they put into growing the trees. It was the art of nurturing the saplings that was different from other villages, a secret that was passed from generation to generation in this village only by the Elders. The Elders were the ones going around and cultivating the orange trees, giving orders to the younger generation.

For a man to get into the Elders' venture of orange tree grooming, he had to be over the age of forty, and he had to be one of the wisest men whose word had weight in the village's life. Most importantly, he must have shown some skills in the orange to be accepted as one of the Elders in the future. The young people would follow the Elders' instructions obediently, grooming the trees, with the hope to learn the secret, and one day, near their golden age, be received as one of them.

The Elders also made sure to rejuvenate the existing orchards or start a new one from time to time. They would help to start a new orchard in a virgin terrain, not used for a few years with the purpose to enrich the soil before using it again for a new plantation. They would bed out the seeds in the new orchard as well as in the existing ones. The seeds were carefully selected and preserved by the Elders from particular trees that gave the sweetest and the biggest oranges. There were no guarantees that the seedling would be identical to its parent, but the experienced Elders were very successful in their selection and the outcome. A seedling would take from two to fifteen years to bear fruit. It was a process that would keep their orchards on the top of every village around and would provide—for the generations to come. The Greek merchants would come by—way before the season was over—to make their pick on different orchards by testing an orange here and there before the ripening process was at its highest. Harvesting oranges when they just reached the proper size before starting to ripen was done to prevent spoiling during transportation to Greece. The timing of harvesting would vary by the variety and growing area. Whoever was lucky enough to seal the deal of selling directly to Greek merchants made a better profit than the ones who ended up selling to Komnenis, that made a huge profit selling their oranges as the middle man.

Following the track of her thoughts, Mariána realized something she had never reflected on before. People in her village put more of their time and energy, their art, and their love, into grooming the orange and olive orchards, the hives, and the grapes than into raising their children. The expression "It takes a village to raise a child!" made sense, and it was applied in such a practical manner. A child would spend more time with other children playing around the village than with the parents; not taking into account the fact that some of them did not have their fathers around much for various reasons. The villagers never discussed how to raise a child. But long talks on how to groom an olive or citrus tree, or how to cultivate the bees and build the best hives to produce the finest honey, make the best wine or construct a solid house took place routinely. *It is so sad that people put more time and thoughts in things that do not possess a spirit than on their offspring, who do have one*, Mariána thought.

She raised Andrea differently. Her Andrea was raised by the village as much as he was raised by her. She smiled, picturing her son's face. He had sent two photos recently, one for her, one for Ana. She took his picture out of a thin wallet she kept in her dress pocket. She looked at his handsome face for a while. Putting the photo back into the wallet, it hit her that survival played a significant role in why people would deal more with materialistic aspects of life than how to raise their children. The need to put food on the table for their own flesh and blood, she realized, was more vital to people. It took all their time, dominated their thoughts, and absorbed their energy; it made them almost incapable of properly caring for their children's spirits. *It had been that way forever*, she reflected. *The need of survival shaped people's lives!*

One morning Mariána woke up with a bad flu and high fever. The fire was out, and it was cold. Chilly shivers went through her spine, her bones were aching, and she felt an unpleasant twinge in her throat. She called for Ana.

Ana woke up hearing Mariána's voice calling her name. She would never call her so early unless she was in some kind of trouble. Worried, she threw her wool shawl around her shoulders, and rushed down the stairs in her night robe. She found her quivering in the corner next to the fireplace. Mariána's face was red, and she was feverish. She ran quickly to the kitchen, and made her aromatic mountain-herb tea and cooked her a hot meal.

The harvest season was at its high peak, and both women were working hard for the whole month of September to get every orange into the baskets that the Greek merchant had provided for storing them in. The cold season was sneaking in; the sweating and the hard work, the long hours, and the tiredness finally got to Mariána. She had never felt sick like this before. One of the things that had helped her to endure all the struggling years of loneliness and hard work was her good health. But today something gave up in her body. *I guess it is part of getting old*, she thought.

Ana decided to stay with her mother-in-law and take care of her for the rest of the day, but Mariána insisted she was feeling fine. She told Ana to go to the orchard and do as much as she could to harvest more oranges. Ana felt reluctant. She asked again to stay with her, but Mariána dismissed her plea. Ana knew, once her mother-in-law made up her mind, nothing could change it. She put her hand on Mariána's forehead. It was burning. Ana looked at her, and begged her to stay one more time. But Mariána just opened her mouth and, without releasing any sound, said, "Go!"

Ana put up a good fire in the fireplace and brought more logs inside. She prepared more of the mountain-tea and placed the teapot with a tea cup and the sugar container next to Mariána's mattress. She also cooked a light soup quickly and put the pan, along with a bowl, a spoon, and a napkin next to the teakettle. She gave Mariána another concerned glance, kissed her on the forehead, and left the house. As she was walking away, her concern grew stronger. After she took the path that brought them to their orchard, she made a quick turn and walked back to the house.

She found Mariána sipping tea. Mariána gave her a weak smile, and waved her hand as if annoyed telling her, "What are you doing here? Go! Go! I am not dying!" Ana stayed at the door for a bit, unsure of what to do. She knew how stubborn Mariána could be when it came to matters related to her own self. She shook her head, gave her a worrying look, closed the door, and reluctantly left the house.

Mariána took several naps during the morning, but it seemed the fever was not backing down. When the church's bell chimed in the air, announcing lunchtime, she picked up the bowl and poured some soup. After she ate the hot tasty soup Ana prepared for her she felt a little better. After a while, she heard someone walking outside the house and wondered who that might be. The front door opened slowly with a squeaking, annoying sound. She had to put some oil on the screws, she thought. Then she heard some steps inside the house. The fire-room door opened a little bit, and she saw a head peeking inside. It was Ana. She had come by to see how she was doing. Mariána made an angry face but inside she felt good. Her Ana was a good-hearted person. She worried about her the same way she would worry about her mother. The soup and Ana's appearance made Mariána feel better right away.

"You startled me my dear!"

"How are you feeling?" Ana asked.

"I am fine," Mariána said. "And, please, do not stand there! Come and have some soup!" she told her daughter-in-law with a warm tone, looking concerned at her tired face. Ana smiled, went to the kitchen, warmed some soup, and with a cup in her hands came back and sat next to Mariána. She put her hand on Mariána's head and felt the hot forehead in her hand.

"Ouch!" Mariána exclaimed, annoyed by Ana's cold hand.

"I am sorry!" Ana said with a sense of guilt on her face.

After finishing up her soup, Ana did not move.

Mariána stared at her and said: "I am fine! Go now! Hush! Hush!"

Ana shook her head, gave her a kiss on the forehead, a warm pat on the shoulder, and left. She heard Mariána's voice behind her:

"Ana, don't work hard, and come back before sunset!"

Ana headed to the orchard with a bad feeling inside her chest. *I shouldn't have left her alone*, she thought.

After Ana was gone, Mariána regretted asking her to go back to the orchard. She was young. A few more oranges would not make a big difference. The fear, she was turning into one of those old ladies who were hard on their daughters-in-law just for the sake of it overwhelmed her at the moment. People often did not realize that the cruelty of life's reality had a way of changing them. It made them harsh and strict on their loved ones, even when there was no need to be. As she was feeling guilty about sending Ana back to the orchard, the fatigue and dizziness from the fever, made Mariána doze off.

When she woke up, it was almost dark. It took her awhile to get used to the surroundings in the darkness. She looked around for Ana but did not see her in the room. She waited to hear the sounds of Ana's steps, but she heard no noise of any movements in the house. Maybe she was in the back at the bathhouse, or in her bedroom. She called Ana's name, but no one responded. The fire was out, and she was freezing. She called again.

"Ana, come down, please!"

She did not get any response. She felt weak and cold.

Worried, she picked up the coat Ana had left at the side of the mattress in case she needed to go to the bathhouse and tried to get up slowly. She felt dizzy, but she managed to stand up. She shivered. She put the coat on. She felt weak but made it to the second floor, leaning on the banister. She entered the bedroom, but Ana was not there. She lit the candle Ana kept on the table next to the bedroom door and looked around. The bed was untouched. She slowly went down and, opened the main door. She called out Ana's name. No one answered.

Panic engulfed her. Ana should have been home by now. It was too late to work in the orchards. No one was around, and it was dangerous for a young woman to be alone around the orchards at this time of the day. It was cold. She picked up the wool shawl hanging on the wall, covered her head with it, and made it out of the house and looked in the darkness. Not a sound came to her ear, to show if anyone was walking toward the house. A cold chill ran through her spine, but she did not go back inside. Slowly, she moved around the corner and headed to the bathhouse. No sign of light in its windows. She swung the door open. Ana was not there. Her shaky legs took off to the road, and she dragged her feet toward the orchard, calling Ana's name from time to time. Maybe Ana had been so taken by the work; she did not realize how late it was. At that point, she didn't know what to think. *I have to be easy on her*, Mariána thought with great concern. She was sweating. The cold chills became stronger as she reached the grove.

She looked around in the nightfall but couldn't see any sign of Ana. She called out her name again and listened to the sounds of the night. It was a scary, silent darkness. It did not respond to her, just echoed her voice. Not even a bird's singing or the trees' murmur in the air. Not even the slightest wind whistling.

Terrified, she called and called her name loudly, but the darkness just echoed her voice over and over.

The night was obscure, and she did not know what direction to go. Finally, she gave up, turned around and walked back to the house, hoping that Ana was already home. Her limbs were aching and her nose and head were burning, but she managed to get back home. It was very dark, and she was choosing her steps carefully. When she reached the house and tried to open the door, her feet stumbled on something. She looked down.

A body lay at the doorstep.

She leaned over and touched it. Her hand got wet. A strange odor reached her nose.

Finally her eyes were able to see clearly. It was Ana. She was covered in blood. Her face was badly hurt; her eyes and lips were swollen. Her body was cold. It did not move at her touch. A dreadful sense overcame her.

At that very instant, Mariána thought her Ana was dead; she felt completely out of it. She tried to get her body away from the door, but it was as if she were moving a rock. A noise at the gate made her turn her head, but she couldn't see a thing in the darkness. Looking carefully, she saw a shadow going away toward the orchards. Whatever it was, she did not have time to think about it; she had to take care of her Ana first. She had forgotten about her sickness, her fever, and her aching bones. She put together whatever strength was left in her body.

She found Ana's hands, pulled them over her shoulders and lifted her. Although her body was quite heavy, she was able to drag her slowly to the bathhouse. When inside, struggling, she put Ana's body in the wooden bathtub and went to the house. She got some candles, matches, and some of the logs Ana had brought earlier inside and walked back to the bathhouse. She lit the candles and put up a big fire in the fireplace. She placed the copper pot they used to wash their clothes and heat the water over the fire on the steel support. On the side, she spotted the water jar. She picked it up and spilled whatever water was left inside the pan. Then she went back and forth many times to the stream in the back of the house to bring enough water to fill it.

Not a scream came out of her mouth. Not a tear dropped out of her eyes. She was not sure if Ana was alive or not, but she went on doing things as if she was. When the copper pot was full, she covered it with a lid. She went back to the stream to bring water to fill the big water container in the corner. After done with that, she waited awhile for the water to get warm enough. Meantime she undressed Ana. Terrified, she noticed bruises all over her body and especially big black bruises around her thighs. In the back of her mind, she knew what had happened to her poor Ana, but she did not want to think about it at the moment. She tested the water with her fingers to see if the water was not too hot, to avoid harming the lesions and wounds on Ana's skin.

When she thought the water was warm enough, she started to pour it carefully over Ana's body. It turned red right away. A bad smell spread in the air. She poured enough water over Ana to clean off most of the blood and dirt. After, with a small pot, she took the filthy water out of the bathtub. Then, she poured more warm water. When the water covered half of Ana's body, she picked up the aromatic soap

Andrea had sent for Ana, the squash sponge, and began to wash Ana's body very gently. When she was brushing lightly against her rib cage, Ana released a groan.

That sound came as a sweet melody to Mariána's ears. *She must have a broken rib*, she thought. She looked for a second at Ana's face, and then, kept cleaning the rest of her body. Ana was severely damaged in her private area. She could not use the squash sponge to wash her there. She closed her eyes and with her hand, trying not to hurt her, cleaned her injured genitals carefully. She made believe she was washing a baby girl instead of a grown-up woman hurt by evil.

After she was done cleaning her body, she reached to wash Ana's long, curly hair. It was unusual for a woman in the village to have curly hair, but Ana had it—long, dark brown, shiny, and curly. She usually wore it in a big ponytail nicely braided.

When she finished washing the hair, she took out the dirty water and threw it in the back of the bathhouse, making several trips. She used some old clothes to soak up all the left water. Next, she poured water over Ana's body again to cleanse whatever dirt was left on her skin. This time she poured some scent from a bottle Andrea had sent from America especially for Ana. A nice fragrance filled the bathhouse. She took a deep breath.

If someone could have seen what was going on inside the bathhouse, they would have thought a ritual was being carried out.

After she rinsed Ana's hair one more time and wrapped it up with a towel, she waited a while for her body to warm and relax. She emptied the bathtub again. Mariána could not possibly carry Ana's body to the house. With a piece of cloth she dried the bathtub of every drop of water and wrapped Ana's body with dry, worn-out sheets and towels, and last she covered her with an old blanket they kept in the bathhouse. She put another one underneath, moving her body sideways. Then she placed a pillow under Ana's head and finally sat down on a small stool next to the fireplace, staring at the flames. She felt as if someone else was doing all this instead of her. She felt numb inside, and all this seemed like a bad dream.

She did not know how long she had stayed there, just staring without any thoughts in her mind. She was not sure if she went to sleep or not, but when she heard the rooster's first crow, she felt as if a lifetime had passed in front of her eyes in one night. In a while after the high-pitched crow, the sound of church's bells spread over the village.

She got up and looked at her poor daughter-in-law. Her beauty was gone. She couldn't see her features; that's how terribly swollen her face was. Her body was curled into the fetus position and looked crippled. She seemed to be in great pain.

Unable to bear the view in front of her in the daylight, she left for the house. She went to the fire-room and opened *musandra*[4]. From the shelves, she picked up an ointment that the midwife had given her to heal Andrea's wounds when he was little. Andrea used to get hurt a lot while playing with his friends around the village as a little kid. She went back to

---

4   Musandra - large closet in the wall of the room where mattresses, quilts and other garments are kept.

the bathhouse and applied the ointment carefully on Ana's face first and on the places mostly bruised. She needed a lot of ointment. She decided to go and ask the midwife for more.

She did not remove Ana from the tub for five whole days. She was running a high fever. She used cold compresses to keep the temperature down. Mariána guarded her twenty-four hours. She made up some diapers out of clothes that she threw away every time she changed Ana right there in the bathtub. Mariána fed her as one feeds a child, pouring soup and a mixture of herbal teas in her mouth three times a day, changing the sheets she was wrapped with when they were soaked wet from fever sweat.

The sixth day, after her fever broke down, she thought Ana was healed enough to be moved to the house. She waited until it became dark. She carried Ana carefully to the fire-room and accommodated her next to the fireplace. She brought another mattress and put it on the other side so she could watch over her poor Ana during nights.

The next morning she went to the midwife for more ointment. The woman looked at her suspicious over such a request for so much ointment. Mariána told her that Ana fell from the ladder at the orange orchard while picking up oranges and was bruised badly.

Days passed, and Ana began to heal bit by bit. Mariána had the impression that Ana had become conscious for a while now but behaved as if she wasn't. Mariána did not blame her. If she had been in her place, she would not have the courage to face her mother-in-law either.

Under the Orange Tree

Mariána sat down next to her one evening and spoke to her softly. She said she loved her, that what had happened was not her fault, and Ana should not feel shame or blame herself for that matter. But Ana did not react to what was said. It was as if she did not hear a word. She seemed lost in a place that Mariána couldn't reach. She kept her eyes shut and passed as she was asleep when Mariána was around. Mariána, on her part, didn't know how to find the right words to make the young woman feel safe and get out of the state of mind she had fallen into. What could she possibly say to wipe from her mind, spirit, and body what had happened to her that horrible night? She wanted so badly to, but Ana lying next to the fireplace, motionless, was a fact she couldn't dismiss.

The third week after that weary night, Mariána took a step further. Ana was recovered enough to sleep in the bedroom and have some privacy. She was not sure if this was the right thing to do, but it seemed right at this point. After she brought Ana upstairs and put her in bed, Mariána set in order the fire-room, cleaned up, and went out. The brightness of the sun hurt her eyes. She walked fast and sat at the bench under the mulberry. She looked at the view in front of her. Nature around the house seemed so peaceful, so harmonious, and so beautiful—it hit her as unreal. She stared at the greenness of the trees with a few oranges left on and got lost in her chaotic thoughts.

The day was warm. The sun was hitting the front of the house at a particular angle. It seemed as if a magic light was surrounding the house. Mariána felt the warmth in her bones. Her being absorbed it all, and she felt a strange calmness. Her mind slipped in emptiness for a bit.

Suddenly she jumped. *Ana did not get her monthly bleeding!* A voice screamed inside her. She ran in the house, stood at the bottom of the stairs for a bit, gazed up as if she was looking at some bizarre view, then frantic rushed upstairs. She opened the bedroom door. Ana was staring at the wall with her back facing the bedroom door and did not move even after she felt her mother-in-law's presence.

Mariána looked at her for a while. An outcry was rising inside her. She wanted to blurt out what she was thinking, but not a word came out of her mouth. She closed the door slowly. Her eyes were wide open as if they had seen a monster. Slowly, she went downstairs, almost stumbling. She leaned on the banister. She stopped in the middle of the stairs, turned around, looked toward the bedroom door with a twitch on her face, and then continued to go down the stairs even slower. Finally, she ended up outside. The terrifying, cruel fact was right there, inside the house.

She began to walk aimlessly. Her brain for the first time started to recollect the pieces. The missing period made her finally accept that what had happened that night was real and not just a bad dream. She did not have the time to think much about it while taking care of Ana. In fact, she didn't want to. She had been in total denial of the hideous incident. All this time she could not acknowledge the fact that Ana had been violated in a way a woman shouldn't ever be. And she knew it wasn't just by one man, but by many. Her physical condition indicated that much. She felt a sharp pain in her stomach.

She couldn't bring herself to say the word! And why didn't she think of the possible pregnancy from the beginning? How could she have not?

The herbal tea! She thought. She could have given it to Ana right away. She ran up the path that brought her to the wild part of the mountain and did not stop until she reached the area filled with herbs. She found the particular plant that many women had told her they used to terminate an unwanted pregnancy. She began to collect feverishly, as if she was under the effect of an unusual spell. After she had picked up enough, she ran back as quickly as she could. She couldn't acknowledge the fact, as the things were; it would not make any difference no matter how slow or fast she went. The child was conceived already! But the agitation of a possible child, not her son's, had bewildered her such that her reasoning was not functioning. Her thoughts were contradictory and disorganized.

For months, after Andrea left, she had hoped so badly for Ana to miss her monthly bleeding. She had observed her carefully at the time. When Ana eventually missed it, ironically she let her guard down. And, now, she was rushing like crazy to stop a process that she couldn't possibly reverse. She was walking as if she was under a domineering force she could not control. When she finally got home, she was all sweaty. She prepared the tea right away, waited until it cooled enough for Ana to be able to drink it, and rushed upstairs.

When she entered the room, Ana was in the same position. She kept her composure, approached the bed. She sat on the side of it with the tea in her hand.

"Ana dear," she said to the young woman. "I brought you some tea."

Ana, who kept her eyes closed when Mariána was present and, as always, obediently did what Mariána asked her to do; raised her head and opened her mouth slightly. Mariána put another pillow under her head and poured the tea with a tablespoon in her mouth in small doses as she did every day, feeding her liquids and soups mostly. When the tea went down Ana's throat, her body shivered.

"Yes," Mariána said softly. "It is bitter, but will do you good." She paused for a bit. "Please, you have to drink it all, dear!" she said with a calm, warm, but firm tone when she saw Ana keeping her lips tight.

Ana opened her eyes, looked at Mariána as if she wanted to say she knew what the tea was all about, but did not release a sound. She raised her head, sat down, took the tea cup slowly from Mariána's hand without looking at her, and with huge gulps, swallowed all of it down her throat. Another shiver went through her body. After that she gave the cup back to Mariána, lay down on the bed, turned around, and faced the wall. Mariána knew what that meant. She got up and left the room.

For the first time, she thought about the day it happened. Ana had begged to stay home and take care of her several times. Instead of listening to her pleas, she had reacted like a stubborn, difficult old lady used to never accepting help from others. With her foolish pride, she sent Ana to the orchard, and although the poor girl even came back for lunch to check up on her, headstrong, she sent her back again. She felt the salty tears on her lips and cried violently. She finally came to a realization; she was solely responsible for ruining her precious daughter-in-law's life.

She thought about the cliff at the end of the village, and she took off in that direction and walked and walked. At some point, she stopped. Ana was alone in her bed, disoriented, not capable of understanding what was actually happening to her; with no one to take care of her, lost to the point she did not comprehend most of the time what was occurring. Mariána made a swift turn and, almost running, walked back toward her house. She entered Ana's room, went to her bedside, wrapped her arms around her, and brought her close to her chest. Ana did not react. She just stayed in Mariána's arms like a dead log. Her numbness was unbearable, but Mariána did not give up. She rocked and rocked her gently like a baby until Ana's mind went to slumber. Mariána put her gently back on her pillow and quietly tiptoed outside the room.

The next day Marina heard a light knock on the front door. She went to open it wondering who was showing up so early at her doorstep. The church's errand boy, little Martin was standing a few feet away from the door. As usual he was jumping on his feet.

"Good morning Martin!"

"Good morning *Zonja Mariána,* Mrs. Mariána! You have a letter from Andrea. Father Niko said you could come tomorrow by noon to pick it up."

"Good day *Zonja Mariána*!

He waved his hand and left in a hurry not waiting for her response.

"Martin, wait! Let me give you a few oranges!" Marina called on him and quickly went inside to get some.

She heard his voice:

"Thank you, *Zonja Mariána*! I love your oranges. They are the best in the whole village, but I am in a hurry. I have a lot of errands to run. Maybe next time. Good Day now!"

She showed up at the door with the oranges in her hands, but the boy had gone way too far on the road. He waved his hand before turning the corner and disappeared.

Standing at the door with the oranges in her hands, she wished that Andrea had stopped sending letters at this point just like his father did.

Since all this happened, Mariána hadn't gone even once down in the village. But with the arrival of Andrea's letter she had no choice. If she did not respond right away to the priest's call, as she and Ana always did, she would draw suspicion. She went and sat on the bench outside looking at the oranges in her hands. What would she say to the priest about Ana not coming with her to hear what Andrea wrote this time? She needed to think of a good excuse. Everyone in the village knew how anxiously Ana waited for the letters to arrive.

Mariána couldn't think of any reasonable explanation that would not draw curiosity. She had to come up with something. The ironic part was, everybody in the village was fascinated with Andrea's letters to the point, that many came by to hear in person the priest reading them. The news always spread quickly. By now, they would be by the church waiting for her and Ana.

The arrival of Andrea's letters had become an exciting event for the village. Their reading was turning into a sort of a ritual. People were drawn by the tone of the letters and the impressive knowledge he provided. No one had written such long letters before with such interesting information. Sparking a good spirit, they created a nice atmosphere among the listeners.

The pride she felt about her son, the wit and wisdom of his letters that made people to come by to listen and talk about what he had to say—the contentment she felt about her son being different from all other men who migrated to America—all was wiped away by the news of his letter's arrival. In that very instant she wished he wasn't that smart. At that moment she wished they were not in the spotlight—his amusing writing had brought them to. Right there and then, she wanted to be someone who no one ever noticed.

After she locked the front door, she took the road to the church with a heavy burden in her chest. She noticed from afar the usual crowd waiting for her and Ana to arrive. They would wait outside for them to come out afterward, and ask what Andrea wrote this time. Some were bold enough to try to follow her and Ana inside, but she politely had stopped them. In the way out, Ana, who had an excellent memory, would recite the letter to the impatient comers, skipping, of course, those parts she thought were too private.

What now? She thought. *What should I say about Ana?* She couldn't think of any excuse.

When she reached the group, they greeted her cheerfully. They were waiting for the news from America. Andrea had written lately about other Albanians who lived in Boston since he learned his writing had become so popular in the village. *He never mentions his father*, it occurred to Mariána.

Her thought was interrupted by their greetings. She saluted back.

A woman asked about Ana.

"She does not feel that well lately," and suddenly she surprised herself by adding, "She had the grippe with a very high fever and it left her a little off."

A kindhearted "Ohh!" came from the group.

Everybody knew what "a little off" meant. The unusual high fever of this terrible influenza was often associated with some strange negative outcomes. Sometimes it caused even death, even mental illness, and was very common at this time of the year.

"Yeah!" one woman replied with a sad tone. "It is spreading around lately."

"How bad is it?" another woman asked.

"She…" Mariána paused, thinking carefully what to say. "It is bad! It's awful. It seems as if she is possessed by the evil spirit," she added with a distressed tone. "That's how bad it is."

A tear came down her cheek when she said that. The woman who asked put her hand on her shoulder and looked at the group.

"We are going to light a candle and pray for her spirit!"

she said.

Everyone's face showed sorrow. They were in dismay to hear about Ana being possessed. Ana was a sweet girl, and becoming Andrea's bride, she got into the hearts of the villagers. After an awkward moment of silence that followed the bad news, Mariána asked everyone to follow her to the priest's quarters.

"Why don't you all come inside with me?"

They understood. She wanted them to fill Ana's shoes that day. Honored, they followed her inside.

Mariána felt relieved. With that move, she killed two birds with one stone. She avoided being alone with the priest, and, her lie saved her not only from today's uncomfortable situation with Ana not being present, but for probable, future readings too. And, she knew, from now and on, they would follow her inside every time a letter from Andrea arrived.

While entering the church, her eyes caught the silhouette of a young man at the corner of the church. She turned to look but no one was there. She shook her head, thinking she was seeing shadows lately.

Life in the house became unbearable as the days passed. Despite the herbal tea Mariána had given Ana to end the pregnancy, nothing was happening. Noticing Ana's skin had become slightly green the past few days, but no sign of blood showed in her underwear or bed, she decided, continuing to give her the tea was of no use. Mariána began to fear that the baby might be born deformed. It had happened to Fotinía three years ago. She drank a lot of that tea. Fotinía had six children and couldn't afford to have another one. They were poor, and the children were a year or a year and a half apart from one another. Her husband barely managed with the earnings from the orchard he had left. He worked for the Komnenis too, but it was tough for him to support his big family decently. One more mouth in the house meant reducing the portion of food for the rest of children. But the herbs did not help Fotinía stop the pregnancy. Finally, the child was born, but something was terribly wrong with the boy. He was disfigured. People used to say the midwife had nightmares after his birth. The child did not live more than three months. That came as a relief for the ones who were superstitious about the infant. People addressed him as "It." His appearance had instilled fear even in folks who had never seen him. Some women blamed the famous tea.

Whatever happens, it's in God's hands now, Mariána thought. She had no power to change what took place and what was going to happen.

After Ana had stopped drinking the tea, her face regained the color little by little, her cheeks became rosy, and her beauty, once so famous, surfaced on her young face. But her mental state stayed the same. She was not responsive emotionally, and she did not speak a word, and that, worried Mariána tremendously. From time to time people would bring their favorite foods for Ana. Mariána gratefully would thank them but begged them not to go through the trouble, Ana did not eat that much.

Soon the morning sickness became a regular part of

Ana's daily routine, and her belly began showing little by little. What Mariána came up with at the church about Ana being left with a certain mental confusion after the grippe, and the mention of possession of evil spirits, came in handy to conceal the pregnancy. People were superstitious. If out of curiosity someone would come by and ask to see Ana, Mariána would casually bring up the famous expression "possessed by an evil spirit." That was enough to make the most curious person back off.

Gradually, Ana began to move around and do simple chores. Mariána had her eyes on the young woman constantly. Once she had to go to the village for some errands. When she came back, she found Ana with her wrists cut. The blood pouring out of her veins terrified Mariána. She tied her wrists immediately and ran downstairs to make her some chamomile tea. After that day, she prepared for her concentrated chamomile tea every night. At the same time, she put out of Ana's reach all sharp objects. Ana did not try anything like that again, but the fear she might was constantly there. The thought of losing Ana created in Mariána an immense painful emptiness. When it was time to go to the church, she had to tie Ana to her bed. She did not feel at peace doing it, but the fear Ana might try something foolish again while she was out was a good enough reason to justify the tying. While she would be tying her, Ana would look at her with sorrow in her eyes, but would not protest or complain about the brutal solution.

The winter was over, and the spring was sneaking in. Mariána did not have much left to do. She took care of Ana, the sheep, the hens, and the house, and she went to the church to get Andrea's letters every time Father Nikos sent news of a new mail.

Andrea's letters became everyone's knowledge in the details. Mariána was grateful to the small group that went along with her to the church for the reading routine. She told the priest to write Andrea something about Ana's illness, not enough to worry him, but enough to let him know that something was going on. Andrea responded he was very hopeful of coming home soon and taking care of Ana. Instead of feeling joy, Mariána felt sick to her stomach every time Andrea wrote about it.

One day, when Ana felt the first kick, she quietly approached Mariána, took her hand, and put it on her belly. Mariána felt the kick and looked up to Ana. She had the impression she saw an invisible smile in Ana's lips. She smiled back at her. She moved her hand gently over her daughter-in-law's belly for a few seconds to feel the kick again and then left Ana alone with her discovery in the world of motherhood.

From that moment, the concept of the child became real. Up to that time, it was an indistinct notion in her of the offspring actually existing. It was like a bad dream, which would and could disappear as every bad dream did. But now, it was a sure thing. It was alive and moving. He was giving signals of existing and being active inside his mother's womb. He was sending his mother the secret, universal baby love talk.

He was telling his mother he was real, and he was coming soon into her life. He was getting her ready to welcome him. He was preparing her to love him dearly, no matter what, when he finally would come out of her body and breathed the same air as she did. He was revealing to her that soon he was going to rest in her hands and on her breast, giving her the most sensational feeling she ever felt in her young life. *Was Ana sensing all that from the child growing inside her?*

Mariána sat down. She felt utterly lost. She felt almost paralyzed. She hadn't thought what would happen when the child was born. Taking care of Ana, making sure that Ana was going to survive all this, took away all her energy, attention, and concentration. Ana's well-being absorbed every drop of her strength, and she did not have the state of mind to think of the far outcome.

But that far future was getting so close, and she had no clue what would happen and what she would do. She had no clue how to explain the existence of the little one to villagers and most of all to her son, Andrea. She felt a panic attack. A dreadful feeling shook her. For the very first time, she thought of the attackers. A sharp, dark shadow flickered in her eyes.

Mariána didn't attend the Sunday Mass in the past months, using Ana's illness as an excuse. She did not dare face the Saints, especially *Shën Thomai*. The Sunday after the kick, she felt the urge to go and worship her favorite saint's portrait. She needed so badly to tell *Shën Thomai* about the whole thing. She had to get the burden off her chest to find some tranquility and absolution for the first time in long, anguished months.

It felt as if it had been a lifetime since all this happened. She felt ancient. For the first time in her life, she understood why people got old at such an early age. Hardship in life aged people more than anything else. She felt like one of the Elders. Up to now for some reason she had unconsciously blamed the saints and God for not protecting her Ana from evil that day. Lately, she came to the terms, she had no one to blame, but herself.

At the Sunday Mass, Father Niko noticed her strange behavior around the saints. He saw her whispering to *Shën Thomai*. She looked older. For the first time, here and there, bunches of visible gray hair could be seen from afar on her head under the sunlight beams. *Poor Mariána,* he thought, *Ana's illness has been harder on her than I have imagined.* He approached her to give some solace, but Mariána moved away from him as quickly as she could as if he were the personification of a sinister force.

He felt insulted and backed off. If someone else had reacted that way, he would have thought there was a problem in that person's life, and he would think hard how to help the parishioner. But with her, he always failed to be the shepherd.

Nevertheless, he couldn't help noticing that, despite all the hardship she was going through, her features as always preserved the beauty she once owned. She just seemed tougher, older, and very distant. Although, he had to admit, she looked more striking with her gray hair and with her vulnerability in a way she never did before. It was her inner strength that always had attracted him. He made himself a promise a long time ago, if he ever decided to get remarried, Mariána would be the only woman to take the place of his late wife. However, she never sent out any sign to empower him with enough courage to ask her to marry him. Today he felt as if he was looking at a stranger. There was nothing of the old Mariána in her.

He saw her leaving the church as if someone was following her. He walked out of the church and stood tall, in his black robe, at the top of the stairs for a while, watching her silent, burdened silhouette disappearing into the road up to her house. *There was something else about her today though*, he thought, *some kind of furtiveness I cannot put my finger on.*

Kozmái was puzzled by the young man's arrival. He said he was sent by *Zonja Mariána* from the village of Kalasa. Yes, he knew who Mariána was, but he did not understand why Mariána had asked for him. He had heard her son's bride was possessed by an evil spirit. He racked his brain, but he couldn't figure out why she had called upon him. The young man had given him her message: Mariána didn't want anyone to know she had requested him. He had to go and meet her for an important matter, but, the young man emphasized again, no one had to know about them meeting. He learned through the conversation; the young man used to be best friends with her son.

Not for a second did it cross his mind that this one was a call from a woman looking to taste his famous lovemaking. He knew somehow this was a serious matter, but he did not find any clues about the reason behind it all, and why exactly she chose him, no matter how hard he tried. They'd never met, although he was sure she had heard of him and his sorry attempt to see her. *Well*, he thought, intrigued, *I am going to find out.*

His curiosity grew as he packed a few things into his backpack. He put inside some clothes, bread, a piece of feta cheese, three onions, a few garlic cloves, and a few smoked fish for the trip to Kalasa.

There were no inns between his village and Kalasa. The winter was over for good, and spring was fully in. He had a pleasant and intriguing trip ahead of him.

Lately, Ana had been doing much better. Her belly grew bigger, and, as she was entering her seventh month; her facial expression became softer and sweeter. Mariána caught her often looking at her own belly and talking the baby language to the child inside her, but the moment she'd realize Mariána was around, she'd stopped. It seemed, she was afraid Mariána would despise her for loving the unborn child.

But since Ana's health had turned around for the better, something else was going on in Mariána's mind. Mariána could not explain why she thought of Kozmái and not someone else. Maybe with him she felt safe; he did not have any connection in the village. She sent for George, Andrea's best friend, with the excuse she needed help to fix the fence around the house. She made him swear, what she was going to ask him to do was going to be between him and her. She made him swear on his friendship with Andrea.

George and Andrea grew up together. They were inseparable when they were little. If she sent for Andrea, George would be right next to him. They looked like twins as children. They dressed the same, spoke the same, as if they were an imitation of each other. They would sleep over at each other's houses, eat together, and steal a few fruits or vegetables from other people's backyards just for the fun of it. What they stole was the same as what they had in their back or front yard, but the pleasure and the thrill of secretly eating something from other people's gardens made it worth getting punished if caught.

Their favorite story was the one when they stole from the priest's garden. He had chased them with a thick stick until they disappeared from his view into the citrus orchards. If he had been able to catch them, they would have ended up for sure with at least ten good lashes on their behinds. Many boys who had tried to take from his garden before them had experienced some whipping on their little behinds.

Father Niko was very fond of what he grew in his backyard. He had the best of everything cultivated in his garden. People said he used human waste to fertilize the plants, when the rest of them used animal waste. The priest had denied such a thing, but people who worked for him swore he did indeed use human waste to fertilize his fruits and vegetables.

The youngsters made a bet with their friends to see if they had the courage to steal from the priest's garden or not.

Others had no desire to pull such a stunt at the priest's expense, but Andrea and George had the guts to go for it. A few kids did not want to be part of the bet. They made a face just thinking what was used to fertilize those trees.

No one believed they would go through with the bet, but they did. They managed to get into the priest's yard and steal a good deal of oranges, grapes, and lemons, even tangerines, which the priest had sworn were the best tangerines in the area. Afterwards, they tasted whatever they were able to get hold of. They offered to share their small fortune with their friends, but the other children did not want anything to do with the priest's fruit. George and Andrea claimed solemnly that they were the best fruit they had ever tasted.

Although they had been two little troublemakers since a very young age, the villagers loved them. As they would do crazy things, such as testing their neighbors' forbidden fruit, at the same time they would be helpful to anyone who asked for their help. Since they were grown enough to be able to lift something or carry out simple chores, they went out of their way to help anyone in need, in particular, the elderly.

The Elders, used to say often about the duo, "Those little rascals!" And then, in a lower voice, they would add, "All that stuff is part of their upbringing and becoming real men. Those two are for sure the ones who one day will replace two of us." A satisfied smile would appear on their thin lips, which barely covered their mouths with no teeth, while saying, "Of course, when the time comes for one of us to go!"

They were twelve when they pulled off the crazy stunt

on the priest's backyard. After that George and Andrea had been considered young adults; the days of that kind of fun were left behind.

They both grew up to become fine, handsome young men who did no more look alike. However, their friendship grew stronger as they got older; and there was nothing that would spoil their bond. They would help each other working together on their families' groves. They went together to all the dance holiday parties in the area. They were famous among the young girls, and favorite candidates among mothers who had daughters. But they both, in very early age, fell in love with two beautiful young ladies, ruining the dreams of many mothers. They were more brothers by choice than brothers born from the same womb ever were. *George would keep his lips sealed,* she thought.

Andrea's departure was not hard only on Ana and Mariána, but on George too. He missed Andrea as much as Andrea's mother and wife did. From time to time, he would pay them a visit, but he did not show up much lately. He got married and had a child recently. Visiting a house where the evil spirit was around was not something a parent would do deliberately.

George was puzzled by Mariána's request of contacting crazy Kozmái, but he knew his friend's mother would never go out of her way without having a very good reason. So, he did what she asked him to do without raising any eyebrows.

After he had delivered her message to Kozmái, she had nothing to do but wait for the outcome. She had all the time she needed ahead of her for what she had in mind.

In a week or so Mariána heard an unfamiliar knock. It was getting dark, but one could see clearly outside. She went to the door, having the feeling Kozmái finally had responded to her call. Instead, when she opened it, she saw a stranger standing there, three feet away from her. Mariána looked at him, surprised. The man was very young. His beard was not even fully grown. He was about twenty years old. He did not make eye contact with her; on the contrary, he looked around. He seemed uncomfortable, shuffling from one foot to the other.

"May I help you, young man?" Mariána asked when she saw he was not going to open his mouth if she didn't ask.

"Ehhh, I am sorry to bother you, ma'am! Would you give me some food? I am really famished," he finally spoke, seeing sideways. He looked frightened, and she had a feeling he was trying to peek inside the house. Mariána became a little suspicious, but he had an innocent face, and seemed harmless. Nonetheless, Mariána could not afford to trust a stranger.

"Wait over there at the bench!" she said with a firm tone.

The man peeked one more time inside the house as if he was waiting for someone to show up, and then slowly turned around and headed to the bench. Mariána locked the door with the heavy handle she kept at the corner and went up to check on Ana. She was in her room embroidering her baby's outfits, something she occupied herself doing lately, and it seemed it did her good. She had been cutting, sewing, and embroidering several baby garments this past month along with the cloth diapers and covers and sheets for the crib with a lot of love—Mariána could tell. Making the baby's clothing was helping Ana keep busy.

Ana, as always, although feeling Mariána's presence in the room, did not turn around to face her.

Mariána closed the door slowly and went down to the fire-room. She put a piece of fresh baked bread with some cheese and a small onion in a napkin. She opened the window and put the wrapped meal on the outside sill. She called the young man to come and get his meal. Then she closed the window, securing it well and stayed a little on the side next to the window to watch him. He looked lost right there on the bench, and it seemed he was not in a rush. He got up slowly, approached the window, and peered through it for a bit. Mariána knew he couldn't see her.

He picked up the packed food, glanced once more through the glass, said nothing, not even a thank you, and left slowly. He stopped at the fence before he took off. A slight move of his head made Mariána think he wanted to give another last look at the house, but he did not turn his head. Then, he went up the road towards the orchards. In the, meantime, she noticed, he did not open the modest meal she had prepared for him. He did not seem to be either in a rush or hungry.

He came for some other reason, she thought. Maybe he was a thief. Maybe there were others with him, who sent him for information on who lived in the house. She had an unpleasant feeling. She opened the door slightly and looked around. After she felt secure no one was around, she went for the gong, fiercely banging the big copper plate that hung outside next to the front door. She used it to alert the neighbors in case of need or danger. The last time she had used the gong, had been when the frost was falling on the orange orchards, and it was three years ago.

Her house was a little far from the village, and that was another reason to have the gong in the house. Others would to go to their door and call loudly the neighbor. At least, with hitting the gong she would scare the thieves if they intended to do anything. How much she wanted at that moment to have a man in the house! She never felt fear in her life. She considered her village the safest place to live. She had heard horrible stories happening in other villages, but never in Kalasa. Since what happened to Ana, the fear and uncertainty were her constant companion. *Maybe*, she thought, *it is the same here too, but people keep their secrets under wrap as I have been doing with Ana.*

Ana showed up at her bedroom door with intense fear on her face, but Mariána told her to get inside and not let anyone in the room no matter what. Ana closed the door quickly. Mariána noticed the terror in her eyes. "This damn life!" she cursed for the second time in these past months.

In a short while her neighbors turned up, and she told them about the stranger. The men took off in the direction she pointed the young man left. The women stayed with her outside, chatting about Ana and their own children. Mariána started to fear that Ana might come out of her room, and her well-kept secret would blow up. Finally, after a while the men came back. They found no one.

"Maybe they got scared of your gong sound," one of the

women said.

"Would you like one of us to sleep over tonight?" her neighbor Lefko asked.

"No! Thank you, Lefko!" Mariána said. "I am okay! I will secure the doors and windows, and if anything happens, then I will use the gong again."

Her friends stayed a little bit longer as the men watched around one more time, and then they left, asking her to call them right away if she saw something suspicious. Mariána felt relieved. For an instant there she was more mortified that the neighbors would find out about Ana than dealing with them thieves.

Worried about the stranger's appearance, Mariána went to bed fully clothed and barely slept, but nothing else happened for the rest of the night. In the early morning, right after the rooster's crow, she fell asleep.

She'd had a few hours of sleep when she heard a knock on the door. She jumped out of bed, fixed her dress, passed her hands over her hair, and with her eyes not completely opened looked outside the window. A big, tall man, with long, dirty blond hair was standing a few feet away from the front door.

Kozmái, she thought. She turned around, looked at herself in the wall mirror, combed her hair in the back, wetted her fingers and pressed them on her eyebrows, and gave herself one more look. Pleased with what she saw, she opened the door. They looked at each other for more than a few seconds. They did not need an introduction. He greeted her first as if they had known each other for a long time:

"Good morning, *Zonja Mariána!*"

She greeted him back and invited him in.

"Please, do come in, *Zoti Kozmái,* Mr. Kozmái!"

Nodding his head in respect without saying a word, he walked in. It felt awkward going into a strange woman's house—not that he was not used of doing it—but with Mariána it was different.

She had aged a little since the day he saw her going to the Sunday Mass. He noticed deep lines around her eyes, gray hair here and there, and there was an expression on her face that gave him a clue of something very grave going on underneath. But, goodness, wasn't she beautiful! Her deep, hazel eyes had a spark in them that sent an instant surge in his body. *Forget about her lips!* He thought. He caught her reproachful look and reminded himself that this was a strictly a business-like call.

She pointed at one of the chairs around the table for him to take a seat and sat across him. She gazed at the squares on the tablecloth for a while then raised her eyes:

"You might wonder why I took the liberty to call upon you," she started. He waited for her to explain, nodding his head. "Unfortunately, I have a strong, subtle reason. I do not want anyone else to know what you are going to hear from me."

She stopped, inhaled deeply, lowered her eyes, and with her head bent to the side, not looking at him, she continued:

"First and foremost, I want to apologize for making you come all this way! And, you have to forgive me for involving you in a private matter, as I couldn't involve any of my fellow villagers for help in the delicate matter I am going to discuss with you. I am going to ask you to do something for me." She was silent for an instant, and then kept going, "I don't want my *paesanos* to know about this, and whatever you are going to hear from me today, is going to remain just between the two of us. You have to promise me that before I —," she did not finish the phrase.

She became quiet again as she wanted to recollect her thoughts. She raised her head and looked Kozmái straight in his eyes, waiting for a signal to continue. Looking at her attentively as he was studying her, he gave his approval with a slight nod of his head.

"I thought about you for various reasons," she continued. "You are a man of integrity, you move quite around, and it is easier for you to learn what I need to know. I hope you will understand and allow me to rely on your aid. But first you need to hear the story behind all this!"

She took another deep breath and, afraid that Ana might hear their voices and come down in the fire-room, she whispered for the rest of the conversation.

Kozmái couldn't help observing Mariána's face as he listened. When he heard, "Would you help me?" he closed his eyes, took a deep breath, opened them again, looked her straight in the eyes, moved his hands over his head down to the back of his neck, and said:

"It's going to be a difficult task."

Mariána was silent for a few seconds and then got up and said:

"Please follow me!"

She went up the stairs, and he walked after her at a fair distance to the second floor. She reached the bedroom door, opened it slightly, and waved for him to approach.

When he reached the threshold, he looked inside and saw the massive body of a young pregnant woman lying on the bed who did not react to the cracking noise of the floorboards.

Mariána closed the door slowly, looked at him, and went down the stairs. He followed suit, and when they were back in the fire-room, she stood on the other side of the table and said:

"She has been like that ever since."

She expected him to say something right away, but he did not. Although she understood the whole thing was a bit awkward, and he was put in a tough spot, anxious, she pushed by asking:

"So, are you going to help me, *Zoti Kozmái*?"

He looked at the woman in front of him, and for the first time in his life he couldn't help thinking, *Yes! She is the one! She is the real thing!* But, at the same time, he knew he was too late. He somehow had missed his chance.

"I will do everything in my power to help," he heard himself saying. He looked at her with a considerate, worrying, caring look and slowly said: "Good day, Mariána!"

He opened the front door and before leaving, added:

"You will hear from me as soon as I find what you asked. It might take some time, though." He looked at her attentively. "Take care of yourself!"

He walked away without turning his head. She watched him until he disappeared around the corner of the cobblestone pathway that led to the center of the village.

Mariána closed the door, went to the kitchen, sat down, and broke into tears. The tension of the conversation with a man she never met before about such private matter, the tone of his words, "Take care of yourself!" and his masculine, warm voice, made her feel vulnerable. It had been a long time since a man had looked at her that way. Not with a lusty look, but the look of a man who cared, the look of a strong man who was concerned about her well-being. She realized how much she had craved for that look. And the way her name sounded when he called her candidly, Mariána! It had a very intimate tone to it.

It had been a good twenty-two years since a man had called her just Mariána. At the moment, she came to understand, that she had, so terribly, missed having a man in her life, a man who was considerate and attentive. Simply, she just missed hearing a man's warm, caring voice.

The invisible wall she had surrounded herself with, had just been shattered by some candid words and compassionate looks. More tears came out of her eyes, and she cried until her lachrymal glands ran out of fluid.

Mariána was watching her very carefully. Ana's face showed serenity that she did not have before. She sounded dreamy and calm. Her face looked babyish, her lips were full and red, and everything else was huge, her arms, her breasts, her legs. Mariána was concerned about what she was going to do when the day came. In her estimation, Ana was due at the end of the month.

She couldn't afford calling on the midwife. She had to do it herself, and she was nervous. A lot of women had complications during childbirth. Many times the baby's cord would be twisted around its neck, or the child would be positioned backward. There were rumors of a child born with a lucky shirt that almost suffocated. There were cases of infants not being able to break out of their mother's body, and both the child and the mother losing their life in the midst of childbirth. That reminder gave her a real scare.

Only once had she assisted the midwife with one of Fotinia's children, and it was an easy delivery. Sometimes, not even admitting to herself, deep down, she wished for a stillborn. But the growth of Ana's belly did not give any indication of that baby not being alive. *And, boy, the kicks he threw! It must be a little chappie in there!* it crossed her mind.

She realized that, all this time, she was thinking about a boy, not a girl. "*I guess it's an old habit. It is easier having a boy. He is physically strong, and he does not get pregnant,*" she thought out of nowhere.

But she couldn't help thinking what she would do after the child's birth. She managed to conceal the pregnancy, but how could she keep an infant secret from others? How would she stop a baby from crying, or in a year prevent him from running outside? How would she hide the child from the village or Andrea for that matter? She shook her head to get rid of those questions. She did not want to think about that at all. She did not have any solution. She hoped everything would be resolved when the situation presented itself.

The most important thing was Ana's well-being. Mariána

prayed every night that Ana would have a natural, normal labor, and the birth would not create any health complications. She was not even aware that the child was not part of her prayer.

One early morning she woke up hearing noises coming from the second floor. Ana was moaning loudly. She got up, put the cloak on, and ran upstairs. She found her standing in the middle of the room with a puzzled face, looking down at her wet feet. A small puddle of water was growing on the floor. Ana raised her eyes and looked at Mariána as if she was asking, what was happening with her. Then she put her hand at the bottom of her belly and groaned loudly. Fear showed in her eyes, and she eyed Mariána, as if asking to be rescued. The fluids were flowing down her legs, wetting her nightgown. The poor girl did not know how the whole thing would play out. It was Mariána's duty to tell her about the process of giving birth, but they did not talk about the pregnancy as if it did not exist.

Mariána stood frozen at the door with panic. Ana's water had broken, and she was going into labor. Never had she felt such fear in her life as she was experiencing it at that very instant. What if something went wrong? What was she going to do with the baby? What if the child died during birth? Maybe so! That would have been a solution to all this. But, what if Ana died in her hands? Should she send for the midwife?

Her brain was restless, and she didn't know what exactly

to do. But one thing she knew; the midwife was out of the question. She pulled herself together and in a composed voice addressed Ana as calmly as she could:

"You have sit down, my dear! It will be all right! You will be fine."

She helped Ana to sit on a stool in the corner of the room and opened *musandra,* the closet in the wall, and took out all the old sheets and old clothes she could find. She ran downstairs to get a big piece of a green, plastic cover. It was a spare item from the war. She did not remember how it ended up in their house. They used it to protect the lemon tree in the front yard during the winter. When she came back upstairs she covered the bed with it; then she put layer after layer of some soft, old sheets over it. And then she brought all the pillows they had and put them at the head of the bed.

She noticed the water had stopped flowing from Ana's legs. She asked her to take everything off and gave her a clean robe. She left the room to give Ana some privacy. When she came back, Ana was sitting on the corner of the bed, looking towards the door with her eyes wide open, waiting in suspense for the unexpected to come. Mariána helped her to lie down on bed. Obedient, Ana did everything she was asked to do.

Mariána positioned Ana carefully over the pillows and told her to bend her knees and stay calm. She covered her legs with a blanket, gave her a kiss on the forehead, and went downstairs to put up the fire. The water needed to be boiled. She placed a big pot filled with water over the fire. It would have been easier if Ana gave birth in the fire-room, but if someone came knocking on the door, the secret she had kept under wraps for nine good months would get out. She went out to the bathhouse and looked for Andrea's baby crib. She found it behind a pile of old things in the back of the bathhouse, cleaned it up, brought it back into the house, put the wooden handle behind the main door, and ran upstairs. She took out from the *musandra* a pair of clothes Ana had made for the child, and some towels Andrea had sent from America with a man who came to visit his wife a few months back. She put everything on top of a small table in the corner of the bed.

Ana's contractions were progressing steadily. Mariána told Ana to breathe deep and exhale out each time she felt the pain coming. She explained the breathing would ease the pain and make the contractions functional. She went downstairs to check on the water. It had been boiling for a while. She threw a pair of scissors in the pan to be sterilized. Then she poured some of it from the big pot into a smaller one, covered it with a lid, and carefully walked up the stairs. She made a few trips up and down the stairs. In the last one, she used a long wood fork to pick up the scissors from the boiling pot and threw them in the small pan.

Ana's moans became louder and more frequent. Her forehead was covered with sweat. Mariána lifted up the blanket and tried to picture what the midwife did when assisting Fotinía's childbirth. She put the stool at the end of the bed, sat down, and looked carefully. She thought this would feel awkward, but everything was coming very naturally as if she had done this many times before. Daring, in a challenging situation, was always a life saver. She realized that Ana was fairly dilated, but the contractions were not that frequent yet. Wiping Ana's soaked face, advising her to breathe deeply, and checking if the child's head was showing up into the cervix, Mariána was working on the clock.

In a short while, the contractions became more frequent and stronger. Ana became dilated enough to start pushing. The moans grew louder. Mariána begged her not to scream. The neighbors could hear. She saw Ana biting her lips and struggling to push. After a while, it seemed as Ana was becoming passive. Trying to hold the screams, she was not concentrating her strength into pushing. The baby was not emerging.

"Please, breathe deep and push!" Mariána pleaded. Ana looked at her with tired, passive eyes and turned her head to the side. She was giving up. Mariána saw the death wish written all over her face. She panicked.

"Breathe deep and push!" she suddenly spoke loud.

Ana looked at her with her big, troubled eyes, and, instinctively pushed a little.

Mariána's face showed anguish. The fear of losing Ana induced an insensible anger in her and her voice became sharp.

"Breathe deep and push once more!" she yelled this time scaring Ana.

Frightened, the young woman did as was told and pushed harder.

Finally, Mariána saw the baby's head. She asked Ana to push even harder with the same harsh tone. It was the only way to get her out of the passive state she was falling into. Ana gave it another try. She breathed, focused, and pushed with all the strength she had left. Little by little the infant's pink body, covered with blood and all kinds of other secretions, emerged from his mother's body. Mariána's heart was pounding slightly, and she was experiencing a sensation she never had before; the miracle of a child being born, the miracle of life, the miracle of creation. At the instant she completely forgot how the little creature was conceived; she forgot about Ana's pain and shame. She forgot about her own turmoil about the child for the last nine months. Tears streamed out of her eyes when she held him carefully by his petite arms and carefully helped the tiny body to emerge. She opened her palms and the baby that just fell on them. It was a very small, wrinkled, pink boy.

Holding the baby in her left arm, she picked up the scissors from the hot pan, cut carefully the umbilical cord, and put the infant on a clean fabric over the table in the corner. Then she washed his skin from all the thick secretions and the blood with a soft wet piece of cloth and put him on another clean sheet. She tied the cord prudently as near to the infant's tummy as she could, and cut most of it close to the knot. She poured a little bit of *raki*[5] cautiously at the end of the incised cord to sterilize it. The infant released a cry.

Then she wetted a clean piece of cloth in warm water and wiped his body gently again, and with a dry one absorbed the humidity of his skin afterward. She wrapped the little boy in his cloth diapers and put him in Andrea's crib.

Suddenly she turned around and faced Ana. Taken aback by the tiny infant, she totally forgot she was not done with Ana. She was lying on the bed uncovered. The baby-sack

---
5 raki - a strong alcoholic beverage distilled from grapes or other fermented fruits

had not come out yet. Ana was shivering violently. Her teeth were gritting, her legs were shaking, and her knees were clashing. The cord was hanging out of her body. By now the sack should have come out. Mariána remembered that some women lost their lives because it did not come out on time, and their bodies went cold and the cervix went back to the usual width. They had a very high fever in the incoming days and passed away. Terrified she picked up the end of the cord hanging out of Ana's body and pulled it carefully. Her body was warm enough, and her cervix was not yet back to normal. She found resistance. Ana moaned, and Mariána said to her softly:

"Push one more time, my dear!"

Ana's body was contracting again, and finally she saw the sack coming out. Mariána felt relieved. She brought the pan with warm water close to the bed and began washing Ana's injured private parts and applied some of the pomade left from her injuries. Afterward, she asked Ana to move a little. She pulled underneath her the plastic cover with all the sheets and clothes she put under her to absorb the blood and all the fluids that came along with the childbirth. She changed Ana's robe, which was soaked with sweat, and placed a thick cloth pad between her thighs. She put a new nightgown on Ana, clean sheets on the bed and covered her body with a white linen and two thick blankets.

She saw the plea in Ana's eyes, but she behaved as if she did not notice.

"Close your eyes and try to get some sleep!" Mariána added with a warm but firm voice. She wrapped up the dirty sheets and clothes with the plastic sheet, went to the door, looked at the child and the mother for a second, then left. She went downstairs, left the bundle of the dirty clothes in the hallway and went to the kitchen to prepare some boiled water with a little sugar and salt for the child to drink. She washed her hands, poured water in the *ibrik*[6] to boil, and put it over the fire. Then she went in the back of the house and dug a deep hole at the end of the garden. She went back inside, picked up the bundle of clothes, quickly ran to the backyard, and threw it in the hole. She covered it carefully with soil. After she had leveled the ground around the hole, she straightened up, released a deep sigh from the pain in her spine, wiped her sweaty forehead with her arm, and went back inside.

She went to the kitchen, scrubbed her hands with soap thoroughly, rinsed them carefully, then threw a handkerchief in the boiling water. She grabbed the tea kettle and went back up.

She found Ana feeding the infant. She shouted, "No! Don't!" She put the *ibrik* on the table and grabbed the child away from her. "Your milk is not yet ready, and you cannot get used to feeding him!" she said loudly, almost screaming. Stunned, Ana raised her head and gave her a bewildered look.

But Mariána knew better. The instant a child was breastfed by his mother, a mutual bond, mother and offspring, a closeness that was stronger than any other connection created among human beings was established between the two. She couldn't allow Ana to feel that unique bond; she couldn't

---

6   ibrik - teakettle

let her Ana get fond of that little creature. *It wasn't enough she had to carry him in her belly for nine months, but she had to feed him now?* A voice in her head blurted out. She ignored Ana's terrified face. She could sense the alienation and frustration mirrored in her sad, beautiful eyes while wrapping the baby in a thick blanket.

She had no idea what she was going to do, but deep inside she did not want either Ana or herself to feel attached to the little one.

She was acting as if under a spell. Some strange power was leading her on a path she had never thought she would be headed. She finished wrapping his tiny body leaving only a small area for him to breathe, and ran down the stairs and out of the house.

Ana watched her mother-in-law with troubled, nervous eyes that turned into misty ones full of tears when she saw them out of the door. She could sense she was not going to see that tiny pink face ever again. She felt the urge to run after Mariána, but she couldn't move from where she was standing. She was not capable of revolting against what was happening. She had lost the ability to react these past nine months. She was staring at the door, listening to the cry of her child in the distance until the sound faded away, without being able to fully comprehend what had actually happened.

Mariána ran in the darkness. The nights up here in the mountains were chilly, and the cold kept inside even young people who usually would sneak out of the house to meet their sweethearts. *Not one soul will see me tonight*, she thought. Suddenly she found herself on the west side of the village, next to the edge of the infamous cliff. Many stories were connected with this cliff. A young lady, who had lost her honor to a stranger passing by the village, had jumped off the cliff when she found out she was pregnant fifty years ago. There was an old story about four hundred years ago. A group of women also had done the same, sacrificing themselves to escape from being captured and turned into sex slaves by the Ottomans.

The night was pitch-black, but her eyes, used to the darkness, could see clearly. She stood at the end side of the cliff looking down at the deep obscurity underneath. *They are not going to find a sign of him if I take his clothes off,* she thought in that hazy mind of hers. She put him down and uncovered his face. The cold hit his tiny face, and he started crying again.

Mariána couldn't stand his cry. She put the corner of the blanket back over his face, left the child on the ground and started to walk around like a sleepwalker with her hands crossed over her chest. She was in an unusual state of mind. Certain gloominess was taking over her brain. She had to do something, but she did not know what exactly to do. She made two more rounds back and forth from where she put him. The little wretch did not stop crying. The third time she grabbed him and started rocking him gently. The infant, feeling the warmth of her body, became quiet. When she did not hear his voice, she walked toward the very borderline of the cliff. She extended her hands and held the child up high with her hands shaking. Her face was stoned. She didn't know she was capable of all this. She did not know she had it in her. An unknown fear grew inside her.

"*This baby is not my flesh and blood!*" she thought, trying to convince herself and justify what she was going to do.

"This child was conceived by a vicious act!" she screamed into the night, not being able to bring herself to say the exact word.

"He is not ours!"

Her shout echoed down the cliff.

"His creation is not sanctified by love or marriage," she wailed, shedding tears.

Looking at the dark sky and the indifferent stars, a weeping whisper came out of her cold, dehydrated lips as her tears were getting almost frosty.

"We cannot keep this child! We just cannot!" she cried. *He might be just like his creator. The apple does not fall far from the tree!* Her inner voice muttered, aiding her guilty, perplexed conscience.

She was holding the child in her arms, not knowing what she was going to do next. The infant moved inside the blanket and released a sharp cry as he sensed the danger he was in.

The motherly instincts made her bring him closer to her chest. A warm feeling swept her body when she felt the little tiny body pressed on her bosom, and she rocked him again gently.

The infant stopped crying. She looked ahead of her. She saw the thick blackness below the cliff and felt horrified. She felt dizzy. She felt as if her body weight was being dragged by a pulling force toward the side of the abyss.

"May God help my soul!" she whispered.

She did not remember how long she had been standing on the ground when she came back to her senses. She shivered. It was bitter cold. Suddenly she felt a motion next to her chest. She realized the child was right there with her, and his little limbs were pushing the blanket. "I did not do it!" she whispered with a weak voice. "I did not do it!" she repeated. She got up, and keeping him tight, swiftly walked away from the cliff, petrified of what could have happened a while back there. She walked faster and faster—she did not have a clue for how long—and somehow she stopped.

She didn't know what she was doing or where she was going. Once, she thought of herself as a person capable of making the right decision on everything no matter how difficult the situation was. But since the violent assault on Ana, she had lost her aptitude of thinking straight. She had lost the ability to be strong; she had lost the capacity to act on in the right moment, and know what the right thing to do was.

Suddenly, she found herself in front of the church. She felt the warmth of her tears and she stared at the church's heavy wooden door. The deacon used to close the gate every night around six in the afternoon, after darkness would spread over the village, and opened it around six in the morning.

Maybe he forgot to close it tonight, she hoped. She needed a serene place to think. She wanted to get inside the church very badly. "*Të lutem më ndihmo, Zonja ime Shën Maria,* Please help me, My Ladyship Saint Mary!" she prayed in a low, weary voice.

She heard a squeaky noise coming from the heavy door, and she walked up the stairs toward it. She reached the metallic handle and pushed it hard. By some mere luck, it was not locked. She could not be sure if the deacon had left it open or her Ladyship had heard her prayer. She entered the church and slowly approached the altar. She bent her knees, closed her eyes, and began praying. She prayed for a while. Her soul needed forgiveness. Back there at the cliff, she was at the breaking point of committing the sin of her life by throwing the frail, defenseless infant into the abyss.

She heard the infant cooing and then the sucking sound of his tiny mouth on his own thumb. She knew if she removed that blanket to see his little, lovable face or spend one more minute with the child, she was going to take him back to Ana. But she couldn't do that, she just couldn't! She couldn't bring this baby home!

Unconsciously she had hoped, here, inside the church, she would find an answer. But she did not! She desperately needed to decide what to do with the child she carried in her arms. Every passing moment made it more dangerous for her to make a decision. On the other hand, someone could walk into the church and find her with the infant. And, the longer she held him in her arms, the more difficult it would be for her to make the harsh decision. Unable to move, uncertain and confused, she stayed there with the baby in her arms, staring at the statue of *Jezu Krishtit*, Jesus Christ—searching for a sign. Christ's head was leaning on his right shoulder, and his face was showing suffering and penitence.

But, there was no sign or premonition! Mariána's mind

had gone blank for a long while. Suddenly she got up, placed the infant on the bench in front of the altar, kneeled, made the sign of the cross, and whispered, "*Mëshiromë o Zonja Shën Mari!* Forgive me My Ladyship Saint Mary!" and she turned around and walked out of the church in a hurry without turning her head, although she had a strong urge to do so. Afraid to cause noise, she closed the door slowly behind her and left. She rushed through the cobblestone road without looking back with any thoughts or feelings. A total numbness had overpowered her mind and soul.

In a while, she felt emptiness in her arms. She had the strong desire to have the baby in her chest, but she did not turn back. She walked away as fast as she could until she ended up in front of her house. Suddenly she fell to her knees, closed her eyes, put her hands over her face, and stood that way for a short while in the coldness of the early morning—not having the strength to enter the house empty-handed. Driblets of tears came out through her fingers, fell on the grass and mixed with droplets of the morning dew. When her body got too cold and sharp shivers ran through her spine, she slowly got up and went in.

She approached the stairs and looked up. She stood there for a bit undecided if she should go upstairs or not. But, she knew, she couldn't face the fragile, shattered young mother at that instant. Poor lass! She just had brought in life her first child and Mariána had taken her newborn from her arms before the hapless mother could feel the unusual sensation of her first child's breastfeeding. She had snatched the infant from her arms; right after the young woman had experienced in the blink of an eye the feeling of motherhood. She had taken from her the only possession that was simply hers, and only hers, Ana's.

Deep down she knew; Ana wanted to keep her child, and she had no right to stand in her way. She knew if someone wished to make a woman their worst enemy, it was to harm or take away her child the way she did. She remembered as a child when a stranger had kicked their golden retriever's puppy; how her parents had to intervene to save the rude man when the mother had fiercely attacked him.

But she had to! She had to! She had to, for God's sake! She had no choice! The screams echoed inside her.

Crushed, she went back to the fire-room, rolled out her mattress, laid down on it without taking her clothes off, and covered herself with the quilt. She gazed at the ceiling for a long time until her eyelids became heavy.

The child is safe in the church. Somebody will find him and will take care of him, was the last thought that crossed her mind before she fell into a troubled sleep.

In the following days, Mariána couldn't bear the young bride's face. They avoided being in the same room longer than they needed to be. Worse part, Ana's breasts were constantly lactating. She remembered hearing many women using parsley to stop the milk flowing after the child had grown enough to be fed with regular food.

Mariána went to the garden and to pick some parsley. She washed each stem carefully, pulled out leaves one by one, put it all on a plate, and brought it upstairs. Looking at her with remorse, she asked Ana to put some parsley inside her breast garment and also eat some of it. Ana did not respond, and she did not make any attempt to get the parsley either.

In the evening, Mariána went back upstairs to check up on her. The parsley was on the plate untouched.

It was the first time Ana did not do what she had asked her to. It was her first rebellion since she had put her foot in this house. Ana, in a very submissive way, trusting her mother-in-law blindly, did exactly what Mariána had asked her to—up to this morning. And, when she saw Mariána's disappointed face, she got up from her bed, gave her a very odd and cold look, passed by her without saying a thing, left the bedroom, ran down the stairs, and stormed out of the house. Mariána ran after her and saw her heading to the bathhouse. She understood, Ana wanted to be left alone.

In a few days, Ana went back to her withdrawn state of mind. Mariána started to worry about her. What was going on in the village about the baby did not disturb her much. Her concern for Ana was greater than the stir that was provoking her fellow paesanos. The fear that Ana might try something drastic against herself again absorbed her attention and energy. She watched her every step. The progress she had made at the last stage of her pregnancy regressed quickly. Mariána's mind was under pressure, and she did not know how to deal with her new withdrawal.

Fotinía heard a knock on the front door. She opened it, and she saw Mariána at the doorstep.

"Wow, Mariána! It has been a long while since we saw each other last," smiling, she invited Mariána in.

After they talked about Ana's health, the conversation came around to the abandoned child.

"That's why I came by," Mariána said. "I need your advice on something!"

"Oh, sure, sure Mariána, anything for you," said Fotinía, surprised—many women would go to Mariána for guidance, but Mariána never asked advice from others.

"I heard all this noise about the infant left at the church, and I thought about my Ana and her sickness." She paused for a brief moment, and then went on: "She isn't herself since her illness. This child is causing so much stir, and I was thinking maybe taking this unfortunate child in our home, could help Ana recover. She seems lost in a strange world since Andrea went away. She was not as lucky as a lot of us have been, to be impregnated during her prime with Andrea. And after the influenza, she had become worse. She is too young not to be able to enjoy motherhood. She needs an infant in her arms. And who knows when Andrea will come back." She sighed and looked at her friend with worry in her eyes and went on:

"Am I out of line here? What do you think, Fotinía?" she finished, looking at Fotinía, hoping for approval from her friend.

Fotinía observed her for a while, not sure what Mariána was really trying to say, and then, shocked by the realization of what she heard, asked:

"Are you sure you want to take this child in?"

"Yes!" she said. "The baby will be a good thing for both

me and Ana. I, too, miss having a child around the house. But most important, the infant will occupy Ana's time. The baby is going to be a *melhem*[7], for Ana's troubled spirit."

Fotinía looked at her friend for quite some time and thinking about Ana's illness, asked again:

"Do you want the child for yourself Mariána, or for Ana?"

Mariána released another sigh and said with a sad tone, "For both, Fotinía, for both. We both are very lonely."

She looked at her friend with a sad expression on her face.

"We both need a child in our lives," she continued. "The life in our house is becoming wearisome. All we have is an empty home, no joy, no children running around, no children's voices, no children's laughs, just Ana and I. We cook, but for who? We work hard without any purpose. We do not have a child to bring a smile to our face. We face each other every night at the dinner table, and we don't know what to say to one another. There is nothing to talk about anymore. We are like two mute people with no words left to give voice to. We go to our rooms with no motive for the next day. It is not a normal house Fotinía, and it is unbearably quiet, not to mention Ana's illness."

Hearing Mariana, Fotinía looked at her friend surprised, but couldn't help herself continuing the line of her thoughts by saying:

"So, you think it is going to be a good thing for both of you?" Fotinía asked with a hesitant voice. *It was unheard of, taking in and raising a child who no one knew where it came*

---

7   melhem – pomade, ointment – figure of speech - a healing for a spiritual wound

from. It would have been different if the child was blood-related or from their circle of friends, she thought. Moving her eyebrows up, unsure about the whole affair, she continued,

"And, you think, Ana will be able to take care of him given her condition!?"

"Yes, Fotinía!" Mariana responded, and thinking, *"Did she hear what I said?"* Her eyes filled with tears, but she found the strength to continue, "And, I will be there for her; I will teach her everything she needs to know about bringing up a child. I will help her to overcome any problem she might face with the kid."

Fotinía looked at her face as if she was seeing Mariána for the first time in her life. The words she said earlier started to sink in with her. She noticed the solitude of the long, lonely years in her friend's eyes and a picture of her and Ana alone in the house crystallized in her mind. With Andrea gone, and with a sick daughter-in-law, with no child around, it must have been difficult for her friend.

"How many years have passed Mariána?" she asked suddenly.

"Twenty two lonely years!" Mariána answered with a low voice.

Mariána's head was slightly bowed, and her eyes were gazing at the wall. The pain of all those years was written on her face.

Fotinía realized how much she had changed since her son's departure. Her head was covered with gray hair. She realized her friend had been hurting deeply inside for a long time. *How didn't I notice it before?* She thought worried for her friend.

"Mariána, dear!" Fotinía said, her voice expressing sincere concern. "It has been years you did not have much happiness in your life. Andrea is gone and Ana wasn't fortunate to have a child of her own. I think you both deserve to have the joy of a child in your house. I am not concerned what others will say; the only thing that really troubles me is, how will Andrea to take all of this?"

She looked at Mariána and added, "It is hard for men to understand how we women feel when it comes to children even if they are not our own."

Mariána raised her head, looked at her friend straight in the eye.

"Andrea is not here!" Her voice became harsh. "God knows if he will ever come back! When I wrote Ana was ill, in his next letter he wrote he would come home soon. Since then, I received two other letters with the same promise. But he isn't here, is he Fotinía!?" Tired, she sighed deeply, lowered her voice, and with her eyes gazing into space, continued, "I am going to explain to him in the next letter why I decided to take the child in." Shaking her head, she spoke with a tone that did not show any hope of Andrea coming home any time soon. "Andrea is a good son, and he is a good man too. I am sure he will understand."

Fotinía looked at her friend with compassion, put her hand on her shoulder, and said softly:

"Okay then!" she said. "Let's do it! Let's go to the priest and place the request."

She thought for an instant, and said:

"Wait for me here! We need more than two people to go to the priest with such a request." She put her coat on and left the house.

That was the help Mariána was hoping for, and she was glad Fotinía understood and acted as a longtime, good friend. Quite some time went by, and Mariána began to worry about Ana being by herself in the house, when Fotinía showed up at the door with four other women.

"You are doing the right thing Mariána," one of the women said. "That child deserves to have a real home, and who better than you can provide one for him."

"And," another one added, "it is going to be good for you and Ana too. That poor young woman needs a child in her arms."

"So, what are we waiting for?" asked Fotinía. "Let's go to the priest and ask him to give the infant to our Mariána."

The group of women walking toward the center of the village attracted the attention of people within their homes, and almost everyone got out in the street, curiously asking about what was going on. When they heard what it all was about, some women joined the group. Krisúlla, the tallest, and the strongest woman in the village was among them. She had a huge body, and she was known to be very competitive with men when it came to hard work. Her participation in the group drew more interest as the women proceeded through the main road of the village and made people more curious. More women tagged along. A few men, curious to learn the outcome in first hand, followed in the distance. When they arrived at the church, the group had drawn fifteen women altogether, and a bunch of men tailing them.

Under the Orange Tree

The priest heard a powerful knock on the church door. He went to open it, and, surprised, faced Krisúlla. With her big fist up, she was ready to pound the door one more time, although the metallic door knocker was right there in front of her. A group of women were standing solemnly behind her on the stairs of the church. He looked startled as he didn't expect at this hour the arrival at the church of a bunch of women. It was an unusual time for villagers and especially women to show up at the church's door unless something imperative had transpired.

The group of women looked powerful and menacing. They resonated such vigor that he felt as if he was pushed back by a strong vibe. *Did they come again to inquire if the child is mine?* He thought distressed. *The midwife checked already the maid and did not find any sign of childbirth or lactating. So, what exactly do these women want from me now? What else should I do to prove them I have no relation, whatsoever, with the child?*

For the first time, he felt powerless. He, the one who had the absolute power over this village, the one who had its people in his palm, and represented the mighty God for his parishioners, was being accused of committing the sin of fornication by the very people that trusted him with their most personal problems and secrets. He was being scrutinized by the men and women whom he guided throughout their lives from birth to death. What surprised him most was Mariána's presence in their midst. His eyes became blurry. *Mariána! What is she doing with them, the gossipers?* – he thought. –*Why is she getting involved in all this fuss?*

What Fotinía saw in his puzzled face was uncertainty. Sensing his worrisome thoughts, she addressed him quickly.

"Father Niko, we came here with a humble request. You know how much our Ana has suffered since Andrea left. Both she and Mariána are all alone in that big house, and they need the comfort and the happiness of a child to fill it. A house without a child is not a real home. It's a home with no joy, a home with no life."

The priest felt an instant relief when he realized they did not come by to inquire if he was the father of the child. They were here to take from him the little boy for the sake of Mariána's daughter-in-law.

"Father Niko!" He heard Mariána's voice. "This infant does not have a mother, and my Ana does not have a child. He needs a mother, and my Ana needs a son. God sent this little boy at your doorstep for my Ana. She was not lucky enough to have a child from Andrea, and maybe God thought to fulfill her motherhood through this child! The little one deserves to have a home, and I will be a good provider for both child and mother. We came here with a humble request to take this child in for my Ana." She stopped talking for a bit. Looking at her friends, seeing support in their eyes, she took a deep breath and found the courage to continue. As she was weighing the words, she begged with a trembling voice, "This child will be like a *balsam*[8] for my Ana's illness."

The priest was listening with his head bent slightly to the side. He avoided looking at Mariána's face afraid the other women would notice the worry in his eyes. He understood

---

8   fig – balsam – balm, a fragrant ointment or preparation used to heal or soothe the skin

immediately this solution was going to bring the affair with the child finally to a reasonable end for the unexpected, grave situation it brought along. He looked at the women without actually seeing them. His mind went back inside his quarters.

These past days he had visited the infant a few times a day, looking at him over the crib, tickling his chest, playing with his tiny fingers, and addressing him with a baby voice. His maid had darted some funny looks in his direction, but he had ignored her.

He had seen quite a handful of children in his lifetime—he had baptized all the children born throughout his priesthood—but this baby had been like a little miracle dropped in his church for him to cherish and to hold. The third day he even took the baby in his arms. He started to talk to the child and tickle him. The reaction of the child was priceless. Amazed, as he was discovering something unique, he beamed.

Too excited, he addressed his maid:

"Nisa, he is smiling at me, and he is giggling!"

The maid, rolling her eyes, looked at him and shook her head.

"The little boy is not smiling at you Father Niko; he is reacting to your tickling and the sound of your voice."

He waved his hand in disregard in Nisa's direction.

"Look for yourself Nisa! He is actually smiling at me."

The maid put her hands on the side of her waist, raised her eyebrows in mockery, sneered a little, and looked at him in disbelief.

"Ooh sure, sure? What do you know about infants Father Niko?" and, as an expert she continued, "Infants cannot see clearly for two to three months after they are born! They react only to sounds and touching."

He made a face after her remarks and went around with the baby in his arms, smiling and laughing with him.

For these three past days, he had genuinely thought of raising the child as his own. The idea had warmed up with him as the days went by and he got used to having the tiny boy around. He even thought to name the child after his father, Alex. But he knew he could not refuse the request of fifteen women, and especially Mariána's plea.

Mariána looked at his face, and what she saw there made her think he was going to turn her away.

The priest stood silent for a few seconds; then he raised his head and said slowly,

"I also, as you all know, did not have the luck to have a child of my own." His voice, became frail, and sounded like the voice of a man beaten by a heavy load in life. He breathed deeply and went on, "My poor late wife, may her soul rest in peace, did not bear me a child. I, too, dreamed of taking this child in and raising him as my own. I grew fond of him these past days." He stopped, bending his head more to the side as if a profound burden was weighing inside his head.

Startled, the women looked at him and saw their priest in a light they never had seen before. They didn't think of him as a man that had a vulnerable side as all they did. They didn't regard him as a human for that matter. They seemed taken aback. He was their priest, and he was not supposed to reveal his weaknesses, some of them thought. The rest were touched and felt empathy for him. They came to him with all kind of requests as he had the supreme power to solve all their problems. To their surprise, they realized he could not resolve the only problem he had in his entire lifespan, having a child of his own.

The priest perceived the compassion coming from the women and felt emotional. He composed himself and said:

"Ana is young and she needs this child more than I do. I am confident you are going to take good care of this child, Zonja Mariána."

At that instant, their eyes met.

"God bless you for doing this!" he said, keeping his composure and putting his hand over her head.

It was the first time he had physical contact with Mariána. He had dreamed often putting his hand on her arm or shoulder, but today, the warmth of her head felt purely spiritual. He looked at her and something in her eyes made him squint his own as if he saw something he shouldn't have.

Mariána noticed the flickering in the priest's eyes, but she didn't know what to make of it. Did he sense her uneasiness and became suspicious that some ulterior motive hid behind her request? She hoped not, but she did not want to make any more eye contact with him. Even if he became slightly doubtful about her intentions, she should not give him more reassurance, and she knew her eyes would betray her.

She thanked him for his blessing and asked him if he could bring the infant for her to take home to Ana right away. The priest nodded his head, looked at her intensely as if he wanted to ask why was she in such a rush, but he couldn't catch her eyes. He looked at the other women; he saw impatience and determination in their faces. He stood unsure in front of them as he wanted to say something, but the expression on their eyes did not give him a choice. It did not give him a way to ask for at least one more day with the little one. For the first time in his life, he felt powerless and vulnerable to take charge and dominate the situation as he normally did. And all because of this group of ordinary and simple village women! *If not for them, the child would have been mine!* He was hurting. He wanted that child so desperately; he could not help himself at that instant, but allowing his wounded sentiments to overpower his thinking.

With an abundant emptiness in his chest, he turned around and went inside the church, walking slowly.

The women were quietly chatting when he showed up again with the child in his arms and a bag full of baby clothes. Mariána's eyes lit up. Cautiously, he handed the child to her. Mariána took the infant from his hands and brought him close to her chest. She looked at his tiny face, and her eyesight became blurry. Fotinía gently touched her on the shoulder and took the bag from the priest. Mariána raised her head, and looking at him, she said smiling through her tears:

"Thank you, Father Niko!"

He was unable to reply. Her voice was different this time, and along with her smile, it went through his senses as it never did before. Facing his last hope of raising the child as his own vanishing in the thin air, he stood there unable to do a thing. For an instant, he had the urge to ask her if she would name the child Alex after his father, but couldn't get a word out of his mouth.

Women looked at him and associated with how he felt.

"God bless you, Father Niko!" Krisúlla said. Sensing his sorrow, she put her big palm on his shoulder.

He felt the weight of her hand. Her gesture made him feel not only helpless but small too. He was taller than every man in the village, but Krisúlla was taller and bigger than him and every man in the area.

On another occasion, the women would have had a good joke about the view of Krisúlla and the priest, but at that very instant no one was in the mood for such remarks. Every woman in that group felt part of the most important mission they ever had done in their humble lives.

Mariána and Fotinía thanked the priest again, turned around slowly, and walked away. The procession of women followed them, keeping a certain distance from the two leading ladies, not waiting for or expecting him to say anything. The surprising realization he was as much human as they were, after all, made them think of him for the first time as one of their own.

The priest stood in front of the church's door watching them leave. They looked like a group of crows flying away, and the little one was being carried away from him amongst them. *Why did I compare them with the crows?* He asked himself. He did not understand at the moment, but his mind was unconsciously out for some small vendetta.

Although, it was the first time he had seen so many

women getting together and so close to one another and moving along collectively, he thought. *It is their clothes,* he realized in a bit. He had seen these women for most of their life but never had paid attention to the way they dressed, or maybe he was just used to their outfits. In church, they sat on the benches and they were lost in the midst of the aisles. He could see only their heads from the altar and never paid attention to the way they dressed. During village celebrations, they put on their national costumes which were very colorful. At the moment, he noticed that their outfits were all black or gray. Life is tough up here in the mountains, he thought. The deaths of loved ones in family circles were so common; the women did not stand a chance of wearing anything else but black. One mourning was, before long, followed by another. And if they were not in a mourning stage, which was usually a year for close relatives based on the unwritten communal canons, they would wear a black, brown, or gray dress with tiny white little designs. With time, dark-colored clothes had become a way of fashion in these parts of the country.

The memory of a summer bright color dress, Socrates had bought for his fiancé in the city of Vlora—Mariána used to wear it when she was betrothed to him, and after they got married—the remembrance of the way the dress showed Mariána's curves, became vivid in his mind. With his eyes fixed on her tall, shapely, elegant figure, which stood out of the group if one could ignore Krisúlla's huge, tall body, he realized, that the hope he had for years of having Mariána as his wife one day, was lost along with the infant. He acknowledged that two of his biggest dreams, fading away in that path to the north of the village, had come to an end at that very moment; having a woman like Mariána at his side for the rest of his life, and having a child, a boy, to raise as his own; a son to whom he could have passed his legacy as a priest, even if the child was not the creation of his own loins. He didn't know how to explain it, but on some level he knew the little one tied Mariána to a world he would never be able to be part of. He had desired her for so long. He had wished and hoped year after year that one day she would be his. Ironically, his hopes went up in flames a few minutes ago when he put that child in her arms.

Krisúlla turned her head and saw the priest standing on the top of the church's stairs watching them walk away. "He really wanted this child, didn't he?" she said.

The other women expressed their approval by nodding their heads in silence in respect for the lonely man they left behind.

When the women got close to the road that led to Mariána's house, finding the excuse that it was becoming late, and the infant needed to be fed, groomed, and put to bed, and it would take Ana a little time to get used to the baby in her condition, she thanked them:

"Your help today meant a lot to me, my dear friends."
"Anything for you, Mariána!" Krisúlla said.
"Please, give Ana a month or so to adapt to the new situation before you come by and pay us a visit!"
"Sure Mariána, we understand!" they answered almost at the same time.

"Mariána!" Krisúlla spoke unexpectedly. "How are you going to feed the child?"

The other women froze. Krisúlla was known for her genuine, blunt talk.

Mariána looked at Krisúlla as if she was asking a silly question and said: "Dear Krisúlla, that's why God gave us the sheep and the cow!"

The rest of the women chuckled, although the question was burning in their minds too, but they did not want to pry and ruin today's sacred memory with ordinary questions.

Mariána smiled at Krisúlla. "Didn't we always manage in our most difficult situations in life, my dear friend!?" she said as if she wanted to say to her, *Forgive me for my rude reply to your concern.* "But you are right. I thought about it," she said kindly to soften the unpleasant moment. "I will boil the sheep milk, and thin it with water to make it appropriate for the newborn as many women have done before in unfortunate cases when as mothers they were out of breast milk."

"Take care, Mariána! This child was a kismet, destined for you. *Zoti[9] të bekoftë ty dhe Anën!* May God bless you and Ana!" Fotinía said, ending the conversation, fearful of any other unpleasant exchange.

"Amen!" the other women said in chorus. They wanted to go away with a pleasant feeling about the great deed they had been able to carry through that day.

Mariána smiled in appreciation, showing her gratitude.

"I always will be in debt to you, my dear friends," she said, looking at all of them in a very grateful manner. The

---

9   Zoti- God, mister.

women nodded subtly. Their faces showed contentment.

Politely, Mariána turned around, holding the infant carefully in her arms. She walked away as calmly as she could as if nothing was bothering her. When she turned the corner, and her friends were out of sight, she couldn't help herself; she moved the blanket to see his tiny face. The baby looked at her with his cute, little eyes. Although she knew he couldn't see her, she instantly felt the love every woman feels when looking at an infant. She gave him a light kiss on the forehead. The worry about the priest back there showing suspicion in his eyes, or if the women suspected anything at all about all this, a concern that had been the entire time in her perplexed mind, got instantly wiped out from her thoughts. She pictured Ana holding the child in her arms. She smiled for the first time in a long while.

Ana was sitting on her bed with her hands around her knees, rocking back and forth and staring at the bare wall. She heard Mariána entering the house. A hideous flickering passed through her eyes, and a nervous tic went through her face. Her gaze became intense when she realized Mariána was coming up the stairs. Her rocking became more frequent, and she buried her face in between her knees. She heard the door opening and Mariána's steps approaching the bed. Then, a sound, a cooing sound, made her raise her head abruptly.

Her baby was in Mariána's arms! Stunned, Ana jumped out of the bed. She looked at the infant with her eyes wide open as if she couldn't believe what she was seeing. She did not move. Then she looked at Mariána with an inquiring look, and then back at the little one again. Staring at his face, she raised her hands. Mariána put the baby gently in her arms and stepped back.

When Ana felt the tiny limbs, his little body, next to her flesh, and saw his hazel eyes gazing at her, his tiny fists pushed in his mouth, she felt serene for the first time in nine months. An enormous joy flooded her. Mariána put her hand over her arm and patted her tenderly.

"Feed him, my dear!" she said softly.

Ana, who was focused on her son's face as if she couldn't get enough of him, looked up at her confused. But what saw in Mariánas' face, understood she meant it. Smiling timidly, she sat down on the corner of the bed, arranged her little one in her arms, and slowly, blushing, lifted her blouse, exposing her breast. *It is her first time*, Mariána thought. *She is going to get used to it.*

Ana took the baby's fists gently out of his little mouth and softly lifted his head close to her breast. The milk aroma entered his senses, and the infant moved his head nervously around her nipple until his lips found it. His small mouth began eagerly sucking his mother's flowing fluid as all babies in the world do when they feel the silky softness of their mother's breast, and they sniff the scent of their mama's milk.

Both mother and child looked content and lost in their tiny, enormous world. They radiated such divine harmony and serenity, Mariána couldn't get enough of the view in front of her. There was a painting of the Virgin Mary with

Baby Christ in her arms in the church. Mariána wished for whoever had painted it, to have had the opportunity to see the scene revealed in front of her very eyes at the instant. What she was witnessing was far more beautiful and heavenly than anything she had ever seen in her life. She stayed a short while watching them and then left the room quietly, leaving both mother and child in a world that was beyond the understanding of whoever was not destined to experience such a blissful bond. Going down the stairs, for the first time she realized why men were so different from women. *God did not grant them the gift of bringing a child into the world or nurturing an infant,* she thought.

At the same time she couldn't help thinking, although it was an incredible bliss to be capable of carrying a child inside your body, sometimes it was also a curse. Her poor Ana was the proof of both.

The inner pain she had been feeling all these months flashed through her eyes. But the serene scene of Ana and the little one came upon her and she went out to get some water to prepare Ana's first baby bath.

Part Four

Mariána was cooking in the kitchen. The weather was pleasant, and Ana, taking advantage of the warm day, had gone outside to play with her son. After the news about the child, in the next letter, Andrea showed understanding and approval for his mother's gesture and asked them to name the child after his great-grandfather Dionísi. He wrote about his longing to have a child of his own. He hoped one day, when he would get back, Ana would be able to bear his children. He expressed the dream of how good it would be for the forthcoming children to have a bigger brother.

Mariána felt relieved by Andrea's acceptance of the child and his supportive attitude. It had been a year, and Andrea had shown a great deal of interest about Dionísi. In each letter, he asked about him, requesting details about his first words, his first step, his first walk.

She looked out of the window. Mother and child were playfully chasing each other and laughing loudly.

Dionísi grew up to be a very healthy child with no mental or physical defects as Mariána had greatly feared. He was adorable and very loving. He made her heart melt every time he looked at her with his big hazel eyes. He was very vivacious too. They had to put away all the things he was able to reach around the house. When Dionísi for the first time called her Nana, she almost fainted from joy. His first mumblings were "ba," then "ma-ma." When he reached the age of one, he said, "Mama," full mouth for the first time, and then, a month later, running after her, he called her, "Nana." Mariána felt reborn. Dionísi's voice was a sweet melody to her ears. As the memory of that day flashed through her mind, she smiled as she chopped onions in the kitchen. The tears from the onions were mixed with tears caused by the echo of the inner sound of the word Nana.

Ana had been doing well too. Dionísi filled her days, her nights, and most importantly her spirit. Around the child she was an entirely different person, joyful and talkative, but very quiet and withdrawn with other people, including Mariána.

Mariána understood and did not hold a grudge against her daughter-in-law. She had gone through a lot and Mariána was happy that the hideous act did not do enough damage in her young spirit to destroy her state of mind. She often seemed lost, but the child kept her on her toes, and she did not give her much time to fall into despair of the horrid remembrance. She asked herself many times what would she have done if she were in Ana's shoes. That day, it could have been her instead of Ana. Just thinking what her poor daughter-in-law had gone through sent chills through her spine.

She heard Ana calling her. She wiped her hands on the apron and opened the window. Ana pointed out in the direction of the narrow passageway, that connected their house with the roads of the village. A stranger was coming toward the house. He was tall with long, blond hair.

"Take the boy and go inside!"

She recognized Kozmái from afar and sighed. A grim look passed over her face. It had been awhile since his last visit, and she had not thought much about the task she had asked him to carry out. But deep inside, she knew it was far from over.

Ana grabbed the child in her arms, and looking strangely at Mariána rushed inside.

"Go upstairs!" she asked Ana as gently as she could.

Without saying a word, Ana took the stairs.

Looking in Kozmái's direction, Mariána closed the window. She went outside and walked to the fence.

Kozmái noticed the motion in the front yard and saw the young woman with the child going inside. As he approached, he observed Mariána carefully and realized she looked much better than the last time he saw her. There were more gray hair and the crow feet around the corners of her eyes had deepened more, but she looked much, much healthier; her skin had regained color, her body was thinner, but, nevertheless, she looked beautiful. The mature beauty always attracted him, and she possessed a beauty he had never seen before. If she had been another woman, Kozmái would not have any problem making an attempt to get acquainted with her, but somehow she was different from any other woman he had ever met. With her, he didn't know how to be flirtatious.

"Nice meeting you again, *Zonja Mariána*! How are you?" he greeted her when he got close enough, and bent his head in respect.

"Nice to meet you too, *Zoti. Kozmái*. I am fine! Thank you for asking!" she replied, opening the gate for him to pass through. "Please, do come in!" she said, pointing inside the yard politely.

He arched his body slightly to create space between her and himself and walked into the front yard.

"Please, forgive me for not inviting you inside the house!" she said and pointed toward the house, implying the mother and child were there.

"I understand!" he said.

The dust on his clothes, the strong scent of his sweat, made her realize the long journey he had taken to come to meet her. She led him to the bench under the mulberry tree on the right side of the front yard. They sat down. Silence followed for a few moments.

"Mrs. Mariána," Kozmái said at last. "I was able to learn something about your query."

"Please, speak softly. The echo of your voice could be heard inside the house."

Ana was watching her mother-in-law and the stranger from her bedroom window. The appearance of an unknown visitor in the house raised her curiosity. Who was the man Mariána was meeting with? Maybe he was someone in her life she did not know about. But that was impossible. They spent every single second together, and if there were a man in her mother-in-law's life, Ana would have known by now. She'd never seen him before, but she had the weird impression she had a recollection of him from somewhere.

Looking at him, a vague memory of a cracking door sound, Mariána's and a man's voice, and the echo of heavy steps down the stairs gradually started to sink in. She recalled the image she had seen leaving their house that day that resembled the man at the bench. "What business could link Mariána with this man?" she asked herself. Her mother-in-law was a mystery to her. She knew Mariána had a good heart, a strength that few people possessed, and she had gone through a lot in life. Mariána had been there for her in some very difficult moments, but Ana was never able to understand her mother-in-law. There had been a short time when they reached some closeness, but it did not last long. The moment she had taken Dionísi from her arms, despite the fact that she had brought him back a few days later, had created a deep gap between them. Mariána was too complicated for her perceptions.

She saw Mariána taking a small wrapped package from the man, getting up, and walking in the house. Mariána came out a few minutes later. She gave him a bag with food, and another very thin, small one as well. She noticed he refused to take the second one. Ana wondered what must be in there. The only thing she could guess, it was money for the package he had brought her. *But what was it? What did she buy?* She wondered.

Dionísi was trying to get her attention for a while now.

She turned around and picked him up in her arms and squeezed him lightly. The toddler giggled. She looked at him and smiled. It was a waste of time to try to make sense of the way Mariána did things. She would never be able to understand. She gave her son a kiss, put him down, and began to play with him around the room.

The giggling noises of mother and child reached the bench. Mariána and Kozmái turned their heads toward the window. Kozmái noticed the sudden transformation in Mariána's face. It brightened up right away at the sounds of the little one's voice. During their conversation, her face expression had been dreary and firm.

He wanted to talk about something else with her, something not related to what they discussed and what he came here for, but he was not capable of carrying the words out. He had thought of what he was going to say to her so many times in his way here. He repeated those words over and over, changed their order, figured out better words, and felt confident he would be able to say how he felt when meeting her.

He looked at her face. He thought about the instant change he noticed a few moments ago, when the child's voice sounded in the air. Then, he realized that this was a world he knew nothing about and probably would ever have a chance to identify with. He acknowledged, that if he wanted to get into Mariána's world, he had to have the insight of this surrounding, of her world, which he did not. He felt juvenile. No other woman had made him feel that way. He felt as if his life did not have any direction at the moment.

He had lived an empty, pointless life, with no worries, a life that revolved around his crazy stunts, nature, and beautiful women. He realized, his innate, narcissistic, self-centered ego was keeping him away from the only thing he very badly wanted to have in his life, and he probably could not ever have. This time around, he was on the other side of the aisle; he was the one having the strong desire, and ironically it was not reciprocated.

Mariána had an impression she saw moisture in Kozmái's eyes, but being distracted by her inner emotions, she assumed her mind was playing games. On another occasion, her woman's sixth sense would have given her the insight into what was going on in Kozmái's spirit, but captivated by thoughts far from the actual reality, he was not under her female perception at that very instant.

Kozmái looked at her, and for the first time in his life he was capable of taking in the significance of a woman's feelings.

"What do you plan to do, if you do not mind me asking?" he heard himself saying. Mariána looked at him, as if she had totally forgotten he was there, inhaled deeply, and said, "I don't know!"

"Why did you want to find out, Mariána?"

His question caught her off guard. She looked at his face and felt an instant, strange, crazy desire to kiss his lips. Her gaze made Kozmái uncomfortable. He instinctively made a slight move back. His reaction brought Mariána back to reality. She looked as if awakened from some daydreaming. She regained her composure.

"That was back then," she said. "Many things have

changed since last year. I don't know why I wanted to find out. I really don't know what I was thinking at the time."

She lowered her gaze and drew a line on the ground with the tip of her shoe. That move showed Kozmái either she was feeling discomfort because of his questions and did not want to answer, or from him being too close to her.

"Well, now it is time for me to go," he said. "But if you ever need any help, or whatever it is, you better send George for me," he added with a firm tone. Then he did something unexpected. He reached out, cupped her face softly with his hands, looked deep into her eyes, lowered his head, and gave her a profound, long kiss.

It happened so fast, it took Mariána aback, and did not give her time to reject him. She just closed her eyes and gave into the kiss. It had been a lifetime since her last one. Her memory had lost the aptitude to recall even if it ever happened.

Kozmái gently released her head and looked her in the eye. Long traces of tears were reaching her jawline. He used his big thumbs to wipe them; he kissed her one more time lightly on the lips and said, "Please, do send for me!"

Giving her a last kiss on the forehead, he turned around and walked out of the gate. With big, quick steps he went his way as fast as he could. One more minute with her and he knew he might do something so crazy he would regret it for the rest of his life. His body was aching, and he felt a strange longing he had never felt before, but did not look back. When he was out of her view and no one could see him, he loped like a man who runs away from peril.

His kiss and his deep, masculine voice reached a deadened place inside her body. It thrust thousands of fiery, tiny sparks in a deep, secret profoundness that had felt no sensations in a while; sensations she had managed to suppress throughout the years. She thought she would never feel that way again. Numb outside and with a flare of fire set inside, she sat down on the bench, put her hands over her face, and sobbed for a while.

Ana looked out of the window and saw her mother-in-law sitting at the bench under the mulberry tree. The way her body was leaning forward with her elbows leaning on the table, and her head between her hands, made her think that something had happened between her and the stranger. Her figure embodied the image of someone frail and feeble; a part of Mariána Ana didn't perceive till that instant. It resembled a subdued shadow of the woman she thought she knew very well. It reflected the loneliness of years and years without a companion to lean on. It revealed the vulnerable side of the strong woman she shared every day of her life, but who had never shown the slightest weakness in front of her.

She empathized with the woman on the bench.

It seemed at the moment, the memory of the life she had led in her parent's house had gone somewhere distant, and she no longer could associate with. Her youth felt too far in the past as if it never existed. Even the memory of Andrea didn't emerge much in her mind lately. It was pushed in some peripheral area of her brain. It was just her, Dionísi, and the woman on the bench. Her life was linked with Mariána's in a twisted, strange knot, she thought.

She picked up Dionísi and went downstairs.

Lost in her world, Mariána felt a small, round, soft hand over hers. She raised her head and took the little hand in hers.

Two big, hazel, marvelous eyes were looking at her with the curiosity only a child possesses, the spirit of inquiry for the mystery of the unknown in the grown-ups' world. His toddler's senses were telling him that Nana was not feeling very well.

"Nana?!"

His childish voice went all the way through her heart. She lifted him and put him on her lap and looked at him, smiling. The toddler put his chubby palms on her face, looked at her with a cheerfulness only a child might nourish, and gave her a kiss with his adorable lips on the cheek. Mariána put her arms around the little one and brought him closer to her chest. The child arched his small hands around his Nana's neck and leaned his angelic head on her shoulder. She embraced him back, and they stood that way for a while.

Ana saw the stream of tears coming out of her mother-in-law's eyes and sensed that the grandmother and grandchild needed some privacy. She left quietly toward the house.

Mariana felt grateful for her gesture. Caught in the world of her grandchild's embrace, absorbed by the serenity of the peaceful moment, relieved from the demons that had conquered her earlier, she was unable to thank Ana.

Dionísi's soft little arms wrapped around her neck, the feel of his head on her shoulder, bliss she had never counted on, pulled her out of her misery. She looked toward Ana.

The young woman stopped at the door of the house to

look back at the harmonious union of grandmother and grandchild.

Their eyes met. The words were unnecessary; they understood each other from the distance.

The nice spring weather, the aroma of the blooming flowers, the fresh air—the child, who blessed her and Ana's life—all entered Mariána's senses and made her feel like there were no worries in her life after all. She got up, put Dionísi down, and started to walk away from the house holding his hand.

Dionísi looked at his Nana's face and understood something in his little head; his Nana felt much better because of him. A big smile showed on his little face. He squeezed her hand, and she responded in the same way.

The child and the old woman walked out of the gate side by side, with their heads high, feeling a great deal of love for each other.

Dionísi's little puppy, Piku—which Fotinía had given him a week ago for his first birthday—wagging his small tail, followed them at a decent length as he knew his place at the moment—showing he was happy just to be a distant part of the little group.

The season of the harvest of the oranges was getting close. Mariána couldn't afford to do the job by herself this time around. Her physical vitality was not the same. The events of the past two years had weakened her strength. Having Ana working in the orchard was out of the question. On the other hand, Ana and the toddler needed her constant supervision. She could not risk leaving them alone for long hours.

Last year George and two of Andrea's other friends had helped her with the harvest. She paid the other two, but George would not take the money she offered him. This season she could not accept his help anymore. He had a growing family to take care of. Mariána decided for the first time to hire seasonal workers, although she was not very thrilled with the idea. She had put aside a good deal of money from what Andrea was sending them lately. *Sometimes the money is worth spending to keep your health and your sanity*, she thought.

She hired a group of men who Fotinía recommended. She came to an agreement with them about the payments, including their meals. They lived in a village three hours away from Kalasa, and the meal was usually included when hiring workers coming from far away. As for the hours, most of the seasonal workers, with the intent to get the work done quickly, would work around the clock. They would sleep in the orchard where they were hired for labor, and would work from the wee hours till very late at night until they were too tired to carry on.

Ana and the toddler were playing outside as Mariána prepared the meals for the workers. It was the middle of October. It was unseasonably warm for this time of the year. Mariána looked out the window. Dionísi had a shirt with short sleeves on, and his small trousers were folded up to his knees. He looked adorable moving his cute arms in the air chasing butterflies. Piku, jumping next to him, got in his little master's way, and Dionísi stumbled. Falling on the ground, the child and the whelp rolled together, one laughing and the other, grunting and licking his human's friend chubby face. Then, Dionísi got up, and leading Piku on, ran around, as the puppy followed alongside barking.

Mariána smiled. The child was crazy about the puppy. They had become inseparable since Fotinía brought the whelp a month or so ago. They couldn't separate him from the cub even in his sleep. The puppy was the only creature smaller than him, not counting the hens and their chicks, but the effect he had on the toddler was remarkable.

One night Dionísi had a high fever. As they were trying to keep his temperature down, Mariána and Ana were amazed when he, feverish, was calling the doggy's name, "Piku! Piku!" instead of theirs.

Mariána never understood the fascination of little boys with dogs, especially puppies. She peeked again out the window and saw Dionísi rubbing his nose with the youngling.

Observing him, she wondered if Dionísi would be lucky one day to have a sister or a brother. She sighed, thinking she had to go to the orchard to bring the meals to the laborers instead of playing with her grandson. Although, he seemed not to need much his mother's company or hers since the little doggy had become an important part of his life.

Approaching her orchard, Mariána could hear the voices of the seasonal workers. Her orchard was not a big one.

One of the workers saw her from afar and gave the signal for lunch time. When she finally got there, the four of them were settled, waiting for her to hand out the meal. Since the first day, they praised her cooking. In the beginning, she would bring the food and leave right away. But, little by little she began to feel comfortable and give them some company during lunch, exchange with them her experience about grooming or harvesting the oranges. When were done eating, she collected her pots to come again the next day at the same time.

"*Mirëdita Zonja Mariána!* Goodday Mrs. Mariána!" the oldest of the workers greeted her. "*What did you make for us today?*"

"*Mirëdita!* Oh, nothing special," she replied. "It's lamb with rice for today."

"Mm! I am famished," the youngest of the workers said and put his hand up with his own cup.

"Be polite and wait your turn!" the middle-aged worker said, looking harshly at the young man, reminding him of the age rank.

"He is young," Mariána said, feeling sorry for the young man. "He is hungrier than anyone else. He reminds me my son when he was his age."

"Who are they?" somebody asked.

Everybody's heads turned around. A group of seven workers were coming in their direction. They were walking in line one after another. The leader of the crew was ahead of the group. On his left side, a man was moving slightly behind him. Two others were pacing a few feet back. The rest were strolling in a fair space. Everyone had the impression that there was a particular hierarchy followed in that group. At the end of the group, a young man, way behind the others, closed the procession. Something in their appearance gave out a quirky feeling about who they were.

"These men are bad news," the foreman said and addressed his men, "Do not get into a conversation with them; just give them a formal greeting."

He turned around, facing Mariána, and a little embarrassed asked her politely, as he was apologizing for being rude, to go behind the big rock on the left of the orchard.

"They better not see you Zonjë, ma'am."

Mariána, who did not have a good feeling herself since she saw the group coming, did as told, and went to hide behind a big rock.

"*Mirëdita!* Good day!" the one in the lead, who looked like the capo of the group, greeted Mariána's workers when they approached.

"*Mirëdita!*" the whole group greeted back in unison.

"I am Yorgo, and this is my gang," the capo said and stopped in front of everybody. "We were hired by the Kondo family. I never saw you in these quarters. Who is your employer?"

The members of Mariána's crew did not respond right away.

"The Sotiri family!" the foreman said after a short pause without introducing himself. With people like them, he thought, it was better not to be too familiar.

"I never heard of this family, and I have been working in this village for a few years!" Yorgo insisted.

"What do we know? It is our first time around here," the

oldest man said. "We don't know this village very well." "As long as we do the work and get paid, we don't want to know much about anything else," a middle-aged guy came to his aid. "We go around, do our jobs, and go back to our families. We mind our business."

"I was under the impression that you were working in beautiful Mariána's orchard," the capo said, looking at the rest with piercing eyes like he wanted to find out about something not being told. "Maybe she sold her orchard," he said, looking at his men with a sly smile. His men were following the interaction without much interest. They looked tired, and it seemed as the only thing they desired at that moment, was to go to their assigned grove, sit down somewhere, grab a bite, and lay down.

Kristo, the foreman of Mariána's crew, shrugged his shoulders.

When Yorgo did not get a response, he waved his hand and walked on as the rest of his men followed him, dragging their feet.

When he was at a fair distance, Kristo released a sigh.

"I was afraid he was going to say something stupid about *Zonja Mariána*," he spoke in a low voice, wiping his sweaty forehead. The rest of men approved with a simple move of their heads, looking in the direction of the new crew, relieved that the first contact with them went smoothly.

Mariána heard the whole thing from behind the rock. When the group of men was passing the corner of her orchard, she came out from behind the rock slowly. She looked in their direction, and her eyes flickered. She saw the back of the last man. For a moment, had a feeling she was familiar with that body posture.

"Anything wrong *Zonja Mariána*?" Kristo asked noticing something in her face.

"I thought I have seen the last one, the young man before!" she responded pensively as her face looked puzzled.

"Maybe he looks like someone you know!" the oldest in the crew replied.

Not taking her eyes off the end of the road, thinking she might have seen the youngster somewhere, she responded:

"It's possible."

"We owe you an apology, *Zonja Mariána!*" Kristo said. "We did not want to put you in this position. But with that kind, you never know."

"No need for apology, *Zoti Kristo*," Mariána said with her eyes transfixed in the direction of the other group disappearing into the orchards. "Starting today, you have to send one of your men to get the food. It is better if I do not come around from now on. I want you to take care of everything, the orange baskets and their transportation, and if something does not sit well with you, please stop by my house."

"I couldn't agree more," said the foreman, relieved. He had thought the same thing after the earlier exchange, but afraid he might displease *Zonjën Mariána*, by being forthcoming, did not say it. "It's a done deal," he said. "Alexis is going to come every day to get the food." He pointed toward the youngest of the group.

"May I have a word with you on the side, *Zoti Kristo?*" Mariána said. She greeted the rest of the men and walked ahead. Kristo followed her for a few yards.

When they were far enough from the rest, she stopped.

"*Zoti Kristo,* what do you know about those men?"

Kristo scratched his head; he did not want to talk about those individuals with her. But he noticed the firmness in her eyes, and said uneasily, "They are indeed the worst kind, *Zonja Mariána.* We heard they do improper things where they work, especially at the end of the season. The word around is they beat and rob people if they find someone alone far from the villages where they work. Two years ago, they spread rumors they hurt a young woman here in your village. But they are very sneaky, and no one has ever caught them. No one wants to deal with them unless people are desperate to hire someone. There have been speculations they even killed someone in the village of Borsh. They always get away with it." He paused and added, "I don't understand how people continue to employ them."

"It seems as if their infamous reputation has not reached this village yet," said Mariána and her face turned gray.

Kristo felt uncomfortable. *These are things one does not tell to a decent woman,* he thought.

"I am very sorry you had to hear all that rubbish ma'am!" he apologized. "We are honest, hardworking men, struggling to provide for our families. Vile men like them make it difficult for the rest of us. That's why we try to keep to ourselves. People look down at us because of those lowlife criminals."

"No need to apologize, *Zoti* Kristo. People should know about these men. They might hurt someone again if people don't know." Her voice was husky. "I am thankful you told me. By the way, you and your men are doing a great job. The oranges are preserved very well in the baskets."

"*Faleminderit Zonjë,* Thank you, ma'am!" Pleased, Kristo put his hand on his chest in respect and bent his head slightly.

"You are welcome, *Zoti Kristo*. Send your man for the meal tomorrow. And *Zoti Kristo*," she said, "before I go, what was the name of the capo of that crew?"

"Yorgo, ma'am."

She thought for an instant, looked in the direction of Kondo's orchard, and then said, "I'll see you soon! Have a good day, *Zoti Kristo*!" and took off at a quick pace.

"The same to you, ma'am!" Kristo said and went back to his men, giving orders to resume the work.

Ana noticed Mariána had not been herself since the last time she visited the orange grove. She was silent and withdrawn. It seemed something was in her mind, but she did not express anything to her. The question if she did anything to disappoint her mother-in-law crossed her thoughts a few times. But she did not find any wrongdoing on her part to associate with her mother-in-law's distress. It was something else, she finally concluded.

Mariána hadn't gone back to the orchard from that day and on. A young man from the crew came every day to pick up the lunch.

As always, Ana stopped guessing about the ambiguity of her mother-in-law's behavior. She went on with house chores, constantly keeping an eye on Dionísi.

The child kept quite a balance between the two women. They respected each other, but their communication suffered a great deal. The strong bond they used to have was not there anymore, not since Dionísi's birth. *Once trust has been ruptured, it can be difficult to regain;* Ana remembered an old proverb. Nevertheless, they were always polite with each other. Ana yearned to have a closer relationship with her mother-in-law, but something inside her did not let her open and warm up to her, and Mariána did not make it easy with her discreet behavior.

Part Five

The men in Kondo's orchard were picking up the oranges and talking loudly. The conversation was all about dirty stuff as they put the oranges in big baskets with layers of dried grass and straws in between. As they were working, they played around with one another, and constantly picked on the youngest of the crew.

Rocco, the capo's right-hand and most trusted man, pulled pranks on others more than anyone, and especially on the young one. Many times he did it for his own enjoyment, but most of the time just to satisfy Yorgo's sadistic delight in seeing other people miserable suffering, or being maltreated.

Rocco knew he was brutal in his own terms, but he had a limit he never crossed. Today Yorgo didn't need his help. His malicious humor was hitting on everyone and others were trying to keep up with it just not to get him madder than he already was that day. They knew if he had not been with a woman for a while, his madness would reach a high point. It was very difficult to deal with him when he was at that phase. He became irrational and bad-tempered to a level of madness, unless he did not get his frustration on something, whatever made him quickly snap; an animal, an object of some sort; or even someone who might say or do something to make him go off in a maniac wrath of ranting or abuse.

Often one of them would get a beating they would never forget when Yorgo would reach his edge. Later he would apologize. They knew he didn't want to lose any of his gang members and accepted his apologies. He understood there was a breaking point after which people could leave him, and he badly needed the spectacle of the followers to feel the power of his domination. They knew all about it, but there was no other place for them to go either; better to say they were a distorted shadow of his image. He was certain they would stick with him for as long as he was able to keep a cool, friendly balance, as he understood in his terms the concept of well-intentioned behavior. They had no other choices.

Years back, Yorgo had gone to the unthinkable max; he had raped an orphan boy who, just for survival, had joined the crew. They all heard the screams and the cry of the little lad coming from the bushes, and Yorgos grunting noises, but did nothing. And, that was everybody's worst nightmare. For days, they did not even look at one another in the eye while Yorgo went around looking straight at each of them with menacing, bloody eyes. A short while after "the alleged rape", it was said, the boy had slipped off a cliff. And no one made a comment or ever talked about it.

Yorgo's temper and all those incidents and rumors made

everyone be cautious around him when he manifested the signs of his insanity.

Today was one of those mad–crazy days. No matter how bad each of them was, Yorgo made them look like angels. He was picking on everyone, and Rocco did not escape his scrutiny. At one point Rocco got tired of his dangerous, brutal kickers and his "friendly", hard punches; they were too much to put up with if not played on others. Yorgo was a sturdy man of medium stature, with the strength of a bull.

He needed a break. He decided to go for a leak just to get away for a little bit from the swirl of his insanity that was driving everybody nuts. As he was taking off up the hill, to show Yorgo his irrefutable loyalty, he threw a joke in the air at the rest of men:

"Come on you despicable vagrants! You are being too slow today. Move your short, ugly hands!

Yorgo erupted in laughter and pointed at Rocco.

"My man!"

Rocco waived his hand and hurried up the path to escape from him even for a few minutes.

The moment he couldn't be seen, he took his time walking as slowly as he could. Although he had been Yorgo's closest friend in ages, and always considered himself as his shadow; even he had a hard time handling the cruelty and the madness of the man in days like this. Yorgo was ruthless, vicious, and merciless, even with the closest people to him when in his nasty mood.

Rocco decided to go a little further than usual just to prolong the break. He reached a rock far from the orchard—behind which he could urinate in peace.

Under the Orange Tree

He heard a noise and turned around. Suddenly, some man with an odd, unusually clean, well-shaved, womanly face, with a wide black hat on, was standing a few paces behind him with a gun in his hand. Rocco froze, incapable of reacting and covering himself. Although in an embarrassing and unusual position, Rocco, couldn't miss noticing the man had on a very strange outfit that did not suit him. And the gun he was carrying seemed out of place in his hand. Rocco lifted his pants quickly but couldn't button them. The man moved his left hand swiftly, and Rocco saw another pistol in the man's other hand. He managed to say, "Hey, man, what are you doing? I don't even know you!"

The man kept staring at him, saying nothing.

"What do you want?" Rocco said again to break the silence.

"Your wallet!" the man finally spoke with a throaty, weird voice.

"My wallet?! No! Not in your lifetime!" he heard himself saying, fuming with anger, not grasping the fact he was not in a position to use that tone.

"Do you have anything else?" the stranger asked.

When Rocco did not reply, the other lowered his look down at his loins.

"The wallet or your manhood!" And he pointed the pistol at Rocco's crotch. "Your choice!" the man said calmly with a stern voice, looking Rocco straight in the eye.

Rocco looked at him, amused, not fully comprehending

what was actually happening to him. He had been on the other side of this scene many times, but up to now no one had dared to approach Yorgo's men for robbery. The man acted like a professional, but he did not look like one. *It is his first time*, Rocco thought, *and he is very good at it. Maybe we should recruit him*!

He looked for a second in the direction where the other men were working, but realized he had walked too far. For now, he had to survive; later on, he was going to hunt this rookie down and not only get his wallet back, but also kill the inexperienced fool for humiliating him. Hating what was happening, swearing he was going to make this rookie pay; he pulled his wallet from the inner pocket of his jacket and threw it on the ground.

His brain had surrendered to the situation, but his instincts had not. As he threw the wallet, his other hand went for the pistol in the holster in the back of his pants.

The other man had anticipated his move and pulled the trigger.

Rocco felt a sharp, burning pain in his loins. Screaming, he fell on his knees with his hands between his legs, looking startled by the quick turn of the event. His eyes were red when he looked at his perpetrator, stunned.

The man lowered his head and muttered in his ear with his strange-sound voice, "From now and on, you are not going to be capable of violating a woman. Your miserable life is already over." Then he looked at Rocco as if to catch in his eyes any sign of comprehension of what was happening. Seeing none, weighing each word, he added, "You are not going to harm a woman or anyone else ever again!"

Rocco's pupils widened and when he finally acknowledged this was not a robbery; he made a minor move forward. The man gave him a sharp kick with the tip of his boot, right on the head. Then, what Rocco saw, left him speechless. The man took off his cap, and he saw long dark brown and gray, beautiful hair falling below his shoulders.

The killer was a woman, Rocco realized, terrified. Although being in awful shape and not able to react in a similar fashion, the thought of being brought down by a woman gave him a surprising strength. He instinctively made another move to get up to challenge the strange broad in front of him, when he saw a glaring light coming from the woman's left hand and felt a tremendous ache in his abdomen. He looked up petrified. His body wobbled back and forth, but he did not fall. He kept gazing at her in disbelief.

The brightness blinded Rocco's eyes. The loud sound of the shot sent a sturdy wave to his ears. He felt his chest exploding. The woman glanced at his distorted body, and her face showed repulsion.

The moment she laid eyes on him she realized she was dealing with Yorgo's right-hand man. Looking in the direction of the orchard, she picked up his wallet and took off very fast, leaving the thug in his misery. She was not sure if he was dead or not, although he looked pretty much dead to her, but she couldn't risk staying there any longer. On the other hand, his immediate death had not been her aim. Suffering and an elongated agony before facing the death was her goal.

The men heard the first shot and got into a heated discussion about where it came from. After the second one, they all agreed that it came from the direction where Rocco was headed awhile ago. Yorgo started to run, screaming to the others to follow him. The men jumped to their feet and bolted after him. When they reached Rocco, he was convulsing, and streams of blood were coming out of his mouth. He was covered in gore. His guts were out of his abdomen. The bad smell reached their nostrils, and they all stepped back, putting their hands on their noses. Terrified they realized he was also shot in his crotch. The view left them speechless. It was beyond anything they ever had seen before, and they have seen the worse. "Man!" Yorgo said at one point with an unemotional, controlled tone. "Whoever did this must have had some grudge with Rocco."

The others did not say a thing. They had learned in a hard way to keep their mouths shut in front of Yorgo. He always twisted their words and threw it back in their faces. And, sometimes, he hit them with whatever he had in his hands if he did not like what they said. But at that moment, it was the shock that left them unable to articulate a word.

They knew they had done a lot of horrible things. And this looked to most of them more like revenge than a simple robbery. A shot sounded in the air. They looked around, and one of them even ducked. The rest followed suit instantly hiding behind the bushes.

"Oh, you little pussies!" They heard Yorgo's sarcastic laugh. "Whoever did this is running like a dog. By now he is too far to harm you little women. Get up and show some dignity, men! Whoever fired that shot, did it to scare you girlies." he shouted to cover his own alarm.

He felt fear too, and it was a first for him. Rocco was his man. What he had in front of him was far worse than anything else he had seen in his life. He was a master of criminal acts, but this went beyond the best job he ever had done himself.

Convinced by his words and assuring tone, they came out one by one, but they didn't even want to look at the mess that once was called Rocco. A moan came from Rocco's mouth.

"He is coming out of it," one man said.

"He is trying to say something," another man noticed. They turned and moved a little closer, holding their noses. Yorgo, closer to Rocco's body, bent and focused on his lips. They were moving, but only blurry sounds were coming out, and he did not understand a thing.

"Are you getting what he is saying?" he asked without turning his head.

"Whatever he is trying to say is stuck in his head and is not going to come out of his mouth," the oldest man observed impassive.

"He is finished," another added.

Rocco gave it a last try; his head moved, he released a strange sound, and then his head fell as if someone had cut it with an ax.

The men stood silent. Shock and numbness were their companions at the moment. Everything had rolled so fast; they were not yet fully grasping how something like that could have happened.

"May his soul rest in peace!" Yorgo said. A weak "Amen"

came out from the mouth of the others. Finally, one of the men dared to ask, "What are we going to do with him?"

"Dig a grave and bury him, what else you fool!" Yorgo said angry, raising his eyebrows and staring at the one who asked. Then he added with a murky tone. "We have to give him at the least his last, resting place!"

He felt restless about Rocco's murder but did not want to show it in front of the others.

"Go and get the shovels," he ordered the youngest in the group raising his voice. The young man, glad to get away from the smelly, horrible scene, ran fast toward the orchard.

"You! Go cut some branches!" Yorgo ordered the rest.

He looked at Rocco one more time carefully before covering him, trying to find clues to his doubts. "Didn't he keep his wallet in his pants' pocket?"

"Yes, he did," one of the men answered.

"Then we have nothing to worry about," Yorgo said with a steady tone. "We are talking robbery here. We just have to be careful from now and on."

But the others were not convinced. The shot in the crotch was not something a mugger would do, unless another Yorgo was born probably from a seed he had planted maybe a long time ago, a few of them thought.

She watched the men from afar. She knew she had the upper hand this time. Astonishment and shock was her plan. The unexpected attack gave her superiority over the thugs. *They will be more cautious from now on*, she thought.

For the first time in two years she felt fervent, she felt avenged, she felt in one piece. She looked down one more time, fired another shot, saw them ducking and left.

At a certain point she stopped behind some bushes, pulled the dress out of her pants, took them off, and fixed herself. She brushed her hair, put the pants, jacket, the pistols, and the hat in her backpack, and avoiding the paths close to the orchards she left in a hurry. She did not want anyone to see her in this part of the village. She heard the echo of far-off voices asking about the shots.

Walking home, she relived the events of the day. She was satisfied and thoughtful at the same time. Next time, she needed a prompt attack and a quicker retreat plan. No time for drama! Just a swift action, an unexpected appearance, and immediate withdrawal! But she had to let things calm down first, until the thugs, convinced it was a random robbery, would let their guard down.

Mariána heard a strong knock on the main door and went to open it. Kozmái's appearance startled her.

He had an angry face on and skipping the proper greetings, he said upfront:

"You have to stop this!" He sounded very upset and furious.

"Good to see you, *Zoti Kozmái!*" she said, squinting her eyes to give him a clue he had forgotten his manners.

"This is not a joke, Mariána," he said, ignoring her cold tone. "You are putting yourself in great danger. You cannot take the rest of those men down on your own!"

"I don't understand." She looked at him with a puzzled

face. "Why are you here, *Zoti* Kozmái, and what are you talking about?" she asked calmly. "And please, do call me *Zonja Mariána*!" She looked him straight in the eye, defiant.

He saw the strength in her eyes and he understood he had to be careful while addressing her. But he was sick to his stomach. When he heard about the first two killings, he jumped to his feet and hit the road. The fear that something might happen to her if she went for the rest of the men gave him the courage to take the trip up here again, without being called upon. He wanted to stop her spree of revenge. On the way here, he had heard about a third victim.

"*Zonja Mariána*," he said, using a slight ironic tone, "I am talking about the killings. Please, drop the act with me. I know it was you who did it."

"How could you even think it was I committing those crimes, *Zoti Kozmái*?" she asked, showing the perfect anger of a wrongly accused person. "Don't you think there might be other people who have reasons to kill them? I hear they are a bunch of no-goods who did a lot of other ugly things."

"I can't think of anyone, at least in this village, who had a stronger reason than you did. The way they were killed, ma'am; it is obvious it was you."

"I am moved you think so *Zoti Kozmái*. But I have nothing to do with the killings. Am I glad that three of them are dead? Sure I am. Very glad indeed! I would like to know who did it. I would like to thank and shake the hand of the man who took them out. It would be nice if you would be able to get that information for me," she said with a distant, perfect voice showing no emotion whatsoever.

Kozmái looked at her in disbelief. How could she lie

right to his face, after he came to her with their names, told her what they did, and supplied her with two pistols along with a whole box of cartridges?

"*Zonja Mariána,* please let me continue what you started," he pleaded toning down his anger. "You want revenge to the last thug; I will do it for you! But you cannot continue what you started. You did what you had to do. You had your vengeance. You killed three of them. Let me take care of the rest. It is dangerous for you to continue like this. You don't know Yorgo. He is ruthless, cunning, and a very dangerous man. You have no idea what this man is capable of." His eyes were full of mixed feelings, anger toward her for jeopardizing herself, worry, and uncertainty of what would come out of her mouth next.

"No, Zoti Kozmái! No! You think I don't know! I do know! I know firsthand!" suddenly, she lost her composure and raised her voice as if he was the one who had hurt her. "I did not get my revenge yet. The person responsible for Ana's attack, the capo of the mob, is alive! The monster lives like he never hurt a fly in his life. The one you described as a cunning, ruthless man walks on this earth like nothing can touch him. The one responsible for all the crimes committed by that pack of wolves, and for my Ana's dishonor is alive. The rest of them are just a bunch of voracious, common criminals with no brain who follow that animal everywhere and do whatever he asks them to do." She paused, stood quietly with her head down, then raising it, said: "I am sorry I got you in the middle of this! I have to thank you again for your help. I had no one else to turn to in those moments. You seemed like the perfect stranger who could help and go on his way. You have no responsibility whatsoever to get involved in this matter. This is not your fight, Zoti Kozmái," she said with a tired voice, "It is mine. You should not have come here!"

"I am in the middle of it, *Zonja Mariána*," he spoke in a low voice. "I like it or not, I am involved. I have knowledge on what is exactly happening. I am the only person who knows who committed the killings and the only person who knows why. That puts me in the middle of it, and I cannot allow you to risk your life any further."

He stopped, and looking at her worried, he took her hands in his palms and continued:

"We come in this life for the sole purpose of existing and having a small and maybe a micro role in this planet. We are like ants who work all day long, day after day, to save food for the next day, for the next month, for the next year, and we go on and on and on, just to survive until our big day comes; then we disappear from the earth in an instant without leaving a trace, at least not one that weighs much over others." After he said that, he instantly thought about the trail he would leave behind.

He stopped and, very composed, observed her carefully to see any thoughtful reaction to his words. He saw none. He was good at reading women's minds and understanding their souls. But there was no indication whether his words had affected Mariána in any way. He felt like he was standing next to a statue made of unbreakable rock. Nevertheless, he was determined to soften the icy coldness she protected herself with, and bring the feminine tenderness and the resilience out of the rigid, tough woman she was.

"Whatever we feel does not have a weight on this world's decisions," he continued, "We beat ourselves up by suffering for things; we cannot even have an impact on. We cannot change the world; we cannot change how it functions; we cannot fix the big injustice that is everywhere, all around us. But we can try to be happy in our small world, live honestly, not harming others, not hurting any other human being, just making the best out of this life. We all have our individual dreams, and you and I have at least more than a quarter of our lives ahead of us on this earth to fulfill them. Life is given to us as a great gift. Our destiny is to follow our dreams and achieve something as individuals if possible, and be happy about it," Kozmái finished, surprising even himself where all that came from, realizing, what he just said, represented his life's philosophy. He took her hands in his palms and felt their warmth going through his fingers.

She was standing there silent, as if she did not hear a word of what he had just articulated to persuade her. Her reticence made him continue.

"Please! Stop this!" he pleaded again, looking her attentively, and trying to dive in her beautiful hazel eyes. "I swear I am going to finish the rest if you want all those men dead!"

Mariána was looking at him as if she was seeing him for the first time in her life. His soft, concerned voice that showed fear for her own safety, his thoughtful words, the beautiful way he expressed himself, the level of intelligence she didn't know he had in him were breaking her firmness. For an instant, she began to consider what he was saying. Yes! Her life had gone through a rough, bumpy path. Yes!

She undoubtedly needed a break. She needed rest; she needed peace within her soul, and she needed some serenity and normality in her life. She needed someone to take care of her for once, and she needed, and deserved, to be loved. She was so tired of taking care of herself and others, without having someone in almost twenty-four years to look after her. And there he was; handsome, strong, and sweet, the most intelligent man she ever met, offering to help, and caring for her. She could feel the warmth and the strength coming from his hands. Hm! How long had it been that someone took her hands and kept it that way?

She was trembling inside. A sweet, pleasant feeling was spreading within her, making her feel more feminine than she had in a long time. She never thought a man like him existed. She felt leaning on him, feel his masculine warmth on her skin, putting her palms over his chest, feeling his arms around her shoulders, and allowing him to be part of her life. As she was experiencing all those feelings, the words "I swear I am going to finish the rest!" made her heart beat faster.

All of a sudden, his following words, "if you want all those men dead!" incited a strong disturbance within her and everything else vanished.

She abruptly withdrew her hands from his palms. An angry outburst swelled in her chest, and she blurted it all out:

"If I want all of them dead?!" she asked, fuming. "What do you know about life, *Zoti* Kozmái? Do you know anything about suffering? Do you have any idea what my Ana had to go through? Do you have any idea how I felt seeing my son's bride desecrated? Do you have the guts to continue what I started? What exactly did you do in your life, Kozmái? Did you ever suffer any tribulations?"

She began to walk back and forth in front of him.

"You have jumped off cliffs; you have swum with dolphins; you have gone to the most dangerous places and challenged yourself against everything called forbidding or impossible. You have done things other people cannot even imagine can be done in a lifetime. You did all these unthinkable things for pleasure. You went through a path in life that does not have anything to do with reality; and that's all you did in your life, Kozmái."

She made another round, stood in front of him and said, "What do you exactly know about real life, Kozmái? What? Could you tell me?" she asked with an irritated tone. "Living life the way you do is so pretty damn easy. No children, no responsibilities, just pure fun!" She paused and looked at him. "Yes, it is true, Zoti Kozmái," she said, emphasizing the "Mr." part this time, "we are like ants, working hard all day, providing for the next, and the next, and the next day. Providing for and protecting our offspring; we do not have the luxury to enjoy life the way you do. You are nothing like an ant or the rest of us, Mr. Kozmái. You live your life carelessly. You live life as if there is no tomorrow, as if the existence in it is a mere joke. You live in the instant, but the rest of us cannot afford to do so. We are exactly like the ants you just described, but you are not one of us! We struggle and survive throughout our lifespan; while you relish yours!"

She stopped, looked somewhere behind him, and shook her head for a while.

"You have the nerve to come out here and tell me to stop.

You have no right to!" She paused, deep in her thoughts, trying to find the right words to say. Looking him straight in the eyes, she added, "Beautiful words come out of your mouth, Kozmái. For a moment there I almost—" she stopped, looked at him, and continued, "In another lifetime, I would have run with you, followed you everywhere, leaving everything behind just because of those striking, powerful, persuasive words you spoke earlier. I never met a man who talks the way you do. Father Niko is the most educated man in our community, but I reckon that life has taught you valuable lessons, and you sounded smarter than he ever had delivering his Sunday Sermons."

She became thoughtful while speaking. It seemed as her rage had subsided. She was weighing every word.

"A woman would have done everything for a man like you, Kozmái." She dropped the "Mr." again. "She would have gone to lengths she never had gone before in her life. But," she paused again and took a deep breath, "I have a young woman in that house scarred for life. I have a toddler in there," she pointed inside the house, "a child who will become a man one day. And when he does, he will ask me the logical question, how did he come to be in this life. And you—you are telling me to stop!" and she repeated, "You have no right!" She paused and looked away from him for a second to hold the tears that were ready to burst.

"You are different, *Zoti Kozmái*. You are not like the rest of us. You are not real. Your life is bizarre and superficial; it does not have any significance. It does not have any depth. Your life has nothing to do with reality." She surprised herself as she said the last harsh words to him.

The tone of her voice was strong and deep as she continued unable to stop. All the bitterness that had accumulated inside her was pouring out. "No, *Zoti Kozmái*! I am not going to stop until the last member of that mob dies." She pointed in the direction of the orchards. "And," her voice rose, "you have no business in this. That's why I wanted to pay you upfront, but you chose not to take the money, and you chose to get involved. And you shouldn't have!"

She paused, breathed deeply, looked him straight in the eye, and told him firmly: "Stay out of this! Keep out of my way! Do not ever come again to contact me!" Her voice reached a high pitch, and she sounded as if she was finally releasing the last drop of her anger.

She knew she was unfair and harsh on him, and she was perfectly aware, she had no right to do so. The man had no obligation concerning her, and he was just trying to help. It was a first time that someone was showing some compassion toward her; but she couldn't stop the outburst. She knew her rage had nothing to do with the man in front of her, but she couldn't help herself.

One thing though she knew well: she had to uproot whatever he had been able to embed in her a few moments ago with his subtle words. She could not afford feeling soft or weak. She could not afford to allow this man's well-spoken language to enter her thoughts and sneak into her senses, creating some unrealistic hopes in her.

There was no room for him and his words in her life.

She was the only one responsible for what had happened to Ana. She had to undo in some ways what went terribly wrong. She had to change how Ana felt. She had to eradicate the fear inflicted deep in her daughter-in-law senses. She had to bring back the zest that once had characterized Ana. She had to restore her faith in life. She had to continue what she had started.

Kozmái listened, his head slightly bent, looking at her sideways. Her voice penetrated his subconscious. It entered his senses, and he felt anguish in his chest for the first time in his life. Her words disturbed him. And he never had been troubled by anything before. She, the woman he felt so foolishly compassionate for in an irrational way, despised him. No woman had spoken to him in such a way before. For that matter, not a single soul! He had known only love radiating from a woman's spirit and body. He felt feeble and sat down on the bench. He was staring at her and hearing her voice as th e voice of his alter ego.

As she was talking, the flashbacks of his life went in front of his eyes. Up to this moment he thought he had had a wonderful, beautiful life. Up to this instant, he had believed he had lived his life to the fullest. He had tried and done everything a man could not have dared and even dreamed off. Other men migrated to find the unknown through hard labor. He found it and discovered it here, in this beautiful land, in the fresh air of the Ionian Riviera, in the glittering waters of the Ionian Sea. He had crossed the boundaries of the community's unwritten ethical norms in effort to explore the undiscovered purity of nature.

He felt elevated every time he had accomplished a new challenge. He felt a new dimension was added to his social stature. He had created new ethical norms on his own terms.

He had built new boundaries for a man to overcome. He had been able to find beauty in everything, in nature, in women, in people and all creatures of the earth. A rock, a leaf, a flower, a small insect, fish, the sapphire color of the sea, or the dolphins would get his full attention the same. He would study objects, creatures of the forest, and human nature with the same passionate curiosity. He would tune out things not related to his interests, and happiness had been his purposeful companion. He knew he was different from others, but he felt good about it, and it had made him unique, up to this moment.

No, he never went through hardship in life. He lived life in the way he wanted to without any restriction from others; he had crossed lines others did not.

But for the first time in his life, he felt emptiness, barrenness. He recognized his complacency. He couldn't make sense of anything he had done in his life at the moment. His conceit had thrown him out of her life, and it came from the core of his being.

His stories would survive beyond his death. People would tell stories about a crazy man who swam with dolphins and did extravagant and extraordinary things, but the memory of his name would disappear into nothingness as time would go by.

Mariána looked at him attentively, somewhat perceiving his thoughts. Nevertheless, she could feel neither pity nor admiration. There was too much in her life to deal with for her to feel compassion for the man in front of her.

She had reached a point in her life where she couldn't

stand men who abandoned their wives, or raped young, defenseless women; and for that matter, those who lived life as if it was a mere joke, as the man in front of her did. She did though; deep down knew that the anger inside her was addressed toward the wrong man. But she was not in the right state of mind to rationalize anything regarding him at the moment.

Her head was sizzling; she needed to splash her face with cold water.

Saying nothing to Kozmái; she turned around, walked away, and made a turn at the corner of the house heading to the water stream—leaving him there; alone with an enormous emptiness engulfing his spirit.

The tension among Yorgo's men had reached its limit. They were on watch twenty-four hours—taking turns. Yorgo kept a brave face. He was less cautious than others, but the rest of them were guarding him more than their lives mostly out of the fear complex he had inflicted upon them over the years rather than out of respect. Though, deep down, they knew, with Yorgo alive, their chances of survival were greater. Two weeks had gone by after the third killing, and then nothing. They didn't notice anyone suspicious approaching the grove. Probably the killer had it only with those three; they comforted themselves.

Other seasonal workers avoided going near their orchard. Many groups worked day and night to finish their task, get the money, and get as far as they could from the area where the killing occurred. Even the head of the Kondo family, their employer, did not show up lately at the orchard.

Mariána woke up early. She wanted to get in the area before Yorgo, and his men would wake up. She opened her chest, took out Andrea's trousers, shirt, jacket, and put them inside her bag. She put on Andrea's winter boots, then pulled from the bottom of her chest the two pistols and the box of cartridges. With one full gun she would be at disadvantage, she thought. She could not afford to refill the gun in case she needed to take another shot right away after the first one. She needed to be precise, quick and fully prepared. She put a bullet in each pistol. She was conscious it would be more difficult this time. By now, Yorgo and his men were armed and ready for whoever they thought was chasing them down, and that made it more dangerous for her to accomplish her mission. But she was determined to go ahead with her task. And, she still had the upper hand. They did not know yet; their pursuer was a woman. When she left the house, Ana and the child were soundly asleep.

As she had reached the site, far from the one she had been in the three other killings, she positioned herself behind a massive rock over Kondo's orchard, with a good view of the surroundings. She could watch the men's moves from where she was. They had just woken up. Their loud, malicious conversation reached her ears. She frowned and picked two leafs from the bush next to her, rubbed them between her hands until their texture became soft, made a small ball out of each, and put one in each ear. The moment when one of them would separate from the group would come. She knew she had to be patient. Two weeks and a half had passed since the third killing. They were cautious, but, in due course the moment would come when one of them would make the wrong move.

The smell of the oranges, the fresh air, and the beautiful view of her village did not get her attention today. Her focus was on the crew down in the orange grove. It was around noon. No one had come her way. She was standing there for a long while now. It was the third day in a row she was watching them. The sun was bothering her. Andrea's cap was helping at least to keep her eyes out of the intense sunlight of the midday. Two of the men left the orchard and started walking up. She did not move. She couldn't take out both of them at the same time. The men went into the bushes, took care of their business one at a time—one on watch looking around—and left. Her only hope was that the next one would come alone. A few hours went by. She was feeling tired. Her limbs were getting numb. She moved off the rock and made a few rounds behind it to stretch her legs. In a bit, she positioned herself again. It seemed as no one had the courage to go too far from the orchard today.

The day was getting close to its end. *It is better if I leave for the day,* she thought. She picked up the bag and moved off the rock. She took the leaves out of her ears, threw the bag on her back, and headed back to the village.

Suddenly, she heard a noise. She turned around to see if any of the thugs had pulled away from the crew. One of the men was moving her way. The other men were teasing him, and he was replying joyfully. No one was with him. The man was so full of himself; he did not think he needed backup. She took the spot behind the rock. His whole appearance had the stamp, Yorgo! *Finally*! She thought with contempt; *the thug is walking towards his death.*

Slowly, he was getting close at a fair distance.

Yorgo reached a rock a few yards down from hers, pulled his pants down, and bent to defecate. A vile thought went through Mariána's mind, and she whispered, "You will rot in hell!" She moved quietly and stopped at a rock ahead of him. The smell of his stool was suffocating. She took her handkerchief out and covered her nose. *The man must eat like a pig*, she thought, and waited until he was done.

Yorgo picked some wide leaves from a bush nearby and wiped himself; with the other hand he held his nose. Whatever he had ate made his stool stink like a skunk.

Suddenly, a beautiful woman with long black and gray hair, dressed as a man, was standing right there in front of him. He froze with his pants down and his hand in his behind. He had dreamed about a woman so badly these past days. At night, although he knew no one dared to go out of their homes after Rocco's death; he had roamed the outskirts of the village with the crazy hope that a woman would make the mistake to go around by herself somehow. Even Rocco's murder and the two other crew members' hadn't quenched his growing lust for a woman. And there she was, beautiful, tall, with thick hair, dark features, breathtaking hazel eyes, and long eyelashes that created a shadow over her eyes that made her more attractive. Exactly the kind of a woman he preferred. Especially her long hair! "Uuf!" he sighed.

He forgot where he was. The lust in his eyes became quite visible. She seemed middle-aged, but he liked ripened women, as he put it. They did not resist as much when he attacked them. It was the young ones who put up a desperate fight. He got excited just thinking about the prospect of having her.

The woman oddly lowered her eyes at his thing while he was unable to move all aroused and ready for her. Wanting so eagerly at that moment to make this woman remember for the rest of her life what a real man was, his hands were shaking. *She has never tasted a dirty macho like meself,* he thought. He had dreamed so many times about the appearance of a female lately, and this one had just fallen from heaven. He would have taken any woman at the moment, but this one topped it.

When he finally came to his senses and managed to straighten up to fix his pants, he saw a pistol appearing in her hand.

He froze. Although he had been ready to meet the murderer for weeks, he was not prepared to face a woman killer. All these days he had played in his mind how the killer would show up in front of him. He had visualized how he would have taken the poor bastard down, and how he would kill and butcher him for anyone to remember. Unfortunately, his mind was set on an entirely different plot.

The appearance of the woman with a gun in her hand caught him completely off guard. He wanted to go for his pistol, but for some reason he didn't. The woman was constantly staring at his thing. "What are you looking at?" he asked displaying anger and frustration. The woman continued to eye his loins in a very bizarre way as if she had never seen one. But there was nothing sexual in her look. It was something else. Her face showed an intense loathing.

Yorgo felt very awkward and had an unpleasant feeling. Never in his life had someone else put him in such position, let alone a broad. He had been the one staring at female crotches, but a woman catching him with his pants down and aiming at his thing with her eyes? He never thought in his wildest dreams that a piece of a dame would be the one to humiliate him and end his life. A gypsy fortune-teller had predicted once by looking at his palm that a stranger with long hair and a smooth face would kill him one day. At the time, he thought it was all gypsy rubbish, and he did not even think twice about what she said. He had forgotten all about it. Today he wished he hadn't.

The woman moved a step forward, and suddenly he noticed two guns in her hands. His numbness grew stronger, but he managed to say, "Hey, why are you doing all this? You have killed three of my men, and now you are going to kill me?! I don't even know you!"

Mariana, having the upper hand of the situation, spoke with a husky voice:

"You know my daughter-in-law!"

As he tried to reach for his gun, he saw one of the pistols aiming at his knee. The flair of the shot, the excruciating pain in his kneecap sent powerful waves in his body, and he fell to the ground. The shot and his squeal scared a bunch of birds that came out around the bushes and flew in the air.

He had been taken down by a woman, he thought in disbelief. He never counted on such thing, ever in his wildest dreams. He had his nightmares, since Rocco's murder, about facing a huge bastard with ugly features and nasty skin, a man who never bathed. He never thought that the killer was a beautiful, delicate, pale-skinned woman.

Although the pain was unbearable, his right hand reached for the gun. The woman kicked his hand hard. In that instant, Yorgo realized who the woman in front of him was.

Mariána! He said inwardly. The realization sent another wave of shock into his senses.

The scene of Rocco's mutilated body appeared in front of his eyes. *That's why she is staring!* The realization of what was coming next terrified him.

His eyes opened wider and showed fear, terror, and alarm as if he had seen the devil's face. *It had been her all this time,* he realized. His guard had let him down. He looked at her terrified. *I should have guessed,* he thought angry at himself. *She is avenging that beautiful piece, daughter-in-law.*

Another shot sounded in the air. He heard the deafening sound, saw the light bursting out of the pistol, then a terrible, painful, burning pain crushed his crotch. He screamed like an animal. Petrified, he looked down and put both hands on his loins. The blood was pouring through his fingers down his legs, and he fell back, butt naked, in his own pool of stinky feces. The pain was agonizing. He couldn't help pitying himself. A weak "please" escaped his mouth as the spasms sent shivering waves in his body for the second time.

He hated himself for pleading, but his manhood was

slipping away through his fingers in such a horrific way, and the pain was beyond anything he had felt before. He was accustomed to pain, it was his kind of thing, but he never had experienced anything like this.

"How does it feel?" Mariána's voice entered his confused senses. Not getting any kind of response from Yorgo, she added with a certain satisfaction and in the same time contempt in her voice, as she wanted to make Yorgo fully comprehend what actually was happening to him by emphasizing each word: "How does it hold up for you, understanding, you, being a doomed, impotent, lowlife bastard for the rest of your stinking, low life, if you will survive this?"

She waited for him to react. But what was left of him was not much able to reflect her words or answer to her.

"How does it seem to be in front of a woman, unable to perform your repugnant act on her or any other woman ever again?"

Not able to say a thing, he looked at her with watery red eyes, as if they were ready to pop out, with his lips tight to hold together whatever was left of his being.

Pleased with the wretched view down on the ground, she continued, "Did you feel powerful when you ordered and watched others forcing themselves on my Ana and mutilating her body?" She waited for his reaction, and when she got none, she said, "Did you feel all mighty when you violated and dishonored a defenseless, fragile young woman in such cruel, sadistic way?" Her voice became hoarse. "Did you feel invincible when you forced your own self upon an inanimate woman, you vicious, despicable, hideous, coward, lowlife creature?" Mariána was standing in front of her victim tall and fearless and releasing on him all the heavy, turbulent, indignant pain accumulated inside her chest since the horrible event.

Yorgo moved his head in disagreement as he tried to mumble a hopeless "No, no, I did not!" At the same time, he couldn't help making another feeble move for his gun in a last desperate attempt.

He saw the light coming from the woman's other pistol, and heard a second deafening shot. He felt a burning pain passing through his right hand. He raised his eyes, looking at her frantically. His right hand hung like a broken branch out of place. He felt pain everywhere. At that point, he knew he was out of luck.

He lowered his head. What he saw, was a distorted view of the edgy brutal he once was, sitting on his own feces.

Mariána was strangely enjoying the wretched view of the man, once an arrogant, presumptuous, vile criminal who had no mercy for his victims.

"This is how my poor Ana felt," he heard Mariána say, "when you butchered her! You shed her blood! You dishonored her! You miserable, lowlife bastard!"

She saw his eyes looking down at the orchard with a last desperate hope.

"Don't even think!" she said. "You are on your own. No one is coming to rescue your pitiful self! You are not valuable enough for them to risk their life to save yours. Those men are not your friends, just some wretched, temporary partakers going along with your filthiness."

He knew she was right. He could picture them, the bastards, abandoning the orchard like the cowards they were the moment they heard the shot—realizing he had been gunned down by the killer. They had tried to convince him to get out of this place before everybody got killed. He saw the urge in their eyes to take off. They would have done so if they were not afraid of him chasing them down or fearing they might encounter the mysterious killer on their path if they made a run for it. They did not even want to wait to receive their payment from the Kondos. They wanted to leave everything and go. They were some frail, scared pussies. He wished they knew the killer was a woman. Maybe they could have the guts to come and rescue him.

At that instant, he recalled how Rocco made an effort to tell him something before he died. He wished he had made a harder effort to understand what the man was struggling to say. But he did not take his murder seriously. He had his suspicions, but only after the third killing did he admit to himself, someone was after his crew, and the whole thing was becoming a serious affair. He wished he had listened to those pussies down there. They were going to be freed from him. He imagined them fleeing for their lives. His face showed repulsion.

He understood a while back that the killer had it more with him than anyone else. Realizing he had no way out and nothing to lose, he gathered whatever strength was left in him and gave himself a push toward her and tried to spit on her. A gush of saliva mixed with blood came out of his mouth but it did not reach Mariána. It fell on his own chest. Whatever power he had put on his mouth's muscles had been not enough to get his last sinister desire through.

Mariána, certain no one was coming to save him, was

taking her time putting new ammunition in her pistols.

Suddenly, as a brute he was, he screamed to inflict fear in her, also hoping desperately that his men would have the guts and the loyalty to do something to rescue him.

She chuckled. An obvious loathing showed on her face.

"Hum! When a man begins feeling overconfident about his affairs, just at that very instant, he begins making his first mistakes. He becomes careless, arrogant, cocky, bold, and he feels all high-and-mighty. He believes he can do whatever he wants, and there is no punishment for him. He thinks he can get away even with murder or violating defenseless young women. He becomes certain he is untouchable, and no one can possibly bring him down, much less a woman. He begins to think, and gradually assumes that the world is under his feet. And, there comes the moment when he starts losing his friends. Then, when he finally goes down, he is certain his old friends would stand up for him and give him a hand. But they are nowhere to be found. He thinks at least the one who owes him dearly, would come to his rescue. And, when he realizes no one shows up in the horizon, he cries out foul like a coward. Ironically, although his scream is shouted at the highest pitch, no one hears his cry. Old pals, who once upon e time absorbed every single word coming out of his mouth, have suddenly turned deaf on him."

Cold and composed, she looked at the smelling, stinking wretch he was. A bloody madness showed in his eyes, and she couldn't tell if he had understood any of what she had just said. She put another bullet in the right pistol. She stared at him just enough, to give him sufficient time to feel both physical and mental pain and to picture what he was going to experience next.

Then, when she could no longer bear the intense, stinky smell—beyond anything she had ever breathed in her life—coming from the mix of blood, opened flesh, and feces once called Yorgo; she raised her hand, pointed at his head, and pulled the trigger—firing her last shot.

She was close enough, for the pistol sound and the light to have a striking effect on Yorgo. His body finally collapsed. Mariána watched him, her face twitching with loathing.

She looked around, knowing no one was going to come to his rescue. Whoever was down there was too fearful for their own life to take the risk to save the villain. Most likely they had fled already. She gave a last look at what was left of the scoundrel and took off.

As she was hurrying through the rocky paths, an old tale came to her mind; the vultures would swell enormously and rupture after eating too much flash and sucking too much blood from their prey. But it seemed it did not work that way for the thug she had just killed. He and his partners in crime were sucking and sucking and getting more greedy, more vicious, more aggressive and ruthless, but nothing had happened to them. No one had stopped their criminal doing. She had to carry out the natural process of vultures' ending, in execution style. She had to take these vultures down one by one and bring to an end to their inhumane demeanor.

After Yorgo had left, the rest of the crew took advantage to unwind. With Yorgo around they had to be on alert all the time. No one ever knew what Yorgo was up to and what might trigger him to come up with some nasty pranks. The sleep was their sole time escape from Yorgo. But even at nights, when he couldn't fall sleep, he had played on them often some wicked tricks.

There were four of them left, five counting Yorgo. He was the only one going by himself lately to take care of private needs. The rest would pair when in need to go. Everybody's pistols had a full cartridge in the barrel. They had become overly cautious.

On the rare occasion when Yorgo was not around, they discussed who was behind the killings. The discussion enforced their belief; the killer was after all of them. It was obvious by now that the killer either knew very well their life-line of crimes, and he was playing the righteous man, or he was somehow related to one of their crimes. They couldn't put a finger on which of their crimes had spurred the revenge, as they had done so many despicable ones.

The fact that the killings were taking place in this village made them think it was about something they had done here in the past. Their first suspicion was about the young woman they messed around with two years ago. But she did not have a single male relative to protect her, they would argue, and it was a long time ago. If someone had wanted to get revenge on her behalf, that would have happened right away, not after two years. That possibility was excluded as with no grounds. The conversations on solving the enigma of the killings always came to a dead end.

It felt good having power over other humans now and then, when they had a chance to humiliate, rape, or rob someone. But since the killing had started, they had come to acknowledge that life did not always go as they pleased. They were scared to death. The fear made them feel an anxiety they had never felt before. Panic became their companion. It made them feel regret for the sins they had committed in the past.

Although they were willing participants in all the malignant things they had done in the past, in moments of penitence, when one on one, they would come to the defense of their own actions. If not for Yorgo, they would say, they would not have gone so far into committing such unthinkable felonies.

Since the second killing, it became apparent their turn was around the corner. They wanted out, but they had no alternative. It was obvious that either a bullet from Yorgo or the killer were their only option. They came to an understanding, they were safer, and they had more chances of coming out alive from this mess—if sticking around Yorgo. They just had to be careful and run for their life when the occasion presented itself.

Following the third murder, they tried to convince Yorgo to consider the danger, but the man was so full of himself, he thought no one would ever dare to come near him. He even started to practice with his pistol, using the youngest one as a decoy. The bullet would go so close to the youngster's head sometimes, there were moments they thought he would kill him. In those occasions, looking at their terrified faces he, satisfied, would sneer chuckling, "I need to be swift with a real target, just in case the killer dares to approach me, so I would be ready for him as ever before." Though uncomfortable with the whole thing, and imagining themselves as his target next, they would laugh along like fools.

Nevertheless, the turmoil had gotten the best of their beings; and they felt trapped in a vicious circle with no way out.

All of a sudden they have become remorseful, a very alien feeling for their persona, the youngest in the group thought looking at the rest of the crew. These past days, he had observed prudently how their behavior had changed in some odd ways since the beginning of this ordeal. The killings had inflicted a state of repentance in their lost spirit. Their qualms were related more to the fear of their own existence than to their genuine regret of what they had done in the past. *Whatever consciousness is left in the depths of their abandoned human souls has been provoked to rise to the surface. Only the fear of being punished could cause such awakening in a criminal's spirit,* the young man contemplated. Ironically, they even have stopped picking up on him lately; he realized surprised.

They heard the first shot. They all stood up and looked at each other. Their faces expressed what they were thinking; this was their fair chance to get away from Yorgo's curse.

Maybe the killer would stop his revenge after taking him down, they secretly hoped. Nevertheless, they were fearful for their own lives. The killer seemed determined. If he had the nerve to go after the crazy Yorgo, for them there was no hope. Whatever they did, they did it together.

A second shot sounded in the air. They thought Yorgo had taken his share of bullets, and their path finally cleared.

The oldest fearfully expressed his thoughts out loud,

"What if he is the one shooting the killer and not the other way around?"

His question didn't startle the other three. They had feared in silence the same thing. The young chap suddenly spoke: "You would have heard his high-pitched voice by now screaming out our names to show his victory over the killer."

The lad's words made sense.

Two of them joined the crew this last season. They hadn't been part of whatever these people had done, and they wanted out. But, they stayed, even though the killings took a creepy turn. They needed the money. They were waiting for the end of the season. They hoped to get their money and go. There was not much work left to be done in the orchard. They thought the killings were not related to them, so no foul, no harm; no one would come after them. Most of the oranges were picked and carefully put into the baskets and carried away by the owner. Only one corner of the grove was not finished yet. It would take only two days to get through this nonsense.

But today, they began fearing for their life. The whole thing was becoming too complicated for them. They had wives, and children to feed. They could not afford to lose their lives over whatever these people had done before they joined their crew. They needed the money desperately, but it was better to go home in one piece than die for nothing and leave orphans behind. They had heard from others about Yorgo's gang's nasty doings. They had gotten an even better hint through their conversations when they would brag about their past endeavors. But they never considered the things they had done were so awful for someone to come after them like this.

"So, what do we do now?" the oldest asked again. He had an urge to run as far away as he could from this cursed place, but the strong fear that Yorgo could appear at any moment from the bushes had numbed his capacity to react. The young lad's rational thinking did not work to relax him.

"I need the money," the rest heard the old man whining.

"We all do," the youngest agreed, motionless, "but we are more secure if we don't move for now. It is safer to stay put."

The two new members looked at each other hesitant. "If Yorgo were alive," one of them whispered, "he should have come down by now, and we would have heard his voice bragging about his victory as the young lad said." They exchanged a look with one another, then turned their heads toward the old man and the youngster. They seemed to have no intention of leaving anytime soon.

"Whether you are getting out of here or not, we are leaving," one of them said suddenly in a low voice. He made a sign to his pal. Keeping an eye on the old man and the chap, both men backed off silently and picked up their belongings. When out of sight, they ran as if a wolf was chasing after them, disappearing into the maze of the orange trees in the north part of the grove.

The old man and the chap did not look in their direction. They both were focused staring at the path Yorgo had taken, waiting for him to appear somehow, or jumping from behind their backs as he often did to scare the hell out of them.

It was awhile before they became aware the new guys had left already. But they said nothing. The oldest often looked up at the mountain path. After a while, he got up and began gathering his own belongings, keeping his eyes constantly to the east where Yorgo had disappeared.

"Why don't we go to Kondos and ask for our money?" he asked, hoping that the young lad would approve and follow. He was afraid to go alone.

"For now it is very dangerous for us to appear at their house's threshold. Everyone is on alert lately. After the shots, I bet every door in the village is locked. These killings have raised suspicions about us, and if we show up after dark at their doorstep after today's shooting, we are probably going to get ourselves killed."

Helpless, the old man, sat down with visible despair on his face.

"Look," he said with a weak voice that showed anxiety and fear, "I've done some bad things in the past, and all that because of Yorgo." He paused a little to see the effect on the youngster's face. "You know how he is." He gave his voice an excusable inflection. "And I am sorry I have treated you in such nasty way," he addressed the young lad, pleading for forgiveness on his part. "Yorgo made us treat you like a —" he mumbled not to say the words that were at the tip of his tongue, and said, "nobody."

He chose the last word carefully, not to hurt the young man more than he had in the past. He watched the young man's face attentively but did not see a twitch. His face was cold, distant, and unresponsive. *I don't blame him,* the old man thought. He and the others had been so cruel to this young chap; he couldn't possibly expect any forgiveness. He was their target on every bad joke or trap they played. The only thing that would have saved the young chap would have been a newbie. They made his life hell, and no one gave a damn about it. They had treated him as the object of their amusement.

He felt fatigued and weak, and then realized; his life was in the hands of the young lad; who, could very well take out on him the daily suffering he had experienced from Yorgo, Rocco, him, and the rest. Even the new crew members began to be part of the pranks they played on him on a daily basis.

His skin started to itch. He knew it was the nervous breakdown. Agitated, he scratched his arms, avoiding looking in the direction of the young man. He found himself unable to make up his mind and just go. He felt trapped in this messy ordeal.

I am getting old and I am scared to death! He admitted to himself.

Somehow a screeching shout came out of the thin air and startled both the youngster and the older man. They jumped to their feet and looked up the trail where Yorgo took off.

The Yorgo-effect was ingrained in their system. They both knew that no one could have released that scream but Yorgo.

It is the squeal of a wounded animal before death that knows its hope for survival is more than over, the young man reflected inwardly. "A beast he was, and as a brute he is dying!" unconsciously he whispered, as the flashbacks of Rocco's death were going through his mind. He knew somehow deep down Yorgo had a similar death if not worse.

"Did you say something?" the old man asked unsure of what he just heard.

The youngster looked at him, and realizing he had said the last words loud enough for the old-timer to hear him, did not answer.

Strangely, he did not feel avenge or pleasure, thinking Yorgo was probably dead. He did not even consider that the killer, perhaps, had avenged him too in some ways for all the suffering he had endured since he was thirteen because of that heartless, ruthless man.

His thoughts were focused on a different direction. The way Rocco was killed had given him a good hint as to who could possibly be behind the murders. And today's killing had reinforced that clue.

The villagers kept away from the orange orchards. Most of the harvest was already in. The only one behind schedule with the orange picking was Kondos' orchard. It was a big one, and the work was going slow there. The killings had created an unpleasant situation not only for Kondo's family but for the whole village. It had inflicted terror on the entire community. Although they knew the killer was after Kondo's crew, no one wanted to take the risk going around by themselves. They had never seen anything like it. People were acting as if in a war alert situation. Rifles and pistols were taken out of their chests and the wall closets.

No one knew for certain what the grounds behind the killings were. When the killing started, some insisted robbery, some vengeance, but the revelations about Yorgo's band's crimes set grounds for stronger concern. Some questioned how the Kondos happened to hire that particular the crew. Did they ask around before booking them? How come no one had heard about them before? And what amazed people the most, was that they had been working in the area for a few years now, and no one knew anything about their shady past.

The Elders proposed to create a small group of men to patrol the village at odd hours in case any stranger tried to approach the village. People were advised not to walk around alone, not even go to homes near the groves. All men were armed. Women and children were confined inside the house after dusk. The only move they were allowed to make was in between the houses that were very close to one another and had a clear path; and that, only under the supervision of the head of the family. The group of men assigned to patrol the village would escort people who had to go on their daily business alone, especially women.

Once, patrolling in the vicinity of orchards, after one of the killings had happened, they met Mariána coming from one of the routes of the orchards.

Fotinía's husband was harsh on her. "Are you out of your mind, *Zonja Mariána* going around by yourself? You should have called on us to see you off?"

She looked him without blinking an eye and replied:

"No one is going to attack an old woman like me. And, don't worry," she added to appease the men, "I carry a pistol on me," and with her hand she hit the pistols inside her bag.

The men shook their heads in disbelief, but who would

argue with Mariána?! They escorted her to her house even though she said she didn't need their attending.

"Our women are becoming like men," one of them observed afterward.

"What do you expect," another added. "She has been living like one for almost a quarter of a century. She is used to take care of herself without anyone else's help."

"It is sad for a woman, or anyone for that matter, to live that way for such a long time!" someone said.

Thoughtful, the rest approved, nodding their heads.

The village's life was paralyzed. The Kondos were advised to deal with their workers out of the village boundaries. They were seen as the cause of this unpleasant torment they had to go through. "Who hires criminals for the harvest?" one would rhetorically ask. "You hire needy, honest people, not lowlife thugs," others would answer to back up the first.

Kondo's explanation about hiring this particular crew was that they began to look for seasonal workers too late, and Yorgo's crew was the only one available to do the job. But the villagers were not pleased. They had become restless with what was going on. Not being able to go about their usual business, they had too much time on their hands. A few strong arguments and fights had broken out among some of the young men. The Elders had to intervene a few times to keep the peace of their quiet, nonviolent hamlet undisturbed.

Today's shooting had brought another round of disturbance upon the village. Things were getting out of hand. People didn't know what to expect. In the late afternoon, two other shots were heard again around Kondo's orchard. The fear among the peasants grew bigger. People locked their doors and men leaned their rifles on their windowsills and stayed in position to guard their homes. No one wanted to get involved with whatever was out there in the maze of the orchards.

Although villagers knew by now that the killer's strike was not aimed at them, the expression "better safe than sorry" made more sense than being careless. They were peaceful people. Wars never made it so far to the height of their village. They had heard only its echoes. They had heard its stories. They had experienced its outcome as trade difficulties, poverty, but never had the wars' hardship tracks gone through their cobblestone roads. They never heard the buzzing of the battles, the bursting grenades, the rattling of the bombs or the explosions of homes.

Their hamlet was positioned far from main roads. It was hard for an army to make it up to their village. Only once, they had a chance to see soldiers in uniform. It was a group of three Italians at the end of the First World War that lost their way and reached their village by mistake; but despite their uniforms, the men were quite friendly and very good spirited. When they marched into the village, they were tired, covered in dust and famished. They were not seen as a threat or as aggressors, or baby killers for that matter as soldiers were usually portrayed during war times. The Italians were treated as graciously as a king would have been. They were surrounded with generosity; they were sheltered, fed, and given the chance to take a good bath.

Their uniforms and their outgoing personality created a festive atmosphere in the village. Such events did not often happen in their humble life and having such gregarious strangers visiting, was a blessing. The soldiers' stories about Italy were fascinating, and their narratives about combat were as close as this village had come to feel the pulse of warfare.

The soldiers spent a week in the village to regain their energy. One of them, Dario, almost decided to stay behind. He fell madly in love with Mariána, but she did not show any sign of mutual feelings. The Italian was fairly handsome and strong. He had a great personality and was the most likable among his comrades. The village was on his side. Socrates had disappeared without a trace. Everyone wanted Mariána to finally give in and accept a good man's love. The Italian had fallen hard for her. He asked her to allow him at least to fix some things around her house without asking anything in return, even when she once more rejected his advances. Mariána knew there were some parts of the house that needed some real work. The house hadn't had the touch of a man in a long time. It was wearing down. She couldn't take care of it by herself. There were major repairs to be done, and she did not have the money to hire a master builder to do it. Mariána felt grateful, but because she could not reciprocate his feelings, she did not want to take on his generous offer. However, under the villagers' pressure, Mariána finally accepted. The desire to show appreciation for the kindness they had received from the villagers made other Italians go along and help Dario to repair the house. They were willing and happy to put to use their skills on things other than war. Some villagers, knowing Mariána would never let them help her, joined the Italian crew, and worked with them side by side.

At one point, the day came when the soldiers had to leave to join their infantry. Their stay had extended to three weeks. The whole village came out to greet them before they left. The night before, the villagers had thrown a party for the Italians. Music—played with the only *fisarmonica*[10] they had in the village—dance, and gregarious joy had filled the village's plaza.

The encounter with the Italians was added to the most important events of the village's told stories. And, that was the face of the war that the villagers had experienced in first person.

With the killings happening all over, memories, going back to that time, had come up in conversations a lot lately. Thinking of it, they realized, they never had a black sheep among them to cause troubles, at least not from the time the oldest Elder could recall.

With the latest murders, the sounds of the shots, for the first time the villagers were brushed with a little touch of the unpleasant emotion of fear and restriction the real battlefield conflict usually brings along.

---

10   [6] fisarmonica – accordion, a portable, box-shaped musical instrument with a keyboard and a hand-operated bellows for forcing air through small metal reeds, squeezed together with two handles operated by the player—carried in front of the chest

Part Six

He had seen her eyes. He had seen the strength and the determination in those eyes. Deep down he had expected and hoped unconsciously for this day to come in a long while. Since the first killing, his qualms had been put to rest to some level, and a certain peace had embraced his soul. He calmly waited for his own punishment on his involvement in the sinful crime.

He grew up obeying Yorgo and not once had he raised his voice. Not once had he objected to Yorgo's and his men's low wrongdoings. Not once had he thought to leave the bunch he loathed.

He was at peace with the fact that one day his punishment would come, and he would face death. Since the beginning, he knew, this execution was about the filthy, odious act he and others had committed in this village. All of a sudden, he ironically realized something. It would have been much easier if his death had come from Yorgo's hands. It would have been an honorable death at least. If he for once had stood up for what he believed was right or wrong, he knew Yorgo would have killed him. But, to save his worthless life, he kept enduring humiliation and doing unto others, everything a human being should not accept to commit.

He accepted the abuse of others and he did harm others in return; not for the satisfaction of it as the rest of the crew did, but out of fear, out of weakness. Always, he realized sadly; he had lacked a backbone as human being, and he deserved to die. The fact that he was forced into immoral acts did not excuse his strained participation.

He did not have a single friend in this world. He did not have any family. His own mother had left him in Yorgo's hands when he was very young. He didn't know where to go after the ghastly experience of a lifetime crime with Yorgo's crew. He was a weak young man who until now never had the blessing to know a better way of existence than what Yorgo had provided and displayed in front of him day in and day out. It never crossed his mind to reject that life. He accepted it as it was laid out for him every day of the week, every week of the month, and every month of the year. Years followed the same, and he dragged his feet after a bunch of villains.

I was a child then, his inner voice whispered in his ears. But he knew his childhood had been over for a good couple of years now.

What about now? He heard the other internal reply.

It is too late, he almost said out loud. *I have to face the punishment! Remorse cannot make up for it.*

Today, tomorrow, or maybe in a week, he was going to be gunned down as a lowlife, a rapist, a villain, and a coward, which he had been all those years of his worthless young life. He had missed his fair opportunity in life, and he would never have the chance to make up for what he had done. He had reached the years when one was considered a man indeed. Other young men his age were already married and had children, but his fate had followed such an unfair path. And he did not try to change it. He did not grab the chance that was presented in front of him so many times. Probably, he did not have it in him. And, ridiculously, he would be gone before he could have a run for a better life. With Yorgo dead, he could've had that pass. But, caught in a web of vile strings, he never found the strength to break out of it; and Yorgo's death had come too late for him to escape from those twisted, invisible threads surrounding his existence and keeping him hostage of the vile man, even after his death.

The old man was watching the young man's face but couldn't read anything. The chap could have beaten the hell out of him by now with no one else around, just the two of them. The young fellow had grown to be a strong, healthy grown man who could knock down everyone, the old man admitted surprised. He hadn't noticed that fact until now. But who paid attention to him? He was the weak, mute toy of the crew and nothing more.

Lad's inanimate face was far worse than a cold pistol on the forehead. Silent men like him were sometimes more dangerous than Yorgo's type. With Yorgo, one knew what to expect. With this one, he couldn't figure out what to anticipate.

He decided to keep some distance from the chap. *One*

never knows what to expect from quiet, mute people, he thought. After a long silence, he dared to ask.

"What do we do now?"

The chap looked at him blankly, like he did not exist.

"We better rest for the night here," he responded without showing any emotion, fear or panic. "Then tomorrow morning we try to finish what is left, and maybe go and ask the Kondos if they would agree to pay us, which I doubt they will, after all that's happening."

He finished and turned around, going to his corner, giving the old man the clue he did not want to be bothered any further.

The old man nodded. He was afraid to leave. He didn't know which way to go. He felt more comfortable being in the company of this strange young man. Although he feared the chap might do something to him during the night, deep down he knew the lad did not have what it takes to hurt others. *No,* he concluded, *the chap is not going to harm me.* Looking at his back, he scoffed inwardly. *Hum! He does not have the guts! It is not in him to be a criminal. That's why it was so easy bullying him,* the old man thought with disgust. But, for now, he had no other choice but befriend the weirdo.

It was early in the morning. The sun had not come out yet, and no one was around. The old man could hear clearly the birds' humming and chirping.

He had a hard time sleeping throughout the night. He looked toward the youngster's corner and hated the fact that the lad was sound asleep. He was thinking hard how to get out of this alive. There was no point in waiting for their earnings. The killer would have guessed by now, this would be their last day in the orchard, and he, for sure, was going to strike for the last time this evening. It was just the two of them. This time he was not going to wait for one of them to get away from the other. They did not have back up as the others did. It would not be hard for him taking them both down at the same time.

The young man was good for nothing, and he was too afraid and too old to confront an experienced killer. Hesitant, he got up, grabbed his bag, and started to walk away looking attentively back at the young chap.

When he reached the side of the road, he stopped. He looked both ways undecided which one to take. *The north or the south?* He thought reluctant. He looked at the red rooftops of the village down south of the road, then toward the path headed north. He seemed fearful and uncertain. He started to head up north slowly. He walked for a while. At one point he stopped, turned his head scouting the area nervously. Suddenly, he spun around, and walking fast, headed back inside the orchard.

When he got nearby the young man, he shook him hard and told him they had to leave. The killer might be in the area at any minute. Leaving early this morning might be their way out. They had a great chance getting out alive.

The young man barely opened his eyes. It took him a bit to be fully awake. Finally, he understood what the old timer was saying to him. He wanted them to get away and leave everything behind. The old man had a point.

As always, he obeyed without saying a thing.

"What difference does it make, where and how it might happen?" he impassively said. He was certain it was going to befall on them in a matter of time.

"What did you say?" the old-timer asked suspiciously not sure of what he exactly heard.

The chap looked at him and said:

"Nothing!"

The old man shook his head. The kid was really weird.

The sun was coming out slowly, but the light was dim. They managed to look around. They gathered their belongings, grabbed a bite from what was left from yesterday's meal, and finished their business right there in the orchard.

Although he knew, the young man was good for nothing, he was too afraid to leave by himself, and too old to confront an experienced killer. Hesitant, he got up, grabbed his bag, and started to walk away looking attentively back at the young chap.

The silence of wee hours made them walk faster. Most of the laborers in the other orchards were gone by now. They were the only ones working around.

When they were up north at a fair distance away from the orchard, they felt a sense of relief. They were out of the dangerous zone. At that very instant, something startled them. They heard a noise, and someone jumped in front of them. They saw a man with long hair and two pistols in both hands.

"Are you in a hurry, boys?" the person asked, looking at them with repugnance. They saw his face was sickened at the sight of them. The older one was looking at the long hair, then the face of the man, and he realized, astonished, that the man in front of them was a woman, and a beautiful one!

Women usually kept their hair combed in the back in these parts of the country. You could see men with long hair around, but not women. The old man was stunned. Slowly he was coming to the realization that the woman in front of him was the killer.

"Mmmmm, Good Morning ma'am!" he said stammering, "We are going on our way, and we do not want to get in the way of anyone's business, especially of a woman, ma'am." He spoke as politely as he could as if he had been a gentleman all his life, but he was unsure if his words would get him and the young chap out of this safe and sound. The chap, he couldn't help but notice, was strangely calm, as if he had been long prepared for this. He looked like he was ready to accept his death sentence. He did not see any fear or shock on the young man's face. *What a creep!* He couldn't help thinking.

Mariána noticed the reaction of the old man and turned her eyes to the younger one. He avoided looking back at her. She thought his face looked vaguely familiar.

The last executions had distressed her in some strange way. She had moments when she asked herself if she had gone too far. It became harder every day finding excuses to go for the whole day, to disguise herself, watch the thugs for hours, and wait for the right time to attack. Many times, tired she thought, *This is a man's job*, and it would make her almost give up. But she knew she had to go on!

After the first killings, she came to understand—she needed a good reason to pull the trigger while facing her foes from now on. She had to implement some other ways to confront her adversary in order to accomplish her task. At one point, she thought her womanly looks would shock them at first sight. They would not anticipate the killer to be a woman; then, the idea that they had more chance to win against a broad would provoke them, and they would go for their gun. That would give her enough reason to fire. She saw the old-timer reacting exactly the way she expected him to.

The old man saw her distraction and took it as his opportunity to end this madness. He reached for his gun in the back of his pants' belt, but unfortunately he was too late. He felt a sharp pain in the middle of his chest's left side and crumpled to the ground. Meanwhile, his gun went off, the bullet hit a rock on the road a few yards ahead, ricocheted, and hit him right in between his eyes.

The view was not a pleasant one, but lately Mariána had set her eyes on worse than what was displayed in front of her at that instant. *One more left*, she thought and turned to face the youngster, who had made no attempt to leave the scene or reach for a gun if he had one. He didn't come across as someone who would carry a weapon or use it even if he had one.

The young man had watched the whole thing as if it was a scene not related to him. His face did not show emotion, as if he was not even there. He felt her eyes upon him but avoided to look back at her. He was staring into the emptiness of the air, waiting for his destiny to be fulfilled.

"On your knees!" she said firmly.

Very calmly the young man complied.

"Put your hands behind your head!"

He did as asked.

Meantime, she couldn't help noticing a strange similarity between him and Dionísi. The big hazel eyes, the curly, light brown hair, the nose. And looking at him carefully, she recognized the young chap who came that day at the gate asking for food. She also had a strong impression he was the same one she saw once at the corner of the church. That's why she thought she knew him from somewhere when she saw the crew for the first time. And all of a sudden she thought, *He was the one who had brought Ana home that dreary night!*

Looking at him, for some reason she felt a certain pity, but did not show it. She asked with a rigid tone, "Tell me what happened."

Not expecting that particular question instead of a bullet in his head, the young man opened his eyes in terror and looked at her as if she was asking the impossible. He shook his head as if saying, "I can't!" The pain he had held inside his chest for almost two years and couldn't get out in front of others poured out. Tears suddenly began to stream down his cheeks. He was glad no one from the gang was around to see him at the moment. He chuckled inwardly *"They are all gone you, idiot!"*

Taken aback by his last thought, he realized, he had lived under their terror for so long that, even now, when they were all dead, he couldn't detach himself from their constant, brutal abuse. Even dead, they existed in his head. Though, not in person, they were around him! He could feel their presence. Their judgment and their voices were imprinted in his mind permanently! They were never going away! Even if he were lucky to get out alive from all of this, they were going to be a constant part of his being and continue to live inside his brain, nevertheless the fact that they were physically inexistent. "Hum! Lucky!" he thought.

He felt the coldness of the muzzle of a riffle in his forehead. He raised his eyes. He had recognized *Zonja Mariána* right away underneath the man in disguise, the first he laid eyes on her. His suspicions that it was her right from the start, proved right.

"Where did it happen?"

He looked at her puzzled. *Why does she want to know?* He thought. *"Why it matters to her where it happened?* But sensing her willpower he blurted it out.

"In the middle of your orange orchard, under the big orange tree."

Mariána felt a sharp pain in her chest. *That damn tree!* a voice echoed inside her.

"Tell me what happened," she asked again and pushed the riffle.

He looked at her one more time, begging with his eyes. He saw the determination in hers. He stood silent. He felt the pressing coldness of the end of the muzzle again. He did not feel fear; he just did not want to talk about it. But for one thing he became aware, *Zonja Mariána* was not going to kill him without learning what happened to Ana that day. Blurry words started to come out of his mouth.

They had been watching her and Ana for a while. They were waiting for the opportune moment. They saw Ana coming to the orchard by herself twice that day. Picking the oranges, Ana had lost track of time. They waited until dusk and then attacked her.

Listening to him, Mariána felt the remorse all over again for being the sole person responsible for what happened to Ana. His voice took her to a place she couldn't afford to be. It was not the right time to feel that way.

Ana put up a strong fight; the young man continued, but she did not have the strength to fight their masculine power. He, himself, was terrified. He witnessed those men robbing and beating people, but never violating a woman. If they had done it, they had done discreetly.

He was more than terrified; he was petrified.

As he spoke, a constant pleading to not continue showed in his eyes. But every time he paused, she would press the muzzle harder on his forehead, and he would keep going.

They gave him the privilege, as they put it, to be the first to have her, but he couldn't possibly do it, he continued. He never had been with a female prior to that day, and he didn't want to have a woman in considered circumstances, not in the way it was happening. He had seen Ana before, and he had a crush on her. He had dreamed about her, but he knew she was married. What was happening in front of his eyes was like tearing up in pieces his first, sweet dream about a woman in the most vicious way. After they had realized he was not going to act on her, they began to make fun of him. Then, they pulled her clothes off, grabbed him by his arms, and two of them took his pants off as the others were screaming and laughing, and pushed him on his knees over Ana.

He swore to Mariána, he would never treat a woman like that, but that day he did not have a choice. They pushed him, shoved him, hit him until he acted on Ana. But he did not know how. That made the men go wild and scream and laugh like animals. They said things to encourage him, but their words had the opposite effect and made him incapable of performing. Her terrified eyes, her screams, and her pleading for him to stop made him more nervous and ineffective, and he had a hard time entering her. If he did not, Yorgo and his men would not give up until he did. Rocco even went down on his knees to see if he was actually doing it and pushed him. Finally, he had managed.

They kept watching him until they were convinced he was done. He was not sure what exactly had happened with him that day, but he lay on her for a while after he felt some release, just to avoid more cruel jokes from those brutal men. Yorgo said to him afterward, "Now you are a real man!"

Ironically, he did not feel like one. In contrary, that day was the worst day in his entire adult life, and he had had many bad ones. That day he felt less than a man.

He had dreamed of being married in the future to a beautiful woman, possibly as beautiful as Ana. But what had happened that day had gone beyond his imagination. That day had destroyed the best part of what he had preserved inside him, his desire for having a family one day. He imagined maybe with Ana, if her husband did not come back, and having children with his beautiful, future bride, lots of children. That dream kept his mind off the ugly things Yorgo and his men did or said. But the cruel world had designed a brutal fate for him.

Hearing his words, listening to what had happened to

Ana, Mariána clenched her teeth. She needed to be strong and hear the whole story. She saw the pain in the young man's face, but she knew she had to know it all. She had to understand. She had a young woman back home who was in constant pain, and she had to fully grasp the extent of her anguish. For as long as she did not know, she would never be able to figure out the length and the depth of her son's bride's spiritual wounds and be able to help her. She would never fully comprehend her torment, and the nightmares that seemed to never stop. She would never fully be able to make sense of the nature of the horrific screams that came from the room upstairs from time to time at night.

Seeing the excruciating pain in her eyes, he tried to explain to her again he was not like the others. He told her how he had gone back later to where they left Ana when everybody was asleep. He had dressed her, lifted her up, and brought her back to the house.

Then he told her how he used to come to the church, to see how Ana was doing, but he never saw her at the church after that horrendous day. He told her, he once came by their house last year to see Ana, and how his behavior made her suspicious.

Then again, the young man pleaded with her not to go on, and stopped from time to time; hoping that Zonja Mariána would come to her senses.

While revealing what happened, he was reliving every single detail of the monstrous day. The enormous pain and the guilt that he had suppressed deep down surfaced again sharp and unbearable. He felt anguished and at the same time embittered. Sweating profusely, he did not make any attempt to raise his hand to wipe the sweat trickling down his forehead reaching his lips.

He looked at her troubled. She was asking way too much of him. She was treating him the same way Yorgo did; he couldn't help thinking. Being naive, inexperienced, honest, and orphan, he had been treated with no regard whatsoever since he was very young. Turning a blind eye to his pleas, *Zonja Mariana* was ignoring how it made him feel feeling speaking about that day. How miserable he felt for each word coming from his mouth. She was forcing him to spill out every single detail. He could not endure going on. How could he continue to tell her all those horrible things they did to Ana? It was the most difficult and challenging thing he was ever being asked to do, besides that horrible day. The dreadful truth, coming from his mouth, was painful to the point, telling it, was intolerable. He preferred at the moment a bullet in his head to end this insanity so he can rest in peace at last for what he had done that day.

But she kept shoving the nozzle. Not understanding why she had to push to the extreme extent to know every single detail, frustrated, seeing she had no intent of shooting him until she heard it all, he had no choice but continue to tell the whole ordeal.

Afterward, they made him watch them. When he attempted to leave the scene, Yorgo grabbed him by his hair and made him kneel and look at the act, keeping his head at the proper level for him to see everything. He vomited quite a few times while the others were performing. He turned his head to the other side to avoid seeing, but when he did, Yorgo pulled his hair hard and kept his head sideways. When he closed his eyes, Rocco, standing by and keeping an eye on him, hit him hard every time he did. Others made fun of him, laughed at him while watching one another over the filthy act.

Yorgo had watched every single man performing on Ana; then when his turn came, he asked Rocco to hold the young man by his hair in case he tried to avoid looking.

That day had become his torment. Not only did he have nightmares over that day, but he was also bullied afterward for his cowardly, pathetic behavior, as they called it.

He swore that day had been his first and the last encounter with a woman. Since then he could not possibly think about being with a woman. The torments of that evening would follow him to the grave. He wanted to leave Yorgo's crew, but being an orphan, Yorgo, his mother's lover, had replaced his deceased father. His mother did not care to listen to his constant pleading to not let him go with Yorgo's crew. He couldn't bring himself to tell her about nasty things Yorgo and his crew did. Yorgo had sworn, if he did, he and his mother would be a dead piece of meat somewhere eaten by vultures.

The monstrous details of the rape were affecting Mariána like a poison and getting inside her veins slowly. The details of Yorgo's act on Ana were even worse. What he had done to Ana was beyond everything she could have possibly thought had happened to her poor son's bride. As the young lad was talking, at the end of his forced, disgraced narrative, she couldn't help replaying the violent act.

She was visualizing the scene of the monstrous rape. She was feeling a dreadful pain and the mayhem her Ana had gone through. She was looking no more at the young man's face but at the horrendous acts performed on Ana.

Detached from actual reality, set back in time, she was incapable of hearing any further details of what Yorgo had done. She was staring at the face in front of her without actually seeing it. The face of a different man was emerging in her eyes.

Suddenly she had a strong, physical convulsion. Her hand moved violently as a result of the powerful commotion inside her. The pistol went off. She had pulled the trigger.

The young man's head exploded. Blood and scattered pieces of his brain splashed all over her clothes.

She had no intention whatsoever of pulling the trigger on this one.

Mariána had killed not the young man in front of her, but unconsciously, Yorgo all over again. She saw what was left of the poor lad and felt ill. She began to shake. She felt a strong churning feeling in her stomach, and threw up.

Her task had ended here; she had accomplished her mission, but did not feel the pleasure of victory over this one as she felt over the other killings. This young man was the one who brought Ana to the doorstep of the house. He was the one she had sensed at the corner of the church. He was the stranger who showed up at the house to make sure Ana was all right, and she had killed him. *He is the one—. He is Dionísi's—.* A thought began to take form in the depth of her brain but did not fully crystallize. At that very instant, she was not ready to face the truth and accept the fact that had just unfolded in front of her a few moment earlier; whatever the accuracy of it was.

She had killed a young man who was at the prime of his life and was forced by a despicable creature to commit an evil act on another human being. She had killed a young man who had the decency of being remorseful for what he had done.

Did she kill the only one who had not participated willingly in Ana's assault, just because she was reliving the monstrous act through his narrative, or did her rage get out of hand? Or, maybe, she did kill him unconsciously because he was the last proof of Ana's dishonor, and his face was the only affirmation of how Dionísi was conceived? At that moment, she was not capable to fully comprehend why her hand had pulled the trigger on the young lad. With the others, it had been easy. She was conscious when she shot them. She was full of vengeance, and she had killed them with no remorse, but not this one.

Mariána looked one more time at the corpse. She felt sick and left the scene in a hurry.

Walking away, she prayed that life, as it was in the cards for her, would not challenge her with such hardship ever again. With blood all over her, she felt a crawling feeling over her skin. She headed to the closest stream, not far from her house, to clean up.

She had to uproot whatever was imprinted a few moments ago on her, at least from outside. She knew one thing; the horrific details of the rape would never go away.

Part Seven

In the distance, a man was following Mariána. He was walking carefully behind the bushes throwing his step cautiously making sure not to be seen by her. He noticed her walk was not natural. She was going a little side to side as if drunk, but he knew she wasn't.

He had watched the whole scene back there. He saw the old man going down. Then he had heard the whole story coming out of the young chap's mouth.

He was appalled and sick to his stomach by what he had heard. At first, he thought she was not going to kill the young lad. While hearing the revelations of his account of the incident, he noticed her body's response to the tremendous pain that she felt within. He saw the twitch on her face. He sensed the grief she was experiencing by the way her neck was jerking. There was a moment back there he had feared that the young man would take advantage of her distraction, and he took aim to take a shot in case he would make a move. But the lad, telling about the horrifying occurrence of that day, was as lost as she was.

He, himself, had goosebumps listening to the horrific details. Then he saw her hand shaking, and right away he heard the gunfire. He saw the young man's body crumpling to the ground and Mariána's distressed behavior. At the end, unfortunately, she did kill him.

Following her afterward, trying to make it through the bushes without being seen, at one point his long hair got trapped in a branch full of thorns. *I should have cut this hair short*, he thought. He pulled his hair off the branch and continued following her.

He had followed her since their last conversation. He had never left the village after that heartfelt talk. Used to spend time in the wild, he had camped in a wooded area above her house. He couldn't bear the thought leaving her all alone in her impossible endeavor to avenge her daughter-in-law, thinking about the danger she was getting herself into. He kept discreet distance while attending her comings and goings. But fearing something might happen to her while she was confronting a bunch of nasty thugs; he followed her and had her back during her dangerous attempts.

He never thought she would be able to pull the whole thing off. But she did. What he saw, while following her, astonished him. She acted like an experienced killer; like she had been an assassin for hire all her life. Watching her all this time he had realized that hardship and vengeance made people do things and develop skills they never would in normal setting. They pushed a person to such limits one could never reach if their life would have gone by the usual course.

Such tribulation could take a long toll on a person's life. He would never have believed that a human could do such atrocious things to another human being, especially to a woman if he did not hear it with his own ears. For him, women were only to be loved and respected.

Although he was furious and remorseful for being a man after what he had heard, he felt great admiration for the woman who had avenged her daughter-in-law. How much he wished he could help her right now; clean the blood from her face, change her clothes, console her just by holding her in his arms. How he desired to caress her forehead gently until she could relax, and her soul could find some serenity.

He would have given everything at that instant if he could erase from her mind the memory of the brutal account she just had heard about her poor Ana. But he knew the only thing he could do for her, was keep her safe from the world around and make sure no one would find out who was behind the killings.

Kozmái followed her until she reached the stream and stayed put. He guarded the vicinity to make sure no one would come her way. He knew the villagers had gone into hiding the instant they heard the shots. But the fear someone might be crazy enough to go out and see all that blood on her, made him wary of the surroundings.

Mariána scrubbed her hands for a while. Even when there were no more stains left on her hands, she kept washing. Then she cleaned her face and her hair. The process of clothes' changing was going slowly compared to other times. The killings had taken a toll on her. After she was done, she sat down, put her elbows on her knees, and stared at her hands, turning them slowly up and down as if she was seeing pieces of brain and blood of the youngster stuck in her skin. Then, she gazed into the emptiness for a while.

At some point, she came to her senses and got up. She took her time digging a hole away from the fountain with a small shovel that was hanging in the back of her belt. She took off the stained jacket, picked her dress from her backpack, and put it on, then, pulled off the pants from underneath the dress. She cleaned up the pistols and put them in the bag. She folded the messy, bloodstained pants and jacket carefully and hurled them into the hole. She picked up the shovel and started to throw soil over it with high-intensity moves. When everything was covered, she leveled the soil over it, hitting it with the back of the shovel then stamped hard on it with her boots. She picked up some grass and covered the ground over the hole.

She straightened up and looked down at the spot. Her eyes were fierce. The secret that was tormenting her in more than two years was buried there. Her Ana's concealed incident would remain such forever. *The family secret is finally safe*, a voice whispered in her ear.

She stood motionless for a minute then went back to the fountain. She washed the dirt off her hands. When she was pleased with their cleanliness, she wiped them with the end of her dress, grabbed the backpack, and took off. Her pace became steadier as she approached the house.

Kozmái tailed her cautiously until she reached her house gate. He saw Ana coming out to greet her. The young woman showed great concern for her mother-in-law's condition. They exchanged a few words, and they both disappeared around the corner of the house. She was safe at last. Her ordeal was over. The dangerous task had been accomplished.

Finally, he could take a deep breath and rest a little. These past weeks he barely had a quiet moment. The constant fear that something would happen to her had been a frequent torment. There were moments he almost unveiled his presence when he thought she was in a vulnerable situation. But she did it! And, she did it all on her own without a scratch on her. No wonder this village held her to be special. Now he knew why.

He arranged himself among two rocks, a comfortable place he had found in the wooded area. He put his coat underneath, covered himself with a blanket he carried in his backpack and looked at the sky for a while. His job was done. He had a long road ahead the next day, and he needed some rest. Last night he barely slept.

He knew, today was the last time he'd seen her. He was going to keep her secret sacred for the rest of his life. Maybe, in the far future, in his wandering journeys, when he would stop in some far village, he would be able to tell her story. For now, while watching the sky at night, he would tell the stars the story of the woman he fell madly in love with. He would tell how he dared to do things for her, he had never done before. He would tell the story of the woman he desired so much, but he couldn't have as his lifetime mate. Looking at the bright stars in the deep sky, he would say, she was as far away from him as the stars were from the earth.

Life, with its unpredictability, persistently challenges the resiliency in some of us with its unexpected, on-again, off-again brutal defiance and strikes, his thoughts started to wander, thinking about the twists in Mariána's life. *Though, on the other hand, the opportune moments that life constantly throws at our feet, are there for us to reach out and grasp, and dive in the opening window of a new life, a new adventure,* he further pondered. *But, for some strange reason, most people do not. Most people are afraid of the unknown they might encounter in the new path; several, with time, become comfortable with the way things are in their life and become incapable of even thinking about change. It is difficult for some to reach to the new, as they often overlook what is in front of their eyes. They become immune to the surroundings. For others, although they are conscious of the opportunities that exist for them out there, it is their destiny that determines what direction their life-path journeys takes. It is as if their life is designed by mere fate, which throws more obstacles than opportunities in their paths, and it makes their life a constant struggle with no possibility of a different future.*

After a while, his eyelids felt heavy, and he fell asleep.

Ana was putting Dionísi to bed when she heard a creaking noise. She approached the bedroom window and saw her mother-in-law coming through the front gate walking oddly.

She ran downstairs and opened the door. Mariána looked horrible. Her dress was wet and wrinkly; her hair was damp and messy. Her face was pale. She looked as if she had seen the devil. She had never seen her mother-in-law this way.

"What happened?" she asked, worried.

Mariána was standing in front of the house, unsure whether to go inside or not. She looked lost as if she was unaware of her surroundings.

"I neeed a gooood, hot baath, my dear." she stuttered, her teeth rattling. She took a deep breath and then went on, "Please, heelp me preepare it." Her tone was weary. Slowly, she turned around, and wobbling, heading to the bathhouse, she disappeared at the corner.

Shocked, Ana did not follow her mother-in-law right away. She did not regain her composure yet after Mariána's sudden messy appearance and her request for help. She stood at the door looking in the direction Mariána left.

The rumors of the killings, Mariána's latest early morning disappearances, her strange, late arrivals on the very same days when they happened; had made Ana wonder if there was any connection between Mariána and the men who were being killed. She suspected. There were four men murdered among the seasonal laborers, and with today's shootings, the number very well might have reached five or maybe six. Deep down, Ana knew perfectly well what was happening. And, who better than her would know what the entire ordeal was about?

She has never asked for my help before, she thought suddenly, *she had never asked me for anything for that matter!*

The words, sounding in her mind, alerted her about what she had to do.

She hurried upstairs to check on Dionísi. He had fallen asleep. She closed the door slowly and went down the stairs so quickly she almost stumbled. She ran after Mariána and found her standing in the middle of the bathhouse. She took the backpack off Mariána's shoulder and put it down. She felt something hard inside it that made her wonder, but it was not the time to be curious.

Mariána was almost motionless. Ana helped her take off the dress slowly. It smelled of vomit. Mariána was shivering under the wet, long white undergarment. Ana helped her get into the bathtub and covered her with an old towel. She put up the fire and brought water from the stream outside. . After she placed a big pan on the fire to warm the water, she rushed back to the house to check on Dionísi. The child was awake and playing with his wooden toys quietly. His dog, sitting next to him, watched him attentively. He looked at his mother, gave her a big smile, and continued playing. Beaming, Ana stood there for a second, not getting enough of her son, then ran quickly back to the bathhouse.

Mariána's eyes were closed, and her teeth were still chattering. The water was warm enough, so Ana poured it in the bathtub. When the tub was filled, she started to wash Mariána's hair. After a little while, her teeth stopped rattling. Ana noticed Mariána was keeping her eyes tight to hold tears ready to burst.

Ana's concern and her warm-hearted care broke the thick layer Mariána had built over the years. She couldn't keep the tears inside any longer. It was the first time in two decades someone else was taking care of her. Streams of tears finally came down Mariána's cheeks.

Ana acted as if she didn't notice a thing: she kept washing

and brushing her mother-in-law's hair. Her eyes, too, became blurry.

At the very moment, the roles were reversed. It was Ana, for the first time in their relationship, taking care of Mariána, the woman who had replaced her mother, her father, and her husband these past three years. Mariána had been her provider, her protector, and today she had been her savior. She had lifted the terrible burden Ana had carried inside these past two years. She suspected that something related to her ordeal had happened that day when the first shootings began. When others followed this last month at the orange orchards, she knew. All of it had ended an era, not to be remembered ever again. Her mother-in-law had avenged her to the last thug.

She felt like the wicked weight she had held within, trying hard to hide it from Mariána, had finally gone away. The heavy burden that was desiccating her little by little every day, especially at night, had been lifted off her chest. For the first time in almost three years, she felt relieved. She felt liberated from the profound, painful load she had carried for so long. She knew that complete healing would take time, but the enormity of the weight had been lessened significantly.

In response to her thoughts, her fingers squeezed Mariána's shoulder instinctively. Mariána's hand moved slowly over hers. The touch of their hands sent a silent, compassionate message to both mother and daughter-in-law. A sense of calmness overcame them, and they felt at peace at last with each other. The unspoken secrets they shared, the dreadful, untold truth that had overshadowed their life no longer stood between them. The unbreakable wall had been lifted.

Their cohabitation had been challenged severely but had survived the test. Their human boundaries had been crossed, and they had come out of the shadows of their realities' obscurity, to relive their simple life all over again modestly and humbly. No words were exchanged. No explanations were necessary. It was the silent vocalization of their souls taking place in those moments in the simple ritual of bathing one's body that helped the purification of the soul of the other—liberating their spirits from what had so heavily burdened their coexistence for so long.

Serenity would follow the turbulence that silently shook the walls of their house. They felt it in their hearts. They felt a warm closeness and bonded all over again. They both knew this time it was for life. And they both knew they would guard against it, they would protect it, and they would not allow anything to destroy what they had reached at the end of that abrasive, intense road of these past three years.

They heard Dionísi calling their names. "Go! Go my dear! Be with him!" Mariána muttered.

Ana understood her mother-in-law needed to be alone. She slowly moved Mariána's head from her lap, positioned it carefully over a folded towel on the side of the bathtub, gave her a light kiss on the forehead, and rushed to the house.

She found Dionisi at the bottom of the stairs. She smiled at him, and lifted him up in the air and whirled him around. The child started to giggle, and mother and son burst in laughter.

Hearing their voices, Mariána smiled. She closed her eyes in wonder and let her body slip further into the coziness of the water, feeling the warmth entering her bones.

As she was falling into peaceful sleep, her senses taking in the keen orange scent coming from the wicker baskets full of oranges at the corner of the bathhouse, her body preparing to bounce back in to its normal routine the next morning; a single thought crossed her mind, *Dionísi was conceived by a good seed!* and her brain slipped slowly into the oblivion of nothingness.

Rina

A little girl lost in womanhood before her time!
May 2007

In Aníta's backyard, a group of young men were digging trenches. Aníta's oldest son, Fatòni, decided to add three more rooms in the back. His kid brother was about to get married, and he needed his separate quarters. He had a bunch of children on his own, and space in the main house was becoming tight lately.

As the men were working on the ditches for the foundation of the new rooms, someone's mattock came across something hard in the soil and bounced back, almost throwing the man to the ground. He called another worker to give him a hand to enlarge the ditch around to see what was underneath. After a while, they discovered a headstone. No script was on it. Everyone surrounded the ditch, looking down curiously at the finding. The ones down in the trench kept digging. Briefly, a bone was seen.

"Dig carefully, use your hands!" the foreman said.

The two men continued carefully to remove the dirt around the bone, and it took awhile before a skeleton came into the view next to the headstone. Judging by the length of the bones, it seemed that whoever was buried there was either a youngster of fifteen to seventeen or a woman of small frame.

What was that skeleton doing in his backyard? Fatòni thought. As he recalled, he never heard of a sister or brother passing away or any old stories of that kind for that matter. Years ago, an uncle, who lived in the same house, had moved out after building his own. Even if someone had died in the kinsfolk circle, they would have been buried in the church's graveyard. Was there a family secret behind this finding he did not know about? What was behind the headstone and the skeleton?

The hired crew men were whispering with one another. The peculiar discovery greatly provoked their curiosity. Some hidden family secret was unfortunately revealed by accident.

Fatòni felt a great deal of discomfort. It was as if their unasked questions were whipping him in the face. His mother had passed away a few years ago, and his dad had been not that well lately. He had memory loss, recognized no one, and often did not understand what was spoken to. He had a hard time articulating words these past weeks. His eyesight had suffered too. However, determined to find the truth, Fatòni went to fetch his father and brought the old man next to the trenches.

The elder had a good walk to get to the backyard. When he reached the ditch, his son pointed at the bottom. It took the old man awhile to focus on what was down there. Somehow he made a vigorous attempt to get away from his son's grasp and stepped back, waving his hand in the air as if he was pushing away the shadow of a ghost chasing him. His face showed dismay.

Aníta's son was taken aback by his father's reaction. He wanted to find the truth about the skeleton in his backyard. His father was mumbling something unclear. Fatòni felt certain his dad knew the mystery behind the eerie skeleton.

The foreman, a man in his mid-forties, heard something familiar from what Fatòni's father was saying. He went closer to the old-timer and listened carefully. Uncertain of what he heard, he asked the elder, "Rina?" The old man shook his head violently, and his eyes showed anguish.

"Take your father inside!" he ordered Aníta's son with a firm tone.

Perplexed by his rigid tone, Fatòni took his old man gently by his shoulders and headed to the house. He came back in no time, and the question, *"What in the world is happening?"* was apparent on his face.

The rest of the crew members working in the backyard were around Fatòni's age. They had a faint recollection of Rina's story. They were small children when the whole ordeal had happened. They were dying to learn what was behind this skeleton thing. They formed a circle around their master and waited for him in suspense to start clearing up the mystery of this unprecedented matter.

The foreman was very thoughtful. He knew that curiosity was killing the rest of the crew, but he was taking his time, merely because he was puzzled by this strange finding himself. Who would have removed Rina's grave and remains, Aníta or her husband? He slowly began to tell the obscure story as best as he could remember. He had been around eighteen at the time, and the story had been taboo for many years. People did not speak about it, but he heard certain things here and there. Finally, addressing Fatòni he said:

"I don't think your mother did it! Even if she had removed the headstone, something she could not have done by herself, she would have never touched Rina's remains, and she would never have reburied Rina in her backyard. She hated Rina's guts. Your mother was a respectable woman."

"Then, who would have done it?" one of the men asked. Silence followed the question.

Cautious and pensive, the foreman said regretfully: "If I were to speculate, I would say, it might have been your father!"

Fatòni looked at the man as if he had said a profanity. He was talking about his father doing weird things, goddamnit! He almost said, *"How dare you!"* but he stopped just in time under the man's sympathetic look. A hard knot tightened his throat.

"But why on earth would my father do such a thing?" he blurted out.

The foreman shook his head slightly.

"Who knows? But one thing I know for sure. The men of this village were indeed possessed by that woman Rina. Maybe your father more than others."

Unable to say anything, Fatòni stood quietly with his head bowed down with a great burden on his chest.

"I do not get it! Why on earth would he unbury and rebury her remains in the backyard of his own house along with the headstone? And why on earth he had to remove the tombstone? Why not leave it behind? That is unheard of and inhumane! It is totally insane!" one of the men exclaimed.

The rest of the crew, although thinking the same thing, looked sharply at the man for saying such an insensitive thing in front of Fatòni.

The question hung in the air. No one could give a reasonable explanation, and everyone's eyes were on the master. The foreman shrugged his shoulders. His eyes were gazing into the hole below their feet. He seemed lost in the past.

"I heard men did some very strange things back then when it came to Rina," he said suddenly. He sounded pensive. "And this is one of those things, I guess." He continued slowly, weighing each word. "From what I've heard at the time, their obsession with Rina was like an addiction. Alcoholics hide their bottles under the mattress or everywhere they possibly could, so they can get a sip when no one is looking." He stopped and looked at the remains. "I am sorry to say, but there is only one possibility no matter how one sees it." He was considering his words carefully not to hurt the young man. "Your father must have been the one who hid her remains in the backyard Fatòni. Maybe, your old man was more distraught with her than anyone else, and his obsession must have driven him to this. Perhaps he hid her remains in his backyard so he could have her close to himself. Pointing at the trenches, he said, "I am sorry again man, but there is no other logical explanation for this. But," he shrugged his shoulders, realizing, he was being too blunt giving such a definite opinion in front of Fatòni for something he didn't know for sure, "what do I know! I have no clue what exactly has happened back then! The only one who knows the truth is not capable to tell us."

The men shook their heads, perplexed by the bizarre story. They were young. They could not comprehend the whole affair. The "bottle under the mattress" thing was not enough of an explanation to make them understand what had transpired at the time. The act of a normal, family man going out of his mind after a mischievous woman to the point of committing such an unthinkable offense like the one laying in front of their eyes, sounded absurd to them. They were talking about the remains of a dead person here. Why on earth would a man degrade himself and dig up the grave of a fallen woman, and then bury her remains in the backyard of his home, next to where his children and wife lived? There was no sense in this. They felt bad for Fatòni. Not much of good luck had fallen on his rooftop today.

Fatòni gave the men the day off. He was not sure at this point, but he did not feel like going ahead with the construction of the three extra rooms over the soil tainted by this old, bizarre saga. It was not a good omen.

He asked the foreman to stay behind. Shaken and uncertain what to do with this thing falling on his shoulders from nowhere, he asked him, "What should I do with the remains?"

"We have to ask the Elders," the man said, reflecting. "This is something beyond us. You and I cannot take care of it on our own. It is not your affair, Fatòni! The trouble is not simply yours. Do not take it personally! It is a much more complicated and deeper matter than it appears. It is a village business. Only the Elders would know how to handle this."

Fatòni looked at him powerless. The foreman's words did not make him feel any better. His house had been tainted with disgrace. Not only with the dishonor of unburying a dead body, but having the remains of a fallen, lewd woman reburied in his backyard by his very own father, the father he had worshiped, and respected as an icon!

Every man in the village had been with that woman, but after the finding in his backyard, people would only remember his father's name connected with her, and, unfortunately, his. Discovering by bad luck the remains of that woman, he had opened the gate to this ancient, forgotten, and forbidden affair of which, the whole village was ashamed of. Now, he was the one humiliated, and far worse, dishonored.

"Please, make this thing go away, would you?" He pointed toward the big hole with a nervous tic. "Would you go to the Elders on my behalf and resolve this as soon as possible? I cannot face anyone right now," he pleaded to the foreman, not looking him in the eye, "and, I cannot stand these remains any longer in my backyard. I want them gone before nightfall if possible. Please tell them that." His tone was apologetic. "I cannot even look at the bones, much less touch them," he said with disgust. "I cannot even think, God forbid, going through the night with that skeleton out in the open in the back of my house. I feel like it is stuck in the back of my head already." His body jerked as he said the last words. Embarrassed, he realized he was talking too much, and stopped.

The foreman put his strong, heavy hand on Fatoni's shoulder, squeezing it in a gesture of deep empathy, and left at a steady pace toward the house of the alderman— feeling bad for the young fellow.

The day went by slowly. Fatòni stood by the front gate of

his house waiting. He couldn't go inside the house without making sure that this business was taken care of before the sun set.

It seemed as if he had been there waiting forever since this unfortunate morning. Finally, near dusk he saw three unknown men in black outfits, looking like gravediggers, approaching his house on a horse wagon. Their appearance gave him the feeling of a funeral escort.

He opened the gate.

After a formal greeting, they walked quietly toward the backyard without asking questions.

Not having any desire to follow them, Fatòni went inside the house. His father was sitting in his favorite crisscross leg position next to the fireplace, lost in his world of oblivion. His eyes were gazing at the flames. He did not seem to have any recollection of what had happened earlier in the day. He looked undisturbed. His only concern seemed to be the fire-flames. He picked up the blow-poker and began thrusting the burning logs, inciting more flares and sparks. He moved closer and stretched his palms in front of the fire, enjoying the extra warmth in his old bones.

Fatòni stood at the door, pitying the helpless old man. His father looked like a nomadic stranger who had knocked on his front door for an overnight stay. He didn't feel sitting next to him as he usually did every evening, but he did not want to face the gravediggers on their way out either. Without any other choice, he sat on the other side of the fireplace, poking the fire with the iron rod and gazing at the flames taking off. His father did not seem to be aware of his presence.

He heard the noise of the wagon wheels and the trot of the horse fading away. He got up and he went out. The wagon was at the end of the street turning the corner. He went in the back of the house.

They had covered the trenches and had leveled the soil. He felt thankful. It would have been hard for him to move that dirt by himself standing over the empty trenches, especially today, and they had figured that much out. The long day's wait had paid well. He knew the use of the backyard would be out of the question for a while. It must have obtained a name in the village already, "the tainted soil", or probably, "the wicked backyard."

The insinuation of it hit him hard. He was a grown man and felt uncomfortable just looking at the dark spot surrounded by the green lawn. He left with hard, grave steps, carrying a heavy burden on his shoulders.

Time heals everything, but for now he had to deal with the enormous weight that fell on him. He had to live with this twisted, unprecedented present that was very hard to swallow. He did not know how he was going to explain all this to his young, fragile, innocent children, who loved their grandpa to death. They were going to hear the twisted version of the bizarre story from other children if he did not tell them the unpleasant truth upfront.

He needed time to think through how to break this mystery to them. He had to choose the words carefully. It was going to be hard for their little minds to comprehend the rationale of how and why their dear grandpa did what he did.

First and foremost, he had to process the whole thing himself. It had not sunk in completely with him thus far.

He was not even close to having a reasonable handle on it. However, he had a vague feeling the odd news would reach the ears of his children way before he was ready to sit down with them to explain.

He had to plant some grass over that black spot tomorrow, he thought as he headed to the front of the house.

No one had been able to learn where the three men had buried Rina's remains, whose discovery had caused such a stir two decades after her death.

The word was, the three men who took care of the whole affair, hired from where no one knew, had sworn secrecy to the Elders' Council. And, not a word had been heard about them or the remains since. Even the Elders, people would say, did not know the last destination of their orders, but they knew one thing for sure: the orders had been carried out precisely as instructed.

Rina's story—the perplexing story of the ordinary young girl turned into a woman of ill repute by mere fate or bad luck, whose life ended in a tragic way—faded again in the midst of the years and decades, not to surface again until now, almost eight decades later in this storytelling.

Rina,

The widow of the village

(Two decades earlier)

Everything began on the first day of spring, *Ditën e Verës*[11]. Spring Day, which marked the anticipation of summer, was usually observed on the fourteenth of March. It had been celebrated year after year, since times, no one remembered, with great anticipation and preparation. It was the celebration of the new. The most important activities in the village usually started with *Ditën e Verës*. The cold days were over. The fruit trees had blossomed in colorful buds. The flowers in the front yard were flourishing ecstatically.

---

11   *Dita e Verës* —Summer Day is a significant holiday in some regions of Albania. It marks the beginning of the new season after winter, and it is observed on March 14th. Although falls on spring, traditionally, it is called Summer Day, in this story is adapted to *Spring Day*.

The sun shined with a new light, and the greeness of the leaves and lawns came to life with a fresh emerald nuance, giving the surroundings a heavenly touch.

In every house, in the weeks prior to Spring Day, people did some radical cleaning. Every corner of the house was scrubbed thoroughly; all winter clothes were washed and put away. The walls covered with the gloomy gray color that chimney smoke had brushed the inner part of the dwellings during the winter needed a new coating. The homes were painted inside out with slaked, white lime not only for cleanness but also to give houses a new look to welcoming the breathtaking spring.

Those who could afford it would loom-weave colorful new curtains for the windows. Many would modify the old ones, and embroider something new on them to show the festive spirit of the new season.

The soil, enriched to its deepest core during the fall and winter, was ready to be plowed, welcoming the new season of vegetables and grain seeds.

A week before Spring Day, the men would go out in the fields first thing early in the morning to clean their acres from weeds and other invasive plants to prepare the land for new crops, while the wives stayed home making the special meals and desserts for this remarkable, happy day. Villagers felt much more hopeful about the future after the first day of spring, and life sounded full of promise.

Anita's home was joyfully noisy. All her relatives were gathered at her house to celebrate Spring Day. The happiness of the festive day had engulfed everyone. The sun entered every room and gave a feeling of delight even to still objects in the house and made it pleasant staying either indoors or outdoors. Some of the women were gathered in the Good-Room, *Odën e Mirë*[12], sitting on floor cushions, creating a circle around the fireplace and chatting and joking blissfully about their daily whereabouts. The rest were around the kitchen cooking and exchanging spicy gossips, while carefree children went in and out of the house, chasing one another and playing hide and seek. Quietly, Anita observed around the house making sure that everything was going smooth.

The young girls, who were between childhood and womanhood, had created a group of their own. Some of them were gathering wild, colorful flowers and daisies alongside the fences. The rest of them were sitting on the benches outside the houses and making garlands and wreaths with the gathered flowers, saving for themselves the one with the white daisies. They put the colorful ones on the heads, necks, or wrists of little girls. Only the small boys younger than five years of age accepted such an honor from the hands of their cousins. Away from the girls, the rest of the boys were playing soccer in the street in front of the house with a rag ball.

The women in the Good-Room grew attentive. Suddenly it became quiet outside. The sounds of the children's voices stopped. One of them approached the window and looked outside to see what was going on.

The children had stopped playing. They were facing the south part of the road. Two boys were chasing someone from afar and calling out something. She opened the window and

---

12 *Oda e Mirë*—the Good-Room or guest parlor.

asked: "What is it?"

One of the children, a girl of age seven, pointed out a woman walking away from the house.

The woman couldn't tell who that was, for she was short-sighted. She squinted her eyes and noticed a woman down the road swaying her hips.

"Rina!" she exclaimed. "That snake!"

The name sneaked inside the Good-Room and froze the joy in the air. The rest of the women came out slowly. Their faces were menacing.

"That lowlife creature!" one of the women whispered, but the children heard her. The little girls raised their heads and looked at her, bewildered.

Anita murmured, "Where does she find the nerve to pass by my house?"

"I can't stand the sight of her!" another woman said loudly, so she could be heard in the far distance.

"Who does?" a voice in the back added.

"If I knew that my husband visited her," one of the women said in a low voice, "I would make him forget what a female is."

The rest of women turned their heads and looked at her, scoffing.

"What are you going to do? Castrate him?" the jokester of the group replied, not expecting an answer.

The woman did not answer. She did not want to concede the fact that she was one of many. She had a tendency to pass herself off as if she was better than everybody else. But they all knew. Her husband was one of the many culprits. He was as much a wrongdoer as every other man in the village. Not one of them was an exception. They were all entangled in the same mess.

They just could not compete with that ill-mannered woman. They did not stand a chance to win over her. They were usually exhausted by nightfall. Between the children, the hard household chores, often helping their husbands in the fields and carrying out their dutiful acts during the nights, there was no time to take care of themselves.

Even the most honorable men had lost their minds over that lewd woman. Some women accepted it as a fact of life and did not sweat it. But many of them dwelled on and on. They felt miserable about the fact that their husbands would prowl at night to go and "visit" that broad.

Some men were even quite bold about it. Many times, they would leave the fields during the day at the peak of the work, finding excuses just to go visit that vulgar female.

The women—working hard under the burning sun or cold wind or even rain,—knowing where their men were, and what they were doing, perceived themselves as unworthy. Their good-for-nothing spouses had no clue how their behavior made them feel. She wasn't even pretty. *What did men see in her?* They would often ask themselves. But deep down they knew what made their husbands go and lay with that woman.

That no-good woman did not need to work! Every man in the village took care of her. There were gossips that she was visited even by men who came from faraway villages. Her skin was as smooth as a baby's behind. Her flesh was soft, and she was all curvy while they were all muscles and thin like a dry tree in the wintertime. The skin of their faces had turned into a thick, wrinkled, full of deep creases, tanned from the neck and up from exposure to the sun, resembling a dried plum—and it embarrassed them deeply.

If she were not there to remind them of all this, they would not acknowledge they could look like her, have smooth skin and all. But she did! She reminded them every time their foolish, infantile spouses disappeared into the house at the end of the village.

Prior to "Rina's Era," everything was normal. Everyone was like everyone else, but since Rina's husband died, the village had not been the same. Rina's threatening silhouette was over the roofs of every house. No one was safe from her allure.

Before Rina became the desired woman and made men go out of their minds, their husbands usually would sleep right away after they finished their dutiful acts with them wives. But lately, not only did they not touch them most of the time; they would stay there with their eyes wide open next to them, dreaming about Rina.

In their matrimonial beds, the women, faking they were asleep, could sense how their husbands' thoughts would fly to the outskirts of the village. They imagined Rina lying on her bed, all plump and sensual, ready for them, giving them pleasures they could not, doing with them things they could not. They could sense a strong desire in their men to leave the bed and go. Most of them, tired of the long day, did fall asleep on the trail of those thoughts.

But some women could not help themselves watching in silence how their husbands would crawl out of the bed, quietly put their clothes on, and creep out of the room like thieves. A few of them were haunted by the whole sneaking out thing, to the point that they would stay awake—waiting for their husbands to come back. Sometimes it happened that they did not till dawn.

Not one woman had dared to say a thing to her husband about the dirty affair. Many of them would wet their pillow at night, disheartened that their husbands would go out there and find pleasure with that ugly woman. Especially after they, had given them a handful of children, for them, the women, to be busier and busier after each child, and not have a single moment to themselves. And the ironic part was, that lewd woman never got pregnant all these years with all the affairs she conducted with men. The thought, to go and ask how she managed not to, had crossed the mind of a few women, but they did not dare act on it. Being seen at her door meant the worst.

The children were staring at their mothers. The shadows they saw passing through their faces made them despise the woman who caused their mamas' distraction. They weren't able to fully understand what they saw, but their little minds had grasped one thing: their moms were suffering because of that strange woman. They also could tell that they hated the woman at the core of their soul. It was such an intense hatred, combined with pain that twisted the expressions on their dear mamas' faces. Perplexed, the children turned around and watched the woman, who was going away slowly. They were curious to know what it was about that woman that made their dear mamas suffer. They could not figure it out. But into their small, innocent hearts, hate tiptoed like a thief that took possession of their purity, leaving behind a repugnant sense about the strange woman.

"Let's not let her ruin our day!" Anita said loud interrupting everyone's thoughts. "Let's go back inside and celebrate this beautiful day!"

"Oh! One day, she is going to pay!" the woman, who pretended her husband was not part of the whole indecency, whispered with a bizarre voice.

The rest of them disregarded her remark for their sake and the sanity of their spring celebration. They went inside, trying their best to go back to the festive mood of Spring Day. Any other day, they would have lingered on, but today was their day, and they did not want to be ruined for whatever reason, much less for that woman.

After their mothers had gone inside, the children returned to their games. Their small voices filled the atmosphere with joy, and the spirit of the holiday recaptured everyone. Ruined for a few moments by the sight of the outcast woman, the day regained its magic power.

Rina was walking away from Anita's house with streams of tears running down her cheeks. When she first approached the house, she felt the joy of Spring Day. She felt the warmth of the sun and the vernal breeze on her face. As she got closer to Anita's home, she felt a wild desire to open the main gate, go inside, and mingle with the other women, and be, for once, one of them. She couldn't even remember the last time when she had participated in such festivities.

Lately, she had been craving that kind of camaraderie with other women. She did not have any in her lonesome life.

Yes! She was lonely and isolated from village life, and it did not occur to her until this Spring Day.

She did not have anyone to confide with, or chitchat with about relevant or even insignificant things. What could she possibly talk with them about? Her lovers or the way they made love to her? Her life had never been pleasant, she strangely came to realize at that moment.

Her mother had ended up a widow a few years after she had Rina. She had had a very hard life raising and providing for her only child. When Rina grew up, and without reaching the acceptable age for marriage—she was thirteen at the time—poverty made her mother give Rina away to a man who asked for her hand. He was an old, odd man who had no children. His first wife had left him a year after they got married, and he had not remarried since.

Rina, despite her thirteen years, still had the body of a child, and did not have her monthly cycles yet. But, for her mother, life had become a heavy burden. She had to do something. The request for Rina's hand had come at the right moment. Her daughter was going to be in a much better place in her husband's house than in that old wooden cabin where they lived. The food was not enough for both, and the hot or cold wind went through the cracks of the shingles. Throughout the years, she had sold the land and the house her late husband had left her to afford a decent life for her daughter and herself. But the money had run out very quickly, and Rina's marriage came with a handful of money that would help her survive on her own for a few more years.

Rina remembered the times her mother was alive; she and Rina would celebrate the holidays over at other villagers' houses, or they would invite people to celebrate in her husband's house after Rina got married.

But, since her mother passed away, and her old and rusty spouse one day just did not wake up after his afternoon nap, Rina's life had turned upside down. She was not used to working in the fields. She was too young when she got married, and her husband had spoiled her. She had little experience in anything. Initially, she hired a few handymen, on the advice of her neighbor, to help maintain the property and work in the fields, but with time she ran out of money.

She did not remember quite well how the whole thing went rolling down that path. It was one of those things that just happened, and it opened an unknown door she didn't know existed.

She was not attractive. When she was young, she was considered plain among her peers. Those women who shouted insults at her today used to be beautiful when they were young, but not anymore. Their beauty had vanished. They appeared to be close to their own mothers' age. Perhaps, bearing too many children, working hard in the fields, and taking care of their families had taken a toll on them.

On her account, she had sensual, thick red lips and a curvaceous body. She had smooth, soft skin men loved to caress. As a youngster she was very slender. But, after she got married, her thin frame turned slowly into the full body of a woman, and it became very plump in the right places. Her hips swayed slightly from side to side, something that made men go crazy about her. Her nose stood out on her face. It was long, thin, and flashy at the end, but men loved to bite it lightly every time they made love to her. She had thick eyebrows that connected in the middle of her forehead, which was not defined as the trait of a beautiful woman. In time she learned that men, somehow, found it attractive. It reminded them of the fur of a small animal and it excited them. Her eyelashes were long and dense and gave her dark eyes a sense of the unknown and disturbing furtiveness.

When she started sleeping with the men who worked for her, she felt ashamed at first. The morals she was brought up with made her feel great remorse. But, as time went by, she began to enjoy very much being with men. Her late husband did not give her any pleasure in bed. He just did his part, which did not happen very often, and went to sleep immediately, while she would stay awake for hours afterward, not understanding why. As a child, she did not know much of the world she was thrown into, and, she often, would ask herself—how was he able to fall asleep in an instant, while she on her part could not? Only, after his death, when she began to sleep with other men, she started to have a good perception of it all.

One of the men was a big-framed guy and very sturdy. He could go on making love to her for hours. The first time she had been with him, she learned the pleasures of lovemaking and the profound sensation that intercourse could trigger in the body of a woman. When she screamed for the first time during intercourse with him, the sturdy man got more excited, and they ended up screaming in unison. After that, she did not feel any guilt; on the contrary, she began to enjoy making love with different men. She started to seduce them, and with time she became obsessed with lovemaking. Each of them taught her new tricks, and her body experienced things she never knew existed. And she had no problems ever again falling asleep after making love.

The whispers about beguiling Rina went from one's man ear to another and in no time they all poured her way. At one point; she did not pay the men any longer. Not only would they do a chore in her house free of charge, but they would bring her gifts and money. The exchange was silently assumed and consented to. But she considered the vigorous one as her primary man. He was not around all the time, as he had a big family to take care of. He did not have the means to take care of her, but he gave her pleasure no one else could, that's what made him so special. She taught him the new tricks she learned from others, and the hours of their lovemaking became incredible. He was the terrific lover she did not want to lose. Though, her materialistic needs grew more expensive, and she became greedier and greedier with time—knowing his situation—she never asked him for goods or money, just once in a while he fixed something in the house as he was a skilled handyman. Others were just an object of exploitation though she learned a great deal from each one in the bed's affairs.

With time she learned, if she wanted to make men more generous in gifts or money, she had to just look at them with her dark eyes after their lovemaking. She would move her eyelashes slowly, opening and closing them, making the one present feel like he was the only man able to make her happy, and the only man giving her enormous pleasure. And that would do the trick. The outcome was not only an increase in generosity on their part, but they would do a much better job around the house afterward.

Rina lived a good numbers of years using men for her pleasure as well as for her material needs without feeling any remorse or void in her life. She wasn't lucky to have children by her late husband, and she took care not to get pregnant during her affairs with other men. She felt no desire to have or raise children whatsoever. She did not leave her estate very often, unless it was an urgent matter, like exchanging an expensive gift for money or something of that nature. And, she was no longer invited to the village's celebration once her bad reputation became notorious. She lived like a hermit who was visited discreetly only by the opposite sex.

As the years went by, there came a time when the pleasures she had discovered being with men did not fulfill her as they used to. Although she was pretty young, just over twenty-three years old, she began to crave the companionship and closeness of other women. It was quiet around her house; just her, the men sneaking in and out, and the screams of their lovemaking.

She knew the women in the village despised her. But lately, she could not help taking strolls around the village's narrow roads, observing houses, looking at their decorations, the wet clothes and bedsheets hanging over the ropes. She began to learn things about each household's means. She learned about the women's tastes from their clothes, or flowers in their small gardens in front of the house, or the way they painted their windows. And recently she had even started to be interested in children. When she would see a small child in the front yard, she would slow her pace and watch the kid carefully. She found herself amazed and smiling on those rare occasions as if she was discovering the marvel of life.

She would take her walks when everyone was either busy working in the fields or attending the Sunday Mass. This new habit began to thrill her. It enriched her life and gave her the kind of joy she was not aware she was missing till then. During her strolls, despite the fact no one was around, it felt as if she was part of the village life.

Today, though, this particular Spring Day, she did not think much when she got out of the house. Men did not visit her during the holidays, at least not during the daytime. She enjoyed having a day all to herself here and then. But, this Spring Day, for the first time she felt the void of an empty house, a void she did not feel before. Today, home did not feel like home. She felt an odd, strong desire to be part of the big celebration. She wanted to see the unique house decorations that were very specific for Spring Day. She wanted to see people having fun. She wanted to hear the laughter and the noise of the crowd. She wanted to feel the festive mood of her village. She wanted to smell in the air the flavor of the cooked meals coming from inside the houses and the aroma of the freshly baked bread and pie. She put on one of her best dresses, making sure it was appropriate for the occasion and went out.

She went unnoticed till about five houses. Everyone was using the backyard for the festive occasion or had gone over to their relatives' homes. When she reached the sixth house, she faced a bunch of boys of the age of seven to twelve who were playing in front of the house. One of them noticed her and said something to the others. They all froze and quietly watched her going by with a certain curiosity in their eyes. She did not look like their mothers or aunts. She was different, but they didn't understand how or why she was different. When she passed their group, they began whispering in a low voice, pointing fingers at her.

The little girls playing inside the garden became aware of what the boys were doing and stopped their games. It was awfully quiet for a moment. Rina felt chills running through her spine. She could feel the piercing look of the little boys and the gaze of the little girls. In that strange silence, she heard the cracking of a window opening, the women coming out, even the rustling sound of their new dresses and their exchange of words. Right away, two or three boys started to walk behind her slowly and quietly at first, but after a while they became bold and started to call her names.

She felt humiliated, disgraced, mortified; hot tears started to come down her cheeks. It was as if her face was set on fire. She had not cried in years. She could not even recall the last time she did. Ah, yes! It was the night before she got married, and the night of her wedding. She cried on her mother's lap, begging her to not be sent to that old, weird man's house. Despite her thirteen years, she was a child, with no clue on what was going to happen in that house, but she just did not want to go. She wanted very much to stay with her mama. She remembered how, she had put her head on her mother's lap, and her mother had caressed her hair gently as she cried. But she did not say anything to console her or even tell her what was on the books for her on the first wedding night.

She remembered sobbing and sobbing until falling asleep on her mother's lap around dawn. She wasn't ready or versed for any of it. She was just a child sent straight to womanhood without knowing a thing about femininity. Her gut feeling had told her that day; her life would change forever. *But how could a child be equipped to face such a thing?* she wondered. *How do you bring a little girl to step into the world of womanhood without coming out of childhood first?*

Her mother knew what was waiting for her in that odd house and did not prepare her about living with a man. She did not have the heart even to lie to her or say something just to soothe her. Instead, as she could recollect, she kept stroking her hair in silence. She did not even shed a tear for her Rina. She remembered crying uncontrollably as if she knew she would lose her innocence as a child in that house. Oh, what unkind things were done to her on her first time with that strange man! How terrified she felt afterward, when hiding in the wall closet and whimpering not to be heard, with that fat oldster there snoring loudly in bed!

Rina hastened her steps to go as far as she could, away from Anita's home. She took a side route and headed quickly to the quietness of her house on the outskirts of the village.

She felt miserable, and for the first time realized what she was missing in life. Fate had been cruel to her. Other widowed women were lucky. After their husband's death, they would usually go back to their folks and often get remarried in about a year or two. Many stayed with their husbands' family and sometimes were arranged into marriage

Under the Orange Tree

within their mate's kinship circle for the children' sake.

She had no relatives to go back to, or children for that matter to occupy her time. She was all by herself, and no one had come to offer her marriage as a widow. She was all alone in the big world with no one to confide with or take advice from. She was forced into a lifestyle that came against the customs of her village. The only thing she had cared for until lately had been her living needs and the pleasures of her body. Until today, she had not realized how far her small world was from the reality of the lives of the women back there, and how badly she had hurt them.

Even the children detested her. That hurt her more than the women's hate. Maybe they didn't know the meaning of the words they threw at her, but they uttered words they were not supposed to.

Lost in her thoughts, she found herself in front of her house. Suddenly she stopped. Someone was waiting for her on the porch. She saw a handsome, young man sitting on the top of the stairs, smiling at her. She looked at him puzzled. She had never seen him before.

Mixed feelings swept her. She did not want to deal with any man today. On the other hand, she felt grateful that someone was there waiting for her, and she would not be alone. Looking intensely at the man, trying to see any familiar features in him, she walked a few steps and stopped at the bottom of the stairs. She couldn't recognize a thing about him. She smiled shyly and asked:

"May I help you?"

"Indeed!" the man replied with a chuckle. He had a handsome face and very white teeth, an unusual thing in the area. "You are the person I am looking for," he continued. Looking at her with lavish eyes, he added, "I heard you hire men to perform jobs for you around the house."

His tone was arrogant, and he strongly stressed the word "perform." His muscular, well-built body ignited desires in her, and her body made an instinctive move.

He noticed her reaction, and a sly smile went through his lips, but disappeared right away.

She did not miss the invisible, vicious smile. She looked at him carefully. If he had come to her the day before, everything about him would have made her go up in flames, but something had changed in her today. The day before, she would have been in bed with him by now. Today, her body was not responding very strongly to the pungent signals his young, hunky physique was sending her way. She felt a slight vibration through her thighs, but that was about it. She stood there looking at him and sensing a meticulous attitude on his part. She felt nervous.

"Who sent you?" she asked.

He looked at her as if he expected something else. His eyebrows went up. He gave her a malicious look and rudely said, "My father!"

"And who might that be?" she asked as softly as she could to hide the commotion she felt.

When the name of her favorite lover came out of his mouth, the surprise hit her. *He sent his son!?* The question sounded sharply in her mind. Then she heard him saying:

"My father said you were the best patron in the area."

She saw a dark, ironic sparkle going through his eyes. Rina felt tense in a way she never felt in the presence of a man. She always had handled men in a manner that they were the ones feeling unsettled in front of her. Today she was the one feeling uneasy. Something about this young man did not seem right.

"I have nothing for you today," she surprised herself saying. "You can come some other time. Or I might send word for you if I need your help."

The young man did not move. He stood on the top of the stairs looking at her without blinking his eyes even a bit. She looked at him surprised and stood aside as to show him, he must get up and go.

"I am not leaving until I get what I came for!" he said boldly.

Caught off guard she uttered back:

"And what that might be?"

He got up, came down the stairs, stood very close to her, gave her an intensive look with his dark eyes, then lifted her up as if she was a feather and walked back up the stairs. He stopped in front of the main door of the house waiting for her to get her key out and open it. During those few seconds, she was not able to react, say something, or even protest. She wanted to, but she wasn't able to articulate a word. She had submitted herself to this unknown man without understanding how. She took the key out and opened the door, not taking her eyes off his face. He smiled at her, muttering, "Good girl!" and she saw another vile flickering in his eyes.

She felt shivers going through her spine, not because of the words, but the way he said them and the way he looked at her.

"Where is the bedroom?" he asked.

Instinctively she pointed to the left side of the hallway. He turned around and with big steps reached the bedroom door. He raised his right foot and shoved the door wide open. Not being able to react to what was taking place, she felt as if all this was happening to someone else.

He put her on the bed and began to undress her as she watched him with anguish in her eyes.

"I like when women show fear," he whispered in her ear, making her shiver, and then undressed himself.

He was much more vigorous than his father. She could not help but notice in the chaos of their bodies' movements that he had a perfectly built body, well-developed pecs, and abs. She had never seen an abdomen so muscular. He pleased her flesh in a way no one ever did, not even his father. But despite her body's strong response to his lovemaking, which was the craziest she had ever experienced, she felt dirty and indecent the whole time. It felt like something sticky had infiltrated her body, something impure, as if his malicious attitude had entered her and made her feel as if a foul odor had infused her. Finally, he stopped after he had done to her everything she had experienced before multiple times and certain things she had never, ever done before. Her body enjoyed the new, but it was the first time in her lovemaking that she did not feel good about herself. He rolled on the side, gave her a big, malicious, content smile, and went to sleep as if he was in his bed.

She could not fall asleep. A strong sense of discomfort was taking hold of her. She could not help herself staring at his body, looking at his handsome face and wondering how a striking young man like him came to be so cruel and so insensitive with a woman. At one point, it occurred to her that he was very much like her. He took from her what he had come for with a cruel coldness that was typical of her.

Everything happened so fast she did not have a sense of the reality of what was going on around her. Though her body responded to everything he did to her, she perceived it as it was not her in that bed. She had done the same thing with men every day. Unfortunately, today the game had changed. The roles had switched. How, she was not sure yet. She had played hard with men, and somehow, today, a stranger had played with her the same very nasty game and had used her as a worthless toy. The only difference was that she pretended to care, and a lot of the time she did. Despite the fact she used them, she treated men with compassion and kindness, whereas this young man was as cruel as a wild dog. He was not even likely like her.

How did all this happen? She asked herself again, and in that thought her eyelids felt heavy. Slowly, she fell asleep next to the stranger, thinking faintly; today her life had taken a new twist and had entered a different chapter.

When she woke up in the morning, she was in bed alone. The young man, whose name she did not ask for and was not told to, was not there. She listened carefully, but not a single sound came from inside or outside the house. She felt filthy. She pushed the covers away. The bed was in such bad shape. The bedsheets were wrinkled in a wicked way. She stood up and sat on the side of the bed. Her naked body felt unclean. She couldn't stand the way her sticky skin felt. She got up, pulled the sheets off the bed, took the cases off the pillows, and hurled them on the floor along with the bedcover. She tied everything inside one of the sheets, grabbed her bathrobe, threw it over her shoulders, and headed to the bathroom. She tossed the linens in the corner, prepared her bath with very hot water, and slipped inside. She stayed for a long time in it with her eyes closed. Then she rubbed her skin with soap to take away the odd feeling she sensed all over herself. She washed her hair thoroughly to get rid of the smell of his body odor, which she could smell all over herself, and finally got out of the bathtub.

When she went back in her bedroom, she looked out of habit at the nightstand on his side. Nothing was there.

Although men came by, following their regular schedule, and knocking on the door persistently, she did not open the door to anyone for a week. When their paradise gate did not open, they repeatedly came many times during the day as well as during the night with no regard to their set time. She stubbornly did not open the door. It was unlike her, but she did not have any desire to see anyone.

Her reaction surprised many. Men were puzzled by her withdrawal, something that did strike even her as strange. They couldn't understand why the heavenly door was closed on them, and why she did not show up at the entrance when they knocked, giving at least a reasonable explanation. Although, they realized Rina's door was not going to open no matter how long they kept banging on it unless she wanted to; they went away disappointed, only to return the next day.

One of them even spent the night, falling asleep on her

Under the Orange Tree

porch, to no avail. She did not open the door to invite him inside. She knew she could not continue this for too long, or some of them might make an unpleasant scene. She felt their increasing impatience. But she just wanted to be by herself for a while, something she did not feel like doing ever before.

After a week, a strong, familiar knock woke her up in the middle of the night. She knew his beat even in her sleep. It was her favorite, vigorous lover. She felt in high spirits. The man was the sole source of her happiness. She always looked forward to her time with him. If her life had been different, he was the man she would have liked to have by her side.

She got up and ran to open the door. But while she was just putting her hand on the key, she stopped abruptly. Was it the father or the son? She leaned her back on the door to rest a little as her heart was beating hard. She heard him asking her to open the door.

"Who is it?" she asked.

"It's me! Don't you recognize my voice?" he asked playfully. He sounded just like his son.

"Step up to the window!" She moved from the door to look out the window. The moon was full that night, and she saw him standing tall against the moonlight. She felt relieved and opened the door. He grabbed her in his arms and sensed she was a little stiff.

"What's wrong, Pumpkin?" he asked, concerned.

She looked at him for an instant and then moved her eyes away. She loved it when he called her Pumpkin. She liked the overtone of the word coming from his mouth, but everything sounded different lately, even the sweet nickname.

"Okay now!" the man said. "What's wrong?"

"You sent your son here a week ago!" She couldn't help herself saying in a low, quiet voice, although she had promised herself she would not bring this up with him.

"What's wrong with that?" he asked, surprised.

"But he is your son!" she exclaimed, taken aback by his response.

"Yes! And he is a very handsome and vital young man," he said, smiling. "I thought you would be pleased. I knew you were all alone on Spring Day and thought to amuse you."

She did not respond right away. She thought of him as her lover. He thought of her as a good harlot. She felt a sharp ache in her chest but did not show her pain. She lowered her eyelashes so he would not see the obvious turbulence in her eyes and said slowly: "I did not know you had a grown-up son."

"That's because we have no time to talk about my children, Pumpkin," he replied with a seductive voice and reached for her.

She looked at him, not giving in yet to his sensual temptation, although the nickname sounded sweeter this time.

"I never saw him around," she muttered. She wanted to know more about the whole thing. It had surprised her that a father would send his son to a woman he visited for sexual pleasures.

"He has been living in the city of Vlora with my brother for a few years now. He is a fine young man. He is doing very well there. He sends us money from time to time," he said. "He came by to see us for a few days and spend Spring Day with us. Used to city life, he got bored that day and asked me if there were places around here he could go for some fun.

I thought about you being alone, and I sent him your way."

He saw a shadow passing across her face and asked:

"Did I do something wrong?"

She swallowed hard and shook her head in denial. She could not tell him she had disliked his son. She couldn't make herself telling him, his son took her by force. She couldn't say to him, his son was not a decent young man. She didn't have the courage to admit to him; she regarded him apart from others and as the only man in her life. She just looked at him and felt the desire to make love to him, and feel the passion of a good man who knew how to treat her and make her feel—as the rest of the world did not exist. She raised her head, kissed him, and whispered with a sensual voice, "Be gentle with me today, my stallion!"

He looked at her surprised, lifted her petite, plump frame to his chest, and whispered in her ear, "What is with you today, little Pumpkin?"

"Nothing," she whispered and she swallowed some more unexpected tears, "I just want to make love to you." He never saw tears in her eyes. He squeezed her in his arms with affection, gave her a deep, gentle kiss, and they went inside.

She felt warm and cozy in his arms, and a good feeling overcame her. He always knew how to handle her and make her feel special. That's why she cherished him as the one. She gave herself to him with a passion she had never known before, and wasn't just physical.

He felt her ardor and responded back. His reaction pleased her to the point that brought them to the most pleasurable, universal union of two twined human bodies where sexual interaction becomes the essence of existence. Their screams penetrated the walls of the room and were heard far and about.

From that day, she went back to her old routine, but inside her, something was brewing. What exactly? She couldn't put the finger on it. But it felt somewhat different than before.

Women were shunning one another, and men were avoiding their comrades. A bad omen was going around the village. Men seemed tired, and women had the murkiness of an ill person. It seemed as if, a plague had passed through the village and had left behind the pale, gray color on their faces. Nobody had died, though. No flu had passed through, and as far an outsider might observe, nothing visible or important was going on, and yet something had happened, something no one could explain, or understand. The doors of the houses were kept locked to even neighbors or close relatives. Some whispers were floating around, but no one knew what the whispers were about. Words with no meaning were said, warnings were thrown in the air, but no one had a handle on what it was about.

Little by little the words began to have a real meaning and a particular language. The new words, "venereal disease," were sneaking into conversations, although people had a hard time pronouncing them correctly or saying them with a normal voice. The phrase was whispered and repeated in a discreet way like a new wicked word that someone had learned, kept using as if obsessed with it but ashamed to say it out loud.

Being superstitious in saying the word "plague," some felt as if this was far worse than the curse of it. It had brought the discreet, sinful acts to broad daylight. Women, mad as hell about their weakling husbands who couldn't keep themselves away from sinning, finally blurted out their amassed rage. They blamed everything on that lowlife woman, Rina, for the lewd life she had led all these years. But they were angrier with their spouses who brought shame on them, their respectable wives, the mothers of their children.

Heads were turned aside. Fingers were pointed. Loud, heated exchanges occurred. Tasteless, vulgar words never said before came out from the mouths of reputable women and men. Hands were raised. Faces were bruised. Blackened eyes were seen; then the silence followed it all, but the fact remained. The disease was inside their bodies; and no one knew what exactly it was, how they got it, or how to fight it!

The shame became part of the village life. The herbal remedies the villagers had used for generations for common diseases did not work on this one. The humiliation was beyond measure. People kept more and more to themselves. It sounded as if an invisible phantom had swept through their chimneys right inside their homes.

Anita was seen going from house to house, speaking with women on the side. The word was she was giving women a potion of mixed herbals. They had to drink a tea made from the mix once a day and also wash their private areas every night with the same liquid. She also had advised women to either ask their husbands to stop visiting Rina, or not sleep with them if they did not want the disease to get worse than it was.

Mad at Aníta for getting in their family affairs, and outraged at the defiance of their wives, some men forcefully made them lie with them. Not only was the disease not going away,—despite Aníta's effortless attempts,—but it was also bringing out attitudes never known before even in men recognized as decent ones.

Regardless of how bad the disease was affecting the male population and despite the shame they felt for getting it and passing it on to their wives, it did not stop many of them from continuing visiting Rina. They couldn't stay away from the house on the outskirts of the village.

Things were becoming difficult for all. Aníta's husband,—who had stopped going to Rina's house,—under the pressure of other men, had told his wife not to get into other's affairs. Speculations around were, he had beaten her several times and even threatened to pack her back to her folks. But, his handling of the matter did not help. The disease was there to stay.

The village felt dirty. The filth was not in the streets, not in the air, not in their backyard, not in their houses, not in their waste outlet in the back corner of the yard. It was inside their bodies. It was in their most intimate parts. Everyone had a peculiar look, a look that usually comes from a very high fever, but in this case it came from their troubled souls as well from the damned disease they shared.

The beautiful hamlet had turned into a ghost. At one point, one of the men died because of that filth. The rumor was, he suffered worse than anyone. He left behind a very sick widow and five children with no one to take care of them.

His death gave a good scare to everybody. A handful of men finally stopped going to Rina's house, but some couldn't help themselves. The woman at the end of the village was a repugnant attraction that even the disease couldn't make go away. Sad, pale, and gray faces became common. Laughs and smiles had become alien.

Anita was seen over at Rina's house—some voices spread the rumor around—but no one believed it. "Anita would never, ever put her foot in that sinful, devious house," many replied to the buzz.

Rina was resting in bed. She had not felt well for a while. It began little by little. She did not pay attention to the signs at first. Then things became more complicated. Men who visited her complained about the same symptoms she had. The redness, the swelling, the terrible itching feeling down there had become common among her usual lovers. She thought carefully about how and when the whole thing had begun. She never had any disease prior to this.

She decided to go see a doctor in the city. When the doctor spelled it out for her, she almost fainted. He gave her some medication, and told her, "If you do not stop sleeping with men, the medication will not help," and then added with a ruthless, cold tone, "You are at risk to end up dead."

Scared, she followed his advice, but she couldn't keep the men from having her. She locked herself in the house. But every time she had to go out to buy something, they were somewhere waiting for her to come out. They would have her anywhere they could, behind bushes, in the back of her house, behind a fence, behind a tree, wherever they could. Her life became a living hell. Finally, she gave up locking the door. The old routine went back on. She knew, if the end was written somewhere for her, she was going to burn in hell soon.

Her favorite lover came by one day. She hadn't seen him in a while. He looked sick and did not ask to get inside. He sat at the top of the stairs and invited her to sit next to him. He was thoughtful. They stayed silent for a bit looking at the emptiness ahead until he broke the silence:

"It happened on Spring Day, didn't it?"

She looked at him sadly and nodded.

"I should have known better," he said, looking sideways in the direction of the trees. His eyes had lost their blue color.

She put her hand on his shoulder and felt his bony back. In a matter of months, his sturdy body had disappeared. His solid muscles were gone, and his healthy, tanned skin had turned into a grayish-green like color. No sign of the handsome, vigorous man he once had been was left in him. He looked old and weary. He got up slowly as if everything in his body ached, and put his hand over her head. The weight of his hand was ethereal. It had lost his magic power. The touch that made her once tremble with sensuality was not there anymore. He looked at her for a while as if he wanted to memorize her face or apologize for something. But instead he said: "Good-bye, Rina!" with a farewell tone. His eyes were sad and impassive.

He touched the tip of her nose with his index finger, turned around, and went down the stairs. Not looking back,

Under the Orange Tree

he walked away with sluggish steps as if he did not have much energy left to be able to finish the distance between her house and his.

She shivered under his touch. Her eyes were filled with tears. She knew! She was not going to see him again. Not being able to see him walk away like that, she got up and went inside the house.

Three weeks later she heard he had passed away. She cried for hours in her empty house. She cried for the life of a good man gone for nothing. She cried for her life gone wasted. She cried for the unfortunate day that brought things to this point. She cried for lost healthy and happy times, never to be returned. She cried, thinking a man might show up at her doorstep at any moment, and take her forcibly without caring what she was going through. She cried of fear of the last condemnation. She cried thinking that hell couldn't be worse than this twisted reality. She cried for not having a single soul to talk to and look after her in this big, empty house on the far borders of her village.

She felt extremely alone, carrying this life-threatening malady in her body that was making her sicker and sicker every day as a punishment for her sinful life.

One day she had an unexpected visitor. That morning she felt worse than any other day and spent the whole day in bed. Her body felt weak and weightless.

She heard an unusual knock on the door. She knew the signals of her lovers' in all their various moods. It was none of them. It was a cautious, soft tap. It was as if someone was not sure of being at the right house. She got off the bed and sweating, slowly approached the hall window and looked outside. A woman was standing on the porch with her back to her. Rina moved slightly the curtain and asked:

"Who is it?"

The woman did not answer her question. Instead she said:

"Please, let me in!"

"What do you want?"

"We need to talk," the woman said, almost pleading, but seemed very sure about what she had come for. She also sounded a little anxious. Rina noticed she was looking around to make sure no one was in the vicinity to see her being at Rina's house.

Rina opened the door and looked at the woman carefully. She recognized Anita. Not knowing what to do, she stood there motionless. Anita had never come to pay her a visit even in her better times. The flashbacks of a beautiful young woman appeared in her vision. She used to dream of being as pretty as Anita was when she was young. But Anita's beauty was long gone. It just had vanished with no sign that it ever existed. What happened to beautiful Anita? she sadly thought.

"May I come in?" Anita asked.

The question brought Rina back to the reality.

Not looking her in the eye, she moved slowly to the side. Why did she come to her house? she asked herself bewildered.

Afraid Rina might change her mind and close the door

on her face, Aníta went inside quickly. The two women stood in the hall facing each other, not knowing where to start.

Looking at Rina, Aníta felt a strange, weird sensation inside her. The woman facing her was not the same woman she last had seen on Spring Day. It was a distorted image of her. She was covered in sweat. She felt as if she was standing next to a slimy frog. The silence continued for a while as the two women had the chance to observe each other closer than they had ever before.

Finally, Aníta broke the silence:

"Can we sit somewhere?"

Speechless from this unusual visit, Rina showed her uncommon visitor to the Good-Room. They moved slowly. Cautious not to touch, they kept a distance, showing openly, they did not trust each other. They sat down in two different sofas across the room. Aníta observed around for a while thinking how to begin the conversation. It was not easy to address the woman she hated most.

The silence made both uncomfortable.

"Why are you here?" Rina finally dared to ask, breaking the ice with a hissy, weak voice.

"You know why I am here," Aníta replied in a confident, serious tone.

"No, I don't!" Rina said. She felt nervous. She hadn't had a woman visitor in her house since her husband died six years ago.

"You have to go away, Rina!" Aníta blurted. The speech she had prepared had gone out of the window with the sight of Rina. She had thought of a different approach on the way here, but something about the whole thing made her to be direct.

"What? Where to?" she asked, startled by the request. "This is my home."

"You are destroying an entire village, Rina," Aníta said bluntly. "Men have gone out of their minds. Even with the filth you gave them, they cannot stop coming here. Think about your soul. Think about saving it by doing a good deed for once in your indecent life. If you stay here, other people are going to die. You are going to die as well. We all might die from this unthinkable disease."

She paused, then with a cynical, cold tone continued:

"The filth has sickened everybody, and it is not going to cease if you stay here. Look at yourself," she said, squinting her eyes. "You are sicker than most. You have a death sentence written on your face already."

Rina's hands were trembling while listening to Aníta's harsh words.

Aníta noticed Rina shaking her head at the accusations apparently denying them, and then she looked her in the eye as if to prove her innocence. Surprised by the silent response, she paused a little, then ignoring Rina's reaction continued:

"Go in the city Rina! Our men cannot reach you there. They are too poor and too sick to take the road that far."

Anita's directness took Rina by surprise, and her face became red. She felt a choking sensation in her throat. After a while, she said: "This is my home. I have nowhere to go!" An intense anguish showed in her voice, and she continued as if she wanted to justify herself: "This is all I have! This is all that I know! I grew up here! Here is all I—I —" stammering, she couldn't finish.

Anita made her feel confused and unworthy. She felt like the floor beneath her did not exist. She did not fully comprehend what exactly Anita was asking her to do. The solitude of her lavish, lusty life had isolated her from the existing reality, and she didn't know how to react to her blunt talk. She did not know how to speak with a woman and be sharp and abrupt the way she was with men. *Men are much simpler to deal with*, she thought.

Anita lowered her head to hide her anger and frustration. After composing herself, controlling her tone, she made another attempt:

"Sell your house and go Rina!"

Moving her head on the side, Rina looked at Anita bewildered. Absorbed in processing what Anita said before, she did not quite follow her last words and did not reply right away. She seemed confused. Finally, following her thoughts she looked around and said: "I cannot leave. Where would I go? I do not know anything beyond this place! I was born here. I grew up in this land. I—I—" She stopped again, unable to articulate another word.

The anger inside Anita rose. Strong emotions were suffocating her.

"Do you think just a little bit about the lives of people you are destroying?"

Rina did not respond. She appeared lost.

Anita's voice was hoarse when she spoke again.

"Then you have two choices Rina, either leave the village or—" Anita did not finish what she meant to say. Her eyes were intense. Their color deepened as she looked at Rina.

She got up and doing so, she dropped something on the

table. Rina gazed at it. It was a small, green fabric bag, tied tight with a twine. She raised her head and looked Aníta in the eye. Her dark, big eyes showed fear. She felt lost, disoriented. No words were coming out of her lips. In a moment, her eyes were begging Aníta for absolution. Unfortunately, the look in Aníta's eyes was unapproachable and menacing.

Looking into her eyes, Aníta understood why men were drawn to her among other things. They were darker than a night without stars. The pleading in her eyes made them even more disturbing. She felt a shiver going through her spine. She shook her head and composed herself. She came into this condemned house! She crossed the threshold of hell, determined to bring this whole nonsense to an end! She could not allow those gloomy eyes to intimidate her or get her soft on this woman!

"Save your soul, Rina!" Aníta said with a sharp, cold, aloof tone. "You might go to paradise instead of hell if you do this. When you do it to save the lives of others, God forgives you." She gave Rina an intense look to make sure she understood the meaning of her words and realized that the wretch of a woman was not quite receptive to what was just said to her. She looked lost in a remote, strange place. Thinking, she did all she could for what she came here to accomplish, Anita glanced one more time at Rina and headed for the door.

She stopped for a moment there. Their eyes met, and Aníta gave Rina another intense look, nodding her head as if saying, "Do it!" while her eyes pointed coldly at the green bag. Then she opened the door unhurriedly.

She closed it very quietly after herself, not making the

slightest noise as if she were afraid of disturbing a person in the deathbed, and was gone, just like that.

Rina stood there for a while, looking at the door with her eyes wide opened, as waiting for Aníta to show up again, but nothing happened. It felt unreal that Aníta was in her house a minute ago. Was she really here? Did she actually speak to her or were the spirits talking to her troubled soul? The questions pounded in her head. She was sick and feverish, and maybe she dreamt it all.

From her centered, indulged self, she had never been able to see the village as a functioning body with a life greater than hers. All she had cared for, in a long time, had been exploiting its men and fulfilling her pleasures. Aníta's visit, or her vision, whatever it was, gave her small world a hard blow. She felt insignificant. For a moment there, she sensed the silhouette of her mother showing up at the door and muttering to her, "Save your soul, my Rina! Your sins are going to be forgotten if you set yourself and the decent people of this hamlet free from this unforgivable turmoil."

Terrified, she went to the door, put the heavy handle lock on it, and leaned against its thick wood, looking around frightened. She put her hand on her forehead. It was as cold as a chilly January day, and her hand became wet from the dampness of her skin. She felt helplessly paralyzed by panic.

Then, the green bag on the table caught her eye.

No one had seen Rina in the village for about three weeks. The word was out that she had not opened her door to anyone lately. No one had seen her going in and out of her house either. Someone said she might have gone to the city for good.

The men did not want to believe the rumor. Several of them became irrational. They were noticed roaming near her property. A few were seen checking round and about the dwelling, although she was nowhere to be found. The boldest one just sat right outside on her porch. Some arranged a rotation routine. Two or three, stationed along the road that led to the city while others at the corners of her house. One of them even climbed the big walnut tree in the front yard watching and waiting for her to appear somehow through the shutters. Many were seen peeking through her windows, but no one had seen her moving inside.

A high-pitched scream was heard all over the village on the Monday of the fourth week of Rina's disappearance. The scream went on and on and on.

People who had heard the screaming, men and women, following its screechy sound, headed one by one to Rina's house. The front door was wide open and in pieces as if a big bull had charged at it. Someone had used a big ax to break it down. They heard a loud groaning coming from inside. They went in cautiously. They didn't see anyone in the Good-Room. Someone went to the kitchen, but no one was there either. A woman, bolder than the rest, led the crowd to the master bedroom on the west side of the house. The rest followed her quietly.

They heard her saying with a trembling voice, "Oh, *Zonja Shën Maria*, My Ladyship Saint Mary!" Shaking, she added, "Over here!" They followed her voice and saw her leaning on its opened door, clenching her fingers on it with her head turned away from whatever she had seen inside.

They moved a little closer and stopped at the troubled view in front of them. They saw a big dark figure bending slightly over the bed. The broad back of a man blocked the view. He was grunting like a trapped, wounded, wild boar; holding and rocking something in his arms they could not see. They moved slowly to the back of the room.

They saw Rina's petite body in his arms. Her head was leaning inside of his left, wide palm. Her legs hung limply over his right hand. Not aware of their presence in the room, he continued rocking her back and forth and murmuring something.

Stunned by the unexpected scene, they all stood quietly for a few moments watching the sight of the peculiar pair in front of them.

Finally, two men approached him carefully and made an effort to get Rina's body out of his arms, but they couldn't. Two others, from behind him, tried to pull gently but firmly the wretched man's arms. His grip was too strong. He did not let go and kept rocking her. It took a strong blow on his head from one of the men, for her body to slide from his hands and fall softly on her bed. Rina was dead. The crowd released a gasp. Its echo bounced around the awkward silence and made people shiver.

It took four villagers to drag the man outside the room. It seemed as if he was unable to feel, react, or comprehend what was happening around him. They forced him to sit outside on the top of the stairs. One of the men slapped him hard on the face to make him come to his senses, but he did not show any sign of awareness. He did not react—just kept gazing into space without blinking a bit.

"Did you kill her?" one of them questioned him.

He looked at the one who asked with his bloodshot, wide-open eyes but did not respond. The men surrounding him noticed his pupils were extensively dilated. They shook their heads. He was not even able to grasp what was happening around him.

The strongest men in the group were asked to take him home.

As they were leaving with him, they heard him repeatedly saying with a muffled voice, "She was dead! She was dead! I found her dead! I did not kill her! I could not possibly kill her!"

No one in the room could help but stare at the strange bundle on the bed. They noticed a tea cup on the nightstand. Someone got close and saw a small amount of dark greenish liquid on the bottom of it.

The men's faces showed anguish. Their eyes were fixated on what was left of their Rina. She was green-faced. Dried white foam covered her lips, red no more. Her body, twisted after the fall from the man's arm, was in bad shape. Her dress was rumpled up and showed her entangled legs from the thighs down. There were only bones and badly wrinkled skin left of the full, plump legs they used to caress and grasp. The flesh had vanished from her physique. Her plump body no more existed. Her seductive, curves were there no longer. Her once smooth, soft white skin was almost murky and crumpled. She looked like the old, monster witch in rags described in fairy tales.

It was a first for them, thinking that she was repulsive. They had never thought of her being hideous. The odd scene embarrassed them, made them feel awkward. An intense clenching feeling was twisting something inside their torsos.

They felt a helpless guilt. Guilt for what? Guilt, for not being able to identify the bundle in the bed with their Rina?! Guilt for their peculiar emotions and thoughts in the presence of their wives in the room?! Maybe! Maybe it was guilt associated with the remorse they had felt at the moment, by being in the same room, with what was left of the alluring woman with whom they had engaged in pleasurable, lecherous sins—and their legitimate wives next to them. Or rather, it was guilt for facilitating her death in some way and losing her.

They could not comprehend why the wearisome feelings were nagging them, but they were—strongly! The guilt swirled inside their chests.

There was no resemblance left of their flamboyant, enchanting Rina, with whom they had experienced the most carnal, censorious pleasures, right on that bed. And not one of them was thinking of the existence of their wives next to them at the moment. They were absorbed by the view in front of them. The memories that were outpouring in before their eyes suddenly replaced the wretched bundle on the bed.

Finally, they realized what the remorse was. They felt guilt for not having her anymore in their lives. She was gone!

Forever! They had lost her!

Swamped with sensual recollections of the thrilling, erotic old days—this room inflicted in them—incapable of looking at what was left of her any longer or accepting the fact she was gone, they left the room one by one.

Women, curious and absorbed in the twisted event, stood behind to take in the world that had taunted them. They slowly surrounded the bed looking at every small detail on it and around it. The room was suddenly packed with more of them. The news of Rina's death had reached the furthest house. The latecomers filled the emptiness created by the men quietly. The ones in the back tiptoed and stretched their necks to take a peek of the infamous scene.

Their curiosity was stronger than their repulsion. They were in the room where all had happened. They were in the room that lured their husbands away from their matrimonial beds in the middle of the night. Their emotions were intense. Their vengeful thoughts seemed to pour through their eyes.

There she was, on her bed. On the same bed where she had committed the gruesome sins of fornication. Motionless! Moreover, so ugly! Ugly to the utmost degree! Twisted after all! With no more of her exquisite appeal! With no more of the lascivious, fleshy, compelling powers she possessed over their men. Her sinful body was lifeless. Lifeless! Lifeless after all!

After a few moments of silence, they began to whisper to one another, looking at Rina's body although no man was in the room. Maybe they were just muttering out of respect for the dead or, perhaps, unconsciously, did not want to voice their thoughts out loud.

Finally, it was just them, the women. Them only! Them, the casualties of that fallen woman! It seemed unreal she had finally gone. Gone for good! Gone forever! The sound of the word, "gone", was ringing sharply in their head with a vindictive, celebrating undertone.

A certain joy arose inside each of them. They felt strange mixed feelings; certain sadness for the deceased, but the enormous pleasure of seeing her gone, was dominating their emotions. They were not supposed to feel that way in the presence of the dead no matter who that was. However, they did! They just could not help it. A deceased person's body was sacred. However, this was the body of Rina, the abhorrent, not that of an ordinary sinner.

She looked exactly the way they had perceived her all these years. She looked exactly the way she always should have. Their men had seen her at last for what she truly was. A disgusting wretch! A creature whose appearance matched precisely her evil soul! Oh yes! Their men had seen her! Oh, how they savored the moment! Just looking at their men's faces a few instances ago; they felt a guilty, immense elation that stirred a strange, good feeling in them. Yes! Vengeance was the right word! Vengeance, for she was gone! She was dead! Oh, how they had dreamed of, for such a day to come! They had cursed her in their empty, long nights from their half-vacant beds. Moreover, it finally happened! Not one of them was thinking about the costly price they had paid through the years and were paying more than ever as the punishment had fallen on everyone at the end.

But, finally, they had their day! The triumph of the moment was so grand, it made them forget about the suffering and the disease she had inflicted in them and left it behind in their bodies.

The only thing lingering in their minds was the thought, *Rina was gone forever! No more was she going to be their torment. No more was she going to be their agony —day and night!*

"Born an orphan, died an orphan!" a woman muttered in the midst of that twist interfusion of sentiments and looked around guilty.

The word orphan hung in the air. The women turned about and faced her. She felt utterly embarrassed. Unwittingly, she came in some ways to the defense of the wretched woman, who lay in the bed with no one by her bedside to carry out her last, departing rituals.

The disturbing thoughts twirled in their minds for a while after that, but little by little faded away, and they were faced with the reality in front of them. The word orphan had hit them hard. The rational practicality of their simple life slowly took over the complexity of the emotions of this unusual experience. Finally, they saw the deceased right there in front of them, as the dead body of a woman with no one to be there for her at her last split from life.

"We should give her the adequate service of the dead," one of them said in a trembling voice. Just like that, the daring woman approached the bed soberly and carefully arranged Rina's body in an appropriate manner. In the back of the room, someone went to fetch the midwife, who served not only as such, but also as a healer to the sick and as a watcher of the dead. Others observed in silence the movements of the woman with imperceptible curiosity, honoring the ritual.

She moved the body to the middle of the bed, put Rina's head on the pillow, and crossed her arms over her chest, and put aside a bunch of hair covering part of Rina's face. Then she lifted her legs. They were cold and stiff like two arid, broken tree branches. She put them as straight as she could together. Afterward, she straightened Rina's wrinkled dress and covered her body up to the waist with a white blanket she found at the end of the bed. Rina finally looked peaceful, as much as a very sick person in her situation could be after death.

The midwife came pretty quickly. The prospect of seeing Rina dead was too big to take it slowly as she usually did with the dead. She touched Rina's forehead and then put her hand underneath her armpit. She said Rina had died three or four days ago. The women looked at one another, and under the midwife's sign, they put their heads down and inaudibly said a prayer for the spirit of the deceased.

After the prayer, Aníta, who was taller than most in the room, looked around, pausing on each woman's eyes. They nodded their heads. They understood the significance of that silent request. They were going to give Rina a proper, small burial. Just them, the women! No matter what had she done before, she had performed the ultimate sacrifice. Some of them even shed a tear or two for the woman who had made their life a twisted inferno in the past years, but at the end — had committed self-immolation.

The prayer had helped to uplift their souls. In a matter of minutes, she was given confidential impunity in a silent agreement.

Death always had that overpowering effect on people.

It made them vulnerable. It made them accept things they would never have before; it made them forgive the dead for the dreadful vices carried out while alive.

The midwife began to prepare the body for the burial, giving orders to carry out for Rina's last rituals. She asked someone to prepare the bath. The body needed to be cleansed from the filth of the disease. It was a sin to bury an impure body. It was a belief that the bath purified not only the body from the committed earthly wrongdoings but also the spirit of the deceased from its sins.

Rina's last resting place was chosen. She was buried in the Unknown Wanderers burial ground of the cemetery. No one knew who said it to bury her there, but the decision was unanimous. She was buried in that spot. The reason was simple; no one wanted her buried along their loved ones. Moreover, no one could visit her without being seen.

The Unknown Wanderers' parcel had come about many, many years ago. After a strong, frosty winter a shepherd had found a very well-preserved body after the snow melted on the east side of the mountain next to the quarry. The word was sent around to the neighboring villages about the found body, but no one had declared a missing person in the area. Someone used the term "the unknown wanderer" for the unidentified man. It stuck with the dead. They buried the anonymous man in the left corner of the cemetery, a spot not used till then. In respect for the dead, the villagers carved a tombstone and placed it over the grave. The script on the headstone simply read:

> ### The Unknown Wanderer

More than a decade later when they found the body of another mysterious man under the snow, he was buried next to the first. Since then, it was decided to have a separate parcel for the unidentified dead bodies that the unfortunate fate brought in their village's paths. The burial spot acquired in time the name, *The Unknown Wanderers' Turf.*

The same script was engraved on the second headstone, but the villagers realized they had to rank them. The words *The First* and *The Second* were added underneath *The Unknown Wanderer* on each tombstone. Below, they engraved the year each body was found.

> The Unknown Wanderer
> The First
> **1903**

> The Unknown Wanderer
> The Second
> **1919**

Rina's grave became the third in the parcel. Her burial happened eleven years after the second wanderer in an even distance from the first two. In the beginning, no headstone was put over her grave. But somehow, someone had gone through the hassle in the quarry to cut a piece of stone and put it there. It did not have any script on it. Not even the year she was born, nor the year she was gone. It was an unmarked tombstone.

Months later a carving like crow's feet was visible on the unmarked headstone.

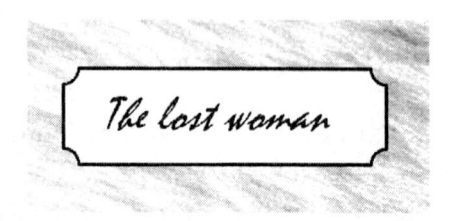

> *The lost woman*

Something happened to the script weeks later. It was scratched to the point, that the writing became unrecognizable. The tombstone went back to being unmarked. It looked just like a simple headstone with the traces that chisels and hammers had left on the surface as it was torn away from the quarry on the east side of the mountain. Only the ones, who knew the script had been there, could notice the visible scrapes of the mysterious chisel that made the script "The lost woman" disappear.

To a stranger's eye, it simply marked the fact that there was a body underneath the tombstone.

The village was never the same after Rina's death. Although gone, she continued to be the tormenting ghost for both men and women of the village. Many men continued to live in the shadow of her memory. Their bodies and minds were under Rina's bizarre spell. For a long while, they did not fulfill their dutiful acts with their wives, not out of a sense of duty over the disease, but as if they were unconsciously mourning her death.

Meanwhile, the women had sworn not to let their husbands have them until the illness was gone, but also as a punishment for their sins.

Things became even worse than when Rina was alive. Mistrust between husbands and wives had become common. Some women would hear their men sob at night, some in their sleep. The men's illogical hope that Rina would appear somehow in her house at the end of the village, to please them in the way their wives never would, had vanished. They felt alone, abandoned, and helpless. Some of them were seen spending hours over her grave when the moon did not shine the gloomy nights. In their mind, they were on a never-ending journey of finding whatever sensual sensation they once had with Rina.

A handful of them had become incapable of acting on their responsibilities as the primary providers of their families. The after death turmoil they had experienced had an everlasting effect. The death of Rina had been their downfall. "She had been and continued to be, their Achilles' heel," a woman that had heard of the Greek legend, said to her friends.

Rina's death had empowered them. They no longer feared their weakling husbands. These matriarchs had a long-lasting effect on the village, but the new generation did not have a clue how this ordeal began.

A year later, a week before Spring Day, a woman went to visit the grave of a relative in the cemetery. She could not help herself but peek at the Unknown Wanderers parcel from afar. She caught sight of only two headstones. She looked around. No one was at the cemetery at the time. She got closer to the infamous parcel. There were only two headstones. A third one was missing. Wondering which one, she became bold and got even closer. To be sure, she walked inside the parcel. She was right; Rina's plain headstone was not there. She looked around, but there was no sign of it. Baffled, she went over to a few other graves outside the parcel with hope to find it somewhere thinking someone might have moved it, but the gravestone was nowhere to be found. In the corner where Rina's grave used to be, the soil was leveled and covered with grass as if there had been no grave.

She thought she had lost her mind and left the cemetery, hurrying as if followed by a ghost. She went around the village, door to door, telling about the wicked fact.

Some people did not believe her story— she was known to blow things out of proportion. Becoming curious, they went back to the cemetery right away to verify her claim. They saw with their own eyes what she said was true. After much speculation, someone proposed digging the soil where the grave used to be to make sure her remains were still there.

The reaction to that suggestion was strong. Most of the villagers considered it blasphemy, and the person who said it felt tense under the scrutiny and did not mention it again.

Such a thing was never heard of before. It was a sacrilege to touch the last dwelling of the dead.

The women gathered at Aníta's house for coffee after the gloomy event and were chatting quietly about the disappearance of the headstone. In the midst of conversation, a voice dropped the known saying, "Out of sight, out of mind!" Some looked around to see who said it to no avail. A few looked for Aníta, but she was not in the room at the moment. They all looked thoughtful hearing it. They had often heard that saying during their lifetime, but that particular day its meaning took a much deeper significance. After a thoughtful silence, someone expressed that maybe it was divine intervention that made the grave disappear.

Weary of the whole Rina ordeal, villagers held on eagerly to the idea of some divine intervention and took it to heart. Neither men nor women talked about Rina again. Her memory had gone with the frosty wind of the winter in an unknown place to return no more.

The people of the village began spending more time outdoors, breathing the spring air, feeling the breeze of the new season on their faces, talking to their neighbors. They were ready to commence the New Year, anticipating the celebration of Spring Day and preparing the enriched soil of their land to plant the new grains for better, profitable harvests. An internal healing had started with the fresh air of spring, and a new hope embraced the atmosphere of the incoming Spring Day. The village had slowly begun its road to recovery

The Awakening

Reaching the impossible
The story of an exceptional man

March 2008

Flora was sitting next to the windowsill staring at the man working in her flower garden. The tragic death of her husband and her son, three years ago, had shaken her frame of mind. Since then, she had been lost too deep in sorrow to relate with reality. Her brain had shunned the outside world. The echo of the sounds within the room or outside noises did not reach her brain at all. She did not utter a word to anyone. The zest for life had long gone from her being. It had disappeared in some hidden, faraway place within her—hard to be found.

After the heartbreaking event, her relatives and her long-time friends came by to help her overcome the grief every day. They did her chores, cooked for her, did her laundry while she stood motionless at the window sill from morning till night. Her immobility became such that they had to bathe her and change her just like an infant, for even taking care of her simple daily needs.

As time passed by, her sorrow did not vanish. She had

gone into a state of mind no one could understand. She did not converse; she did not say a single word as if she had never spoken her entire life. Even her mother could not reach her soul. Flora did nothing but stay still on the sofa of her guest room, leaning on the windowsill, staring outside as if she expected some vision to appear and wake or shake her up. They had to drag her slowly, to make her sit at the table and feed her. But at some point, they gave up. They fed her right there on the couch. Unfortunately, her vegetative response to her surroundings grew stronger and stronger every day, and it became too much to be handled by the people who cared about her.

    Most of her loved ones began to get wearisome by trying to get her back on her feet. Her unresponsive, idle state and her inability to make even the slightest effort, pushed away the most zealous of them. One day, her mother decided, it was time to take her back home. When her father tried to get her up and walk her out of her house, she grabbed the side of the couch with both hands and refused to move. Her older brothers, who attempted to give a hand in the matter, although they were stronger than their father, couldn't make her go with them. She had a small frame and didn't weigh much, especially after the heartbreaking loss, and they thought it would be easy carrying her home. Suddenly she became aggressive. The moment they grabbed her arms, she screamed and kicked. She pulled their hair, bit them and scratched them so badly, they had to give up and drop her on her sofa, where she curled up in a fetus position and became quiet at once. Everyone was utterly surprised by the strange reaction and the burst of energy coming from a woman who barely had walked or reacted to anything for more than a year. After that episode, people felt that their efforts were hopeless. Flora had not shown a single sign of improvement.

One of the relatives came up with the idea of hiring someone to take care of her. Everyone welcomed the thought with great relief. They asked around for someone appropriate and capable of possibly handling everything. The acres around the house needed a lot of work and the season of planting the grain was close. The vegetable garden in the back of the house had a sad look of abandonment—the weeds had grown to the height of a person. Although, a few tried to give a hand from time to time to maintain the flower garden in front of the house, it not did not help much. The flowers were dying.

"It has to be two people," someone said, "A maid for Flora and the house, and a worker for running things around the house, in the gardens and the fields."

The family business had to get going to enable Flora live on the property. Otherwise, it would be bought by some wealthy landlords in the area, whose people were seen looking around the house lately. They watched over estates in bad shape to buy them for nothing. Usually, they went after old folks with no heirs. And, Flora's husband did not have any relatives other than Flora, who on her part was not capable of managing the property. The problem was, no one could afford the wages of two people, despite the fact that many members of the family circle had expressed a willingness to contribute.

The word for hire went around. The news came about a man in a nearby village, who people hired for all kinds of work. If it were hard labor or taking care of the Elders, even children, he would do it. He had even taken care of a paralyzed old woman once. The only thing people knew about him was that he was an orphan whose parents had died when he was an infant. He was left with a distant relative at the age of six by an uncle who had too many children to feed and couldn't afford one not born of his own. After that, the boy grew up going from door to door, under the pity of the villagers. But it did not come to him for nothing. To earn his meals, he had to run errands and carry out tasks for the families who took him in out of mercy. He was moved around from one family to another until he came at the age, no one could consider him a child any longer. Since then, he started to live on his own as a vagrant. In time he became a well-built young man who people hired when in need for an extra hand in their property.

He came to live in the neighboring village at a very young age, and started working as a laborer there. With time, people began to trust him little by little and hired him for whatever they needed. He did not socialize with other people, kept mostly to himself, and took shelter in an abandoned old cabin that did not belong to anyone in the south part of the village. He had found there, his last stop on his odd journey. The villagers had accepted him as a necessary part of their daily life.

The only thing about the man, they heard people saying, was that he was a little slow-witted—some would say absentminded, or soft in the head as some goodhearted people nicely put it. Because of his unusual ways of doing things, his lack of communication with others, his habit of not looking people in the eye or responding to their questions, someone had called him "the Retard", and the nickname had stuck with him. The name did not have an unkind connotation, and no one heard him complaining about it. If he ever had a name, it was forgotten.

Despite that, he was a great worker and a great caregiver—from cooking to gardening, to working in the field, to fixing roofs or walls, doing the laundry, and even taking care of babies. The villagers were amazed how quickly he learned new things and how precise he was in what he did. Bottom line, he was very skillful despite his lack of interaction with others. Many considered that an advantage. Not being like other people in many ways, he surprised everyone with his workmanship, punctuality, and neatness. They also learned he had never complained of anything, and there were no incidents reported from the families—he had worked for either.

He came across as a hardworking laborer and a decent person to be trusted; it was the final word. People, who had hired him, said, he could be trusted with a child's life. The decision was unanimous; he had to be employed to take care of Flora and the house. When it came down to the payment, they were told he always asked for the top wage. He had a good sense of money as if he knew his worth somehow, and he never was out of jobs.

They offered him higher earnings than he was getting in his current job, to convince him to work for Flora, and he accepted the offer. The fact that he would live in a barn in the back of the house and take care of a mute woman—as they put it—made him jump at the opportunity.

He inspected the house carefully in and out the first day they brought him in, and he started right away with no one telling him where to begin by fixing the front yard and the flower garden. People who came by to visit a few days later to check on him and Flora were amazed at the tidiness of the house inside and out. The house was immaculate inside. He had cleaned every corner and thrown out a lot of unused things that had piled up in the rooms. As the weeks went by, everyone was surprised by colorful flowers blooming in the front garden. He painted the house white, inside and out. He spruced up the roof tiles, almost black, which shined afterward with a deep redness under the sunlight and outlined the windows in a light green.

The house, which was old and falling apart, in a few months of his hiring seemed as if it was built not too long ago. The meals he cooked were delicious; Flora's relatives began to stop by during lunch time just to get a taste of his fine cooking. They often found him feeding Flora with gentleness and treating her with caution.

Flora's parents were very pleased. Everyone in the family thought he was the perfect solution for Flora's circumstances, especially since the man barely spoke. He did not look them in the eye when they addressed him, and he left right away to do something outside when they visited. He knew he did not need to take care of Mrs. Flora for the time they were, and it was obvious, he felt uncomfortable around people.

It was as if he was invisible, but his touch was everywhere, and his job was done impeccably, they noticed every time they came by. He was capable of doing an excellent job no matter what task he took on, people commented. Now when they referred to him, they would say "the Retard" with a tinge of respect. With time, the word acquired a distinct connotation for great esteem.

Little by little the house, the vegetable garden, the flowers, and the acres of grain came to a great shape. It seemed the property had found its master. The pilgrims going through the village would stop for a few moments just to look at Flora's house. It gave everybody a sense of beauty, peace, and perfection. The word went around, and people came to see with their own eyes what the Retard had done with a house at the breaking point.

With time, the outsiders who used to do business with the villagers noticed quite a change every time they visited. A sense of beauty and peace had overpowered the village. Each house looked better, and the flowers in the front yard were flourishing. A pleasant aroma spread out around the village. It was springtime, and that made everything better. People were more generous and open-minded. Strangers could not resist stopping by to ask for a rose or a carnation while passing in front of a house. The Retard had impacted people's lives without their being aware of it.

As the village's face changed in time, Flora's house stood out. One day, a new carved wooden fence surrounded the house. It was a work of art. Each piece was beautifully engraved with elegant patterns. The rails, the poles, all sculpted in shapes people had not seen before. Villagers also noticed changes in it from time to time. People would say to one another, "Let's go over to the Retard's to see if he put any new carvings in his fence." The fact that it was Flora's house, the one they were referring to, was unconsciously fading in their viewpoint.

In a holiday gathering, a man commented, "No matter what we do, we cannot beat the Retard. He is always one step ahead of us." He emphasized the word "retard," and his tone showed a degree of resentment. A few people looked at him thoughtfully. After a while, an old woman said, "What God takes away with one hand, He gives with the other!" And, pensive as she was, looking at everyone, she added, "We should not put ourselves in rivalry with God's challenge!" Most nodded in agreement to the wise remark and everybody went on with their holiday business.

Many things had changed since the Retard was hired as a caregiver for Flora, but not Flora. As the village was influenced to a great extent by his creative work and her house was thriving, she continued to sit motionless on the sofa with her eyes fixed out of the window noticing nothing.

One day, Flora's mother, during her routine visit, found two fresh, red and white roses next to Flora on the windowsill. She looked for any sign on whether Flora had noticed them. Sadly, she found none. Her daughter was clueless of the existence of the flowers next to her. Her mother sighed, took the flowers, put them in a small vase, and helped her daughter eat the meal the Retard had prepared for his matron.

After she had finished feeding her, she stayed awhile, looking at her once beautiful girl. She looked like someone she just met.

"What has happened to you, my dear child?" she whispered, not expecting an answer from the woman next to her. Flora gave her mother a brief, blank look and looked away toward the window. Such a reaction took her mother by surprise. But, it was so brief, as if it did not happen. Her visits to Flora's house had become shorter and shorter lately, and it saddened her.

They had a strong mother-daughter bond prior to the accident. She grew up without a sister, and once Flora entered womanhood, she became the sister she never had. But now her beloved daughter was gone. Her child's spirit was wandering places unknown to her. Oh, how she wanted to help her dear child come back to life! How she yearned to hear her voice, how she longed to tell her things, tell her what was going around the village! To show her how the Retard had fixed her house, and how the village itself had followed suit! How badly she wanted to hear her daughter respond! Just a single word! But, sadly, nothing came out of Flora's mouth.

In the beginning, she often spoke to Flora like she used to in the past. But she was faced by a stranger in a still body and mind, an unfamiliar, inert, silent, impenetrable person who sat, immobile, on the sofa. With time, she grew tired and stopped conversing with her beloved daughter.

She looked one more time in Flora's direction, hopeful for a sign, a blink, a motion of her lips, the movement of a finger, but all to no avail. Great sadness overcame her. She looked at the roses, back at her daughter again, and slowly left the room.

As she walked away, she felt no desire to come back anytime soon. She came to realize she wanted very badly to keep the memories she had with her dear daughter as they were before her misfortune. The sad view back there was replacing her memories of her daughter and her image little by little. *The only way to prevent that,* she thought, *is to stay away from the sight of the stranger at the windowsill.*

The day was almost over. Flora's caretaker was finishing the chores outside before going in to take care of *Zonja Flora,* when he heard a whimper. He stopped. He tried to figure out where the cry was coming from. For a while, he did not hear anything. Being sensitive to noises, he kept alert. Then again, the sound of a strong sobbing infiltrated the air. He straightened his neck and turned his head in the direction of the house. The sound was coming from there. His brows went up in bewilderment. He did not see anyone going in the house. Who was crying? *Zonja Flora* never cried. In the two years he had served her, he had never heard her crying. So, who was it? He approached the house slowly and cautiously opened the front door.

Usually he would find her in her typical position—sitting on the sofa, looking outside as usual with her hands on the windowsill. That's how she stayed all day long. He had made it a habit of glancing in the window's direction to check up on her during the day when working outside. She never moved. But today, not only was she weeping; she was loud.

Her shoulders were moving up and down in convulsions.

She had never done that before. The Retard stood at the door of the Good-Room, not sure what to do. Lately, her relatives' visits were infrequent. It seemed they had become forgetful of her. Most of the time, it was just Mrs. Flora and him. But that did not bother him a bit. It made it easier to carry out his tasks when no one was around and be himself. Visitors made it always complicated for him. He felt impaired when they came by as if his dimensions were diminished, and he couldn't go about his chores as usual. He had worked with people before, but, in this job, he had established a well-balanced routine that included only Mrs. Flora, not anybody else. And he got used to it. Her relatives sudden arrivals in unpredictable days, when he least expected anyone, threw him off. Everything different disturbed his routine and disoriented him. He needed the very same daily routine.

He did not have the freedom to do things his way in his other jobs. People who had hired him in the past used to explain him constantly what to do, when to do it, and how to do it. Some even used to tell him how fast or how slow he had to do certain things, presuming he did not know how to get around different tasks. They treated him as if he was incapable of doing much on his own without their constant supervision or instructions. But, he knew better; he had to obey their commands and do whatever he was told to do, although he had mastered everything that had to be done better than most ordinary people did. It was called survival. But here in this house, for the first time in his life, his fate had taken a different course.

Zonja Flora was quiet, and she did not resist his caregiving. It was as if he were taking care of an infant with no one telling him how. He did not like when people paid attention to him, bossed him around. *Zonja Flora* did not give him any orders. She was oblivious of his existence, and that suited him fine. He liked his new job very much. It gave him the freedom to do things his way.

In this house, he did everything at his own pace, in his own fashion. No one accounted for what he did, how many logs he chopped, what he did first and what he had to do next. He completed the chores around the house in his own order. It gave him great pleasure to take care of the flowers in the garden, work in the fields, or fix what was broken without having someone breathe down his neck. What he had enjoyed the most so far while taking care of Mrs. Flora was working on the new fence. It gave him a satisfaction he'd never experienced before. Carving the pickets, the rails, and the middle poles and then assembling everything together so nicely, panel after panel, creating a different view, became his new thing. Just looking at his creation every morning gave him enormous joy. He did not think ahead what to do or how to carve. It just came to him, and he did it on impulse.

He never felt this way before, so content, so at peace, and so fulfilled. The greatest moment for him was when people stopped by and took an interest in his work on the fence. His hedge gave the villagers such pleasure. He would observe them from afar, talking to one another. They pointed at the head of each picket, looked at the details of his carvings, compared them and, surprised, they would discover the differences between the panels. Not one was like the other. Their attention made him work on new pickets or hedge when he had time and replace the old ones one by one around the house. He made sure to keep up their curiosity. He knew they would come back as long as he put newly carved posts or new rails every so often on the fence. Although he did not like having people around, he took great pleasure in the consideration his work was getting and the villagers coming to see it. He would stay far from the fence and watch them going around and inspecting the new details on it. That inspired him to do more things.

It came to him to carve a wooden table with four wooden chairs one day. It took him two months to finish the whole set. The backs of the chairs were high and full of details. He took his time with every detail. Each showed a different relief of carved figures. He portrayed animals and birds in miniature in tiny detail. He engraved flowers and houses, mountains and rivers on top of the table, creating an amazing bas-relief. When he was content with the work he had done, he put the set on the right side of the front yard. The amazement on people's faces when they saw the table collection gave him great joy. He heard them saying the set lived up to the standards of a king. He did not know what a king was, but he knew by the tone of their voices that it was the highest compliment ever given. A broad smile stormed his face the day he heard it. It was his first smile in a lifetime of weariness.

He had made it a habit of bringing her flowers lately. He would pick two roses of different colors, switching them every day. He would leave them beside her hand on the sill each morning. It gave him pleasure doing it. He did not know why, but it did. She never touched or looked at the roses, but he did it regardless, every day.

At the end of the day, when he came to serve her dinner and put her to bed, he found the roses exactly where he put them in the morning. He would feed her right there in the couch. And, the only time she would allow him to put his hands on her, lift her up, take her away from her favorite corner on the sofa and put her to bed, was the evening. It was dark outside, and nothing out there for her to stare at but darkness, which meant for her, no apparition of sorts.

He would tuck her in the bed carefully as he would a child, waiting for her to fall asleep. Afterward, he would leave the bedroom, take the flowers from the sill, throw them away, lock the house from outside, and head to his barn.

He would again put fresh flowers next to her the morning after. He always found Mrs. Flora at the window no matter how early in the morning he got in the house. That was the only thing that had thrown him off at first. When he took care of a child, he had to get the child out of bed in the morning. But not with Mrs. Flora! The moment the first rooster's crow was heard in the air, she was out of bed, all dressed, up to the Good-Room, and curled at the window sill. It happened a few times; he would see her coming out of the bedroom and walking by him as if he was not there. She would enter the guest room, make herself comfortable next to the window, put her hands on the sill, and sit there for the rest of the day staring at the route headed to the village. It was the only thing she did as a grown-up.

Lately, he had also started to put a bunch of flowers in a vase in the middle of the dining table every other day. He had noticed women doing so in the houses where he had worked before, and he felt the room looked prettier with the fresh flowers in a vase.

Except, tonight he was faced with a new challenges—she was crying. The sound of Mrs. Flora's cry brought him back to reality. His wandering thoughts switched fast to what was happening at the moment.

She was not supposed to cry! What was expected of him to do about this sudden new occurrence? It was easier to take care of her when she was quiet and curled up in her corner. He rocked her like a child for a while every night before bedtime until he heard her regular breathing. Then he put her on the bed slowly, carefully removing her dress, and tucking her under the cover with only her embroidered chemise on. After that, he would watch her for a while, making sure she was in deep sleep, and her breathing was rhythmic. Only then would he leave, content his day had gone by without any complications.

But today was different! *What was required of him to do with her nonstop crying?* He asked himself again. He didn't know how to make her stop. He was not equipped with such knowledge. She was not a child. She was a grown-up woman. How do you stop a woman of age from crying? The crying part was not noted to be one of his duties when he was hired. *Zonja* Flora was supposed to be quiet. That's why he took this job, to serve a quiet woman, and that's what he liked most about this job. For the first time in his adult life, he had a job where he could be himself. His matron was a woman who needed care but did not give him a hard time. He knew precisely, what he was supposed to do from morning till night, and what *Zonja* Flora needed. He did everything to the dot, with high accuracy, and maybe more than he was supposed to do because he liked it here. He was content with the way things were up to this moment. But right now he felt confused.

He did not approach her. His instincts spoke of the danger. Her loud cry and the convulsions of her body scared and agitated him. Not able to stand it anymore, he left the room.

He went out and made rounds after rounds about the house, shaking his head constantly and waiting for the sobbing to stop. But it did not. Every time he reached the front of the house, he could hear her lurid, nonstop cry.

Suddenly, while he was taking his nervous tenth walk the vision of something that had happened when he used to work for a couple in the other village, materialized in his mind. The young, new bride used to cry often, especially when it was bedtime. He did not understand why, but it was her thing to cry every night. The sight, he once had observed what the husband did to calm her down, came upon him.

That evening he was fixing something inside the house. Whatever was happening around him, it was usually caught by his peripheral vision. The blurry image revealed the hubby lifting his missus in his arms, bringing her in the bathroom, and giving her a hot, long bath. Then he brought her back to the bedroom.

That's what he needed to do. He relaxed. The revelation

was clear. Mrs. Flora did not have a husband, and he was the only one around to take care of her. So, it was his duty to stop her from crying. *If woman cries, that is what a caretaker is supposed to do, give her a hot bath*, he decided.

He felt calmed right away and went back to the house. He usually bathed her every other night. Tonight was not her time. But he had to change the routine. He had no choice. He couldn't bear the sound of her crying. He prepared hotter water in the tub than other nights. Then he went to fetch Mrs. Flora. He approached her carefully, put his arms around her body as usual, lifted her, and took her to the bathroom. He undressed her as he did every time he bathed her. Today he took his time to wash her body, caressing her flesh carefully. Her weeping seemed to fade away. After he had sponged her body thoroughly, he started to stroke her skull as he was soaping her hair. That's what the husband of the weeping bride did. Mrs. Flora's crying turned into small whimpers and somehow almost stopped in irregular light sobs. When he was done bathing her, he wrapped her up with a big towel, and with her in his arms, he walked toward the bedroom. He put her on the bed. Her sobs became weaker. He made an effort to think about what else the husband did to calm his wife.

People, he worked for, did not regard him as human when he was around. He did not exist for them. He was invisible to their senses. They would do things in front of him they would not in front of other strangers. Careless, hubby had left the door of their bedroom opened as he went in with his wife in his arms that night.

He recalled seeing him putting the missus in bed, taking

the towel off and exposing her bare body. He remembered the husband getting undressed and getting in bed with his wife and lying on top of her. The image of the two bodies slowly becoming one was vivid in his imagination. He remembered watching the scene as if from a remote distance, as he was not there but far, far away.

Another sob from Mrs. Flora's mouth interrupted his thoughts. He had to do it until she would stop crying. He undressed slowly, taking his socks off last as the man did that night. Then he sat at the side of her bed and lowered his head toward her face. Now he was not thinking anymore what the husband of the crying lady did. Different images were flashing in his memory; men kissing women, embracing them, holding them tight.

Up to that moment, to him, they were just images lost deep in the unconsciousness of his brain. His intuitions guided him to pursue similar ways with Mrs. Flora to relax her. He put his lips over hers and pressed on them gently. He found it likable and pressed his lips a little harder against hers. She did not react or move her head aside. She just let him do it. His tongue found its way inside her mouth. He started to devour the sap in it. It felt as he was licking and tasting a sweet, juicy fruit, and he kept kissing and kissing her and searching with his tongue. He felt something happening in between his legs and making him uncomfortable. He stopped caressing her and looked at himself. His manhood had become hard, and it was up. He did not notice anything like that before in his body. He straightened up and looked down in wonder. His thing was coming out like a stick. What is it? He asked himself. But then he remembered that's how the hubby's organ was when he brought his missus to bed and got naked.

He opened the towel covering her, put his arms around her shoulders, and moved to accommodate himself on top of her like he saw the husband do with his wife. Mrs. Flora's body, although very slim, was warm and soft. Her skin was smooth, and he liked the feel of her skin against his. He moved his body over hers very gently; for he was heavy and was afraid he would hurt her.

After a while, he felt her legs opening up and he sensed his thing finding a soft, fleshy spot underneath in between her legs. He liked when his manhood touched the softness of the flesh between her legs. He began to move up and down there a little faster and loved the way it felt, and somehow he found himself entering a soft, sweet, and very wet hollow inside her body. He felt a quivering sensation through his abdominal muscles, and he moved faster. Her body responded to his movements. That excited him more, and his movements became very rapid inside her soft opening.

She began to moan, and he felt like groaning himself. He tried not to, but in a while they were both crying loudly. Their bodies started to sweat profoundly. He was moving in and out of her sweet place, fervently, and he felt her body arching to accommodate his movements. There came a point when he screamed and in response she screamed too. Their voices grew louder and louder and reached in resonance a very high-pitched sound, after which he felt a throbbing, sweet release at the end of his organ. A strange weakness overcame him, and he fell over her body, powerless.

Realizing his weight was too much for her slender frame,

he removed himself from her with some difficulty as he felt weak, and he lay on his back beside her. He had done some very hard work in his life, but he never felt as tired and relaxed at the same time as he felt that instant. He noticed his organ became flat as it usually was. He smiled at the view of his naked body. What had happened earlier was a very strange reaction that had never occurred to him even once in his life. He turned his head and looked at her attentively. Her eyes were open, and she was looking at him sideways. He bent over and gave her a kiss. This time it came naturally to him. He had never kissed a woman—or any human being for that matter in his life, not even a child.

The images of husband and wife disappeared. It was just him and Mrs. Flora. He turned on his side facing her and began to stroke her hair gently with his right hand. Her breathing became peaceful. He looked at her. She had fallen asleep while he was caressing her head.

He felt very pleased that he was able to calm Mrs. Flora. Sleep was overcoming him too. He got up, put his clothes on, and left the room in silence. When he arrived at his bed, he fell over it like a stone. The sound of his snoring reached the rooftop of the barn.

He opened his eyes. There was too much light in the barn. The day had begun already. The sun had almost reached the zenith. He jumped off the bed. He searched for his clothes, but they were nowhere. He looked down at himself and realized he was fully dressed. He ran out of the barn terrified. It was too late for assisting Mrs. Flora's morning necessities.

He stormed in the house but stopped at the sight of Mrs. Flora inside the guest room, sitting at the window. He noticed a plate on the corner table with some crumbs of bread, with small driblets of cheese and jelly, and drops of milk on it, and an empty glass.

"Good morning, Mrs. Flora!" he said in a nasal-sounding voice. He did not often get the chance to hear his own voice, and he had never greeted her before.

She turned her head, glanced at him for a moment with a surprised look, then kept gazing outside the window. He had the impression he saw an invisible smile on her lips, but she did not greet him back. He took the plate and the glass from the table and left the room. He went on with his usual daily routines. Somehow he found himself whistling. It was a beautiful, sunny and warm summer day.

Flora's mother decided to go and see her daughter. It had been awhile since last she had seen her. She had missed her very much lately. She cooked Flora's favorite meal, packed it in a small pan, and left in a hurry, trying to get over to her daughter's house before lunchtime.

She found Flora alone, at the corner of the sofa, staring through the window. She approached her and kissed her forehead. Flora moved a little, glanced at her mother straight in the eyes, then returned to her accustomed daily position. Her mother thought she imagined what she saw. Something about her daughter today was different. She decided to ask The Retard on her way out if he had noticed any changes in Flora lately, but she realized he would not answer her question. She sat there beside Flora, fed her, and enjoyed looking at her daughter, whose face didn't look as pale as it used to be. Her cheeks wore a rosy skin tone. She smiled and started to tell her about the village's latest news, about her father and brothers. She had the impression Flora was listening this time, although she did not show any sign of it. She left an hour after she arrived with a slight hope that her daughter's recovery was on the way, and soon she would be okay.

He avoided all day passing in front of her window or going inside the house and did not even bring Mrs. Flora flowers as usual. He was happy when he saw her mother coming. That released him from the lunch obligation.

In the evening, although his sensory faculties spoke of danger, out of the sense of duty he approached the house. He stopped—dreading of hearing her cry. Everything was quiet. He headed for the front door and went inside, tiptoeing with an unexpected fear of hearing the unusual weeping sound.

Flora was sitting in a position half way from the window as if she was waiting for him. Her head was tilted toward the door. She was quiet. He looked at her sideways, and went to the kitchen. In a bit, he brought her a piece of freshly baked bread with a layer of butter, a piece of feta cheese, one boiled egg, and a cup of yogurt on a tray. He put the platter on the sill to see if she would eat on her own and sat in the corner. For a while, Flora did not make any move toward the food.

He waited. He had a feeling—today was the day for her to start doing things on her own. She had prepared the breakfast and had eaten by herself. That was her first big step. He had learned to be composed and patient back then while caring of little children. He knew when they were ready to feed themselves. He had found out, if not given enough time to dare taking the first step, they will not be able to learn how to do things on their own. It was the rule he followed when dealing with them, and Mrs. Flora was one big child. She was different from all other adults he had known.

Finally, she moved her right hand and took the slice of bread, and then the cheese with the other one. She held them for quite a while, looked briefly in his direction, and coming to realize he was not even tempting to feed her, she took the first bite. Then the second, the third, and little by little she finished the whole slice. Then she looked at the egg. Waiting for him to pick it up and peel it for her, she did not move. He did not either. Staring at him, she extended her hand slowly, picked up the egg, and hit its bottom against the side of the sill until it cracked. Then she removed the eggshell piece by piece, and, after glancing one more time in his direction, started to eat it. When finished, she looked at the yogurt cup, and then, wondering, at him. His gaze diverted toward the window. Understanding he was not raising a finger to help her; she reached for the cup and the teaspoon next to it. She ate the whole thing and put the empty cup on the platter.

He got up, picked up the tray and headed to the kitchen. When he went back, Mrs. Flora was not in the Good Room. He heard a noise coming from the bathroom at the end of the hall. He raised his brows. Mrs. Flora was surprising him today. She was no longer acting like a big child.

He sat down on the sofa and waited for her to finish. He heard the splash of the water. Mrs. Flora was taking a bath! He stood there for some time, but she did not come back in the guest room. Uncertainty and hesitation showed on his face.

He waited a few more moments and went out in the hall again. It was quiet. There were no noises coming from the bathroom. He saw the light of the candle coming from underneath Mrs. Flora's bedroom door. The door was slightly opened. He put his ear close to it to listen if any sound was coming from the room. He heard something he did not understand. He pushed the door slightly, and he saw Mrs. Flora lying on the bed.

She was not covered, and she was naked. Her eyes were closed. She did not react to his presence in the room. She appeared asleep. *Mrs. Flora always sleep with her cloths on,* he thought puzzled. He approached the bed, picked up the quilt at the end of the bed and covered her body. He sat on the side of the bed looking attentively at her face. She seemed very peaceful.

It was time to go. He moved to get up. Her hands came slowly from below the quilt and gently grabbed his. She opened her eyes and looked at him in a way no one had ever looked at him his whole life. He averted his eyes. *What does she want from me?* He thought, a little alarmed. *She is not crying tonight!*

He was facing things he was not accustomed to these past two days. She pulled him down slowly. Her hands reached for his face. They were warm and soft. He liked the feeling of his face buried in her palms. Then she drew his face close to hers, and she kissed him lightly.

He did not respond at first. She kept kissing his features one by one. He stood still until a warm sensation came over him, and he reacted. He kissed her back. She took his hands and put them over her breasts. They were so warm, so tender, and so round! He very much liked the touch of her bosom. It reminded him of sponges when wet. He saw women feeding their infants with their breasts but never thought they would be so warm and mushy. Until this moment, in his view, they were a source of food for children. Tonight he was discovering they were much more than a fountain of milk.

It is much better than carving wood, he thought. He felt the touch of her fingers on his chest as she unbuttoned his shirt. The hardness of his organ was very visible by now over his pants. *She is not crying tonight!* Crossed his mind, but it went blank under the spell of her hands, and he helped her take his shirt off. Mrs. Flora pulled the quilt off her body.

Vaguely, he understood what was expected of him. Mrs. Flora wanted him to help her relax like the other night. *But she is not crying,* the thought kept pounding in his head. He stood up, having second thoughts, but her eyes were so intense and inviting. Keeping eye contact with her feverish eyes, he slowly took off his shoes, pushed down his pants, and then his underpants. He stood naked next to the bed looking at her. Then he sat on the side of the bed. She rose, put her hands around his neck, and pulled him slowly toward her. He let himself go, and in a bit found himself upon her.

Afterward, both pleased, they lay next to each other, feeble but content. He was on his belly, his head facing her. She looked beautiful, he thought. Her cheeks were dark pink, and her eyes had a glow he had not noticed previously.

She too was looking back at him, studying his face, and found it a handsome one. She gave him a slight, sweet smile.

Her smile pleased him very much. Leaning on his elbow, he stood on his side and looked at her face. He put his index finger between her eyebrows. Moving it gently down, he reached the tip of her nose. He moved further down to the upper lip until his finger rested on it. With his finger, he examined her mouth from one corner to the other, feeling the softness and the pleasant invisible jumping curves of her lips; as his senses were very perceptive to details. He pressed a little on the bottom lip and found out it was pleasantly smooth.

She was very slim and had small features, and she had nice-shaped, soft pink lips. He was exploring her body the same way he would examine a piece of wood he intended to use for carving. He knew certain woods were good for working. They had to have a pliable texture, and enough sap to make incising easy. And Mrs. Flora's body was just like that. Her flesh was soft, and she had a lot of sap inside her. His finger went unhurriedly over her chin, her neck, and then began to draw a coiled line between the smoothness of her breasts. An invisible smile showed vaguely on her lips, and her eyelids closed slowly. He continued to move his finger around her breasts with no rush as if he was studying the texture of the wood on a tree. He touched the tip of her nipples, and he felt their hardness underneath his fingers. Her body arched as he moved his finger down over her stomach, drawing small circles right and left on her sweaty skin and stopping at her navel. Amused, he played with her navel for a while; then he opened his hand and rested his palm over her tender, warm belly. The softness of her skin sent a hot sensation through his body.

Her eyelids moved up, and she looked at him with passionate eyes. He felt his hardness again as she invited him by moving her legs apart. He moved over her, kissing her, caressing her until he found his way again inside her supple, wet, very hot, magic place. And they both, got lost in the ecstasy of lovemaking.

When it was all over, he felt weightless and lay next to her. His eyelids felt heavy. He pulled the quilt over, covering her body as well as his own, and with his left hand over her belly, curling around her body, he fell asleep right there in Mrs. Flora's bed.

He woke up sweating profoundly and found himself in a strange bed. He felt the warmth of someone's body leaning on his. He was in Mrs. Flora's bed, he realized, and she was next to him.

He was not used to sleeping with someone next to him or in someone else's bed. It was dark outside. It was almost the middle of the night. He jumped out of bed and immediately realized he was naked. Disturbed over the fact, he got dressed quickly and ran to the barn as if someone was chasing him away. He got into his bed. The familiar scent, and the comfort of his bedsheets—his body was accustomed to and so habituated with— gave him solace. Sleep overcame his senses right away.

The next morning he avoided going into the house. Something was not quite right. The whole thing was new and entirely different from other things he had done and experienced before. The change of the regular nightly routine gave him great discomfort. It felt good helping Mrs. Flora to relax, but in broad daylight what had happened the last two nights seemed very alien and remote. It had been uncomplicated the first night when it was dark, and Mrs. Flora needed comfort. But he seemed troubled and perturbed about last night.

Around lunch time, he went back to his usual regimen, as he always had a hard time to change what he was accustomed doing every day. He put together a lovely bouquet of flowers in different colors and entered the guest room.

When they were finished eating, Mrs. Flora picked up her plate as well as his and headed to the kitchen. He sat in his chair with a puzzled face. Everything was changing so quickly, and he had a hard time keeping up. Confusion was the word to describe his state of mind. He used to eat in the kitchen after he fed Mrs. Flora, and he was the one who washed the dishes. In a very short timeframe, too many new things were happening. He needed some time to absorb the most recent changes and incorporate all of it in his well-set-up twenty-four-hour routine. His eyes caught the bouquet;

he got up, picked up the flowerpot and took it to the kitchen to put some water in it.

Mrs. Flora was finishing washing the dishes. She did not hear him enter. He always moved like a cat, making no sounds, giving no indication he was present despite his heavy body. He had learned to be invisible to others to avoid the annoyance of interaction.

He quietly waited for her to move away from the sink but unintentionally, he touched her. The kitchen was too small for his massive frame even when he was there by himself.

Startled, she saw him and moved aside. He moved the faucet handle and waited for the water to fill three-quarters of the vase. Flora turned the tap off when there was enough water in the pot. She put her hand over his and smiled at him. He turned his head away and left the kitchen. He put the flowers in the jar and went outside to finish his chores around the gardens. He was thoughtful, but he could not solve the riddle unfolding around him. Suddenly he noticed a butterfly wrapped in a spider web at the bush around the corner. He tried to save it, but its wings were severely entangled in the web's strings. He stood there looking at its desperate efforts to get free with no hope.

He felt edgy thinking of the night approaching and what it might bring. He was hoping Mrs. Flora would not cry again.

In the early nightfall, he went to chop some logs in the back of the house. When finished, he did not go inside to help Mrs. Flora get in bed. Instead, he headed to his barn. He washed up and laid back on his bunk. Usually, he would fall asleep right away, the moment his head hit the pillow.

But, he was having a hard time relaxing or dozing off tonight. The avoidance of the evening routine had disturbed his daily regimen. He tossed right and left in his bed, but he could not close his eyes. His thoughts were very much in a chaotic state. What happened these two last days had thrown off the normality of his daily routine and had quite confused him. Everything was fine before Mrs. Flora cried. She was passive and quiet, and that made everything so easy for him. All of a sudden, she cried, then, she started to move around the house, and next, she began to prepare food and wash the dishes; and, above all, she needed him to relax her every night even when she did not cry!

Everything was going wrong these past two days. His mind could not find any rest. His body could not relax. Something in his body was not quite right. It did not feel like his own body, but somebody else's. It was speaking a language that he could not comprehend and was keeping him awake. It never happened like this before, but lately everything was happening in such a chaotic way. He felt agitated and restless. The bed was pestering him.

He jumped to his feet and went outside. He was troubled and edgy. The moon was full, and he could see the grain field clearly. He stood in front of the barn, not sure what to do. He glanced at the house. An indistinct appeal came from that direction. A vague feeling of something soft and sweet was swirling in his insides. His eyes were intense and red. He began walking.

Suddenly, an unclear fear sneaked upon him. His anxiety arose and made him more feverish. Midway to the house, he changed direction and, with huge steps walked toward the grain acreage. His pace quickened and soon his walk turned into a quick run. He ran and ran about the field for a long time until he felt worn out. Finally, as dawn was making its first appearance, he headed back and went straight to the barn.

He hopped into his bunk. Sleep came over him right away and saved him from his worries.

The next day he decided to work on the fence—not *that* it needed any work. There was nothing to do after he watered the flowers and the vegetables in the backyard, and he wanted to keep himself occupied. He had no desire whatsoever to go in the house. The alien, new things in there were too much for him to handle.

He cut new pickets, poles, and rails enough for two panels and began engraving the tip of one picket. He felt calmness overcoming him as he worked carefully with his short knife. The head of a woman was taking shape, but he was not aware of it. He just kept carving.

"It's beautiful!" he heard a woman's voice behind him. Usually he recognized the voice of a person even if he couldn't see them, but today he did not. He turned cautiously his head to see who was behind him and saw Mrs. Flora. He jumped, dropping the knife and the picket he was working on in the ground. He was very skilled at sensing noises around him but did not hear her approaching.

He never saw Mrs. Flora out of the house. *What is she doing outside? Is she meant to be outside? Shouldn't she be inside at the windowsill? And, why is she talking!* The questions swirled in his mind with an unusual intensity. He stared at her as if to solve the puzzle, and then looked in the direction of the barn as his escape.

She picked the picket off the ground and noticed that a person's head was forming on it. "That's incredible," she said. "Can you carve heads?"

Much taller than she, he kept gazing over her head in the barn's direction, keeping his eyes out of her reach.

She put her hand on his arm and said: "Don't be scared! I like your carvings." She looked around and then back at him. "You have done a fabulous job with the house!" She stood quiet for a while and said with a subtle voice as if she wanted to make peace with him:

"I like the new fence and the flower garden."

A slight, involuntary smile brushed his face as he was looking away from her in the direction of the grain field this time. But the smile disappeared faster than it showed.

He moved his head around as if to find a way out. But he couldn't go away. She was right there in front of him, and he felt trapped. He couldn't move. And, she was talking! Mrs. Flora was out of the house, and she was talking! It was another new thing added to the rest. She never came out of the house; she never talked, and she had never addressed him before, that's why he did not recognize her voice a little earlier. He had to get accustomed to all these changes in such a short time. Today it was her coming outside, her voice, and her talking to him. She was not giving him orders though about the tasks and the chores she wanted to be done, he realized. She was talking about him, about his carvings. And—she touched him! She touched his arm. No! No! She was not supposed to touch him! Something was wrong!

The words pounded in his mind. His eyes were rolling, and his head was moving from one side to the other. It shouldn't be this way! Whatever was going on these past days, it was not included in the deal he had signed up for!

He felt lost. It was much better when she did not talk and stood still at the windowsill. Now, everything was so different and strange. It was alien and unfamiliar! Entirely new turf to him! A turf he had never walked on before; a path so unknown, it began to irritate him to destruction. Moreover, she was affectionate to him! He was not comfortable with that feeling. It did not fit in his set-forth-of-rules world. No one, ever in his life, had been considerate to him. He was quite reluctant to everything unrecognizable that was out of his own periphery of comfort. And, it was swarming all around him, and sneaking up on him, entering his quiet world from everywhere.

The whole thing had passed the limits of his comfort zone! Everything was fine prior to her crying. He took such good care of her and the house. He had established his routine, and everything was just flawless. She had never cried before. However, since then, all these new things had happened one after another. She did not say a word before, and now she couldn't stop talking! She never moved before, and now she was getting out of the house. She never ate and bathed by herself, and now she was. Moreover, she wanted him to relax her at night, something she never did till now. Agitated and distressed, he feared of what was coming next. He knew very well from his experience how it would be from now on. Eventually, the following day, she was going to tell him what to do, and how to do things around the house.

What bothered him most was the fear she would cry again. And, thus, he had to go out of his way to relax her, and he did not want to.

He began moving his upper body lightly back and forth, and tilting his head sideways. He wanted to go back to the decent, good life he had for two good years. In these two years, he had finally found his comfort zone. The freedom to do things his way and determine his own routine gave him a solace that came in complete accordance with his being. He had been calm and content with no worries in his mind for the first time in his life. Alas, now everything was going wrong. His head began to ache terribly. *My head*, he thought, *my head!* He felt a keen burning inside his skull. His body movement became more frequent.

Sensing his anxiety, she put her hand again on his arm and squeezed it lightly.

"Sit down please!" she whispered.

Obedient he sat down on the bench, looking away from her.

"You have done a lot around the house, and I don't know how to thank you!"

She put her hands on his face and held it tight, making his eyes meet hers.

"Nothing is going to change," she said. "You are going to do everything as you did before, but there is one thing."

He looked at her, bewildered.

"You don't need to take care of me anymore or do anything inside the house." She stopped, and looking at him with affection, added: "Now, go ahead and keep on carving! And, please come in for lunch when you are done! I am making stuffed peppers."

She got up and left.

He followed her figure moving toward the house from the corner of his eyes. The danger was moving away from him. Finally, he was alone. Suddenly he felt calm. He liked being by himself. He picked up the picket he was working on before she came by and kept sculpting the wood. The shape of a woman's head was becoming more and more visible. When he was finally done, he was surprised by the resemblance of his work to Mrs. Flora's face.

After that day, he established a new routine. He took care of everything that needed to be done outside, but he avoided going inside the house after dusk. His senses had a way of controlling his actions and avoiding the peril. He always kept away from things that caused him aggravation. Everything was going back to a good pace. He was calm and content again. His nights were his, and he went back to falling asleep without any trouble.

He had discovered a new distraction lately. It kept him busy, occupied, and content. With the outcome of the likeness of Mrs. Flora's head, he understood he could work on making heads. He stopped mending new fences. He set out to the forest and searched for a wild walnut tree, as it was better suited for carving. It had a subtle texture, and he liked the color tone of its wood. He wanted to engrave Mrs. Flora's head in its real size.

He knew the forest very well. He knew where the walnut trees were located. Before he worked for Mrs. Flora, he used to take walks in the woods and explore the plants and the trees and watch the birds and the small animals. Wandering about the forest relaxed him and made his anxiety go away. He had enjoyed there the time alone without the humans somewhere to irritate him. He had sought solace in discovering the marvels of nature. It was just him and the harmless plants and animals.

Deep in the forest, he found what he was looking for, the 150-year-old wild walnut tree. He used to come to this tree and sit down at the foot of its trunk and relax, observing the wonders of wildlife. But since he found peace in Mrs. Flora's house, he stopped taking his walks in the woods.

He stood there looking at the huge tree appreciating its beauty; its branches nicely spread created the shape of a huge mushroom. *The forest is a wonder*, he thought amazed. He had no time to waste wandering around though. His head was set to do what he came for. He looked one more time around then examined the tree.

At the bottom, a thick branch, long and round enough that he could carve a person's head, piqued his interest. He cut the branch at its base. Then he cut the branch into logs. Each log was big enough for making a head or more out of it. *Maybe a small animal*, it crossed his mind. By now, he had become confident he was good at carving heads, and he had an indistinct fancy not only to impress Mrs. Flora but the villagers as well. He had recognized they had an enormous curiosity about his carving. He carried the logs on his handcart and pushed it back to the house.

It had become dark when he arrived at the front gate. Quietly, he opened it and, cautious not to make noises, stopped there, and brought the cut logs one by one back to the barn. He chose one that suited Mrs. Flora's head. He began working on it and got lost in his new quest.

The head was taking shape nicely as the days went by. He worked on it after the long day of work. Not only did it keep him busy, but made him forget about his worries. It relaxed him and gave him great comfort. He was pleased with the contours of her features. He had an urgent desire to finish the head as quickly as he could. He even started working at nights. Changing his stern nightly routine was a first for him, but the drive he felt to finish her head was stronger than his self-reliant, established habits.

One night the carving came to an end. He gave the wood some final refinements and the head looked finally, exactly like Mrs. Flora's.

He was pleased with his refined craft. He smiled again. *But wait, something in her neck is not quite right,* he thought. He pictured Mrs. Flora head and remembered she had a mole on the left side of her neck. He sat down and began to work on it. In the end, the mole was there. He looked at his work one more time. He was pleased. He polished it and made it smooth and shiny. He wanted to be a surprise for Mrs. Flora. Thinking of the expression and the smile on her face the moment she would see her carved likeness, he smiled. He stepped back, looked at the head carefully, examined each feature for any imperfection, but found none.

It was time for bed. He was tired but satisfied. He took off his clothes and got in his bunk in his underwear only. It was a scorching summer, and lately he kept the door of the barn locked. He did not want Mrs. Flora to walk in and see what he was doing, although the odds of her coming by were very slim. She had never stepped in the barn.

The next day he got up early, picked up the carved head, and headed to the house. He waited around the corner. The moment Mrs. Flora got out of the house to pick some flowers in the garden, he sneaked inside and brought the carved head into the guest room. He put the head on the table and sat in the corner. He wanted to see her first reaction without being noticed by her.

When Flora entered the room, she stopped abruptly after noticing her likeness in the middle of the table. Pleasantly surprised, she approached the wooden sculpture and looked at it attentively. He even had carved the small mole on her neck! Every detail of her face was so precisely reflected. She brushed the wooden head with her palm and felt the bumps of her wavy hair. He had portrayed her more beautiful than she was indeed. Her eyes! They seemed so alive. He had colored the area of the pupils in light brown, exactly like her eye color, and even her irises had a darker nuance. She looked at each feature carefully. The lips! Everything was a perfect resemblance. She was greatly surprised. Her Retard was very skilled, she proudly thought.

She turned around, saw him in the corner, and beamed at him. Then she approached him, took his hand, and brought him close to the table.

"It's beautiful!" she exclaimed and smiled. He replied by moving his head lightly as a thank you.

"Is it for me?" she asked.

He nodded.

"Oh! Thank you so much!"

She looked around, wondering where to put the carved head. Her eyes stopped at the windowsill. She picked it up carefully and put it on it.

He glanced at her. He had missed seeing her head behind the window these days. Since Mrs. Flora did not sit next to the sill anymore, he could dart glances at her likeness from outside. For two good years, he had seen her every day behind the glass, and lately it had been just an empty, sad space. But, not anymore!

He was content. He walked outside and turned his head. Mrs. Flora's carved head was staring at him. He felt content the windowpane had Mrs. Flora back. Satisfied with his work, he went about his daily chores.

One day, a small lamb began to take shape from a log he was working on. The head appeared first, then the body, the legs and its tail at last. He looked at the lamb and felt an enormous joy. He wanted to be perfect, so he kept working on fixing, what his eyes found as imperfect. He focused mostly on its little head.

The latest discovery of making heads or animals fulfilled him more than anything he had done before. He was appeased. The days were passing by, one just like the other. It suited him well. He liked having the same daily routine. The only thing worrying him was Mrs. Flora's gaze. She made it a habit of coming out of the house from time to time and watching him from afar with her big brown eyes. He did not understand why she was staring at him the way she did, but it made him uncomfortable. Every time she did, he would stop what he was doing and walk away. He did not like people staring at him for no reason.

Everyone was surprised at Flora's progress, but most of all, her mother. She was glad her daughter was feeling better. Flora did not talk much like she used to, but at least she was functioning like a regular person. *Everything in its own time,* she thought.

She began to visit more often. It was pleasant to have Flora back. "Time will heal her wounds," she revealed to her husband. And she told him about Flora's beautiful sculpture. "The Retard is very skilled," she said to him. "You should come with me one of these days to see it. It is strange," she added, "how perfect the head is."

When carved wooden animals began to pop one after another in Mrs. Flora's front yard, the villagers started to pay visits to the house again. The new carvings amazed everybody. The reputation of the Retard's carving skills reached the far villages. Every two weeks a newly carved animal would appear in the garden. The villagers learned the routine of their display, and they came by, close to the day the new carving would show up in the front yard. Some missed it by a day or two but most became pretty good at predicting when the Retard would come out of his barn with the new sculpture in his arms.

People would start applauding, from the instant he appeared at the barn door, till he put the carved animal in its proper place next to the others. With time, the event turned into a ceremonial routine and the most enjoyable

Under the Orange Tree

entertainment in the area. The villagers even bet what animal The Retard would carve for the next round. But he always surprised them—sometimes with a bird of the sort they had never seen in their lifetime, fixed in a dry tree branch. Or, the next time it would be a small animal few of them had encountered in the woods.

They had to admit, since the Retard had been hired to serve in Mrs. Flora's house, life had become far more interesting, and the reason was him, the Retard. The anticipation of the new sculptures had created a certain excitement and liveliness in the area. The villagers even made a habit of calling it "The Day of the New Carving." Usually, the ceremony happened in the early evening.

On one of the predicted days, the villagers, in twos or threes, came out of their houses and headed for Mrs. Flora's house. Little by little they gathered around the fence, waiting for the doors of the barn to open and the Retard to come into view. The discussion among them was about what kind of carved animal it would be this time—they even made it a habit to bet on it.

Suddenly, Mrs. Flora appeared instead with a big tray full of refreshments. It was her first appearance at such an event. The women greeted her warmly. She went around calm and confident. Although she had not mingled in a long time in a crowd, she chitchatted as if she had never missed a village occasion in past years, and waited with the others for the exciting appearance.

People were drinking and chatting gaily, keeping an eye on the barn's door. She was as curious as they were about the new carving. This time it had taken him longer to finish his new venture. He was very stringent about not showing his new carvings to anyone, including her. She had never been in the barn. One day, when out of curiosity she walked beside him toward the barn, he showed strong signs of agitation. Her instincts told her to turn around and head back to the house. The message was clear. The barn was out of her reach. It was his sanctuary. She understood and respected his discretion.

When someone asked her what he had carved this time, she shook her head, "He never shows his work", she replied. "It always has to be a surprise."

They heard the crack of the thick wooden door. Everybody's eyes turned in that direction. He was holding the carving in his arms covered in a white sheet this time. The silence dominated the crowd. Their curiosity rose high. They were anxious to see what was underneath the cover.

The Retard was walking slowly. He had learned how to prolong the anticipation. Their eyes, fixed on him, gave him some power and control over the group. He very much liked having their attention. It was the only time their gaze did not bother him. He didn't need to interact with anyone in those moments. He just had to bring out his work to the front yard. Stepping carefully, he approached the corner of the carved animals. The crowd noticed a high, thick trunk in the middle of the group. That provoked their curiosity even more. The Retard was walking very cautiously as if he was afraid to break what he held underneath the linen. Finally, he arrived at the display corner. He carefully put his new craft on the top of the trunk.

A buzz went through the crowd.

The only thing they could tell was, the carving was a widespread piece of wood this time. He did something under the cover as if he was fixing the craft to the log. After that, he stepped back. He did not look at the crowd. He did not need to. He had mastered seeing sideways. He saw the anticipation in their eyes, the growing interest, the excitement, the eagerness, and the impatience for the unknown that hid under the white sheet. He waited a little bit. When he sensed their impatience was growing beyond more than expected, he extended his hand and very slowly pulled the sheet.

"Wooooow!"

The crowd released exclamation sounds in awe. The usual applause did not take place. They were stunned. What they saw had exceeded all their expectations.

An eagle with her wings wide open, her claws clutching a stick and two heads coming out of her neck base, emerged over the log. One head was stretched to the right, one to the left. Two pairs of glassy eyes that appeared to be strangely genuine stared at the people on both sides of the fence. The eagle looked alive, especially its eyes. Startled, the villagers took a step back. They could see the tongues in the slightly open beaks. The well-formed chest was covered with carved feathers lighter than the ones on the back. It bestowed the impression as their necks were moving to check the danger of a foe around. It was an illusionary effect, but it was very insightful. The carving was a work of art.

Everyone was in a state of shock. A murmur came from the crowd after they regained their composure.

"He carved the eagle!" someone finally said.

"With two heads!" another one added.

"What a marvel!" A shocked voice came from the back.

"You did a remarkable job, Retard!" a young man shouted.

"We are honored and proud of you!" A man's deep, emotional voice covered all others.

"Hail to our eagle[13]!" The applause started on the left side, and everyone joined in a loud ovation. They could see him swollen with pride. They knew he was skilled, but this was the work of a master. And a master he was, their Retard! He kept surprising them in unexpected ways. From a man who no one had noticed before, he had become a sensation these past two years, and today he had crossed every limit imaginable. "To have such a gifted man in the village is a privilege," someone said after the amazement about the eagle display had died down.

"How on earth does he know about the flag's eagle?" someone asked the question everyone had in mind.

"Who knows! Maybe he saw it displayed somewhere during the Independence Day. We assume he doesn't know things because he is different. But, does it matter? He has given this village fame. And today, he carved our eagle," a very excited old man commented. "Our reputation has significantly grown beyond the village's outskirts because of him, and with this," he raised his hand toward the Eagle, "we are going to be famous in the whole region."

Then, the old man did something no one had done before with the Retard. He opened the gate, approached him,

---

13   The Eagle with two heads is the symbol of the Albanian flag

put his left hand on his shoulder, and extended his right. The Retard, surprising everybody one more time, did not withdraw as usual when somebody would get too close to him. On the contrary, he grabbed the old man's hand and shook it hard. The old man made a face from the pain of his firm squeeze. A good-natured laughter burst from the crowd. Others encouraged by the handshake entered one by one and shook his hand. They felt an enormous pride filling their chests for having such a talented man living among them.

He went to the barn very satisfied that night. For the first time, he felt like one of them. He felt equal with the people who stood on the other side of the fence today. He lay down on his bunk and stared at the beams of the high ceiling. In the darkness, he replayed in his mind the scene from the evening, over and over again.

As he lay dreaming with his eyes open, he heard a creaking noise coming from the door. He sat up and recognized the silhouette of Mrs. Flora sneaking inside. Surprised, he looked at her, with his eyes wide open. *What is she doing in the barn?* He felt panic overcoming him. He stood up. *She is not crying,* he realized. But she was not moving either. She wasn't even speaking. *Why is she here?* He wondered.

She saw him freeze and stood at the door not taking another step.

They faced each other in silence. He noticed she made a slight move to head out, but did not leave. Used to seeing very well in the darkness, he saw big tears in her eyes.

She was not crying. She was silent. But the tears were flowing down her cheeks. He stood there, focusing on her tears. They became larger. Instinctively he moved forward.

When he was closer to her, he touched her face and wiped her tears like he did with little children. They were warm. The moisture of her tears and the softness of her face in his calloused hands sent a tingling sensation in him. Their bodies drew closer. He looked her in the eyes and did not feel the usual intimidation by the intensity he saw there. He pulled her close. He felt the warmth and the softness of her flesh on his body. He lowered his head and kissed the tears coming from the corners of her eyes. She clung to him. He lifted her up. She embraced him.

He felt her body pressed on his, her arms around his neck, her head over his shoulder, and her small feet touching the lower part of his body, caressing it cautiously. But, mostly he could feel the softness of her breast on his chest. She was like a little sleepy lamb that had found its way to a cozy place and was trying to accommodate itself as comfortably as it could. He smelled her scent, and his lips reached for the nape of her neck. A moan came out of her mouth.

With her in his arms, he turned around and walked back to his bunk, put her gently down, and began kissing her all over. She responded back. He took his time enjoying her breasts. The pleasure he felt kissing and touching them made him quiver, and his manhood responded aggressively. She opened up to him, and he thrust himself into the now familiar sweet, juicy, soft spot. In an instant, they became one.

It all came naturally to him tonight.

Mrs. Flora made it a habit to visit him every other night in the barn, sometimes during his sleep, and it often startled him. Like everything new, it threw him off at first. He had nowhere to go to avoid her nightly calls, and he had no choice but to accept her intrusions. In no time, he became accustomed to her nocturnal appearances and even began to like it. Once, when she did not come on her habitual round, he woke up in the middle of the night and could not go back to sleep for a long while.

One evening she invited him to dinner. After they're finished eating, she took his hand and led him to her room.

As several weeks passed by, the days and the nights alternated in a customary order and it did not confuse him any longer. On the contrary, he was the one taking the initiative more often than Mrs. Flora did when the sun hid behind the horizon. He would lift her in his arms and take her in the bedroom.

One evening, as they had their usual, peaceful dinner, Mrs. Flora suddenly asked him:

"What is your name?"

Taken by surprise, he glanced at her, then stared at his plate without responding. He did not move for a while. He kept eating. It had been a long while since anyone had asked him about his name.

In the other village, in the beginning, people had tried to get a name out of him, but he never responded to their query. Somehow they stopped asking and just called him "The

Retard." He did not understand the real significance of the given name at the time, but he had sensed; it did not have an ill meaning. At one point, he got used to it and "the Retard" became the name everyone knew him by.

After he had finished the meal, he raised his head and stared at her. Mrs. Flora was the only person he could look in the eye for an extended amount of time. She patiently waited for him to respond. His thoughts were processing the question thoroughly. He had an exceptional memory. He remembered events from his childhood, but he did not know how to explain most of them, and a lot of things were blurry and sometimes confusing. His brain was capable of recalling details of the past if something provoked the locked memory.

An invisible, amorphous mass, minced into pieces, was moving around in his head, by coming and going from the depth of his brain, without taking shape, or a real significance. One moment it was there as if he was ready to say it, and the next was gone. He felt puzzled at what was going on inside his head. He looked at her and shook his head in desperation.

Realizing he was struggling, she pleaded:

"You must have a name! Please try to remember it!"

After her plea, as the sound of her voice entered his senses, an unclear, and at the same time, a familiar name was crystallizing in his mind. Suddenly a word, recovered slowly from the profoundness of his mind, echoed clearly in his head. It was the name his uncle used to call him.

"Tom!" he suddenly said with a muffled voice.

"Tom?" she asked and smiled.

The pronunciation of his name coming through her female's voice awakened an indistinguishable sound in his head. He stared at her bewildered and in the same time receptive. Then, the blurred, remote vision of a woman calling "To-om," a child who was running around, flashed through his mind. Something swirled inside his chest.

He fancied the way his name sounded coming from her mouth. It had the same warm, intimate intonation as the woman's voice that appeared in his vision. He glared at her, and a slight smile appeared on his face.

"Tom," she addressed him again. "Do you have a last name?"

Her voice brought him out of his inner realm, and he looked at her, troubled. He stared at the shining surface of his plate. It was spotless. He always cleaned it up meticulously with bread after his last bite.

"Like a surname," she said. "Everyone has a family name. My name is Mrs. Flora Kastra. Kastra is my last name" she continued when she saw him hesitate. "My maiden family name is Lako. My mother's name is Miriana Lako; my dad's name is Andon Lako. What is yours? Tom who?" she asked with a gentle tone to put him at ease and give him time to think.

He looked thoughtful and lost in his memory maze. It seemed as if his brainpower was trying hard to restore his identity from the long-concealed memory. No one had called him by a last name. He was way too young when forced to live with his relatives. There was a long moment of silence. Gradually something came to him. The retrieved words were taking shape. He remembered his middle name.

Then, he reminisced about what people used to call his uncle. Somehow, his brain put it all together. Taken aback by the strange fact that he had a name like everybody else, he raised his head, and looking at her said slowly, emphasizing each of the names:

"Tom, Adrian, Molina!"

She looked attentive. She repeated: "Tom Adrian Molina!"

He liked the sound of it. He repeated it after her with his muffled voice. "Tom Adrian Molina!"

She looked at him, smiling, and said again: "Tom Adrian Molina!"

Then suddenly, they said it at the same time, repeating it over and over as if they had discovered something amusing: "Tom Adrian Molina! Tom Adrian Molina! Tom Adrian Molina!" It had a good sound in their ears. He had a name, they both thought in a different way. And then, they both began laughing.

After a while, as he was processing the whole name thing, her voice reached his ears:

"Would you marry me, Tom Adrian Molina?"

His eyebrows came together, and he looked at her, puzzled as ever. She understood she had to explain what she meant.

"I want you to be my husband," she said, "and I want to be your wife!"

His eyebrows went up. A worry showed in his eyes. In his low, muffled voice, recalling the words out of his brain slowly he said:

"You mean, like a real husband and wife?" stressing the

words "husband" and "wife" as if to make sure he understood correctly what she meant.

"Yes!" she said.

Emphasizing the same words, slowly and carefully, she continued:

"Like a real husband and wife. I will take care of the house while you will take care of the gardens, the fields, the fence, the roof, and everything I cannot do. We can even have more sheep, hens, and a maybe two horses. You can make fences, tables, and chairs for other people. You can carve people's and animal's likeness. You can make toys for children. You can do whatever you want. And," she stopped for him to focus, "you can sell your work."

He pulled back on his chair and looked at her for quite some time. He seemed very thoughtful, trying to grasp the significance of it all, to process inwardly what she was telling him, and what the whole marriage business meant for him. Up to this moment, marriage had never crossed his mind. It was an alien concept that was not part of his world. He visualized something in his mind, and he suddenly asked, bewildered, "Will we have children?"

She smiled. "If you want to, Tom Adrian Molina, we will."

"Do you want to have children, Mrs. Flora?" he asked her, articulating each word carefully.

"Yes," she answered heartily, "I do Adrian!"

He paused and thoughtfully answered, settling the issue, getting the words out one by one unhurriedly as he was proud of the outcome: "Then, we will have children!"

She smiled. Looking at him carefully, she got up, went

around the table, put her hands around his neck, kissed him on his lips, and said:

"I'd like to call you Adrian."

He shrugged his shoulders. It did not matter to him what she called him, but he liked the sound of the word "Adrian" coming from her mouth.

He loved helping Mrs. Flora relax at night. He had taken great pleasure in doing so every night lately. It gave Mrs. Flora great satisfaction every time he did. He felt happy putting a smile on her face. And surely he would like very much to have a child to take care of. He was fond of children. Everything about them was pleasant, the way they smelled, the way they put their chubby hands around his neck when he took care of them. *Yes!* he thought. He would love very much to have a child of his own and be Mrs. Flora's husband. He liked it a lot. A big smile appeared on his face. He nodded his head, content with the new role in his life.

He looked at her face. It was so close to his. Usually, she kissed him only during the night, in bed. He remembered that men used to kiss their wives around the house during the day too. He enjoyed it very much when she kissed him. He grabbed her face and kissed her back.

She gave him an intense, fiery look, and he knew very well by now what it meant. He got up, easily lifted her like she was a feather and headed to the bedroom. He felt proud helping Mrs. Flora relax. But now he could do it as her husband. His step became steady and confident. He was Mrs. Flora's mate, and Mrs. Flora was his missus from that evening on, he thought! And husbands slept with their wives every night.

A week after, when Flora set down with him, and told him they needed to go to the church to get married, he became agitated. He looked at her, confused, not understanding why they had to go there. They were husband and wife already. They lived in the same house. They slept in the same bed. They ate lunch and dined together like all husbands and wives. And they were going to have a baby soon. He shook his head.

Why the need for the priest and the church? He did not like to leave the house and go to the village, especially to the church. He had gone once when he was a child, and it didn't feel right. Too many people around, the priest spoke loudly, and the music bothered his senses. The space was tight in there—he had to sit between two people who constantly touched him with their elbows. He had an anxiety attack that day and ran out before the Mass was over.

He sought quietness. And, the distance between himself and other people was a must. *No! Not in the church!* he thought. He shook his head restless. He wanted to say to Mrs. Flora he didn't desire to go, but he did not know how.

He sensed something from her facial expression. Mrs. Flora wanted desperately to get married in church. But it was too much to ask of him. He averted his gaze, turned away from her, and started to move his torso back and forth.

She knew, when he got upset about something, he avoided looking her straight in the eye, and would start either rocking his body, walking around, or leaving. She got a hold of his arms; made him stop, turned him around to face her, and took his face between her palms to help him relax. It was the only way to have him focus and listen. She saw the anxiety in his eyes, although they were aiming sideways. Slowly she began to explain.

They were husband and wife, she told him, but for others to see them that way, they needed to get married by a priest in the church. The argument did not sink with him. Then she explained that all people were called husband and wife only after they got married in a church ceremony. She did not succeed with that reasoning either.

She gave him a long, sweet kiss since she knew it always soothed him. After the kiss, he looked at her. He was calmer, but not enough to be comfortable with the idea of going to church. She realized, convincing him on the matter, it was going to be a difficult task. He thought of it as illogical. They were already husband and wife in his book. They did not need a priest to tell them they were. His truth was different from hers. He lived in a different world, and she knew he did not like people around, let alone the whole pack in a closed space like church. And, a wedding, she knew, was out of the question.

As she was trying to read his mind, an idea came over her, and she looked at him.

"What if," she paused in suspense, "the priest comes to our house to carry out the ceremony?"

"Only the priest?" he mumbled looking at her suspicious.

"Yes!" she replied, then added, "And my mama and papa." She looked at him, pleading.

He understood how badly she wanted to get married by

a priest, and shook his head slowly in approval.

"And my brothers," she said fearfully.

He shook his head violently. He couldn't stay still in front of so many people staring at him from a close distance.

"Okay! Just Mama and Papa."

He approved with a headshake.

"Settled then!" she said.

She kissed him on the forehead, and in fear he might change his mind, left the room. Now she had another difficult task. She had to convince the priest to perform the service in their home, not in the house of the Lord. *Would he accept the odd request?* She wondered, and thought she needed to talk it over with her mother first. She rushed out of the house. She did not have much time. She needed her mother's support badly to get this done as soon as possible.

As the word about Mrs. Flora and the Retard's quick, almost discreet wedding ceremony got out; the news shocked everyone in the village. It was like an explosion blew up the entire community. The unconventional marriage dominated the conversations of every household. The revelation of his real name, Tom Adrian Molina, came as a big surprise too. "Does he have a name?" most asked. For others, it brought back the memory of his parents being killed during the worst storm the region had ever experienced in a good thirty or so years ago. "Is she out of her mind?" a handful of villagers asked. "How did the priest let them tie the knot?" others would say. "Moreover, performing the sacred ceremony of marriage out of the church grounds! That is a sacrilege! Their marriage is not valid!" The words came out of the defiant, angry, rebellious spirits of some. "How could her folks allow it to happen?" the rest questioned. But, no one had reasonable answers to convince them otherwise.

Ironically, these are the same people who applauded and highly praised Adrian at the last carving display, Flora thought when she heard about the commotion her marriage was causing. *And now, they are taking the high road against him, the dear man he is?! These are the same ones who cheered like crazy when the white sheet came off to reveal the eagle. They are the same men who threw encouraging words of praise, held him in high regard, and felt honored of having him in their midst, accepting him as a valuable member of their village. These are the ones who, overjoyed with pride, shook his hand. Now, they are opposing his marriage to me?!*

The village had turned into a boiling pot.

"But that Retard marrying Mrs. Flora?!" they would ask angrily. Their clouded judgment could not pass over that name. The high regard they had grown for him these past two years was wiped out from their brains. "But daring to marry Mrs. Flora? And sleeping with her?! That retard?!" The name took a connotation it never had before, even when he was first called by it.

Save for the ones who opposed this union strongly, there were a handful of people who came to Flora's and her husband's defense. The argument that they brought against those who opposed the marriage was, "It does not matter that he does not talk much," they would say. "He is an excellent provider and *Zonja Flora* needs a man to take care of her and the house." Other supporters, mostly women, hinting to their lazy husbands, would say, "The Retard can provide a lot more for his wife than some men who talk too much and do very little to fulfill their own family obligations. Most importantly, he makes Mrs. Flora happy."

Issues on the opposing side went much further than just the usual bragging. A group of villagers, restless about this unsuitable, unacceptable marriage, decided to go to the priest and ask for Mrs. Flora's marriage annulment. They considered it not a valid one, on the grounds of mental retardation. What fueled their objection to this marriage was the fact that Flora's brothers were nowhere to be seen to come in defense of their sister. They had been nonexistent these days. The group felt they had a moral obligation to make things right for the underdogs who were reluctant to voice their opinion—that's how they tried to convince themselves to justify the actions they were taking.

After being very attentive to their argument, the priest, a gentle, old man who had seen a lot in his life, explained, "God has his mysterious ways to accommodate all his sheep. And the Reta—" the priest did not finish the word, "Mr. Molina," he continued, "is entitled to the same rights as you have. He has the right to be married as all men do. All men are all equal in God's eyes!" he emphasized, making a call to their shortcomings of the Bible with a soft, persuasive voice.

Undefeated, and relentless, they brought up the fact that the Retard and Mrs. Flora were not married in front of the altar. They looked at each other, pleased, convinced the priest had no choice but to invalidate the marriage. They were sure they made a compelling argument.

Not only they did not use his real name in the conversation, but they gave the word "Retard" an undertone they had never done before, the priest noticed. They were an angry bunch for some "divine" reasons he couldn't understand, and above all, did not have anything better to do with their lives, he chuckled. For them, Adrian Molina was a slow-witted person, a simpleton, and that was about it. It did not matter what he had done for Mrs. Flora, how he had managed her house, what marvelous carvings he had crafted with his bare hands. It did not matter what impact he had in their lives with his talent, and how the village had changed because of that "delayed" man. It was all forgotten, utterly erased from their memory.

They were suffering from a short memory syndrome, the priest thought, amused by their persuasion of the matter. But he knew better. Wit and humor—that's what he needed for the moment. He couldn't help looking at them with pity. He had to come up with some explanation that would not give them a reason for another objection. He had foreseen the reaction and was prepared for this upshot. With his well-trained voice, which kept them at bay, he brought as an argument a case. Ten years ago he had to marry a very sick young man on his deathbed. The ritual was performed to honor the promises the families of bride and groom had made to one another for their union, although the unfortunate young man was expected to die soon. But, he said, slightly raising his voice, he was given the joy, and the hope of the living before life left his body. His life was celebrated before death took him away. And the gain of one sometimes means the loss of the other, he concluded.

"Life has its mysterious turns," he added thoughtfully, "and the church has always been there to serve its congregation when they were in need of its humble support."

"But this is different," they persisted. "That man was on his deathbed. And," they continued, "And the altar is the altar! Priests leave the church only when people are on their deathbed, or when they are buried. Marriage is consecrated in front of the altar, the sanctuary of God! The Retard and Mrs. Flora didn't have a proper wedding!" And, looking at each other pleased, they shook their heads as if saying, "We got him!"

The good, old priest smiled. He looked at them for a few moments and, speaking gently, as if he was addressing a person on the deathbed, replied:

"Altars, my dear fellow men, are created by MEN. God's shrine is nature. There were no altars when God created the earth and put humans in it. There was only nature!" The good old man raised his voice slightly at the word nature. "And Mrs. Flora and Adrian Molina were married in their flower garden, in God's natural habitat, not in the human's altar! Christ lived a humble life, mostly on the road, among God's creatures. He spoke to the people in God's most natural sovereignty, from the shade of a tree, or the top of a hill, and under the burning sun, but never in a luxurious place. We, humans, have put him nowadays in a high, palatial place we call, the altar." Lost in his contemplation, thoughtful, he added softly as speaking more to himself than to the men in front of him, "We did it to make ourselves feel good and comfortable—not for him!"

In an instant, he became aware where he was. *My mouth is running loose,* he thought, *I am getting old, and age is getting the best out of me.* He noticed their distrustful and confused faces. A slight mockery and certain curiosity showed in his eyes as to what will they bring up next. He waited for a reaction on their part.

When they did not reply back, the priest extended his right hand as saying, his time with them was over if they didn't have anything else to say.

"God bless you my children!" he said softly.

They looked at each other. They couldn't come up with other reasons. And, there was no point in challenging the old-timer's arguments, or bring any other reason disputing any further the "strange, ungodly union," as they put it in their own exact terms. They weren't going to win against their quick-witted priest.

With nothing more to say, a little baffled from all the priests wording, they bowed slightly in silence, then turned around and walked out the church. The priest observed their angry, hunched backs and shook his head with a spark of amusement in his eyes.

They left the church displeased and unconvinced.

"The good ol' man is losing it," one of them said shaking his head as they were walking back to the village. Unsatisfied with the outcome, he added, "And what gibberish was he talking about—the Christ, the altar, and nature? It's time to replace him! We should write a letter to the bishop."

The rest of them did not respond. Walking away from the church had given them time to think about the priest's last words. Taking their frustration and concerns to God's assigned shepherd and listening to his indisputable arguments had helped their heads to cool off somehow and see the whole thing in a slightly different light. Their rage had calmed to a rational degree.

Flora's marriage continued to be a much-discussed topic among villagers for a while. Time, though, having a surprising effect on healing wounds and making the oddest events fade into oblivion—no matter how difficult or sensitive an issue or event in life might be—helped the fury over Flora's marriage die slowly in the midst of ordinary daily struggles. Gradually, everyone in the village came to terms of acceptance with the odd, unconventional matrimony.

Epilogue:

As the months passed by, Flora began to go back to her old ways of doing things. She was seen at the grocery store, at the church, visiting her parents, and once in a while she would take Tom with her. He did not like that very much; however, to please Mrs. Flora, his kind wife, he went along, but she did not make it a habit. With time, she had learned how and when to use her power to make him once in a blue moon take the tortuous trip with her.

Often, when people would meet her alone, a few out of malice, others just of old habit would greet her: "*Mirëdita Zonja Flora*! Good Day Mrs. Flora! How are you? How is the Retard?"

Flora would reply politely:

"Beg your pardon! I didn't catch what you said. My hearing is a little muffled lately. Did you ask about *Zoti Molina*, Mr. Molina?"

The person would blush and ask again: "How is *Zoti Molina*?"

"Why, very well, thank you!" Mrs. Flora would respond, smiling. "*Zoti Molina* gives you his best wishes!"

Most people, feeling uncomfortable, would nod their heads in acceptance of the regards, and embarrassed would rush away. Others would give their regards back. And, the villagers, gradually, got used to the new name.

In time, it was forgotten that once there was a man everybody regarded as the Retard. The talk about Mrs. Flora's new husband, who did wonders with her house and was a very skilled carpenter and carver, was all over. It was said that by a miracle, he brought Mrs. Flora back to life when everybody else failed, even her mother. Meanwhile, he was addressed as the respectable *Zoti Molina*.

His fame as a craftsman made people line up at his new carpentry shop settled inside the barn. A handful came from remote villages. They placed orders for fences, doors, windows, tables, and cupboards with the request to be carved by *Zoti Molina* himself. Some would even order their portrait or the likeness of their favorite animals to decorate their front yards. Everyone knew they were getting a unique work as they were certain, he never repeated a carving twice. Some stopped by just to enjoy the new sculptures in his garden.

In due course, Adrian Molina had to hire a few apprentices, skilled young men from all over the area to help him handle the overwhelming number of requests, and built an extension to the barn to expand his shop. He even created a group that made only children's toys. For the work field he had to hire some workers.

Adrian had taken refuge in his private section of the barn lately and had left the orders to be completed by his apprentices, which he had already trained well how to craft in his style. It happened when Flora's swollen belly began to show. He knew a baby was growing in his wife's tummy. He had seen it before. Thinking of a small boy, of his making, running soon around the shop while he was working, gave him an idea.

He started to spend hours of his free time locked in there. Flora was concerned at first, taking that as a drawback on his part from all the outpouring work he was getting. But she came to recognize that he needed his time away from others once in a while. The retreat in the solitude of his own space was his way to cope with the intensity of his new life.

In the last month of her pregnancy, Flora became very hefty and had a hard time moving around. The midwife had advised her to take to her bed. Adrian took good care of her. He made it a habit of sleeping in the barn to not bother her at night. As a matter of fact, she needed the whole bed to herself. Her tossing in the bed made it difficult for another person to sleep there. She knew she was safe. Adrian had very sensitive hearing and a sixth sense if she needed him or went into labor.

One morning he brought her breakfast in bed. He waited patiently for her to finish eating. When she was done, he took her hand and let her know he wanted to show her something.

Holding her hand, he helped her get out of the bed and walk slowly to the window. She looked at him, puzzled. He pointed outside on the left side of the front garden.

She covered her mouth in amazement. *That's what he was doing all this time in the barn,* she thought. And to think she had moments of fearing his shortcomings. She turned around and hugged him dearly. "It is marvelous! Oh!" she exclaimed. "It is beyond anything you have done before!"

She looked at him with loving eyes.

"Help me go outside. I want to see it up close."

Adrian smiled and helped her move. But she had a hard time taking one more step. Her walk to the window was the most she could do in her condition. She looked at him in desperation. He understood, she wanted to see his work badly near at hand. Without hesitation, he lifted her in his arms. She was heavy, but not for his strength.

In a bit, they were out of the house. He stopped next to what had emerged during the night in the garden, and put Flora down.

The figure of a mother sitting on a bench, holding an infant in her arms, rose magnificently among other carvings and overshadowed everything around it. The mother, as she was breastfeeding her newborn, was looking attentively at the little one as he was sucking her bare breast. The mother's pride and love could be read on her face. The newborn was portrayed unclothed, and Flora could see his gender. It was a boy. Tom Adrian Molina wanted a boy! His eyes were closed, and the little one seemed comfortable and content in his mother's arms, as if he was feeling not only the warm milk flowing smoothly into his small mouth but also the softness and the warmth of his mother's body, and her love. His tiny lips were curled around his mother's nipple. The whole ensemble transmitted a sense of peace, love, and serenity. The portrayed harmony and the close bond between mother and son made Flora shed a tear.

Leaning on Adrian to accommodate herself, as her legs were killing her, she raised her head, put her hand behind his neck, brought his head down, and gave him a deep, affectionate kiss.

"You dear, dear man!" she said with a tender, adoring voice.

He smiled, looking at his wife with puppy eyes. Flora continued to observe the composition closely. Her Adrian had exceeded every expectation anyone had thought possible with this assemblage. She had never heard of anyone as far as she knew doing such a thing. Both mother and child seemed unbelievably real. Savoring the beauty of the pair, the details of the hand of the little one, she reached and touched his teeny fingers. She looked at his tummy and caressed his belly button. She noticed the mother was barefoot, and the nails on the toes were crafted in details. Her body was not covered in a typical dress. It was more like a thin night robe, ruffled here and there, showing her curves visibly. The chemise did not cover the nicely sculpted hands, wrapped around the chubby infant. One could see the shapes of the long legs, the thighs, and well-carved knees under it. On the top, the nightgown was nicely folded over her arm, exposing her left breastfeeding the little one.

The shape of the other breast was visible under the delicate chemise. It showed the erected nipple as if waiting for the little one to grab it once he was done gulping down the milk of the left breast. It was incredible how Adrian had captured all the details in his composition. A crease in between the eyebrows showed the ancient mother's worry about her child.

Every detail amazed her. The woman's figure was a pleasant resemblance of herself. It was, thus far, the best craft her dear husband had carved. He had depicted details of her body on the crafted woman that only a sharp eye could notice.

He had deified her.

She felt the pride stirring in her veins, *Is our son going to look like the little one?* Looking carefully, she noticed the child's face was portrayed very much like Adrian's, but with finer, smaller, chubby features. *He has made the infant in his likeness,* she reflected.

Watching his flawless work, she thought how the villagers would react to this masterpiece. In particular, she wanted to see the faces of the ones who had opposed their marriage. They had not seen the best of him yet. A content smile showed on her face.

Adrian, supporting his wife's warm body as she was enjoying his carving, observed her closely. He caught sight of her tears, the way her expression changed when looking at different details. He saw the visible pride in her eyes, and the smile that sealed her silent insight of his craft. A strong emotion stirred his chest. He lowered his head and gave her a slight kiss on her head.

All of a sudden she felt a sharp shiver going through her body.

"Adrian!" she screamed as her body became suddenly heavy, and she began to slide down. "The baby is coming!"

She appeared in excruciating pain. Her breathing became irregular, and she was grunting soundly. When he tried to lift her and bring her inside the house, she cried louder. He realized it was better not to move her. He accommodated her body right there on the ground, took off his shirt, rolled it up, and put it under her head.

"Don't move!" he ordered with a firm tone he had never used before, without the slightest mumbling, and ran into the house. She looked in his direction, surprised. Was that man her Adrian? He certainly had changed in many ways, she thought.

He came back with a blanket, some linen, towels, and warm water. Everything afterward happened very fast. There was no time to call anyone else. He had to serve as a midwife for his son.

Flora had a very quick, easy labor. With her last scream, a little boy slowly came out of her body. A cry pierced the air.

Tom Adrian Molina picked up his son, wrapped his tiny body in clean white linen, and lifted him up toward the sky. Looking at his best creation, this time in his own flesh and blood, he released a deep, hoarse shout from the top of his lungs toward the sky.

Content beyond any limit for being able to create such marvel out of her body, and exhausted at the same time, the new mother watched with a faint smile on her face the breathtaking figure of father and son.

Biography

The author, Nimfa Hakani, an Albanian-American, writes in both Albanian and English. Her poetry, short stories, essays, and several articles on social Albanian issues have been published in both languages in printed and online Albanian newspaper editions. The short story, **The Blood Line**—*The Story of a Prince* is published in various online newspapers. Her poems, *I refuse, Simply Woman* can be found at allpoetry.com.

Nimfa is the author of three books published in Albanian language, **Pacientja 101**—*The Patient 101*, a collection of short stories, **Luani i Fjetur**—*The Sleeping Lion*, a collection of tales and fables, and **Gjetoja dhe Orët**—*Jeto and the Nixies*, a children's book based on *The Albanian Epic of Heroes*.

Under the Orange Tree is her first published book in English.
The central themes in the short stories of this collection are based in real life stories. The author is deeply drawn to themes of humanity's transcendence in the face of life's greatest challenges. The life of the protagonists of each story had provoked the author's curiosity since the first time she heard about the struggles of four women and one man she never met. Under the spell of that fascination, she wrote **Under The Orange Tree, Rina,** and **The Awakening** describing the life of these ordinary people in an intriguing, interesting way.

The author lives in the state of New York.

CPSIA information can be obtained
at www.ICGtesting.com
Printed in the USA
FFOW01n1412270416
23633FF

9 781478 750536